UNSPEAKABLE FEARS . . .

"Is she the one you was missing?" asked the young policeman who had followed Matt down the precipitous quarry cliff.

"That's Evie," Matt said softly.

"I never seen a dead body."

Matt followed his gaze. Evie Wagner's face was puffy. Her lids were open. The vacancy stabbed into his brain and he had to look away.

"D'ya think there was a perpetrator?" asked the cop.

Matt shook his head.

"She kilt herself?" His voice was a whisper.

"The note implies that."

"Note?"

"Up there, on her books."

The note was composed in a girl's elegant penmanship with a mauve felt marker: *Dear Dad, Mom doesn't believe me. I really am a virgin. Now I will be forever. . . .*

progeny

J. G. MAXON

POCKET BOOKS

New York   London   Toronto   Sydney   Tokyo

An *Original* Publication of POCKET BOOKS

POCKET BOOKS, a division of Simon & Schuster Inc.
1230 Avenue of the Americas, New York, NY 10020

ISBN: 0-671-67908-2

First Pocket Books printing December 1989

10 9 8 7 6 5 4 3 2 1

POCKET and colophon are trademarks of
Simon & Schuster Inc.

Printed in the U.S.A.

CHAPTER ONE

The body in Matthew Chays's arms was lightly slimed with algae. It had no pliancy. The girl was stiffening in the fetal curve of her dead man's float.

The cop grasping her ankles slipped, caught himself, and hiked his hands up on her calves. Dumb to be wearing motorcycle boots, but then the cop didn't know he'd be scrambling around the moss-slicked rocks of Lambert County's sandstone quarries.

"Early rigor mortis," the young cop said.

Coagulation of protein in the muscles: Matt remembered from mysteries he used to read. A strand of her brown hair fell onto his forearm. He couldn't shake it off. It sucked to his skin like a leech from the gelatinous water of the quarry. He was responsible for her: he was the principal of Sand Ridge Junior High and she was supposed to be in her seventh-grade classes today.

"Is she the one you was missing?" asked the policeman who had followed Matt down the precipitous cliff.

They swung her carefully onto the tarp Matt had pitched down from the top of the quarry. They eased her down as if she could notice.

"That's Evie," he said softly.

1

"What now?"

He was the cop, but he was asking Matt.

"You radioed it in, right?"

"Yeah, you said that's how you heard it."

Matt nodded. He'd been listening to the police radio in his car when he heard the cop call in the sighting of the body, and had dashed there from several blocks away. The policeman was a rookie, about nineteen and skinny, hardly older than the thirteen-year-old girl. The boy made Matt feel hefty, strongly rooted in his life. The cop was nervous, afraid he'd make a mistake. They shouldn't allow boys to be cops if they had more than a certain quota of pimples, Matt thought. He made Matt feel as if he were verging on antique at forty.

"Your colleagues'll show any moment," Matt reassured him.

The boy nodded.

"I reckon the easiest way to lift her is by the derrick," Matt said. Gather the tarp up by the corners, hook it through, and hoist it up."

The boy was staring down at the girl's eyes. "I never seen a dead body."

Matt followed his gaze. Evie Wagner's face was puffy. Her lids were open. The vacancy stabbed into his brain and he had to look away. The stare of the dead. He'd seen it before. It was one of the reasons he'd abandoned war reporting. He knelt and closed her eyelids, first the left and then the right, which required three attempts. The muscles of the face go rigid first.

"D'ya think there was a perpetrator?"

Matt shook his head.

"She kilt herself?" His voice was a whisper.

"The note implies that."

"Note?"

"Up there, on her books."

Still kneeling on the rock, Matt waved his hand in the direction of his car and the boy's motorcycle on the lip of the quarry. The car door was wide open, as he'd left it when he leaped out. Static and blurred talk could occasionally be heard from the police radio he had installed out of journalistic nostalgia.

"Wha'dit say?"

"Something about being a virgin forever."

The note was composed in a girl's elegant penmanship with a mauve felt marker. Matt moved a vein of sodden hair from Evie's forehead and lifted a large, rust red oak leaf, the size of a man's hand, from her throat where her sweater dipped in a V. The dank smell of wet wool surrounded them in the chill, gloomy afternoon air inside the deep bowl of the quarry.

"She looks 'bout as old as my kid sister," the cop said.

Matt studied the thickness of the tarp, folding it between his thumb and forefinger.

"You know her, I mean, didja?"

"Sort of. She'd just become a friend of my daughter, Tobie," Matt said, swallowing hard to keep from choking up.

When was Leland going to get here? The color of the ledged sandstone walls varied from light buff to rose. Vegetation on the south side was deep orange. Fall had come late; summer hadn't really snapped until the late October weekend just past. From low, down on his knees, the water reflected red.

"Halloo," a man's voice called.

"Halloo, halloo, halloo," the cry bounced off the air-hardened sandstone quarry walls.

From the south Matt could see two policemen walking and slipping down through the brush from their cars parked in the lot at the North Ohio Building-Stone Factory.

"They're here," the boy said with relief.

"Why don't you switch on your radio and tell them to contact the factory and get the derrick operator over here?"

The boy pulled the radio from his belt, eager to have an instruction, desperate to forget the body that lay at his feet.

Matt could see Cecil Leland's drooping jowls even far across the pool of water. That was, however, the only aspect of Sand Ridge's police chief that resembled a bloodhound. Leland coped with problems amorphously, dulling issues that were sharp or dangerous. If a car was found parked across the exit route of Sand Ridge's fire engines, Leland would be tolerant, assuming that the driver must have had a good reason. Fortunately there was almost no crime in the small town, and Leland's chief lieutenant, Jock Stark, did pass out parking tickets and otherwise organize his boss.

Leland and Stark tightrope-walked across the narrow spit and leaped over the water to the rock where Evie Wagner lay.

"God."

"Yeah," Stark replied, his breath drawing in.

Matt thought it eerie how even the muscles of one's body reacted in sympathy to a newly dead body.

"You think she fell?" Leland asked.

"She wrote a note," the boy said too eagerly. "Up there."

"What'd it say?"

The kid turned to Matt, his ignorance exposed. Matt replied.

"Something like: 'Dear Dad, Mom doesn't believe me. I really am a virgin. Now I will be forever.'"

"'Course she was," Leland said.

"Did you know her?" Matt was surprised.

"No, well, chances are she was," Leland said.

"I radioed Sam up there to gear up the derrick engine," the kid said.

"This is so awful. Do you know the family very well?" Leland turned toward Matt as he talked.

"Only a little," Matt replied. "I met the mother at a PTA meeting. Don't know them well at all. It's customary for the police to inform the family, isn't it?"

"Yeah, but I don't know them at all. At least you do."

"Barely."

Mr. and Mrs. Wagner would read about their daughter's drowning in the paper before Leland would get up the nerve to tell them.

"I'll tell them." Matt sighed.

"There'll have to be an autopsy," Stark said.

The door of the derrick engine's shack groaned and slammed. The motor sputtered into a muffled, distant thud-thud-thud.

Matt explained to the men his notion of lifting the body out of the quarry wrapped in the tarp, since the walls were too steep to carry her out. He suggested knotting the corners together, inserting the hook under them. But the kid, eager to use his shiny new buck knife, was already awkwardly

4

cutting holes in each corner of the tarp for the hook to go through. Stark walked off a short way, examining the scene of the drowning.

"I'll take her books and stuff with me," Matt said.

He realized how cold he was, soaked from jumping into the water to float Evie's body to the edge. He put his coat on as he watched Leland kneel and bend her arm so that her hand lay below her breast in the traditional funeral pose. The other arm wouldn't bend. How would Tobie react to Evie's death? Matt began the trek back across the spit, through the bushes and trees, and slowly back up the steep side of the pit.

Tears squeezed to the edges of his eyes. He slapped his hands together. His shoes squished from the inside. He turned from the brushy area, picking his way carefully higher toward the top.

Tobie had described these quarries once as the belly buttons of the earth. They were numerous around Sand Ridge, excavated over the past hundred years to make grindstones, building stones, soaking pits for steel mills, sidewalks, curbs. It was easy for kids to wander into them, whether they wanted to or not.

On the last toe-push before the very top, he stopped cold. A bullfrog bulged next to his shoe. Matt had practically stepped on him. He hoisted the fat fellow up. The bullfrog sat palpitating between his palms, his bulbous eyes being smeared lethargically by the lids. He was as cold as Evie's body. The throbbing of the machinery now pulsed in the damp air. Matt tucked the creature into the cargo pocket of his army coat and snapped him in.

The derrick on the edge of the quarry was stabilized by guy wires anchored with sandstone chunks weighing several tons. The wires flexed over him, giant water-bug legs. The hook was already down. He collected Evie's books, tucking the note into her biology text. The hook began to wind up, its cable moaning. The load swayed like a folded bundle carried in the beak of a stork. He'd met Helen Wagner once at a PTA meeting. She'd been worried about whether the school's PE program was too rigorous for Evie. Although she'd spoken up in the meeting, she seemed retiring, a bit fragile. If his daughter were dead, how would he want to be told? There was no good way. And, *shit*, that note. He slid into the car and slammed the door. Suddenly he remembered the frog.

"You okay?" Matt unsnapped his pocket and checked: the frog blinked in the sudden light. He unzipped his coat so the pocket flopped loosely away from his body.

He backed the car around, sticking his head out the window. In the rearview mirror he saw the tarp clear the rim of the quarry, swinging slowly, dizzily. A shout. Matt couldn't tell what was said.

He looked again. The tarp flapped down loosely, two of its corners ripped out.

CHAPTER TWO

Yale Kaltmann had spent many happy hours puttering in
the basement of his Victorian frame house on the hill
overlooking Heron Creek in Sand Ridge. It was there that he
had devised his plan for immortality.

The basement's concrete floor was a dusky barn-red and
was waxed until it shone; the sandstone walls and wood
ceiling were painted white. The effect was rather like
standing on a tongue surrounded by teeth.

Yale had even painted white the cylinder of liquid nitrogen that was hooked by hose to the cryogenic capsule, as
well as the dozen or so other cylinders scattered around the
basement, stacked like small missiles on the shelves. The
wrenches, tongs, screwdrivers, and other tools and the steel
cryonic capsule shone brightly, spotless.

When he was in the basement, Yale always removed his
shoes and padded around in hospital slippers. It was essen-
tial that dust be minimized while his experiments were
carried out.

He loved to tinker, freezing various items to test their
reactions and to make sure his equipment was in tip-top
condition. He examined the Michaelmas daisy he was using
in today's experiment.

His mother had loved these flowers, which had grown in the yard next to their tract house in a Cleveland suburb. He recalled the spare leaves, with the asterisk blossoms interspersed like stars, in the way some children remember wallpaper patterns from infancy. His childhood memories were particularly clear, like glass, frozen by the vision of the semi truck that had killed his parents but spared him when he was in third grade.

A few years ago, Yale had had what could be termed a mid-life crisis. That's when he began to buy clocks and timepieces of all sorts. Over a couple of years the idea had crept up on him that he hadn't much time left in his life, despite the fact that he was healthy, strong, and fully capable of living to a ripe old age. He'd begun to think he hadn't accomplished much, especially as a scientist, and hadn't built up great work to leave to posterity. It wasn't so much that life was short, but that it was taking him too long to accomplish great things. He began to think about children, hyper-aware that he didn't have any and probably wouldn't, since he couldn't imagine marrying.

He had hung clocks on each of the basement's four walls and in its crannies to enable him to see the time from any angle. He couldn't stop buying clocks, fantasizing that each new clock meant that much more time was being measured. As a scientist he knew that wasn't so, of course, but he also knew that there was truth in emotions, a truth behind scientific facts. His subconscious clung to the hope time could be stretched out.

Yale laid down the daisy for a moment, sat on an old oak rocking chair next to the lab table, and sipped a cup of coffee he'd brought down from the kitchen.

After his parents died in the car crash, Yale was taken to live with his reclusive aunt in Akron. She'd probably coped with a small boy as best a single woman could: fundamentally, she ignored him and let him do almost anything he wanted. He learned to keep his fears to himself. One particular terror, an understandable fear of semis, was so intense that he would never walk on the main road to school but took back streets to avoid encountering any of the huge trucks. As an adult this contributed to his buying a van instead of a car. He wanted a vehicle that was sure to be seen, even by the truck drivers in their cabs high off the ground.

In retrospect, Yale figured he was not like most kids; he was smart and in control from an early age. He possessed a certain valuable quality of mind—persistence. He was not exactly smart in the sense of grades. But teachers, or anyone else for that matter, don't really know about genius. After all, genius is, by definition, rare and not easily recognized. Yale Kaltmann was a loner, aware of himself, his abilities, his self-sufficiency. He kept it to himself, but he was sure of his genius.

One thing Yale didn't like about death was that you lost control. His aunt babbled at the end. While holding her limp hand, he'd alternated between thinking she was pathetic and hiding his disgust at her condition. He was relieved when she died. Then, finding out how much money she had left to him, he was pleased and surprised. It enabled him to pursue his rather expensive hobby of cryogenics, which he'd first learned about during his stint in army refrigeration training.

Yale took the next to last sip of his coffee. He swiveled in the rocking chair and gazed at himself in the side of the shiny cryonic capsule. It was no wonder girls found him attractive. He had a thin, elegant mustache and his hair was still completely black. Not a hint of gray, even though he was forty-six.

Before she died, his mother had treasured his shiny hair. He vividly recalled her bending over him and stroking his head, stroking ideas into it. He remembered the words she'd repeated again and again: "Always ask yourself, 'Would I do this if my mother was here with me?' Then you'll know if you're doing the right thing." She told him to be careful about strangers and to be very gentle with girls because they could be easily hurt.

He'd followed her wishes precisely. In high school he agreed to go out to a drive-in movie with a girl named Shirley Driscoll. He didn't know she'd cause problems.

"It's not normal, Yale."

He could still distinctly remember her words. She was complaining because he didn't try to touch her.

"And you have such bedroom eyes," she teased.

He shrank away from her on the front seat of her car.

"Your lids are so heavy and sexy." She coquettishly touched his eyelid.

He ducked his face.

"Whassa matter, you a virgin?"

He was silent.

"That's okay. Your hair is black patent, slick like Clark Gable's. You should grow a mustache."

Yale covered his upper lip with his left hand. He half wanted to hit her when she touched him, but he remembered his mother's cautions. He subsequently avoided the girl at every chance.

Yale was proud that the people he worked with at the school considered him a calm person. Only he knew the great stress he had been under until last spring. His stress was so intense at times that sections of his body would go numb, sometimes one thigh or a section of his arm, temporarily blocked by a pressed nerve.

Finally, he'd figured out how to be eternal, a way for Yale Graham Kaltmann, the son of Beatrice Graham Kaltmann, to live forever. When he'd thought of it, an enormous pressure lifted from his mind. It was a plan of sheer genius. Already he had put it in motion, and it was working well. Only one person knew, and she wouldn't tell. No one else would ever find out, unless he wanted them to. He knew his stress would soon disappear.

Yale finished the coffee and stood. He picked up the daisy to carry on with his experimentation.

The only window in his basement was filled with glass bricks, which blocked the view but let in filtered light. He had already checked the backup generator; it would automatically swing into action if the mainline electricity shut off. A green light on the gauge of the capsule showed that everything was functioning properly. A red one would light if the temperature rose. The house's utility meters were placed outside so no one needed to enter the basement. The outside door had been blocked off, and the only entrance to the basement was from the hall of the house.

The compressor for the cryonic capsule hummed loudly, vibrating the nearest four-by-four pillar and the ceiling above it like a dentist's drill. He bent over, still balancing the daisy, peered into the bubble-shaped window, and patted the machine affectionately as if he were actually patting the baby whose swaddled face shone round as a saucer through the window.

Liquid nitrogen in the crock on the lab table was boiling off in clouds. Vapor poured over the lip of the container and disappeared. The basement was cool. Yale grasped the daisy stem with a pair of tongs in his rubber-gloved hand. Turning away from the capsule, he dipped the daisy through the cold steam into the liquid, then lifted it out frozen as a Popsicle. The molecules of the flower had become ice. He rotated it, examining it, and smiled. Perfect. He dropped it into the sink. It shattered. Tiny chips of petals, the yellow fuzzed center, the green stem scattered all over the white enamel, then softened as they thawed.

He picked up an egg that he'd brought from the kitchen. Holding it with his gloved right hand, he cracked the shell on the edge of the laboratory table and dropped the contents into the liquid nitrogen spume. When he fished it out, it was frozen in the tear shape formed by gravity as it fell. The yolk was blurred to a dull mustard through the icy albumen.

One of his laboratory mice had been scurrying around in the cardboard box ever since Yale had brought it down at 3 AM. He purchased the mice from a scientific supply outlet in Cleveland. He picked it up by the tail. A clean, white mouse with the pink nose and eyes of albino creatures, it wiggled and squeaked, twisting its head, focusing on Yale out of one eye, then the other, as he held it up. He lowered it through the vapor. When he pulled it out, it was still and perfect, its eyes still wide open. As he examined it, the tail cracked, and the body hit the table with a bang. He opened the door of the deep freezer in the corner of the room and set the mouse, plus tail tip, on a metal plate on the bottom shelf.

He glanced at a clock. Not enough time to take a jar to school. He had to pack the jars in plenty of insulation and dry ice. Sometimes he took a warm one, but usually he preferred to use the frozen method. He fingered the two bottles on the middle shelf for a second, then closed the door. Really no time. He peeled off the rubber gloves, draped them over the sink, and lifted his white tunic over his head, then climbed the stairs, turned out the light at the top, double-locked the door, and left the house for his job as chief electrician and maintenance engineer at Sand Ridge Junior High School.

The late October sun was tipping over the trees at the edge of his large, fenced-in front yard. Waking up early was another way he saved time. Sometimes he barely slept at all.

Ever since he was little, Yale had known that secrecy is power. Although Lorna Ross might know too much, he'd made sure she would never talk. He understood power and how to use it, because he was analytical and cool, just like his cryogenics. He liked the comparison. He was a happy man. He climbed into his brown van, windowless in back, looked behind the front seat to make sure his refrigeration repair equipment was intact, and headed to work.

CHAPTER THREE

"Olga!" Helen Wagner shrieked, snatching for the towel that was falling off her buttocks. "Close the blinds!"

She was lying on her stomach, naked except for the towel. Her legs were spread apart on the table, and Olga's assistant was stirring a jar of gunky depilatory wax with a wooden spatula, preparing to apply it to the dark hairs along Helen's inner thighs.

"Darling, you shy?" Olga asked, scurrying from the beauty parlor side of the blinds into the waxing salon.

"I don't like people gawking at my ripply thighs," she replied. "You may be Russian and blasé about the world seeing your body, but I'm a prudish American."

"My deah, you've got a fabulous body," Olga said, pulling the cord on the narrow-slatted mauve blinds that partitioned the Olga Beauty Salon. "You shouldn't be hung up. Is that how you say? Hung up? If I had a figure like yours . . ."

Helen laughed. Olga told everybody what a great this or gorgeous that they had, depending on whether the topic was hair, skin, or bodies. Well, maybe Olga was not wrong in her case. She tried to keep herself toned up. Twice a week at the beauty parlor was the most Helen could manage and have Hal not complain about the money.

"I've heard she's not really Russian," Augusta Johnson

whispered. She peered over slyly from the adjacent table and then back at her *Vogue,* looking as if her lips had never moved.

The assistant glopped the warm wax on Helen's left leg and smeared it over the offending hairs. Helen tried not to think about the fact she was being touched, even though it was only another woman.

"What is she?"

"Polish."

"Why does she say she's Russian, then?"

Augusta Johnson shrugged and her stringy breasts wobbled as she raised her chest off the massage table. "Sounds classier to be Russian."

Helen didn't really like to hear the gossip in the Olga Salon. If she could have listened and not been expected to respond, that would have been acceptable. But eventually people always got nosy. Take Augusta. She always talked about her daughter, which inevitably led to questions about Evelyn. Helen didn't want to talk about Evie. Or about Hal. Or about herself. She wasn't shy, she was private. She should be living in a big city. She daydreamed that Hal would move his hardware store to East Cleveland where nobody would notice them.

"My Kim claims the seventh-grade girls all have a crush on two new teachers," Augusta said. "One teaches biology and the other chemistry—has Evie mentioned them? Sounds like the scientists are the heartthrobs this year."

Helen shook her head, kept reading *People* magazine.

"Kim is letting her feather cut grow out." Augusta turned to the assistant since Helen was unresponsive. "Thank God the kids aren't doing those tail cuts anymore. Looked like monkeys. Or coloring their hair acid green."

Helen hadn't heard Evie talk about Kimberly Johnson, although they were in the same class. Evelyn. Up till now she'd been a model child. Helen didn't want to think about the scene this morning after breakfast. But then, Evie had never done anything wrong before. Four months and no period. Maybe it's because she's still young and irregular, Helen mused. Sometimes girls have psychological blocks that affect their biological rhythms. Helen didn't want to think about it. She shifted and motioned to Olga's assistant.

"Isn't it about time?"

"Oh, lord." The woman jumped, glancing at the brass filigree clock above the electric coffeepot.

Helen liked to visit Olga's salon because the theatrical Russian woman (or whatever nationality she was) enveloped her and all the women in a warm bubble of words. Her bounty of undemanding language and her periodic nervous breakdowns made her clients feel kindly toward her and toward each other. Helen sought refuge in the salmon, rose, and sea green parlor, with its row of fifteen plastic dryers lined up like helmeted motorcyclists waiting for the starting gun. She always chose a middle machine, with no one sitting on either side, and listened to the air roaring in her ears. "Blowing your brains out today?" Hal joked on her salon days.

"How's Evelyn?"

Augusta was scrawny but oddly flabby as she wrapped the dressing gown around herself. "Can't be too rich or too thin," Helen had heard Augusta say at a PTA meeting. Problem was, Augusta was thin on top and ponderous-bottomed.

"She's doin' okay," Helen murmured dismissively.

The beautician's assistant held the dressing robe for Helen and twined a terry-cloth towel around her neck. From the corner of her eye Helen watched Augusta leave the waxing room. She sighed out loud, and then felt obliged to explain her sigh to Olga's assistant.

"Sally, what can you do when girls start to . . . notice . . . boys?"

"Ah, I dunno. My mother always said the best thing was to scare the bejesus outta a girl."

Helen grimaced. It was precisely that attitude she abhorred to use with Evelyn. But this morning . . . She felt caught in a spiral, knowing how to be a mother only by remembering her own mother. The assistant's fingers on Helen's temples assuaged her headache, but not her memory. Perhaps Evie needed dancing lessons to help her coordination. Harold wouldn't mind paying. "Anything for my girl." He said it all the time. How could Evie possibly be pregnant? But it was way too long since her last period. And the vomiting. This morning it had made her a half hour

late to school. Shame had prevented Helen from phon-
ing the principal's office to tell them Evie was coming.
She'd been avoiding disaster, all disaster, very carefully
for the last fifteen years, actively working at it. This
was awful; how could it be happening to her? The beauty
shop was a cave of rosy, warm peace, in contrast to her
thoughts.

Helen's elbow rested on the chair arm as she held aloft the
bowl of goo that the colorist was basting on the strands of
hair sticking out of the salmon pink bathing cap. At this
stage of porcupine quill hair, Helen avoided looking at
herself in the mirror. Her mask—"avocado mud," Olga
called it—was smeared on her face and neck, leaving holes
for her eyes. Like a raccoon in reverse. The mudpack was
great: nobody could expect her to talk. It had hardened to
the stage that if she moved her face muscles, it would crack
and spoil the tightening effect.

Olga bustled up behind her, silent for a change. Helen's
head was lowered but she rolled her eyes upward to see in
the mirror. She wondered why Olga bought such silly
mirrors, with frames of carved flamingos, flexed necks
dipping into the glass as if into water. Maybe she liked the
pink.

"Helen. Matt Chays is here. He wants to talk with you."

"Me?" Helen said without moving her lips. But she
wrinkled her forehead and cracked the top of the face mask.

"Yeah, honey," Olga said, lifting the bowl out of her palm.

It had to be about Evelyn. Suppose she'd thrown up in
class. Helen turned slowly, out of habit, so as not to drip the
coloring solution. Everybody in the salon was watching her.
Matt's tall, dark-coated figure looked incongruous against
the hot pink of Olga's taffeta curtains. He paced in the short
space, limping on his left leg.

Handsome, Helen thought. A large, ruddy man with
brown hair, sexy hazel eyes. Helen had a weakness for big
shoulders. He was about forty, gray beginning at his temples. God, she must look like a screaming banshee. She
eased off the beauty shop chair as if she were in a posture
class. The mask around her lips hadn't cracked yet; she
carried her head carefully, like glass.

* * *

Matt had stood unnoticed at first. He'd walked through the door while Augusta Johnson was gathering her coat in the walk-in closet and before Olga had come to the front cash register. The violent odors of hydrogen peroxide, ammonia, a clash of perfumes, and God knew what else swamped him. He had entered the caldron that was cooking beauty.

"Yes, yes, of course, darling, a facial makes everyone blotchy and red. My skin looks like it's been through ten wars after mine," Olga consoled Augusta.

"But how can I walk around like this?" Augusta asked plaintively.

She stood next to the reception desk. Her raccoon coat, with its illusion of extra-spiky fur because of the black tipping on the silvery pelt, lay across the easy chair in the lobby. As she turned, Matt automatically lifted it to help her put it on. She retreated as if jolted by an electric shock. Her reaction was stronger than mere surprise at his presence in a female preserve.

"Mr. Chays, why, what are you doing here?"

She didn't wait for an answer, but launched into a nervous babble about her daughter. Matt scarcely registered her words. Emotional residue from the quarry scene clung to his mind and dulled his attention. He'd gone home from the quarry to change clothes and leave the frog, but he seemed never to have left the cold quarry walls.

"Kimberly hasn't been well, I've been worried sick about her, that's why she's been out of school," Augusta said.

"Kimberly?" Matt fumbled.

"My daughter, Kimberly," Augusta said. "I don't know exactly what it is, maybe I should take her to a doctor, she's usually so healthy, last week she started . . ."

Augusta paused, searching for a word, avoiding another.

". . . she got real woozy, then she was okay again, but I kept her out of school, she'll be okay I'm sure, I always think it's better to play it safe, don't you?"

"Yes, yes," Matt said in his best placatory voice.

Besides being a mother, Augusta was rich; her husband, a major local taxpayer, owned a furniture factory in town.

"I figured it was a type of flu or something, really I'm doing everything I can think of," she said.

By then Olga had walked toward Matt. "Can I help you?"

"Helen Wagner's neighbor said I could find her here."

"She's here. Is it urgent?"

Matt nodded, and Olga glided inward toward the mirrors and sinks. Augusta Johnson sank onto the easy chair. Matt had rehearsed what he would say, but all the prepared words were seeping out of him. He glanced far down the salon and saw Olga talking to a woman, who rose from her chair. He paced across the small lobby several times. Breathe deeply three times: he reminded himself of how he used to prepare for radio news broadcasts. The woman walked toward him. She didn't really look like a person. From that distance, the army green mask made her face into a skull with cupped eye sockets. Her pink bathing cap and erect hair tufts were more alien than human. Her dressing robe was a modern Scandinavian design of target circles.

Helen Wagner stood before him. He fancied he would speak and the words would be a foreign language to her.

"Mrs. Wagner?"

She nodded.

"I tried to reach your husband."

"I'm sorry I look this way," Helen said.

She pressed her palm to her forehead but blew her words through stiff lips, still preserving the uncracked lower part of the mudpack.

"It's Evie, isn't it? Is she sick?"

Where were the words? What was he going to say? He thought of the tarp ripping. The loose, flapping canvas hung in his mind.

"Evie didn't show up at school today. I tried to reach you or Mr. Wagner. When I couldn't, I notified the police."

"Police!"

Her mask was destroyed. Tiny white cracks webbed her face. Like a windshield struck by a rock, the mudpack had shattered but held together.

"Something's wrong. Tell me," she said.

"We found Evie at the quarry."

"Is she hurt?"

Helen raised her hands to her face in horror. Matt nodded and clasped her shoulders.

"No, no, no."

She moaned and swayed back and forth, pulling Matt along with her. He noticed that the coloring paste on her hair was also daubed on her eyebrows.

"You didn't say she's dead." Helen's voice wavered, on the edge of control.

"Evie was drowned."

She stood still.

"My baby . . ."

It was a wail of grief.

"The police are taking her to the Lambert County coroner."

Helen's eyes were glazed.

"There's a note."

Matt fished in his pocket, pulled out the folded notebook page, and smoothed it out on her palm. Helen had to hold it at arm's length to read it without her glasses. Tears balanced on the mud crust.

"Oh, God."

She gasped and Matt could feel her crumpling. He caught the piece of paper as it fluttered out of her hands, grabbed her beneath the armpits as she fell. Her head lolled back.

Matt looked around the room, supporting Helen as she slumped in a dead faint. "Where can I lay her down?"

"The waxing tables," Olga said, and waved toward the back of the beauty parlor.

Helen's arm flopped down as he lifted her. Olga held up the arm and walked crabwise with Matt as he carried her past the line of egg-domed hair dryers, between the shampooing sinks to the massage room. Beauticians and clients cleared the way, staring at them. Whispering rippled as they passed, like the undulating hush of a wave. He eased the limp body onto the table. Olga placed a vinyl cushion under her head.

"She needs to be kept warm," Matt said.

Augusta, who had followed them, laid her raccoon coat over Helen's body.

"This cap, can we take it off? It's putting pressure on her temples," Matt said.

One of the beauticians deftly rolled up the pink plastic until it was off Helen's ears. With coaxing, the spikes of hair slipped through the perforations.

19

"Any smelling salts?" Matt turned to Olga.

"No."

He needed something strong that would jolt her brain.

"A bottle of perm solution," Olga offered.

He took the bottle, unscrewed the lid, lifted Helen's head, and passed the bottle several times beneath her nose. She jumped and drew back, making a face. Her eyes fluttered and opened. The salon full of women was deathly quiet.

"Where am I? Hal, it's his fa—" She covered her mouth. "Hal, I must talk to Hal."

"Olga will call him," Matt said. "But stay still for a while so you don't faint again. You've had quite a shock."

"Evie. I didn't mean anything. I believe you, Evie."

Helen began to sob. She turned her face to one side, raised her hands, and was surprised at her skin's texture.

"Can you take off the mask?" Matt asked the woman who had removed the cap.

It would help keep Helen on the table. The woman started to remove the coating, dipping a small sponge in a bowl of water and, with circular movements, dissolving the caked pea green clay with its varicose cracks.

"Olga," Matt said wearily, motioning the woman away from the table to talk. "I don't want to leave, but I . . ."

"You must go, my dear. You've done all you can. We'll keep her warm and make her stay until we get Hal on the phone."

Several of the women were trying to restrain Helen, who was by then off the massage table and walking toward him.

"Shhh, honey, it's okay. Lie back down."

"Evie," Helen wailed.

Her arms flailed in the air as she struggled to break free. Matt shifted toward the main room of the beauty salon. Helen followed him, trailed by ten or so women moving in a cluster like an opera chorus.

"It must've happened at school," Helen said, the pitch of her voice rising.

She kept turning toward Matt as the women tried to propel her in the other direction. A patch of skin was exposed on her forehead, like a third eye.

"Are you gonna let more girls get pregnant? Evie never went anywhere else!"

Helen pointed at Matt and moaned. "Who was the father? He must know!" she screamed.

"No, honey, he's just told you about Evie. It's not his fault," said the beautician who was holding the face sponge.

Her tone was one used for a small child.

With Olga motioning for him to leave, Matt strode toward the front door between the sleeping hair dryers. He reached into his pocket to reassure himself that Evie's note was there. Why would she claim to be a virgin? To cover up for a boy? God, what would he do if it were Tobie? At the door, Matt glanced back. Helen's pathetic wailing reached out like a ghoulish hand around his throat. His breathing was fast and tight.

CHAPTER FOUR

"Hey, watch ooouuuut!"

The raspy voice made Matt's head flip up. Blair Nelson maneuvered himself aside, rigid as a broom handle, so that Matt narrowly missed mashing him against the wall of his newspaper building.

"Going to a fire?" asked the editor of the *Sand Ridge Daily Oracle*.

"More like I been to one."

Matt pulled his hat down on his forehead against the deepening chill of the late afternoon.

"What's that?"

Blair Nelson was hard of hearing, a drawback if a citizen wanted to give him a discreet, off-the-record tip.

"I said, more like I been to a fire. I just informed Helen Wagner."

Matt took it for granted that Blair had heard about Evie. The editor's news-gathering ability was never dulled by his deafness. Blair's ears were notable in other ways, too: they belled out and served as lodging for endless items. An editor's green eyeshade perched on their tips. An antiquated hearing aid parked in the right ear. Sawed-in-half reading glasses lurched far down his nose, the curves of the frames'

22

temples clinging, like fingertips on a cliff edge, to his ear
spools. A long, yellow, number two pencil was stuck, eraser
end forward, in the groove between his head and left ear.
Now an earmuff sat back of the good ear, while the other
was muffed.

"How'd she take it?"

"Fainted."

"She know about the pregnancy?"

Matt started. Was Blair going to publish that Evie was
pregnant?

"Did the coroner tell you that?"

"Come again?" Blair said.

"I said, did the medical examiner tell you Evie was
pregnant?"

"Nope. I'm on my way to the coroner now."

"How'd you know, then?"

"Leland said you had a suicide note."

Matt pursed his lips. He motioned Blair to follow him
into the arched doorway of the sandstone facade, which
matched the other buildings on Sand Ridge's narrow,
one-block Main Street. The alcove would allow him to speak
more quietly. Matt enjoyed Blair's stance of crusty editor
fighting for the free press. It was a game, often played but
seldom played out. A newspaper editor in a town of just over
ten thousand could ill afford to rub his readers the wrong
way more than a few times a year.

"You're not going to go with that pregnancy bit, are you?
It's a bitch of a story: the mother fainted, God knows what
can of worms this note opens up for the parents, and you
want to make it worse by telling the world!"

"Can't let our emotions color our news sense," Blair said.
"You knew the girl, didn't you? Maybe you could tell me
something about her."

"Yeah, I can tell you she was a sweet kid, neat, good
grades." Matt felt silly, shouting the platitudes. "But this
note . . ."

He patted his coat pocket.

". . . she was confused."

He paused, lifted the note from his pocket, and passed it
to Blair, who shoved his glasses up and read it slowly.

"See what you mean," he said, handing it back.

"I've got to go home and tell Tobie, and I don't know how. She's never known anybody who died. Except her mother. But she was only four when that happened. She can't remember it."

"You got to tell kids right out, be honest," Blair said. "You got to let her grieve. It's part of allowing the memory, allowing the love."

Matt nodded. For a second their eyes held. Sounded right. Like Blair knew. Usually Blair tried to play editor to Matt's reporter, authoritarian, tough, the boss, even though they both knew Matt's journalism days were over. Sometimes Blair dropped it all and was, well, human—really human.

"When's your deadline?"

"Ten minutes ago. We'll put the *Oracle* to bed late tonight. Had to bump off a good page-one story about the Sphinx factory. The factory just got a commission from a library in Texas that wants two sphinxes near the steps instead of the usual lions. A coupla tons of sandstone. The factory hasn't had that big a special order in quite a while."

Enigma Sphinx, Inc., was the oldest business in Sand Ridge. Its main products were lawn ornaments—hundred- to three-hundred-pound carved models of Egypt's great woman-lion statue, as well as the more ordinary lions and a few Buddhas. Enigma also sold sphinx birdbaths, sphinx charcoal pits, and carvings for key chains and charm bracelets.

"Something else I should warn you about since you're going to see her," Matt said. "The tarp they were lifting Evie in tore, and they dropped her from quite a height."

"Shit. It's godawful."

Matt felt drained. He jockeyed to drift away.

But Blair cleared his throat quietly, conspiratorially, and Matt leaned in to listen.

"I hear Augusta Johnson is fixing to sue the Lambert County Abortion Clinic, Dr. Mabrey specifically."

"Yeah? She had a bad abortion?" Matt asked.

Maybe that was why she'd been acting so weird toward him, spacey, like she had just killed all the raccoons that went to make her coat.

24

"Not her. Her kid. Named Kimberly."

"Kim had an abortion?"

"Not exactly, according to my source. Mrs. Johnson says Kim was hemorrhaging, unrelated to a pregnancy, she says. Claims her daughter was a virgin. Says she took Kim to the clinic, since it was closer than the hospital, and that they fucked her up."

"God, that's disgusting. But what's with this virgin stuff? Why suddenly two girls saying this? Like something out of the *National Enquirer.*"

"You want to make a statement?"

"Statement about what? Virginity?"

Blair nodded.

"Right, sure. How about: 'I approve of virginity, especially when it's gone.'" Matt was exhausted, depressed.

Blair raised an eyebrow. "I'm serious. Especially if this stuff about Evie's claim comes out."

"Ah, c'mon, man, Sand Ridge may be a backwater compared to Cleveland, but even yahoos around here know virgins don't get pregnant. With one possible exception."

Matt drew the sign of the cross in the air.

"Precisely. Nobody in their right mind will think pregnant girls are virgins."

"So?"

"So they will look around for the father or fathers."

"Don't look at me," Matt said.

"They are already searching to place blame."

Matt was quiet, peering closely at Blair. "You're not telling me something."

"Maybe, maybe not."

"Okay, so we've drafted statements together for me before. Remember last year, the statement about the teacher who was assigning Kahlil Gibran's poetry? How'd that go? Something like: 'While this poetry may be viewed as suggestive by some, Sand Ridge Junior High believes students today are more sophisticated because of television and movies, blah, blah, blah.'"

"That's the idea. Something to pre-protect your ass," Blair said.

"Okay. How about a statement like: 'Matt Chays, principal, blah, blah, today expressed his deep condolences to the parents of Evie Wagner. He said that all of Evie's teachers and her friends at school are deeply grieved by her untimely death. Mr. Chays told the *Oracle* he will investigate how to tighten up on the monitoring of attendance and will do everything he can to protect the well-being of all children in Sand Ridge Junior High.' How's that?"

Blair had slid a palm-sized notebook out of his sleeve like a circus magician. He scribbled Matt's words in an alphabetic shorthand.

"Can I add 'especially the young girls' to the clause about protecting children?"

"Sure."

"That ought to keep the wolves from baying too loudly. All in your interest."

Blair flipped the notebook shut, nudged it inside his shirt pocket. Instead of turning to leave, he peered at Matt, drawing deeply on his cigarette.

"Look, let me give you a tip, if you'll keep it under your hat: Arnie may be out to get you on this one."

"Shit, what for?"

Arnie Beachley was the town's chinless mayor. Sometimes Tobie called him Dick Tracyless and, when he had one of his chronic hiccup attacks, she said he looked like a snake burping. Matt had a hard time taking Arnie seriously.

"The guy never wanted you to have this job. He had his own candidate, some bloke from Cleveland, crony of his. The rest of us outvoted him."

"That explains it. From the day I moved here I had a funny feeling about Arnie, something weird, cold, about the guy's attitude."

"Under your hat," Blair cautioned him.

"Sure, but why the hell am I responsible for girls who are getting pregnant? Am I supposed to make them wear chastity belts?"

"Hey, don't kill the messenger. Arnie's gonna blame someone, and you've only been in Sand Ridge a year. It's easier to scapegoat outsiders than insiders. I gotta go."

Blair pulled his plastic visor down a notch over a lower forehead wrinkle. The furrows on Blair's brow were so deep that a farmer could plant seeds in them.

"Just a friendly tip."

"Thanks," Matt said. He meant it.

Blair checked to be sure the pencil was behind his ear, gave a curt wave of his hand from next to his head, and said, "I know how much it means to you to be here with your kid."

CHAPTER FIVE

Blair didn't know the half of it, Matt thought as he rolled his cart around the grocery store with the editor's warning festering in his brain. If he lost this job, he could face a custody battle from Glenda's parents, Tobie's maternal grandparents. They just might deliver on their threat.

On good days, Matt found shopping to be an entertaining exercise. On bad days—and today ranked with the rottenest —it soothed him. He shopped even if the fridge was full. To him it wasn't a question of diversion. All his years of wandering around war zones and covering developing countries had fostered in him a quirky appreciation for two things: the belching smokestacks of industry and the wondrous American marketing system that brought him items as different as fresh Hawaiian gingerroot and Boston scrod. He dropped four giant artichokes into his cart. Tobie would like them. They would remind her of Nana and Grandpa in Santa Cruz.

After Glenda died nine years ago, Tobie had lived with his parents in Santa Cruz. Matt's mother had always been more of a mother to Tobie than Glenda had anyway. Somehow his wife had missed out when God distributed maternal instincts. He figured he had more than Glenda had. It always baffled him. Yet he had loved her extravagantly anyway. His feeling for her was rooted in their crazy, early romance. For a couple of years, even after Tobie was born, Glenda would travel with him on his assignments. She seemed not to want to be tied down. He probably never would figure out what had happened, most likely because she'd never resolved her own personality. Then she ran off to Peru with that asshole of a TV journalist. Last Matt heard of her was from the U.S. embassy there. She and the reporter had been killed when their van plunged off a cliff.

When she and Matt were still together, there was something about the precipitousness of Glenda's actions, none of which she seemed to control, that made him feel he had an abyss inside himself. As if it were his own character flaw. After Glenda's death, he'd resolved to settle down, to rid himself of her failure, to raise Tobie. The only problem was that he needed money. His father had been a barber, his mother a bookkeeper in a grocery store, so they had little capital. For six years he'd left Tobie with them in Santa Cruz and traveled the globe raking in good money, paid handsomely for covering wars.

Hazard pay. There were hazards from Ethiopia to Nicaragua to the Western Sahara. Tobie kept track of her father on a large globe. She stuck it with flagged pins, pretending he had conquered and raised the Chays flag where, in fact, he had merely written a story. Hazard pay bought the globe. Hazard pay bought her clothes. Hazard pay bought their house in Sand Ridge and averted the threat by Glenda's parents in Texas that they would sue his parents in Santa Cruz for custody if he didn't come home and take care of his own daughter. The globe was now in the attic, gathering the minimal dust that existed in the humid climate of northern Ohio.

Superb gingerroot tonight at Foodway. Smooth. Better than the usual stuff, which looked like gargantuan toes wrinkled by a hot, three-hour bath. He slipped two large roots into a plastic bag. He'd freeze some.

The threatened custody suit had sped up his exit from journalism, attractive now mainly for its money. Shortly after Matt abandoned the war-groupie fraternity with its sleazy, brave, and shell-shocked but addicted reporters, he'd taken a quick master's degree in education at San Jose State.

Then he taught seventh grade for three years in the Santa Cruz system. Tobie was then approaching those tentative years of puberty, during which, Matt decided, he would rather not be raising a girl by himself amid the freewheeling lifestyle of Santa Cruz.

"I'm flying to Ohio to check into a new job," he told her one day when she was nine.

"That's not a push-me, pull-you decision," she pouted. That was her expression for their generally democratic approach to mutual decisions.

"Nope. Totally totalitarian," he admitted.

He knew she was hiding her worry, but they sat down together with an atlas and an encyclopedia and studied Ohio diligently, as if it were a foreign country he was going to cover. In the end she was reconciled because at least he was taking her with him this time.

For Matt's purposes, Sand Ridge was about perfect. Cleveland was only fifty miles away, with jazz clubs and bookstores to keep him from feeling he had moved to the Australian outback. The only thing missing was women. Several in town made it clear they were "available," but he was careful to keep the judicious distance required of a town notable. Before his marriage and after Glenda's death, he'd been no prude. Few journalists were. But Tobie was reaching a sensitive age when his devotion to her was being carefully scrutinized. Besides, if Arnie the chinless wonder was ready to skewer him on the slightest pretext, Matt would have to play it low-key on the female front.

In only one year Tobie had fit into the town well, for Sand Ridge was not so small that hostility toward a total newcomer was insurmountable. A major plus was that the town was buffered from crime and the too-fast life by surrounding farm country. Cable TV hadn't even arrived in the area. Theft had increased from about nothing ten years ago, Leland had told him once, to the weekly stealing of some item left too conspicuously available. A lot of people in Sand Ridge still didn't lock their doors when they left their houses.

Though soothed by his shopping ritual, Matt still couldn't keep his mind off Evie. Before telling Tobie, he had to ease the fact of her death into his own system, like working new clay into old until they were in harmony. He remembered that he'd told Leland to call him tonight if the medical examiner turned up anything queer about the body. He didn't expect there would be anything. Was it possible Evie didn't know exactly what virginity entailed? Helen Wagner didn't strike him as prudish, but you could never guess about the topic of sex between parents and a child. Wouldn't it be ghastly if Evie'd had a false pregnancy, or was too innocent to be right about the symptoms?

Matt pulled his car into the old garage. Tobie had picked the house. It was a pale butter-colored frame with forest green trim on the eaves and the porch skirting. Her obsession was to have a house with stairs, after knowing only ranch styles in California. Hence the two stories, with an attic. And a huge backyard, in which they'd accumulated a compost heap they named Uriah.

She was home. Light shone through the stained-glass window. Matt liked that window, but he could never decide whether its odd colors were exotic, whimsical, or macabre. The house, he was convinced, adapted to the environment and even to the mood of its inhabitants. He turned the key and called out hello as he noisily lifted the groceries through the door. Quiet. He hung his hat, scarf, and coat on the rack.

"Hello," he called again loudly.

He toted the groceries to the kitchen, flipping on lights as he went. Silence. Not even a radio. He walked back through the living room.

"Anybody live in this house?"

Giggling trickled down from the stairway. He looked up. There she was, stretched out completely, lying along the banister railing, balancing neatly as if she were carved into it like a totem.

"How'd you get there?"

"Easy."

"Yeah. . . . I'm waiting for an explanation."

"I did it real slow."

"Can you get down?"

"I don't know. Ooooh. Help, help."

Matt walked up a few stairs and helped her roll off. She sat on the steps, her long-thighed legs folded up to her chin like those of a praying mantis. Her blond hair, which she had colored in lighter streaks last week, was tousled. She watched him as he leaned over at the bottom of the stairs and removed his shoes.

"Wherever have you been?" she said in her pseudo-put-out tone.

"Shopping. Stir-fry sound okay?"

"Suuuuure. If I can soak the fungus."

"That's for hot and sour soup."

"Can't we put it in stir-fry?"

"I guess we could."

"I told Shadrack the other day that we put this stuff called cloud ears in our food, and that it really was a fungus that blew up like a balloon in water, and you know what he said? He said funguses were like scabs on trees and they probably had pus."

"Scabs are part of the skin," Matt explained. "But a fungus is a plant that usually grows on another plant. A mushroom is a kind of fungus."

Tobie crossed her legs around each other, once at the knees and then at the ankles. Matt thought someday she would surely break, but she was oblivious to her flexibility. Softly she began chanting. At first he couldn't understand her; then the words clarified.

"There's a fungus amungus, there's a fungus amungus."

She sat there picking tiny balls off her wool sweater, examining each closely as if it were a nit.

"What've you done with your glasses?"

"I thought you'd nevah notice," she said in her best vamp voice.

"Well?"

"Well, don't you think I look better without them?"

"I can see your freckles better."

She clamped her hand over her nose. Matt started to walk upstairs, forcing her to shift her position.

"Don't you think I would look better in contact lenses? You could see my speckled beauty better."

"So, it's the old contact lens scam, is it?"

"Daddy, please, please. I want violet ones so I have eyes like Elizabeth Taylor."

He turned and looked down at her long-pulled face.

"Boy, you look lugubrious," he said.

"What's loo-goo—you're always using long words. How're we supposed to communicate if you use words I don't understand?"

"Lugubrious means your freckles get elongated and sad."

"That's ridiculous. I could play softball better."

"You're already better than all the boys on the team."

"Besides, I wouldn't have to wear those nerdy elastic bands to keep on my glasses. They're for dweebs and zods. And . . . I could look out of the corners of my eyes, like I can't now."

Matt looked at her out of the corners of his eyes, and she laughed. Maybe she thought she was winning the argument. Maybe she was. But not for the reason she might think, not her persuasiveness. Perhaps he should allow her to wear contacts, because then she might turn her attention to boys. That would be normal, though he grudgingly admitted he had mixed feelings about the time she would start dating. This local generation of thirteen-year-olds moved in packs of boys and girls. Only a few had genuine dates. That began at about age fifteen in Sand Ridge.

Matt worried perpetually about Tobie's transition out of puberty and into independent womanhood. He had always tried to be matter-of-fact in explaining the biological changes a girl undergoes, but he realized there simply were limits on Tobie's openness in asking him questions. A year ago, he had told her about menstruation before a film was shown to the sixth-grade girls at the elementary school. When she graduated to junior high, she'd attended a series of three classes that Nurse Ross gave to the girls' PE classes. He had given her books to read at appropriate times. But because there was no dominant woman in her life, he worried that she might get warped opinions or be repressed on the subject of sex. His secretary, Audrey, had helped out; she lived a block away and Tobie would occasionally drop in and chat with her. Matt knew this was inadequate, but he hadn't much alternative.

Last May one day when he was working in the yard after school, Tobie had dashed out the back door, slamming the screen, pranced up to where he was planting tomatoes, and came to a screeching halt, placing an arm akimbo.

"Guess what," she'd commanded.

"You finished your homework early."

"Nope."

"You want to go to the movies with Carol."

"Nope."

"Lessee." He tilted his head pensively. "You've resolved not to talk on the telephone for one week."

"Daddy!" she said in exasperation.

"I give up."

"My period started."

He was flabbergasted. What did you do and say when your daughter made an announcement like this? Usually a daughter would confide in a mother, who would then tell the father. "Well, well, well, that's just fine," Matt said. He reached out and shook Tobie's hand. "Congratulations." That didn't seem quite the appropriate response. He'd hugged her, stumbling over the hoe, and they were both shy. "D'ya want a cigar?" he'd asked, and they'd both laughed.

Tobie trailed Matt into the upstairs hallway, a dark-stained, oak-trimmed room that led to the four bedrooms and a bathroom. Upstairs the ceilings were low, and Matt always felt compressed when he was standing up; Tobie liked them low because it was cozy.

"How 'bout if I say I'll seriously consider whether you can have contacts on your birthday?"

"That's ages away," she complained.

"Ages? You call six months ages?"

"It's forever," she said.

Suddenly an enormous *baaarrrrooomp* bellowed out from the bathroom. Tobie's light brown eyes widened in surprise.

"What was that?"

"You didn't see him? I brought him home earlier."

"Him who?"

"That's what happens when you don't wear your glasses."

She spun about on the heel of her sneakers and ran into the bathroom. Matt reached in behind her and turned on the light.

"I don't see anything."

Matt pointed to the bathtub, its glass-paneled door closed except for a crack. Tobie slid it open, and the bullfrog *baaroomped* again. He sat halfway up the tub floor with one long toe tip in the pool of water and a yellow ribbon of pee staining the white porcelain beneath him.

"He's fantastic. He's gigantic. Where did you get him?"

"Out by the—near a pond of water."

He waited for the why-were-you-there. He still didn't know how he would tell her. Blair was probably right: tell her straight out.

"But you're breaking the rules," she accused.

"Am I? Do you really have five animals?"

"'Course I do. How can you break the rules? You won't let me."

"If I'm giving you the frog, I guess you'll be breaking them, too. Let's see, who do you have now? Wig, the cockatiel; Sam Houston, squirrel; Plague, the garter snake; Abracadabra, the chameleon; and who else? That's only four."

"The guppies," she said. She was bending over the tub peering into the frog's slow-blinking, large eye, which was grinding around in a slow pivot. She reached out from behind to touch him. The creature hopped an inch and splatted the water beneath him.

"Squat. Let's call him Squat."

"I think he could live down to his name."

Ever since she could walk, Tobie had collected animals. She treated them as adults—not exactly adult people, but she accorded them respect. The meticulous and extended observation she lavished on them was a form of adoration of life in all its variety. Matt had watched her study turtles, birds, rabbits, even insects for hours. She absorbed their movements, textures, and traits. Early on, he'd limited the number of animals she was allowed to keep to five. Sometimes this fluctuated (meaning more, never less) when one of the animals was tiny. Or sometimes when one was ailing, Matt would arrange for another to appear. From them, Tobie had learned about birth and death, joy and mourning.

"What does he eat?"

"I called Harper, and he said he'd be okay for a day or two. He eats insects, snails, and crayfish. I fed him some spiders from the basement."

"Hello, Squat," Tobie said soothingly.

She knelt over the tub.

"Do you think he can see all around?"

"Probably, with those periscope eyes."

Squat sat immobile on his wedge-shaped back feet. He was mottled, drab gray-green, the color of Helen Wagner's facial mask. Tobie touched him. He didn't flinch. She slowly placed both hands around him and lifted him a couple of inches. He squirmed, and then suddenly urine exploded all over. Tobie dropped him hastily and held her dripping hands over the tub. She looked up at Matt, and they both burst out laughing.

"So you're scared, are you?" she said with a chuckle, addressing Squat.

"Pretty good defense," Matt said.

"What are we going to keep him in?"

"Why don't you take Squat to the old duck cage in the basement and put him in the low pan with an inch of water? I'll be down in a second."

Matt watched his daughter descend the stairs. He leaned against the doorframe, dreading his inevitable task.

God, his feet were heavy. He started downstairs. He'd have to do it. Get it over with. Tobie either couldn't hear him or was ignoring his approach. Halfway down the cutaway stairs, he was washed by the cold, wet air that always seeped through the mortar between the sandstone blocks into the basement. This part of Sand Ridge used to be a swamp. He shivered. He couldn't tell her down here. It was too like the quarry.

Tobie's back was to him. She was bending over the duck cage, murmuring to Squat. The frog was transfixed. Could she really have said something about Evie? He listened more closely.

CHAPTER SIX

"Hi, Squat, you like water? Evie likes water. Do you know Evie? She can swim."

Matt's knees seemed to melt at the joints. He leaned against the stones of the wall. Tobie was whistling "You Are My Sunshine." Wig chimed in from his cage hanging next to the high window that looked out on the ground. Matt continued down the steps. Slowly she turned, sensing that something was wrong. Her eyes, which were the same honey brown as her freckles, copies of Glenda's eyes, searched his face.

Her skin was ashen. Her hands withdrew from the frog. She held them in fists at her sides. Panic shot through him. He rested his elbow on the two-by-four frame of the duck cage and watched her face.

"Evie is dead," he said.

Her intake of breath seemed to be his own. She pressed her lips together. Her eyes roamed away, as if looking for a way out of his statement. She released her fists, tensely spread her fingers, and closed them tightly again.

"I didn't believe them. A couple of boys at school . . ."

She shook her head as she spoke. She shuddered. Her

restraint collapsed. Matt put his arms around her and she folded against him. The tears came, caught in her throat; her spasmodic sobs tore through him. His eyes fogged. He lifted some strands of blond hair off her temple. She had put on her glasses, and as she clung to him, the corner of the frames poked his chest.

"Did she . . ." Tobie choked. ". . . kill herself?"

Matt stroked Tobie's hair. He nodded yes, realized she couldn't see him, and said, "Ummm."

"Why did she do it?"

"I don't know. Suicide is complicated."

"It's my fault."

"I'm sure it had nothing to do with you."

"Yes, it does."

She nodded her head vigorously.

"Last week when we were walking home, me and Evie and Verity, along Elm Street, something terrible happened. Shadrack was dashing back and forth around us on his bicycle as we walked along. He was spitting and trying to just miss Evie's feet."

"Spitting tobacco?"

She nodded her head and swallowed.

"Pretty gross for a preacher's kid. What did Verity say to him?"

"Nothing, she's scared of him, calls him her big brother, sometimes like she's proud. We were just walking when, zap, a squirrel that was hopping along the 'lectric line fell down."

"Shorted it out? That line is fifty thousand volts."

"The squirrel fell in front of Evie. Just plopped. Shadrack got off his bike to check it out. He said, 'I declare this squirrel to be dead and pregnant.' Evie asked if we could be electrocuted by touching it. Shadrack was poking it with a stick, and he started chanting over and over, 'You'll get fried and pregnant, fried and pregnant, fried and pregnant.' Evie began crying and screaming at him. Shadrack chased her for a block, carrying the squirrel between two sticks. It was crisp, Daddy."

"That's Shadrack being his usual obnoxious self. You can't blame yourself for what he did," Matt said softly.

"He's a dick. But I didn't stop him. I didn't follow her like I should've and help her. Shadrack's a total dick."

Matt was jolted but hid his surprise. "Total dick" was a phrase in common high school usage, but it was new to the junior high level. The children didn't know how harsh their words sounded to their parents.

Tobie smeared a tear across her cheek. Matt handed her his pocket handkerchief and she blew her nose.

"But, Tobe, none of this would make Evie kill herself. Almost always when people die, their relatives and friends blame themselves. They wish they'd been nicer, wish they hadn't said certain things."

"Was it like that with you when Mom died?"

"Yes."

"Do you think Mom would've come back to us?"

"I don't know."

"I'm sure she would've."

"One thing for certain, she'd have come back to you," Matt lied.

It was not at all assured that Glenda would have done more than visit Tobie now and then. He remembered right before she left them with that "total dick" of a TV journalist: Matt had walked into her art studio to find her crouched before an oil canvas she'd been working on, crying. The center of it was sliced through so that canvas swatches hung like loose rags. He remembered holding her in his arms next to the flapping canvas. "What is it?" he asked. "I'm shut in—claustrophobic," she'd whispered. "I'll go mad unless I get free."

Glenda was a haphazard mother. She'd never understood about his "father nerve," even when he tried to explain. "It's devastating," he said. "It's an impulse to protect Tobie from everything. No one else can have this particular bond, this nerve, but us. Look, she's got your eyelashes. She's losing her baby chubbiness. Don't you see? Isn't she remarkable! Look, her fingers are perfect." But Glenda didn't find it all as amazing and binding as he did. She'd left abruptly, no explanations.

"She'd've come back to you, too," Tobie said. "I know she would've."

"Well, maybe. But you shouldn't think that you had anything to do with Evie's death. We don't know why she did it. There's probably some logical explanation."

Tobie pursed her lips.

"I should've known something big was wrong when Evie didn't show up for Mr. Harper's class. She'd never miss his class. She had a big crush on Mr. Harper."

"Oh?"

"Yeah. Well. You know we have this club. We invited her to join 'cause she seemed to be pretty nice. It's our club for telling secrets. Her secret was that she liked Mr. Harper. She guessed he was cute. Alice told Evie that if she wanted to belong to the club, she'd have to stop being a three-strapper."

"What's that?"

"Being really straight—carrying your backpack with all three straps, even the one around the waist."

"How're you supposed to carry it?"

"With one strap, just over a shoulder. Everybody thinks you're a dweeb if you use all three. Two is bad enough. Evie wasn't so bad, though, Alice was just being mean . . ."

Matt took her by the shoulders and shushed her. She was quiet.

"Nothing you said or did had anything to do with Evie's death. I'm sure she didn't kill herself because of you or your friends."

"Why did she, then?" she asked softly.

"I don't exactly know, or not yet, anyway."

"Will you tell me when you find out?"

"If I find out."

"Promise?"

"Promise."

He turned toward the various animal cages that stood along one side of the large basement.

"Remember Tip and Nuck?"

"And Kuster and Beaton and Pope I, II, III, ad infinitum," Tobie said, laughing and stumbling over the Latin pronunciation.

"Not exactly celibate." Matt grinned.

The two mice, Tip and Nuck, had caused a population

explosion. First they'd built their nest out of ripped-up newspapers, and every night would drastically rearrange the north-south tunnels to slant east and west, or vice versa. Their cage had been in Tobie's bedroom until the bustling noise of nightly "furniture"-moving caused her to transfer the cage to the basement. Then Matt noticed one day that they and their dozen or so offspring had taken on violent and homosexual practices that one science book said were caused by overcrowding. Finally he convinced Tobie that they should give the mice to a pet store in exchange for some other animal, he couldn't remember which one at the moment.

History. Each parent-child relationship extends back in a helix, the two human beings coiled like sweetpea tendrils around each other. If one should break and die, the coiling was fixed forever. The emotion became a statue. Hal and Helen Wagner's agony must be unbearable.

"Evie's birthday is five days before mine."

"You're shivering," Matt said. "Let's go upstairs and cook the stir-fry."

"Can I bring Wig?"

Matt tilted his head and scratched his throat beneath his ear as if speculating. "Okay."

As she hoisted his cage, the white cockatiel flattened his topknot over his bald pate, which was the color and texture of a pencil eraser. The refrigerator motor shut off the moment they entered the kitchen, and the enormous silence was filled with the chimes of the antique German wall-clock, which began solemnly to bong seven. After the seventh, there was one more gong. Wig had added his own. Tobie laughed. Then, Matt could tell, she chastened herself, remembered Evie. Sweet and sour. Hot and cold, like the burn of dry ice.

Monday night, set up for the kind of living Matt liked, a melded evening when he and Tobie cooked and talked, when she did her homework and he read. But tonight a pathos hung in the house. He'd once read of a survey that found that people who commit suicide are prone to wear and surround themselves with purple. Unprovable, but if he were to characterize the color of his tension and apprehension tonight, it would be purple. The night was not destined to be cozy and reassuring.

Tobie took over the onion chopping, while he dealt with the ginger and the garlic. That way she could allow herself to cry with impunity. The onions were so strong that his eyes became teary, too.

CHAPTER SEVEN

Their new electronic wall phone shrieked. They both froze momentarily, then Tobie jumped to get it. Matt figured it must be Chief Leland with the coroner's report. She lifted the receiver, said hello, and listened. Then she lowered the mouthpiece and smothered it against her stomach. She had to pooch out her abdomen to make the action effective.

"Matthew, for you."

"Who is it?"

She cast her eyes ceilingward. This, plus her calling him by his name, usually meant it was a woman.

The caller identified herself as Niccole Epps, a legal aide working for the Cleveland law firm defending the abortion clinic against Augusta Johnson's impending suit. Blair Nelson had suggested that she contact him. The case was quite peculiar, she said: Mrs. Johnson claimed the girl was a virgin. Matt replied minimally since Tobie was listening. He agreed to meet Ms. Epps at ten the next morning for coffee at Sobo's Family Restaurant in downtown Sand Ridge.

"It's one of those you-can't-miss-it places," he said. "Right across from the *Oracle* newspaper office."

After hanging up, he crossed the kitchen and began chopping carrots into slivers. Niccole Epps's rounded, peculiar pronunciation sounded like a lisp, as if her words were beveled. At the same time, her tone was deep and creamy, a perfect radio reporter's voice. She must be large, like an opera singer, to accommodate such a voice, he thought.

"A mysterious woman?"

"Niccole Epps. I've never met her. She was calling on some legal matter about the school. We agreed to meet tomorrow."

"Uh-huh."

Tobie stood back and surveyed him. She was acting erratically, one minute withdrawn into her repressed grief, the next her normal, cheerful self.

"As your shrink, I think"—she put on an adult tone— "that you really should get married again. It's been a long time. It's not healthy to be alone."

"You call a Tobe and six animals 'alone'?"

"Now, Matthew, I'm serious," she chided.

The phone blasted again. This time Matt got it.

"Hey, Matt, either Hal Wagner is a grief-crazed father or the posse is organizing against me. Or both."

"What's up?" Matt asked.

Matt was half mentor and father figure to Tom Harper, half friend. They were united by being outsiders. Matt had hired Harper last August, convinced he was a fine teacher. He involved the students in biology in ways few teachers could. From his first interview, Matt had liked him. Harper had applied for the job from Boston. He'd never been west of Niagara Falls. He was young, only twenty-seven, but he already knew that his aim was to be a principal. When he took the job, Matt had warned him that Sand Ridge had plenty of residents who were outright creationists. Others ranged from violently against to lukewarm over teaching Darwin and human reproduction courses, as was required by the Ohio state curriculum.

To make the locals even more suspicious, Harper was handsome—olive skin, dark hair, and a neat beard—and single. His predecessor had upset a lot of parents by showing a film about human procreation to the children. After an early warning from Matt, Harper had developed his own tactics. In his file cabinet, he stored a confiscated collection of prurient magazines and lurid literature that would have made the drawer blush if it had been human. There were the usual *Playboys,* as well as pamphlets on "How to Enlarge Your Organ Through Exercise," "G Marks the Vital Spot," and a semi-comic book called "Brunhilda Brutalized." Harper made each boy sign the magazine he was caught reading before turning it over. Upon the proper occasion, these could be produced as evidence of Harper's concern about the boys' morals and his own probity, as well as evidence to parents that their sons weren't blameless. Matt considered the scheme slightly harebrained, but it appealed to him. It had a certain kooky logic to it.

"I assume Tobie is nearby so you can't really talk?"

"Right," Matt said, continuing to slice vegetables while holding the receiver on his shoulder.

"Okay, I'll rattle on and you can be euphemistic. My phone rang. I picked it up. A voice said, 'Is that Tom Harper?' Sounded just like this friend of mine in Brookline. I answered, 'Is the pope Catholic? Do bears shit in the woods?' You know me. Talk about shit. The man on the other end of the phone blew up—burned up the line back at me. Said I lived up to my reputation. Said I taught filth and smut. Said I told kids to take off their pants. He didn't believe in the devil before but maybe he did now. Said he'd talked to some guy named Storm. Forget the last name. Clouds, maybe? Said I was corrupting young boys, teaching them how to jerk off. 'Hey, whoaaa,' I said. Tried to interrupt him. 'Who is this?' I asked. 'Wagner,' he shouted. His name didn't register at first. I defended the state of Ohio curriculum. Get this: he accused me of being a Pied Piper. Whistling them to perdition, he said. Must've been talking about my bird-whistle-identification contest in class. I told him I hadn't said anything about pants, I'd told the kids a joke. You know, how do you tell a boy cell from a girl cell? You take down their genes."

Matt groaned.

"It helps the kids remember," Harper added. "At some stage, dodo here realized that the man had said he was Hal Wagner. Dong. Good thing you told me about Evie when you called about your bullfrog. So I got real soothing, not that I'm the soothing type. I said I realized he must be stunned by Evie's death, and she was a lovely girl. That set him off again on a tirade. Said he wanted the name of every

boy in the class. He was going to track him down. 'Him
who?' I asked. 'The cock-assed, purple-tipped prick of a kid
who got my angel pregnant.' I swear—the very words.
Swore he was going to castrate the son of a bitch when he
found him. Sounds to me like Evie killed herself because she
was pregnant. Afterward, I wondered if Hal Wagner was
getting a bit dramatic for a grieving father. Me thought he
didst protest too much. The wife was ranting at him in the
background. Sounded like she was saying it was his fault,
that he coddled Evie. Then, right in my ear, nearly blasted
me out the front door, Hal shouted at her, 'Just 'cause your
father fucked you!' Whoops. She must have grabbed the
phone and slammed it down."

Harper paused. Matt couldn't think of anything neutral to
say that wasn't ridiculous. He couldn't tell, from what
Harper'd said, if Hal had heard from Police Chief Leland or
the coronor about whether the autopsy had proved Evie
pregnant.

"Sorry about this. But I thought you should know,"
Harper said. "We little fish need to be protected by you big
fish."

"Maybe I should rethink my career," Matt replied. "Maybe I'd rather be an ichthyologist. But I guess fish have
politics too. Terror politics: fear of being eaten."

They agreed to talk more tomorrow and hung up. Tobie
had poured the oil in the wok and set out the hoisin sauce.
She stood with one foot on top of the other in her ankle-high
tennis shoes, rocking back and forth like a mechanical
creature. Her tongue curled up like a tiny taco.

"That sure was a wackoid conversation," she said. "You
didn't say hardly anything."

"I hardly said anything."

"That's what I said."

Matt gave her a slanted you-know-what-I-mean glance.
"It was just Harper telling some tales."

After dinner they settled in the living room, Tobie doing
her math homework and Matt reading his newspapers. She
suddenly asked Matt if she could call Verity to talk about
Evie. He suggested that she see Verity tomorrow morning
before classes instead. It would be better to talk about their
friend face to face, not over the phone.

"When Evie is buried, will they cross her arms like this?"

"Probably."

He thought of the dense clay soil of the cemetery. How worms could manage to move in it he couldn't imagine, especially down deep.

"Did someone have to close her eyes?"

Matt rose from his chair and walked over to sit on the opposite end of the sofa from her. She chewed on her pencil and watched him.

"Yeah, honey, someone did. I had to do it."

She sat there for a long, long minute. It seemed to him her whole body was staring, not just her eyes, trying to absorb the idea. She reached out to him, and he enclosed her in his arms. Such a difference in holding her body after poor Evie, so warm, alive.

"Daddy."

"Yes."

"You know when that friend of yours called last week, that journalist? Do you want to go be a journalist again like he said?"

"No, Tobe, I want to be with you. I made that decision and I don't regret it. The most important thing in the world to me is to be with you. Now, why don't you go check the animals one last time before you go upstairs."

After she had consoled the animals about Evie, she went upstairs and prepared for bed.

The phone screamed through the quiet house for the third time. It had to be Chief Leland.

"The autopsy went quicker than expected," Leland said.

Always putting the best face on things. Matt bet there was not another cop chief like him in the entire United States. No matter how sickening and hideous things were, Leland found the positive. His words rolled around in his jowls before they came out, so they sounded wet.

"The coroner said she was about five months along; must've gotten pregnant in the summer. From what he could tell, the baby was in good condition."

Matt winced.

"Did you talk to the father?" he asked.

"*Talk* to him. Hal Wagner was calling me every five minutes till we got the report. Guess it's understandable, though. I tried to make it easier on him. I told him it looks like she was a good girl. She was cherry. Maybe her note was right."

"You said that to Hal? That she was cherry?"

"Didn't word it quite like that. But, yeah."

"Come on, Leland, girls don't get pregnant just by eating, you know."

"Yeah, but there's something weird going on."

"Like what?"

"Guys were talking at the bar tonight. Something about Kim Johnson being pregnant, too. Her old woman is claiming no boy ever laid a hand on her—or anything else. I'm just saying these ain't no girls you'd expect to mess around. Then there's the Sobo family. Couldn't be a stricter Catholic family. They follow that little girl—what's her name?—around like she was the jewels of Jesus. There ain't no boy 'round that's idiot enough to mess with her."

"She's pregnant?"

"That's the talk."

"Whose talk?"

"Don't rightly remember."

Matt was stunned. These weren't the kinds of rumors people would make up. You'd have to be crazy to invent them.

"Oh, another thing. These guys were mentioning some new teacher you got at your school. Harvard? Harper? Saying he might have something to do with Evie's pregnancy."

"That's really off base," Matt said.

He thanked Leland for reporting on Evie and hung up. Who could be doing this? A gang of boys? The girls would be too ashamed to tell. One thing, Leland was right about the upstanding families. Of course, he was bound to get stuck in the muck of it; he could feel it coming. Harper! God, what next? Mass rumormongering was dangerous. Matt switched off the kitchen light and the one in the dining room and stumbled through the dark of the living room toward the stairs. Tobie's favorite soft rock music floated down. She walked into the upstairs hall from the bathroom. Her long flannel granny gown, with a pink ribbon at the collar, swept over the floor.

"My freckles are moving around," she called as he ascended.

She was trying to be normal again. She drew him into the bathroom so she could locate the freckle in question in the mirror. Matt gazed at her quietly. The bones of her cheeks were becoming more distinct as her face matured.

"I promised I'd tell you why Evie killed herself."

Tobie's eyes showed panic, as if she wished to hide, like a wounded animal. She watched him in the mirror.

"She was pregnant."

She slowly turned and searched his face for confirmation of his words.

"Daddy."

"Ummm."

"How do I tell if I'm pregnant."

He was speechless for a moment.

"Honey, if your period stops. But it doesn't just happen by itself, you know."

"Will I want to kill myself if I get pregnant?"

He looked directly into her eyes, hoping his words would sink indelibly into her mind.

"Nothing is so important that you should ever kill yourself. Besides, I love you too much. If you have troubles, we can talk. Anyway, you're not going to get pregnant till you're a woman and you want to have a baby with someone."

CHAPTER EIGHT

Lorna Ross leaned over to help her baby eat his cupcake. Like most mothers, she half opened her own mouth, to assist by example. She licked the sweet, blue icing from her thumbnail, then ate both cupcakes, for her baby was actually dead.

Her baby would have been ten today. Sometimes Lorna thought of him as ten, but then she would correct herself. She was the only one getting older.

She celebrated Buford's birthday every year, just like today, with special petits fours she purchased at the Good-Dough Bakery. Her apartment with its Salvation Army furniture was located just above the bakery; she closed the air vents, trying to keep out the sweet, bloated smell of yeast from below.

She placed his orange playsuit on the chair, anchoring it beneath the edge of the large, brass-framed photograph of him pink and naked after his bath. Buford had been wonderful from the beginning.

Ernie'd been on vacation from the steel mill in Cleveland and she'd got time off from her old job ironing at Excel Cleaners, "The Uniform People." They were in Louisiana visiting Ernie's mama. It was March and peculiarly hot, even for the South, when they'd gone out for a stroll. Lorna had been fending off her husband for weeks, ever since their last fight. Now she felt listless, wilted by the heat and tired of resisting Ernie's persistence.

In the garden of an old, abandoned house, he'd stopped and commanded her to stand still. She gazed at the tilting building, idly interested in its tattered curtains. She watched transfixed as Ernie searched in his pocket, pulled out a pocketknife, unfolded the long blade, and sliced through the front of her dress until it hung open limply. He pushed it off her arms, and it dropped at her ankles. He cut her bra and her panties. The back of the blade flashed coldly between her legs.

He ordered her to lie down. She did, mashing the tall grass near some peony bushes. The warm air throbbed through the heavy perfume from the honeysuckle vines climbing the wall of the house. The giant, bulbous peonies were purply-red with dozens and dozens of petals. Ernie sliced the stem of a huge flower with his knife, then stood over her and commanded her to spread apart her legs. The petals of the flower tumbled through the air and hit her body without a sound. He cut another and another, shaking them over her breasts and belly. She lay hypnotized, lulled by the warmth, overpowered by smells, entranced by the knife. She reached down and felt the cool flower parts on her body.

He removed his shoes and socks, folded his pants and shirt. She'd never seen him so methodical. He knelt beside her and ran his fingers through her petals. Slowly he edged between her legs, entering her and thrusting in and in and in. She was astonished and shy later to discover some peony petals inside of her. Buford was her little flower.

After Buford was born, Ernie grew vicious, accusing her of thinking only of the baby. The intensity of his anger overwhelmed any good feelings they had left for each other. He'd been unemployed for weeks and drinking hard when he disappeared.

She finished a course in practical nursing and took the job at Sand Ridge Junior High. Those were the happiest days of her life. Every girl should want to be a mother. She would do anything for Buford. Her baby was dearer than her own life.

Lorna touched his photograph. Tears blurred the room. She wondered if a person could tell when his mind went over the edge.

An accordioned, clackety noise filled the apartment and Main Street. The owner of the bakery was yanking down the steel shutter over his shop, closing for the evening.

She set the Bozo the Clown record on the turntable, and the music and story came out scratchily from the old record player. Buford had always smiled and gurgled at that silly kids' record, especially the part where Bozo imitated the elongated guffaw of the circus giraffe: uh-huh, uh-huh, uh-huh.

She remembered that awful night when Buford left her.

Actually, the day had been lovely. Every year she forgot, until it came, that spring was her favorite time of year. The leafless trees were hairy against the sky. Knuckly branches of the apple tree had just begun to bud. Leaves soft as earlobes were popping out on some bushes. Spring was always wet and luscious in northern Ohio. The earth was waterlogged from immediately below the grass clear down to the edge of the fiery burning part. No one could convince her it wasn't; she was a well-traveled woman. She was the most adventurous person in her family. All of her five brothers and sisters lived around Toledo, where her father was a retired farm laborer and her mother was still a domestic servant for a town family.

Maybe she was adventuresome and different from the rest of her family because she didn't really belong to them. Her coloring was different. While they were all reddish-blond, she was dark with olive skin and dark brown hair, which she used to streak with peroxide. Her eyebrows were so heavy that they met across her nose. Of course, no one knew that, because she plucked them. At the age of thirty-five, she had pronounced crow's-feet around her eyes. Her hair was extremely thick and, because Ernie had once said he liked it thick, she'd never let a beautician thin it, but wore it in a blunt cut that caused it to bush out.

That morning a blue jay in the ash tree outside her window had woken her. Its raucous squawking was alarming and made her shiver. The jay kept screaming so long and loud that Buford woke up crying. Lorna jumped out of bed, reached into the crib, and picked him up to soothe him. He'd been sleeping fitfully the past few nights. Later she delivered him to the day-care center and went off to school for her usual four-hour daily stint.

That night at about eleven, three hours after she'd nestled Buford next to his puffy polar bear, he stirred. She'd been sitting in the rocking chair, reading a story in a ladies' magazine; the breeze through the window occasionally lifted a page in a gentle gust and she would smooth it down. In between reading, she thought about last week's bingo game at the Baptist church. And she worried about her job, since that day she'd been asked by the athletics director to provide services for a new girls' tennis camp to be held at the school gym for the first time that coming summer. The gym teacher wanted her to give the eleven- to thirteen-year-old girls checkups and answer any questions about general health and menstruation. The teacher wanted individual visits for the girls.

Out of her reverie, Lorna heard Buford stir. Like many mothers, she was hyper-attuned to her baby's sounds. He coughed and kicked his feet. Lorna placed the magazine face down on the coffee table to keep her place and walked over to the crib. Buford had half woken up and was gurgling and choking a little. She picked him up and began humming a lullaby. He cried fitfully as she carried him back to the rocking chair, murmuring sweet things. Thinking he might need to burp, she gently placed him over her left shoulder as she sat down. He cried for a moment, then coughed as she patted him on the back. Then he was quiet. She felt reassured as she rocked him. Then she realized he was rather limp. She stopped rocking and twisted her head around to look more closely at his face. He was so still. Out of the corner of her eye she saw the curtain blow full into the room and then suck out violently, flattening against the screen, staying there she didn't know how long, because suddenly she knew something was desperately wrong.

She dipped him off her shoulder. His eyes were wide open, staring. What was wrong? She held his wrist. He wasn't breathing.

"Buford, my baby, my darling."

Her words were inquisitive at first.

"Buford, what's wrong? You can't do this. You can't."

She slapped him. She'd read somewhere that people had been shocked back from the dead. No, no, he couldn't be dead. She picked him up beneath his arms and shook him hard. But his head rolled and she couldn't bear it. She put him back in her lap, ripped all the buttons off her robe as she lowered the top, and pressed him tightly against her naked breasts.

Boy babies were more susceptible to disease than little girls, she knew that, and she'd heard of crib death. But he hadn't been in the crib when this happened. She stood up, still clasping him desperately to her body, and the robe fell off. She began pacing across the apartment, saying, "No, no, no." Sometimes she murmured his name and Ernie's.

She gently lowered him back into the crib. Maybe he'd recover, back to where he was before she'd picked him up. Always she kept pacing, passing by and bending over and touching his hair, his back, drawing down the legs of his cotton flannel pajamas. She was a nurse. She should know what to do to help her baby. Her training was failing her. She thought of calling a hospital, but that might confirm her fears. She didn't want to know. She must've paced back and forth for fifteen minutes, tears rolling down her cheeks, sometimes singing, sometimes moaning and murmuring words that would have been unintelligible to anybody hearing them.

She recalled the curtain blowing, first into the room and then abruptly out. That must've been his soul going. She held the curtain against her lips as if it might still have some of his life in it. Then suddenly she went to her closet, pulled out a dress, put it on, tied on her walking shoes, and removed the stroller from the back of the linen cabinet. She squeezed her coat, several diapers, and her jacket under her arm, then lifted Buford out of the crib. She was very quiet outside in the hall. Although only one other person lived in the building over the bakery and he was a man too deaf to have heard her, she was careful. The transformer on the street outside gave a loud buzz, making her jump and draw back until she realized what it was. Holding Buford close with one arm, she bumped the stroller wheels down the stairs as quietly as she could.

On the sidewalk, she looked around carefully. All was quiet. The transformer buzzing stopped. In the pool of light from the street lamp, she awkwardly opened the stroller, kicking it open with her foot while still clutching Buford. Slowly, holding his head up, she eased one of his legs through a leg hole, then the other. She propped her coat and the diapers around him to keep him upright, and put on her jacket. All the time she was talking and singing and crying.

"We're going for our walk. Down by the creek. To see the crawdads. Remember the crawdads, Bu? Remember the way the mama crawdad carried all those little babies under her tail?"

No one was on the street, which was hardly unusual. After all, it was eleven o'clock at night in a small town. The air was cool but not cold. The wind swayed the tops of the big trees, but the small trees were still. Lorna took Buford on their usual walk. She walked a lot because their apartment was small. She had the short, quick stride of a fattish person. She checked Buford as she went along, leaning over to make sure he was still sitting up straight.

Down Main Street, past the gas station, which closed at eleven. The laundromat was dark except for a single light from inside that made the machines look otherworldly. To the creek. Past the creek. She would save that. She wanted to walk more. She wheeled the stroller around the old, disused coal storage building near the defunct railroad. Much of the time she was talking and crying. She could scarcely see for her tears. Whenever she hit a bump she would check Buford. She walked around to the back of the lumberyard. She liked the smell of new-cut lumber. It was cheerful, hopeful, because anybody using it was planning for the future. She knelt to check Buford, calling his name, patting his cheek, adjusting his knitted booties, all the while wiping back her tears. She heard a car, glanced up, and, through the lumber storage area, saw one of the town's police cars patroling. No one noticed her.

She started walking again, back toward Heron Creek, past the high, impenetrable wooden fence around Yale Kaltmann's house. She'd walked by his fence frequently, each time wondering what he did behind there, for she'd heard that he had no family. This time she didn't think of the fence at all. She rolled the stroller down the sidewalk to the public bench near the creek, next to the memorial for the town's Vietnam war veterans. The instant she sat down, she noticed that a gate she'd never seen before was slightly ajar, leading through Yale Kaltmann's mysterious fence. She picked up the entire stroller with Buford in it in her arms and headed toward refuge behind the fence. By now her eyes were dry, the tears drained, and she felt transfixed even though she couldn't have been, for she picked her way through the gate, leaving it wider open, and crunched through last year's leaves on the floor of a small forest inside the fence.

Except for her footsteps and her talking, the night was quiet. The raucous tree-frog and insect choruses of summer hadn't yet begun. The moon sliver that dashed in and out of clouds guided her to a clearing beyond the woods. It was a garden, or would be a garden. The ground was freshly plowed, the heavy clay laboriously turned up in gigantic clods. To one side of the plowed dirt were four upturned crates. She set down the stroller and sat wearily on one, turning Buford toward her while she reminded him again of the crawdads.

His birth, the nursing of him, his laughter suffused her mind like liquid soap sinking into clothes. Tears came again. She buried her face in her hands and rocked herself back and forth on the creaking crate.

"Ho! Who's there? You're trespassing! What're you doing?"

She kept rocking and moaning.

"I said, what're you doing?"

She was still, raised her face, her hands suspended in air. It was a man in jogging shorts. In the dark, she couldn't see his face well. Suddenly a flashlight flamed in her face. Her arms shot up, her elbow hooked over her eyes to shield them. The man's hand reached out over Buford's stroller and yanked her arm down.

"Mrs. Ross."

His hand dropped. She said nothing.

"Why are you behind my fence? What are you doing out at this hour?" The tone of his voice hadn't changed perceptibly on his recognition of her. It was angry, almost nervous.

Suddenly an earsplitting wail slit the spring night, causing Yale Kaltmann to leap backward in shock.

"My baby, my baby," Lorna howled.

Her voice played up and down the scale and she began sobbing uncontrollably. Yale flashed his light around till it caught the stroller. Sure enough, there was a baby, its eyes wide open. Odd, it made no sound. Yale moved to touch it. Lorna screamed, "No, no, no, no!"

"Is something wrong with it?"

Lorna wailed, "No, no, no!" She didn't want anyone to know.

Yale knelt next to the stroller and shone the light at Buford. The eyes didn't even blink. Jesus, her baby was dead.

"Mrs. Ross, I'm Yale Kaltmann, you know, at the school, the electrical supervising engineer. I'm not going to hurt you or your baby."

The tone of his voice had changed dramatically, though Lorna was far too distraught to notice. His instant and profound sympathy made him seem like a different person. The fact that nobody had ever been on his property here had caused his initial irritation. But when he saw Lorna's plight, he was flooded with compassion and curiosity.

"Mrs. Ross, why don't you come inside my house and have a cup of tea or something to drink?"

Lorna didn't stir. Her sobbing had subsided to catches of breath. Yale, still kneeling next to Buford, reached over to shut his eyes. They were stuck.

"No, no, no," Lorna wailed again.

"Shh, shh," Yale said, turning quickly and grasping her arm firmly, the way one did disturbed people.

He didn't know exactly what he was going to do to help, but he was drawn to Lorna's predicament. He loosened his grip.

"You can't just stay out here all night, we must do something. Why don't you trust me? I will take care of everything."

Only then did Yale know what he was going to do; and now that he knew, he could act with utter confidence, giving Lorna courage, too.

"Here, let me carry Buford and you carry the stroller," he said.

He stuck the flashlight under his arm and lifted the baby out as Lorna weakly moaned and murmured Buford's name.

"Here, take the stroller."

Yale wanted her to be busy while he held Buford. He moved off. In a panic, Lorna grabbed the stroller, folding it with a clatter, and followed. In the cover of the dark, and with Lorna behind him, Yale again tried to close Buford's eyes.

One closed.

But he couldn't shut the other one.

God, she'd have a fit if she saw one open and one closed. He'd have to act fast. All the way up the steep hill to the house, he kept trying to ease the other eye down, speeding up his pace to stay well ahead of Lorna. Damn, he'd have to head straight to the basement. He didn't like it when things didn't go his way.

Lorna was trundling along far behind him, shouting weakly for him to wait, wait. Yale strode through his small orchard. The house loomed in the gloom as the moon disappeared behind a particularly thick cloud. His house was gigantic, the kind originally built for a single family, back when families came with ten people, and servants. He kept it in reasonable repair, even replacing the slates on the steep roof himself. He could do all this because he was fit. He prided himself on the condition of his body. Aside from jogging almost every night, late so as not to encounter anyone, he rode an exercycle that he kept in one of the house's multitudinous rooms. People probably thought the house was too large for him, but he wouldn't want a smaller one. Sometimes the overflow of his experimental materials from the basement had to be accommodated upstairs, and he needed storage space for other projects.

His muscles strained as he pulled farther ahead of Lorna. Before she caught up to him, Yale wanted to set the baby down in the light so he could try the eye again. He rounded the corner of the house and bounded up the front steps. He stopped and tried the eye again slowly. It worked. Both closed. What a relief. He removed his running shoes without bending over, hooking the back of each heel with the toe of the other foot and sliding them off. Quickly his mind turned to his plan. He was in his shorts. That would be distracting to Lorna, not to mention to him. He swung open the door, ran up the stairs, grabbed his sweatpants with one hand from the closet hook, set the baby on the floor, pulled on his pants, grabbed the baby, and ran back downstairs as Lorna mounted the front steps. He'd never held a baby before. Of course, this one didn't wiggle or cry, so it was different. But it wasn't too stiff yet. He rather liked holding him. God, he'd have to hurry, though. The baby wouldn't stay fresh for long.

"Mrs. Ross, welcome, do come in."

No one from the town had ever visited his house. He had kept them all out. A couple of delivery men had helped him carry the heavy machinery in, but even the postman never ventured beyond the low front gate, which was fifty yards from the house.

"What are you doing with Buford? I want my baby!"

"I have him. He's just fine."

"Give him to me. Why did you run away with him?"

She was crying again. Her hair was an enormous, tangled bush around her head. She dropped the stroller on the front porch as Yale held the door open.

"Ah, Mrs. Ross, I'm sorry, I must ask you to remove your shoes. I always do that, as you can see. Mine are over there. I hope you don't mind. I'm sorry, could you please take them off out here?"

Dazed and compliant, Lorna backed over to the banister of the porch, leaned heavily against it as she untied her shoes. She let them stay where they fell and headed through the door Yale held open.

"Buford, my darling, here's Mother." She stretched out her arms for him.

"Not yet," Yale said, half alarmed, half soothingly. "I'm strong. I would like you to follow me, and we'll take care of you and Buford."

Lorna began whimpering, pleading. "I want him. I'm his mother. You can't take him from me."

"Come with me," Yale said, again walking ahead of her.

He took her through the hall to the basement door, opened it, and switched on the lights, which blazed forth like daylight. Lorna followed him cautiously down the steep stairs, patting the tops of her breasts disconsolately. As the basement came into view from behind the stairwell, she paused and gazed in amazement. The whiteness was dazzling. As her eyes adjusted, she noticed all the tanks and equipment. It seemed rather like a hospital, so it didn't make her too uncomfortable. There was a vast sound of ticking. Slowly her eyes drifted from wall to wall: clocks everywhere. The only place she'd ever seen so many before was in a store. At that moment, one of them began to bong. One bong. Then another. And another. She couldn't distinguish between them. They were all going off in dozens of tones, chimes, and clunks. She felt dizzy. Then the chiming faded, terminated by one, slow cuckoo.

"It's late," Yale said. "You must be very tired. Why don't you come and sit over here?"

He pointed to a white folding chair tucked behind a machine. Lorna wearily but dutifully took the chair and unfolded it. Maybe if she was obedient, she'd get to hold Buford.

"Please," she said, holding out her arms.

"Sit down first."

She sat. Yale handed him down.

"Ohhh, his eyes are closed."

She yanked him to her and rocked back and forward.

"Buford, are you gone? You can't go."

"Mrs. Ross, he's passed on, sleeping." Yale spoke soothingly.

She whimpered.

"I can help you, if you want."

She looked up at him, running her sleeve under her nose. Yale was disgusted, but she didn't see his expression.

"Why do you want to help me?"

"Because I can, because I have the equipment and, more important, I have the knowledge of cryogenics that can make your baby immortal."

Lorna hadn't any earthly idea what he was talking about.

"You realize, of course, that ordinarily you'd have to bury your baby, your Buford."

"No, no!"

"It's the law. But if you promise absolute silence, if you tell no one, I mean *no one,* I will put your baby in cryonic suspension for rejuvenation at some future date when medical experts will know how to cure him of whatever made him die."

"I'm afraid."

"You don't need to be afraid."

"What are you going to do?"

Was she stupid? he wondered. Maybe she didn't know what cryonic suspension was.

"I'm a scientific specialist. I can freeze your baby so quickly with these machines that he will not be damaged, but his every organ will be preserved in a pristine state. Then years from now when medical science knows how to cure him, they can thaw him and perform the appropriate operation that will save him. You want your baby back, don't you?"

Lorna was staring at him. She nodded. She knew who Yale Kaltmann was from the staff meetings at the school. But all she could remember now was what Thelma Johnson, who worked in the school kitchen, had said about him once: "He's soooo handsome, those eyes, come-hither eyes. You know, it's a crime he's still a bachelor."

He was handsome. And he was so solicitous of her. Not at all like Ernie used to be. Yale was explaining all these things like he really wanted to help Buford. His eyes were deep and mysterious.

"If you'll cooperate with me, we can save him," he said, leaning over to pat Buford on the head. Lorna drew back, shocked by a blue tattoo she glimpsed on Yale's forearm.

"I'm sorry," he said, following her eyes.

He always wore long-sleeved shirts when he went out in public, but now he still had on his jogging T-shirt.

"I got it when I was in the army."

"What is it?"

"These men, bullies really, told the man to tattoo a girl on my arm and then put the name of my girlfriend on it, my girlfriend from the first grade, they said, since they knew I didn't have a girlfriend then."

"That's horrible."

He shrugged. He wanted to pretend it meant nothing to him. He'd never told anybody what else had happened that night, and he never would. He tried unsuccessfully to block it out of his brain.

They had shoved him into a darkened room and slammed the door behind him. When he saw the prostitute sitting with her knees together on the edge of the bed, his first thought was that she'd never get out of the black lacy pants, bra, and chemise she was wearing. She lay back on the bed and, to his shock and disgust, opened her legs. Her panties had a slit in them. He'd seen pictures of underwear like that, but he'd never seen it on a woman. Woman! You couldn't really call her that, he thought. *Whore,* the only word for her. What she made him do! He couldn't bear to remember. He was stunned at his loss of control during the sex act. It was all so selfish and obsessive. He'd become wrapped up only in his own pleasure. Afterward, he was horrified to think how this woman had controlled him, could have made him do anything. He was nauseated. All he could think of was the filth and dirt of it. And the perfume. He thought the smell wouldn't wash off his body. Never again would he have sex. Never.

"What's the tattoo say?" Lorna asked shyly.

"Beatrice. My mother's name. I gave them her name."

"That's nice."

Ordinarily he wouldn't tell anybody even these few things. Hell, ordinarily no one would be in his basement. But he had to get Lorna to cooperate. For her own sake.

"Now, I'm going to have to ask you some questions before we proceed to help Buford."

Lorna squeezed him closer.

"Do you have any family, any relatives near Sand Ridge?"

"No."

"Where does your family live?"

"Toledo."

"Good. Does anybody know that Buford has died? Have you told anybody?"

She shook her head.

"You know that when a person dies, the authorities must be informed and the body must be handled by them and either buried or cremated."

She looked desperate. Buford was all she had in life. Without him there was no meaning.

"Do you go to church?" she asked, looking up earnestly at him.

"Not since I was little," he said.

Her face fell.

"But you see, I believe in God," he hastily added. "I believe that God operates through science. That is why I have spent my life preparing myself just for this moment. I am God's servant in saving Buford for a future immortality."

"What's this stuff you're talking about?"

"Cryonics. You see, a lot of people do it. Some prominent people. You know who Walt Disney is, right?"

She nodded.

"When Mr. Disney died, his will ordered that his body be placed in cryonic suspension, frozen that is, until medical science advanced far enough that there was a cure for what killed him."

Her eyes were looking at him over Buford's head. She was holding the baby up, her lips tenderly pressed to his forehead.

"Now, if you want me to help you, you've got to swear total secrecy. Otherwise it could get very dangerous for you. You could be charged and hauled into court. You must tell no one. Do you understand?"

"Yes," she said, immobilized by his penetrating look as he leaned toward her.

"Then let's begin. Hand him to me."

"No. What are you going to do?"

"Certain preparations have to be made to protect his body. Maybe it would be better for you to wait upstairs while I prepare him."

She shook her head vigorously.

"Then you'll have to let me get to work. We don't have much time left."

Yale reached for the baby and, when she wouldn't let go, they carried him together to a cabinet he used for his experiments. They removed Buford's clothes, and Yale began smearing a special lubricant over the baby's body. Lorna began crying again, tears rolling down her chin and dripping onto the floor. Yale didn't like that—he kept the place antiseptically clean—but he said nothing. She reached out to touch the body, and then helped spread the grease, all the while talking incoherently, as when she was out walking.

Yale worked quickly. After the lubrication, he took special foil from a drawer, spread it out on a different counter, and cut it to fit Buford. Deftly he clipped the foil around the baby, almost before Lorna realized what was happening. Only the face was left exposed. Lorna touched his closed eyes. Yale quickly snatched him up and eased him into the capsule, which had been humming behind him. He snapped the door shut, looked quickly at the body through the protuberant porthole window, checked various gauges, opened a valve, and listened for the rush of nitrogen. He turned, to find that Lorna had crossed the room, slumped down on the stairs, and buried her face in her hands.

"That's it," Yale said. "We've saved him. Now someday you can hold him in your arms again."

He bent over and lifted Lorna up. He didn't like touching her, but she had just enabled him to run the most impressive experiment of his career so far.

"Now, listen carefully. You must promise me that you will mention this to no one. Do you promise?"

She sobbed.

"I said, do you promise?"

Yale was suddenly worried. What if she spoiled it? No, he wouldn't panic. He grabbed her by the arm above the elbow and squeezed it hard, so hard she screamed at the pain. Her eyes looked at him in fear.

"I don't want to hurt you. But you must promise. Say, 'I promise.' "

"I promise."

"I will tell no one what has transpired here tonight."

"I will tell no one what has tra—"

"Transpired."

"—transpired here tonight."

"Now, listen a little more. In two months, you can tell your family in Toledo that Buford died and that you buried him here. Get that? Two months."

She nodded.

"As soon as possible—this weekend—you take a trip out

of town, as if you're taking Buford with you. Be sure to let people know that you've gone to visit your family in Toledo. When you come back, you say you've decided to leave him with your parents for a while. Then in six months you can tell people around here that Buford died and you buried him in Toledo. Repeat it, tell me what I just told you."

She repeated it slowly.

"Good. Now, then, you're very tired. I think you should go home."

"Buford."

"He's saved. You can come and visit him."

He guided, almost pushed her up the basement stairs, then pulled her through the hall and out the front door. He tied her shoelaces after she put her shoes on, then walked her firmly to the front gate.

When the gate clicked shut behind her, she stood shivering there for a minute. Her first footstep alone was so heavy, as if her shoe was glued to the ground. She'd been a single mother with normal mother's fears for her son. Now the worst had come true. But Yale Kaltmann had been nice. He had come to her aid. She'd never heard of this cryonics before, but if Walt Disney had done it, it must be worth something. Mr. Kaltmann had said she could come visit Buford. Maybe Buford would look down on her from heaven and know she still loved him. When Mr. Kaltmann brought him back, she'd have her own soft, sweet one again. Mr. Kaltmann really was very nice and so strong—in character, she meant. Buoyed by the thought of his kindness, she took that first heavy step home without her baby.

Now it pained Lorna to recall that dreadful night, but she couldn't help herself, especially on Buford's tenth birthday. She turned off the Bozo record. She was so tired. She knelt down at the side of her bed, as she'd done now every night for the past seven months, and she prayed that this new cross would be lifted from her before anything terrible happened, before Mr. Chays found out.

CHAPTER NINE

Neither Shadrack nor Verity Ruth Molway told their father about their mother. Verity wasn't sure why Shad never told, maybe because he himself was always sneaking around these days, doing who knew what. Or maybe it was because he was afraid of the biblical wrath of the Reverend Orville Molway. Verity was not the tattletale type herself. She knew how to keep secrets. Sometimes on afternoons like today, Verity's mother wandered in and out of people's unlocked houses. Why she did it was inexplicable. Why her father hadn't found out was another mystery.

Verity hated their house. She was ashamed that its roof was flat instead of slanted, and that it had only one story. Her father often boasted about his humble beginnings. That was why he kept the mobile home, which he called a trailer, as the entrance to the house and tacked on extensions with white aluminum siding. The result, on the vast, flat, grassy lot, was a house that resembled the low-slung, right-angled arms of a Scrabble game.

Verity came home from school and entered through the side door. The TV set was switched on to one of Wanda Molway's favorite soaps; the sound was off. Verity didn't bother to change it. She set her books on the Formica table and swung open the fridge. The mayonnaise was getting low.

She scraped it out with a rubber spatula and spread it on a slice of cracked wheat bread.

"Eating your health food, Vare?" Shad said as he burst through the door.

"Umph," she said with her mouth full.

Shad had called her Vare ever since they were little and still liked each other, before he began to get pimples and to say he wanted a bull neck. Verity figured he would probably get his wish someday.

Shad took the ketchup from the fridge, blooped some on a slice of white bread, and folded it over carefully.

Verity sank into the easy chair facing the TV, looping her long legs over the cushioned arm.

"Oh, no," Shad said with exaggerated disgust.

"What?"

"The old lady's not here; she's going to call that number in Detroit again to catch up on the story she's missed and Dad is going to get mad at her and she's going to deny it."

"The old lady? I think you could be a little more respectful."

"I'm respectful. I never tell on her, do I? Whaddaya think she does in those houses, anyway? The other day Greg's mom said she came home and there was Mom, sitting in her living room watching TV. Greg said she told his mother her bedroom was a mess, that the bed needed to be made."

"I think she wants a two-story house," Verity said.

"That's just 'cause that's what you want."

He stuffed the last of the bread into his mouth and moved his face close to hers, chewing noisily, until she turned her head away.

"You look green around the gills," he said.

"What gills, dummy?"

Shad pulled away and cuffed her on her arm just a little too hard so it hurt, then took off for his room. Verity stared at the television. It was so soothing to float away. She had always stared a lot. She needed to stare a certain amount every day.

Later, after dinner, Shad and her father left for a Scout meeting. Verity and her mother were washing and drying the dishes. The two usually didn't talk much, but when they did it was almost inevitably during dish washing. The ritual called forth confessions, observations, myth and magic. A jaybird squawked into the weird, yellowish last light of day. Jaundiced sky like this always preceded a storm. The wildflowers Verity had stuffed into an aluminum pitcher and set at the foot of her bed had been saved from the coming blast. She and her mother were silent, surrounded by the smell of detergent and the clink of dish and pan. The fifty-year-old Chinese elm outside the kitchen window swayed in the gathering wind. Verity stared up into it as she dried a plate. The branches, bulbous on the ends with clusters of tear-shaped leaves, bounced, flexing against the somber clouds. She felt motion sickness, peering up into it. The branches moved independently of each other. Her brain spun.

"Tonight is the autumnal equinox," Wanda said.

She pronounced it "e-queen-ox."

"What's that?"

"It's when the sun is exactly over the equator. Everything is still then. It's like the earth isn't spinning. I was reading this story in *Redbook*. It said that at exactly the time the sun is over the equator, you can stand eggs up on their fat ends. Do you want to try it?"

Verity shrugged. "Guess so." She had only recently observed that her mother said things to her that she would never say to her father or even to Shad anymore. Usually her mother, who had the same pale skin as Verity and faded blue-jean eyes, moved as if she were apologizing for imposing on the air. She really didn't want to distress anybody or anything. She wanted only to observe. Her shoulders sometimes would square, as they did now, at the prospect of adventure. She was a woman with big bones. She had told Verity ages ago that her mother, who had been married to a farmer in Toledo, was part Indian, accounting for her square cheeks and jaws and wide wrists. Verity removed a dozen eggs from the refrigerator. Two more boxes sat on the lower shelf. Her mother's eyes snapped and she nodded; she had planned this.

"But we can't start until eight thirty-four. That's when it's exactly the equinox."

That meant forty-five minutes. When the last pan was dried and put away, Verity leaned on the green linoleum-covered counter and watched as her mother fit the coffee filter into the pot for the next morning. By now, the room was quite dark. From her mother's silhouette moving around the kitchen, Verity could almost swear she was more confident in the dark. Verity brushed her hands across her forearms and her breasts as a chill passed through her nipples.

"You cold?" her mother asked. "Maybe you should get a sweater."

"Mama."

Verity hadn't used that name for at least a year. She had decided that she had outgrown it. The word hung in the air like incense.

"Mama, do you think I could have a brassiere?"

"Oh, my, already?"

The words were breathy, almost as if they were not quite words. Her mother reached over and pulled Verity's T-shirt tight from behind to get a view of her breasts. The teenager was surprised and embarrassed. Her mother almost never touched her. It seemed ludicrous to be blushing in the dark. Maybe her mother could act out of character because the darkness cloaked all eyes. Maybe this was her real character. Maybe in this obscurity, Verity could tell her mother her secret.

"I guess so. I was hoping maybe you'd be small like me. It's such a drag to be boob-y, I've always thought. I couldn't nurse you and Shad, but I never minded."

"Mama."

Verity's saliva evaporated, like when she and Shad used to hang out the windows of the moving car and dry their tongues in the passing wind. Her mother opened the fridge again to bring out two dozen more eggs. The fluorescent light, cold and the color of lightning, stabbed the room. Afterward the room was deeper black. The word "mama" was still suspended.

Instead of what she wanted to say, Verity said, "How many eggs are we going to do? Five omelettes?"

Her mother laughed. "I don't know. Maybe the earth will stand still for a long time and we can get them all up."

"I hope it doesn't get stuck still," Verity said. "Wouldn't we fall off?"

"I suppose."

Sometimes her mother seemed so blasé about such frightening prospects. Maybe that's why Verity could tell her.

"Let's light some candles," her mother said.

She placed the eggs on the counter and fumbled in a drawer for the black candles Verity had purchased in the grocery store because they were a "wow" color.

"Do you think this will really work?"

"Why not? Stranger things have happened."

Her mother held a candle to the gas burner and the wick flowered. She lit two more and placed them on melted wax in the indentations on three saucers and positioned them around the U-shaped countertop. The two of them sat at the counter on high bar stools. A half hour to go.

"Tell me about how you and Daddy met."

Verity wrapped her long legs around the stool leg and propped her chin on her hand. It was a story she had heard before, but she hoped there would be a new twist, a particular phrase that would expose a secret.

"At a tent revival, you know that."

"Yeah, well . . ."

"He was handsome and much older than me. He was real strong, you know. Used to play football and then he worked in a steel mill. I'd always liked going to these tent meetings, even though my mother said it was only sending words up into the air and that by the time they got to the Lord they would be too thin or too frozen for Him to hear."

"Do you think God knows everything?"

"I guess so. I leave that to your father."

Verity's mother always insisted on buying brown eggs from a local farmer's market because she'd grown up with brown eggs. In fact, they were the color of Band-Aids, Verity thought. She coddled one in her palm. It was smooth and perfect except for a tiny bump like a mole. The kitchen was moistly warm from the meal and the dish washing. The candle flames gasped and fluttered and deposited fluctuating shadows, like ancient cave drawings, on the ceiling and on the walls. Verity girdled the egg with her thumb and forefinger and tried to imagine the equator. She held the egg over a candle and gazed at its ostrich shadow. Verity jumped when suddenly the alarm on the stove went off with its tinny, irritating brrrrring.

"It's time," her mother said.

An excited glow transferred from the candles into her pale eyes, rendering them flag blue.

"The earth is still, can you feel it? Peace . . . peace . . . peace. You're supposed to chant peace."

Verity mimicked her mother's actions, holding the egg and passing her palm over it. But she was shy about the chanting until her mother said, "C'mon, or it won't work." Then she murmured, "Peace . . . peace." She watched as her mother held the egg, pointy end up, and tried to stand it up. Several times she moved her hands gently away and the egg began to topple. Finally, amazingly, on the fifth try, the egg stood. Alone. Still. On its fat end. Didn't fall over. Even after five seconds. Ten. More. It worked. They were very quiet as their eyes met, and they smiled. The very smoothness of everything, the warm light, the silky egg, the improbability, struck them quiet. Then Verity tried it, and after a minute, her egg stood. They moved carefully away and gazed at the two eggs upended. Was this peace? Her mother hid another egg inside her broad-knuckled hands, whispered to it, and stood it next to the others. Slowly they set up one after another of the eggs, murmuring, laughing, joking that it might be easier to crack the bottom when one was stubborn. "Wouldn't Shad like this?" her mother said; Verity wondered. They put eggs on the table, on top of the fridge, on the corner of the banister that went up the three steps into the mobile home part of the house, on top of the Mr. Coffee machine, on the TV set. Before she placed each one, her mother held it up to a candle flame and looked through it. "Look, this one's fertile," she said. "See the dark spot? I wonder if it will stand." It did, and her mother moved the candle flame to see that the spot floated in the bottom half of the egg.

"Mama."

"Um-hunh."

"How does a girl get pregnant?"

"A man or a boy has to know her."

Her mother didn't like to talk about sex. In fact, she had never explained sex to Verity.

"Yeah, but what do you mean, 'know'?"

"Like the Bible."

"Mama," she said in exasperation, her nerves tingling.

"A girl has to go to bed with a boy."

Verity was still, her heart pounding so hard in her throat she didn't know if she could say it.

"I didn't go to bed with anybody and I'm pregnant."

Her mother frowned. Verity knew she didn't want to hear this. Her mother mainly wanted not to be noticed and, most crucial, not to upset her husband.

"It's not possible, then," she said.

"I haven't had my period for four months and I don't feel good a lot."

"If you've been a good girl, there's no trouble," her mother said, and then added, "We'll have to tell your father."

Verity chewed the side of her mouth. Now she felt really frightened. She tried to put up another egg, but her hands were shaking too much. So she sat there, just sat there on the stool staring at the eggs, weird eggs, upended all over the kitchen in the flickering light. She watched as her mother, without a word, put up the last of the three dozen.

"You mustn't put your hands over your head," her mother suddenly said. She spoke without looking at her. "If you do that, the cord could wind around the baby's neck and strangle him."

So her mother believed it was possible she could be pregnant. Verity had been praying she was wrong.

"Do you believe prayer works, Mama?"

"I leave that to your father."

Pickup truck doors have their own high, hollow sound when slammed shut. Verity and her mother sat immobile, the last few seconds sweeter, more bizarre, more intense, just because they were about to end. All these fleshy-brown, smooth ovoids, defying sense, erected around the kitchen like a Stonehenge. The black wind gushed into the house. The flames stuttered, faded to tiny blue dots, and recovered from the whiplash as the door was partially closed. Orville bulled through the door first; he always did, as if to show how everything should be done and thought and said. Shad followed. They filled the living room. Orville's head was only inches below the low ceiling.

"Why d'ya have the lights off? What are you doing? Is this some kind of seance?"

Her father didn't wait for answers. He appeared so strange to Verity. The reddish birthmark on his left cheek looked like someone had slapped him; maybe it was the doctor at birth, she thought. Shad was his bodily echo, a little smaller. At some stage her father had taken over her brother, taken him away from her to teach him how to be a man.

"Wow, that's rad," Shad said, transfixed by the sight.

Orville suddenly switched on the overhead light and slammed the door closed with such force that the walls and floor of the house shook. The eggs began to wobble like bowling pins, and they all, some in slow motion, some in jerks, tumbled over. Wanda, now standing, was transfixed and squinting in the glare. Verity reached to catch an egg, snagged it below the counter, but it cracked and the yolk and albumen dripped through her fingers. It was the fertile one. Orville walked deliberately toward them. Verity imagined that his thick legs belonged to the Colossus of Rhodes. He picked up a fallen egg from the counter.

"What were you doing?"

"It's the autumnal equinox," Wanda said.

"I don't want you ever to do this again."

He spoke quietly and as if teaching a child.

"It is Satanism. It is based on astrology. This is exactly the way the Devil begins his temptation, innocently, seductively. We must defy his beguiling fork-ed tongue."

That was all. He whipped the evil out of the temple with a calmly delivered decree. He was never physically violent to her mother or to her. He repressed it. In fact, he seemed to be a vessel to hold violence, to trap it inside, to keep it from exploding into the world. He strode over to the refrigerator, lifted a gallon jug of milk, poured a giant glassful, and drank it instantly and entirely, as if he had just walked across a desert. Ever since he'd got the calling and given up drink, Orville had guzzled milk this way, thereby perversely maintaining his beer belly. Then he went into the room that was his office at home.

Shad flopped in front of the television to watch "The A Team" and drink a Coke. After Verity and her mother had cleaned up the kitchen, Wanda hesitantly knocked and entered the office. Verity knew she was telling.

"It was pretty rad, wasn't it?" Verity elbowed Shad lightly during a commercial.

He shrugged.

"Well, it was. What's this?" Verity asked, pointing to a large blob on Shad's jacket on the chair.

"Wax," he said, glad to be off the eggs.

"From what?"

"A candle, stoopid."

"What were you doing with a candle?"

"We were having an induction ceremony with four guys tonight. New Scouts."

"With candles?"

"Yeah, it makes it more serious."

"They were all standing up, Shad, all of them. Because the earth was still. It was at peace."

"Ummm."

"You're boring," she said.

He shrugged, but kept his eyes on the TV. She went into her room, shut the door, and read chapter twenty of *Gone with the Wind*. She loved it. It wasn't boring.

The next morning, Verity's father accompanied her to the Sand Ridge clinic and waited in the reception room while Dr. Wilson examined her. She hated going to the clinic, even though Dr. Wilson was always gentle and spoke so quietly that occasionally she missed what he said and had to guess what kind of answer he wanted. The nurse helped her climb up on the table and covered her with a white sheet. She thought of corpses. She was ordered to spread her legs apart, just like when the girls were examined at school. When a nurse or doctor said, "You're going to feel this a little bit," she always tried to think of something else, anything else, to blot out her mind so that afterward she couldn't recall precisely how her body had been touched. This was harder to do with dentists, but usually it worked with doctors.

After she had put her clothes on again, Dr. Wilson talked to her father in a separate room for an eternity. Then the nurse motioned her into the room. Her father's face was odd. She knew she had been right.

"Has any boy ever touched you where I did?" Dr. Wilson asked.

She shook her head, keeping her eyes on her hands twisting around each other in her lap. Dr. Wilson turned to her father. "It was the same with two other girls in town. In none of these cases was the hymen broken. We'll take a test, but it's clear from the cervix that the pregnancy is about five months along."

Verity felt suspended, floating, as if all of her was brain, swimming in its skull.

"I don't want to die," she said to her father in the pickup on the way home.

"Die? Girls don't die from having babies these days. You could die if you had an abortion. But you won't have an abortion. Besides, your dad will take care of you, honey. Nothing will happen to you."

She sank into deep brooding until later that day, when her father called her into his office. He sat her down and explained that this baby she was carrying was from God, a holy blessing, that the Lord was looking down with amazing grace on Sand Ridge by sending these immaculate infants. He said he was praying to further understand this wonderful thing, and that until he heard directly from God, she should not tell anyone but keep the whole thing protected and sacred.

"You must do one thing for me, will you promise?"

She nodded. If he would take away her confusion, she would promise anything.

"You must open the Bible every day, let it fall open to the passage the Lord wants you to read, and pray while you read it, let it seep into your soul. Will you do that for me?"

She clung to the command; she would hold to anything, any authority that seemed to have an answer; she would do anything, if only someone would take away her body over which she had lost control.

"Praise the Lord," her father said, placing his hand on her forehead.

His face was large and radiant, close to hers. She wondered if the birthmark, the slapmark, was hot to the touch. "Do you understand?" he asked. She shook her head and murmured, "No." Although he conveyed an aura of attentiveness, he heard only what he wanted. At least, that's what she figured, because his eyes, with their nearly albino lashes, reacted as if she had said the proper thing, and he sent her out as if she had received the Word of the Lord and been reassured.

Verity had kept her father's order not to tell anyone. She also took her Bible each day, held it as if her fate depended on it, and let it guide her. But every day the Holy Book fell open to one dreadful prophecy after another, or to some absurd section like "the begats": so-and-so begat so-and-so, who begat so-and-so, who was the father of so-and-so. Her father kept a Bible in every room in the house except the kitchen. One day her Bible opened to Revelation, chapter 16:

> *And I heard a great voice out of the temple saying to the seven angels, 'Go your ways, and pour out the vials of the wrath of God upon the earth.' And the first went, and poured out his vial upon the earth; and there fell a noisome and grievous sore upon the men which had the mark of the beast. . . . And the second angel poured out his vial upon the sea; and it came as the blood of a dead man; and every living soul died in the sea.*

The third angel poured blood also, the fourth fire, the fifth darkness, and men *"gnawed their tongues for pain."*

Verity shivered. She knew a vial from chemistry and biology. How could it have in it fire or darkness? And how could you pour darkness? Maybe angels could. She suddenly knew she was a container. Something was coiled inside her. Today she'd gone to the library and found a picture of a fetus, curled there cloudy-vague with veins. It reminded her of pictures of the earth from the spaceship *Columbia,* of frog specimens in jars of formaldehyde, of eyeballs without eyelids. Hideous images, apparitions, poured over her like a spell. The bare tree limbs outside the windows of the house

76

were like dark veins of dried blood. She was half aware of the creaking of the mobile home, caused by the cold making it contract where it was joined to the house proper. Verity tried to pray: "Our Father . . ." Why couldn't her father take all this away? She felt she had no skin, like an egg with no shell, floating, helpless, fated, confined, predestined, fragile, ill.

Suddenly, at a touch on her arm, she screamed, a sound so earsplitting that it seemed disembodied. She had not heard her mother enter the house; perhaps she had come in the front door. Verity slumped, folding her arms in, covering her face with her palms. Her mother bent over her so that they were folded into one another, mother, daughter, embryo. But there was no comfort. Only the shape of comfort. Verity rocked and rocked and sobbed, deep, dry, terrified gulpings for air. The Bible had fallen to the floor, its gilt-edged pages bent and torn. Her mother picked it up, smoothing the pages.

"What . . ." Verity choked.

Her mother patted her head, tucked a strand of hair behind her ear.

"What does He look like?"

"Who, dear?"

"God."

"No one knows," her mother said. "No one has ever seen Him."

"What will my baby look like, then?"

"Beautiful. The Son of God is perfect."

"What if it's a girl?"

Her mother looked at her, speechless. Clearly she hadn't worried as much as Verity about this baby.

"Willie May said in class yesterday that God is black," Verity blurted out.

For a few seconds her mother was silent. "I don't think so; we'll ask your father when he comes home."

That not settled, her mother went to phone the Detroit soap opera number.

CHAPTER TEN

"Hello, sir."

Matt strode past a clump of boys and through the back door. Looked like jocks. Junior high was the age of cliques. Students never hung around the two-story brick building alone or in twos. Young teenagers existed in clumps. Individualism would reassert itself again in the late high school years. Besides the jocks, there were the burnouts, mostly boys from the Golden Acres orphanage. They smoked perpetually. Then there were the cheerleaders, who Tobie said all hated each other but acted like they didn't. The farmers' boys were sometimes called heifers. Who knew what the burnouts called the children of the professionals in town.

"Hello, sirs" followed Matt as he walked down the hall toward the hundred-year-old sandstone section of the school and his office.

"Morning, Audrey," he greeted his secretary.

She looked up from the stack of mail she was slitting open.

"My God, Mr. Chays," she said. "It's awful."

Audrey Tredwell always called him Mr. Chays at school, in case any children were around.

"You know, then?" he asked.

"It's all over school. All over town, in fact."

Audrey had two eccentricities. She always had to have a fresh flower on her desk. Today it was a single bronze mum. The other peculiarity was that her hands were Exhibit A in any conversation. No matter what she was saying, one or both hands had to be between her and her listener. Matt always had to concentrate in order not to fixate on them. Audrey pointed with her long, neat, painted fingernail at the first paragraph of the top letter on the pile.

"Mail: Mrs. Dorcas Anderson says she's worried about her daughter getting pinkeye in the swimming pool. Reverend Orville Molway wonders whether you, as a pillar of the community, would like to speak out at a town meeting on the ban on liquor over 3.2 percent."

"You made up that pillar bit, didn't you?"

"It's right here," she said, smiling. "Evangelicals are eminently upright. Then they look around for fellow pillars to buttress themselves."

"I wouldn't touch that 3.2 percent liquor bit with a ten-foot pole," Matt said. "Maybe with my tongue, but not with a ten-foot pole."

Audrey passed him the mail. He paused a moment, debating whether to mention Katie Sobo. But he really didn't believe that story. Rumors around a bar.

Matt leafed through the mail, noting Orville's slogan on his letterhead: "Bewail and Repent, The Time Is at Hand."

He wondered if Orville'd heard about the pregnancies yet, Evie's and Kim's—if, in fact, Kim had been pregnant. Kim's mother attended Orville's church. The preacher was a force to reckon with when it came to moral issues in the town. He was a huge, going-flabby man. When Matt learned that Orville had overcome alcoholism, he understood him better. Then when Orville told him that his left-handedness had been "cured" by his mother perpetually paddling his hand with a wooden cheese board until he switched to the right, Matt felt sympathetic. Still, the guy had to be watched. He could fly off the theological handle at any moment.

Hell, what a splitting headache. It was so bad that the idea of cutting off his head to stop the pain almost sounded good. Matt dug an aspirin bottle out of the recesses of his old oak desk, shook three pills into his hand, rose, and walked across the room to drink water from the silvery thermos Audrey filled for him each morning.

His neck was stiff. He was tense, bottled up. His left knee throbbed. He knew it reacted to cold; looked like tension worked on it, too. He had nobody he could really talk to. He remembered a Chekhov short story he'd read about a man whose son died. This old guy, who drove a horse-drawn cab, tried to tell people about his grief, about the little details. No one had time. Finally the man had to tell it all to his horse. It wasn't that Matt was lonely. But he couldn't explain to Tobie how it really felt to pull Evie from the slimy water, to force her eyes shut.

The second buzzer went off. He walked over to Audrey's door. The student council president had just come into the reception area and stood next to the table that held the public address system microphone. Matt motioned for him to sit on the other side of the table. The boy read the announcements: the girls' tennis team had beaten Masonville; the Pep Assembly was next week; pies, for the pie-eating contest, could be turned in on Monday. Then Matt took the mike.

"This is Mr. Chays. I have a very sad announcement to make today. Some of you already know. Evie Wagner died yesterday. She was found drowned in the quarry. When a lovely girl so young and full of life as Evie is taken from us, there are no words that can fully express our grief. Therefore, I would like to propose that we bow our heads and close our eyes for a short time. I hope each of you will remember Evie as you knew her. Let's pay tribute in our silence."

Yesterday was so long ago. A spark of anger flared in him. Against whom? The parents. He wanted to blame somebody for this terrible death. And always the memory of her little body in his arms. The phone on Audrey's desk rang. She yanked the receiver off quickly. Matt watched her depress the button to cut off the caller and then leave the phone off the hook.

Matt ended the silence with, "Evie Wagner, you were one of ours. We loved you."

He clicked off the microphone. The school sounded as if it

were completely empty. The student council president had tears in his eyes and left the office in a rush. Audrey's lips were pressed together. She nodded approval. Matt walked into his office.

He didn't know how long he'd been there, turned sideways from the door, typing a draft reply to Orville Molway, when he sensed a heavy presence at his door. He swiveled. Nurse Lorna Ross wasn't exactly fat: she was lumpish. She stood solidly in the doorway, and yet Matt sensed she didn't want to take up any space.

"Mrs. Ross, is there some trouble?"

"Sir, sorry to bother you. But I thought I should get straight to you. There's a girl. She's not feeling too well."

Matt had a hollow feeling in his stomach. He finished typing the sentence he was on, flung the carriage return across too hard, angrily, and rose from his desk.

The extraordinary thing about Nurse Ross was her hair, which was very thick and cut so that it flared in the back and was level with her chin. It looked as if she could have another face beneath that hair with another small, upturned nose just like the one in front.

"What does it look to you like the girl has?"

"Don't know exactly. She came in after throwing up in the girls' room. I took her temperature. It's normal. Gave her some apricot juice, then told her to lie down for a minute."

"Who is she?"

"Amber Smith."

"Don't know her."

"Eighth-grader. New in town."

"Did you ask her about her period?"

"Yes, sir. She said she usually felt okay."

"Could she be late?"

"She didn't say."

He was being alarmist. Shit, there simply couldn't be another girl pregnant.

"Maybe I should go talk to her myself before we call her parents."

He followed the woman out through Audrey's office and into the hall. He had to shorten his step. He'd always considered Lorna Ross an odd duck. She even walked waddly. She had been at Sand Ridge Junior High for seven years before he arrived, and by all accounts did an okay job.

"Did you know Evie Wagner?" he asked quietly as they passed the closed classroom doors.

She started, as if he shouldn't have talked.

"Not very well. It was terrible. Your announcement." Her voice was shaky. "I had a baby who died."

Damn, Audrey had told him that. He'd forgotten. Shouldn't have said anything. Her white uniform and incongruous natural leather, bulb-toed shoes added to the duck image.

"His name was Buford."

"I'm sorry," Matt murmured.

New deaths recalled old. He ought to know. During the past twenty-four hours, he'd thought a lot about bodies he'd seen in the wars he'd covered as a reporter. Never did see Glenda after she left. She died a phantom. Nurse Ross paused outside the care room, one hand on the doorknob, the other spread on the glass door. He liked her hands, capable, maternal hands with thick veins. He followed her into the small room. On the right was a desk, then a window, next to it a small sink, and at its edge a small gas stove. Immediately to the left was an alcove with a cot in it, closed off by a curtain.

"Hello, Amber," Lorna said. "Mr. Chays has come to see you. Is it okay if we pull open the curtain?"

A weak "yes" answered, and Amber Smith's hand reached out to help. Aptly named. Her frizzy blond hair was long and drawn up in a ponytail; it haloed her pale face. She was pretty and small. Matt knelt by the bed.

"Feeling kinda lousy, huh?"

She nodded feebly.

"Nurse Ross said you vomited. Do you still feel nauseated?"

"Yes."

"Do you want to go home?"

"I guess so."

"We want you to get well. The nurse thinks you should see a doctor. We'll give you a note for your parents."

Amber nodded and chewed her lower lip.

Matt motioned Lorna out into the hall, told her he'd have Audrey phone the parents. He thanked her for keeping him informed; she'd done the right thing, he told her encouragingly. Privately, he told himself that his feeling of doom was affecting his judgment. Amber probably had the flu. Needed to be careful not to jump to conclusions. He couldn't suggest to the parents that they check Amber for pregnancy: he could get in trouble for that. Principals got blamed for everything. At least a journalist wasn't considered responsible for the dreadful things he had to report.

Lorna moved away from him and then her eyes searched back, peering deeply into his. Slowly, but with an air of immense strain, she turned aside.

"Is there something else?"

She shook her head too many times and kept her eyes down.

"Are you all right?"

"It's just . . . Evie . . ."

"Are you really okay? I know this is hard."

"I'm okay. It's just Buford . . ."

Matt patted her shoulder, not knowing what else to say. She shook her head back and forth and plodded away, splay-footed, toward her office.

"If you need anything, let me know."

"Thank you, Mr. Chays," she mumbled.

Poor woman, losing her baby. Audrey had said it must've been a crib death.

Back in his office, Matt wheeled the typewriter over to his desk, yanked out the letter he'd begun to Orville, and inserted another sheet. He quickly drafted a notice that the school would be closed until further notice. Since there was no superintendent, he would have to check with the state Department of Education on protocol. He surveyed the note, then pulled it out, crumpled it, and tossed it into the wastebasket on his way out of the room.

CHAPTER ELEVEN

Matt slid into a booth toward the back of Sobo's Family Restaurant and opened the *Oracle*. He was a bit early for Niccole Epps.

Oh, God. Orville was at it again. And Blair was willing to cover it as news. The banner headline read "Preacher Sees Virgin Births." Matt gulped his coffee.

'Fear not, my children' is the soothing message of nationally known preacher Orville Molway. The Reverend Orville will give a sermon on Sunday that is aimed at reassuring our town about some rather mysterious recent occurrences among students at Sand Ridge Junior High.

Oh, shit, what did the school have to do with it? Matt rolled up his sleeves, because the café was overheated.

Several young girls have become pregnant—not so strange in some towns, you might say. But these girls have not been known by any male. At least this is according to the Reverend Orville, who says he spoke to their doctors. The doctors refused to talk to the

Oracle lest they violate the Hippocratic oath of doctor/ patient confidentiality.

The *Oracle* does not know how many girls of Sand Ridge Junior High have been affected or if there are cases in nearby towns. But the Reverend Orville says he knows of four. He will not name them, however.

Four! Matt groaned. Evie, Kim, maybe Katie Sobo, but he was convinced she wasn't. Who would the fourth be? Orville couldn't know about Amber; she didn't even know yet. Even if they were all pregnant, and even if they were from impeccable families, this virgin bit was outrageous. What in the name of heaven had Blair done with the article on Evie? Oh, there, buried at the bottom right with the headline "Drowning in Quarry." Matt's statement on protecting the children was—he opened up the paper—on the jump page.

"Hey, hey, hey!"

The man at the cash register jumped out of his chair and ran to the door. He flung the glass door open and Matt could hear, "Hey, lady, stop! You're gonna mash the meter!"

She sure did, bent it like a nail. She was driving a twenty-foot U-Haul rental truck that stood high off the ground. Matt marveled that the cashier could even tell it was a woman driving. She was peering out between the dashboard and the top of the steering wheel. By the time Matt reached the door, she had braked the behemoth and sat stunned, with her hands covering her mouth. The cash register man, whom Matt had never seen before, stood amazed while Matt knocked on the door of the truck cab.

"Can you open up?"

After Matt had helped her open the door, she sat motion-less, high inside, shaking her head and looking guilty.

"I probably gutted the carburetor," she said.

"More like you emasculated the parking meter."

She looked at him cautiously and slowly smiled, as if to reward him.

"I didn't know these things were male," she said, quickly adding, "I'm not too technical. I always think I'm damaging the carburetor. Sounds important to me, like the jugular."

"You want me to back it up?" Matt offered. "You don't look like you're exactly built to manhandle these rigs."

"Guess I'm in no position at the moment to get irritated at short slurs," she said.

She was wearing a gray wool coat, medium-heeled pumps, and nylons, and was sitting on . . . Matt couldn't tell at first, but she slid out of the cab and two huge law books were exposed.

She was shorter than Tobie. Her hair was the color of new crockery flowerpots, but shiny, and with auburn, nearly maroon, streaks. It was long and precisely parted in the center as with a knife; fuzzy tendrils framed her pixie face. However, the delicacy of her features was completely negated by a large, aquiline nose. The patrician nose went with her deep, mellow voice, even if nothing else did. Matt guessed she was thirty or so. She was chewing gum.

"You'll have to remove the beer can."

She pointed into the truck cab. Amazing: a slightly flattened ale can was attached to the gas pedal with masking tape.

"You use this to get high?" Matt asked.

"I've heard all the world's short jokes," she said wearily.

While Matt eased the truck back off the meter, she conversed with the restaurant clerk. Her arm and body motions were wide and graceful.

"Do you think these things can be squidged upright again?" she asked as Matt rejoined them.

"I doubt it," Matt said.

"Well, whatever its gender, I guess I'll have to replace it."

"Nah, I'll take care of it."

"Why should you?"

"Call it chivalry."

The town council had recently decided that the five parking meters downtown were bringing in little money and had voted to remove them, but Matt wasn't about to explain all that and lose a chance at impressing an attractive woman. He felt a surge of—what? Youth?

"I'm Matt Chays."

"Ahh," she said, stretching out her hand, which was thin with long fingers. It made his own feel absurdly manly. Given her rich, deep voice, he was surprised that Niccole Epps was not a gigantic woman of dowager demeanor.

She glanced cautiously at the other man, making him an

intruder, giving a clandestine tone to her and Matt's new relationship. They went inside and she slipped into Matt's booth in the back, opposite him, chunking her briefcase on top of the table. Uh-oh, a career woman, Matt thought, and caught himself: had he become that provincial already? Then she pulled her gum out and held it between two long fingers.

"What shall I do with this? I was chewing it to keep me calmer. I'm à wreck."

"You shouldn't drive such a big truck."

"It's not that."

She measured him with her eyes. They were limpid brown and slightly too close together. Somehow this gave them the effect of pulling the observer toward her.

"I need a drink."

She didn't look like the drinking type.

"There's nothing stronger than 3.2 beer in this town, unfortunately."

"Oh, damn. Look." She held out her hand; it was shaking.

"God, what's wrong?"

He wanted to reach for her hand to steady her, but he resisted.

"My car was blown up two hours ago in the parking lot of the abortion clinic. That's why I'm driving this truck."

"Holyfuckinshit, no wonder you're shaking like a leaf! How can you be acting so calmly?"

She grinned at his profanity in triplicate.

"Delayed reaction, I guess. And gum."

"Oh, sorry. Here."

He offered her the saucer from under his coffee cup. She placed the wad in the middle.

"No booze at all, then?"

Matt left the table and came back a couple minutes later with a shot of ice-cold vodka. Niccole threw it back quickly, as if she were Russian.

"You Russian?"

"Texan, originally. I didn't expect to be dealing with rednecks and crackers so far north."

She ran her fingers through her long hair and held her hand out level again to test the shaking.

"Sounds elitist."

"Elitist, schmetist. Wait'll you get bombed. But then, I don't know where you stand politically. Here I'm shooting off my mouth, and you could be Jerry Falwell in disguise for all I know." She sighed and continued, "Finally, I thought I would get serious with this job, become a lawyer, have a real career. Maybe I'd be better off as my old scatterbrained self. On the way here, I kept seeing those little white crosses people put at the side of the road to mark a car accident and death. Oh, lord."

She placed her forehead in her hands for a few seconds, then looked up and said, "So?"

"So, what?" Matt asked, surprised.

"So, have I come all this way only to be accused of being elitist?"

"Yeah, well, these people usually have their reasons for opposing abortion. You shouldn't sneer at them."

"I have my reasons, too. Guess I'd better go."

"Sit down," he ordered as she started to rise. "Please," he added.

"What?"

"You seem to me to be too disturbed to go anywhere, let alone drive that monster truck again. Tell me about the bombing."

The attack had occurred about 8 AM in the clinic parking lot, shortly after she had arrived to meet with Dr. Mabrey. The police were exploring leads and said the car looked like it had been blown up by a homemade pipe bomb. After answering the police questions, in a spurt of adrenalin she'd insisted that Dr. Mabrey allow her to hire a truck from the gas station adjacent to the clinic so she could make it to her appointment with Matt.

"I was going to sneak into town."

"In a twenty-foot truck?"

"Well, you know . . ." She paused, feebly searching for an idea. "There are lots of these trucks around. So," she added.

"So, what?"

"So, where do you stand on abortion? Are you going to help me?"

"Where I stand doesn't matter, especially since each case is specific, but what do you need from me?"

Niccole explained that her firm had been hired by Dr.

William Mabrey and Associates of the Lambert County Abortion Clinic because Augusta Johnson and her husband were suing, claiming that the clinic had negligently injured Kim. The defense case would be that someone had damaged Kim before she was brought to the clinic.

Matt gave a low whistle: a shocking thing for this little town. The Johnsons were rich, a fine, upstanding family.

"Can you think of anyone who'd tell me more about the Johnsons? A neighbor, a minister?"

"Augusta's preacher is Orville Molway."

"How do I find him?"

"Look, Ms. Epps, I don't want to stifle your initiative . . . but Reverend Molway has established an organization called Koffee Katch, which is directly inimical to your interests. It is set up to oppose abortions by persuading a woman who has an appointment at a clinic to come for conversation and coffee beforehand. Doctors won't perform an abortion on a woman who has eaten on that same day."

"Hmmm, are these people, this Orville, violent?"

"I don't know. One year he publicly, on national TV, shredded a bunch of *Time* magazines that had a cover story on the permissiveness of youthful morals. But violent, I doubt it. He and I disagree on most things, but, what the hell, he has a way with words. Once when someone asked him where he'd graduated from high school, he said he hadn't graduated, he'd quituated. Not bad, huh?"

"Are you temporizing for political reasons?"

"Is that what I'm doing?" Matt smiled. "And here I thought I was being Christian. You want to know about Orville? Look at this."

Niccole leaned over to read the newspaper that he pushed toward her.

"This is weird. Is he serious?"

"Hasn't a funny bone in his body."

She spotted the article on Evie, quickly scanned the beginning, and said, "Oh, that's just awful. Why did she kill herself?"

"She was pregnant."

"Oh, God, how terrible for everybody, especially the parents. Odd that these things are all going on at the same time."

As she continued to read, Matt wondered if he looked old or paunchy to her, if she had spotted the beginning recession of his hairline, if his face was ruddier than usual, if the gray in his light brown sideburns looked distinguished, if he should grow a mustache, if she had a birthmark, if she liked sex.

"So?"

"So, what?" he replied, startled out of his fantasies.

"So, do you have any suggestions on how I might proceed?"

"Tell you what—if you'll give me a few days, I'll see what I can dig up. How 'bout if we arrange to meet on Friday night? My daughter has a slumber party that night."

"Ummm," she said, surveying him closely. "Are you trying to keep me from nosing around on my own? Of course, you do know people in town . . . and I'm busy at the office. Would the Flats be okay? That is, if you don't mind driving up to Cleveland. I know a Chinese restaurant there, the Wok, quite good."

Matt wasn't sure if he was trying to control her investigation, but he didn't answer her speculations directly; he just listened to her monologue. After she'd talked herself into meeting him Friday, they paid and left the café. Matt roped the beer can back onto the gas pedal of the U-Haul, asked Niccole repeatedly if she was okay to drive, told her she shouldn't abandon the case (what if she just walked right out of his life?), and promised he would help all he could. She climbed into the cab and started the engine.

"So?"

"So, see you."

"One more thing." She lifted her left hand, which had a single gold band on her ring finger. "Strictly business Friday."

He nodded and stepped back. So, a married lady—well, so be it. Niccole had problems getting into reverse gear.

"One more thing," he shouted.

He stepped up to the window and handed her a stick of gum. She stripped it, popped it in her mouth, and roared off down Main Street.

* * *

As Matt was passing the Sobo café again on the way to his car, zipping up his jacket, he heard a loud tapping. Old Emelda Sobo was furiously clacking a spoon on the glass of the door and motioning him to enter. The wind sucked in with him, driving the small old woman back against the counter with a whoosh, her ornate Eastern European apron flapping about her knees. He'd forgotten his newspaper, she said.

"And vhat is zis?" she asked, thumping the paper with the spoon. "How do zhay get zees babies?"

"Probably the usual way, I guess. We all should watch our daughters and granddaughters the way you and your family watch Katie. Then they'd be safe. But we can't believe everything that's in the paper."

He knew he probably was treating it too lightly. A kind of unspeakable, superstitious terror was written all over the old woman's face, mirroring his own sinking spirits.

"It's okay," he said, putting his arm around her. "This is just a fluke. You know 'a fluke'?"

The old woman nodded, her gnarled hands clasping and reclasping each other.

"All these girls pregnant at the same time, it's a fluke. I'm sure we'll get to the bottom of it. Probably some stupid boys messing around. Katie wouldn't be doing that. You don't need to worry. Katie is not going to get pregnant."

She said nothing. Katie couldn't be pregnant. The grandmother surely would know if she was. Her watery blue eyes peered earnestly out of the wonderful wrinkles lining her face. He always hoped someday he would have wrinkles like these, a line for every care, each love, every laugh. Those other eyes swam into his brain, rolled back in agony and dead, eyes there but gone. He shivered with a sudden terror that stabbed into his spinal column, and a surge of anger flooded in to counteract it.

"Katie'll be okay."

His words came out grim. He felt her bones when he patted Mrs. Sobo's shrunken shoulder.

Arnie Beachley had called while Matt was out of the office, and as he sat down to finish his draft of the letter to Orville, Arnie called again.

"You seen the paper?"

The first time he heard Arnie talk, Matt had realized what people meant when they described someone as having a piping voice—sort of related to a piccolo.

"Yeah. Pretty ridiculous, 'virgin births,' eh?"

"Hell, this is serious. You may be a secular humanist, or whatever you are, and I may be religious only on holidays, but you're in trouble, 'cause Sand Ridge Junior High is what all these girls have in common. It's the common denominator. Simple mathematics."

Arnie's voice fit with his chinlessness, as if his whole face were a thin, fluty instrument, maybe a recorder. Over the phone, the sound was irritating.

"Me? What did I do?"

"It's what you didn't do. You didn't stop this."

"Look, Arnie, I'm just as concerned as you."

"Oh, yeah, how come you didn't call me about Evie Wagner, about Katie Sobo and however many hundred more? Just what are you going to do about these girls?"

It was all Matt could do to keep from mimicking Arnie's pitch, because Tobie sometimes did it at home. In fact, he had to deliberately lower his voice to avoid it.

"This morning I was seriously considering closing the school."

With his foot he shoved the wastebasket into view from under his desk. It had already been emptied.

"Close the school?!! Do that and I'll see to it you get fired!"

"For what?"

Blair must be right. Arnie didn't want Matt in the job and was furious his friend hadn't gotten it. Maybe he thought he smelled Matt's blood.

"For avoidance of duty . . . or something. I don't want that school closed."

"Arnie, you're only one of many parents. If you had something other than sons—"

Arnie began to hiccup. It was impossible, Matt noticed, to have a dignified conversation if you were hiccuping.

"Hic . . . Chays, I'm telling you, if you make a move to—hic—you'll never forget—hic. We'll get somebody in that job who'll keep things under control."

He hung up before Matt could try to smooth things over. Guess he'd have to do some groundwork before he thought of closing the school. He checked the wastebasket again. Still empty. Didn't need that announcement anyway. At least, not yet. He might be brave sometimes, but foolhardy he wasn't. Arnie's phone call made him really uneasy.

CHAPTER TWELVE

Yale had let Lorna visit Buford quite a lot during the first six months after he'd taken charge. But as time went on, he gradually whittled the visits down to one a month, then just on holidays, then four times a year, twice a year. This past year, the ninth since Buford's death, Yale had so far only let her see her baby once—on the anniversary of his going.

She wished in retrospect that that visit had never happened. Her troubles before then were nothing compared to what she'd faced afterward.

It had been a violently windy Friday in March. Dried leaves from the previous fall, broken and black with age, swirled as gusts swept through town. Trash cans blew into the streets, clattering off the curbs.

In the morning, Yale had stopped in at Lorna's office at school.

"You can come see him tonight," he said gruffly.

Lorna's face lit up. She could feel it, radiant like a blush.

"You can bring some of his toys, if you want. The front gate will be unlatched, just push it open."

When she'd first visited Buford nine years ago, she'd brought things, toys, to make him feel at home, or perhaps to make her feel that he could tell the difference. Lorna had

94

also begun to attend Sister Rosalyn's seances in north Lambert County to contact Buford. She talked to him, told him she was watching over him and waiting to see him again. Of course, he couldn't answer, since he hadn't yet begun to talk when he was alive. And Lorna went to church. She didn't consider it sacrilegious both to go to church and to deal in the occult. Surely God would understand that she needed to use all possible means to contact her baby boy.

One night in the second year, Yale had blocked her entrance into the basement, although he'd told her she could come visit Buford. He objected to all that "junk." He'd had it up to here, he said, reaching high over his head, with her interminable, messy visits to his pristine basement. He wasn't really mean when he said it, only very rigid, so she knew she had no choice. Men were like that. When women got on their nerves, they either ignored them or ordered them around. He was just like Ernie in some ways.

Yale's permission for her to visit Buford this time seemed a special blessing. As she dressed that evening, she thought that Yale was probably justified in being firm with her. She was consumed by her love for Buford, and perhaps she did overdo things sometimes. She slid some bobby pins into her hair to tame it. Maybe Yale was jealous of her love for Buford. Spurred by the possibility, feeling proud of herself, she put on her red blouse. Men always liked red. She wore her heels, too, not so high that they made walking difficult, but certainly attractive, and her rhinestone earrings. She packed a few favorite toys and icons in her bag—not many; she didn't want to push Yale too far.

As she eased open his gate, she was flooded with an unexplainable feeling of well-being. She loved Buford so much. More than anything, more than herself. She was so lucky to have him. If anything happened to him, her life would be worthless. At first she had been afraid, in awe of the shiny metal capsule. But she'd gotten used to it, until now she felt almost warm toward it. It was big, big enough for a grown man. She liked the notion that Buford had so much room. The capsule was keeping her beloved so he could come back to her someday.

Yale was at the door before she could knock.

"Come in," he said.

Without his usual gruff instructions that she had to remove her shoes, he swung open the door.

"My shoes?" she asked.

He nodded and smiled. He looked pleased that she was happy. Lorna slid her heels off and set them inside the doorway. He closed the ponderous front door and ushered her down the hall toward the basement door.

She preceded him down the white stairs. The ticking of the clocks rushed up at her like a symphony of tiny percussive instruments. She had become used to it. In fact, she thought it was merry and elflike. While still on the stairs, she ducked her head to locate Buford's capsule. Ah, there it was. Yale had moved it to the other side of the room. She hurried over to it, her bag banging on her right hip with her swaying walk. She threw both her arms and her upper body over the smooth side of the capsule, as if she were a mourner and this was a coffin. She was so happy to be near her baby again. Tears rolled down her cheeks.

"My darling, did you miss me? But you and I talked only last week, didn't we? Sister Rosalyn is so good to help us meet. Still, it's better to be here to see you, you know."

Lorna pressed her face against the capsule's porthole window. She could see only the foil wrapping Buford. Maybe she'd said that last for Yale's benefit. She turned to see that Yale was not in the basement. Over the humming of the capsule, she heard footsteps upstairs. There was a slam that sounded like a refrigerator door.

"Hummmm," she said in pitch with the machine. "How are you, my Buford? Is this man taking care of you? He's a nice man, isn't he? He saved you."

She lowered her voice to a whisper.

"What would you think of a stepfather? Just think about it. He's a very attractive man, and we already know he cares about you, don't we? No, no, don't worry, not right away."

Lorna laid her bag on a white table Yale had set out and pulled out Buford's favorite polar bear, a statuette of Mary and the baby Jesus, an occult crystal wrapped in red velvet, and a cross. She heard Yale's cautious footsteps at the top of the basement stairs. She sat in the chair, primly fixing her skirt to cover her knees. He came slowly down the steps, carrying a tray with something on it. A teapot with cups and saucers. This was promising. She felt unusually cozy. Buford was safe and cared for. Yale was being so hospitable. She felt almost at home in this strange basement with its ticking clocks and humming machinery.

"I fixed us some tea so we can have a talk," he began.

"You're being so nice to me and Buford."

As he walked steadily across the basement, she had a good view of him. He was handsome. He wore a black turtleneck. It almost completely covered his tattoo, she noticed as he stretched his arms out to set down the tray. She moved her religious scenery and toys to one side. The thick hair on his wrists was as dark as the black patent of his hair. His eyelashes were long and curly. She'd never noticed till now a deep, single crease that slashed vertically between his eyebrows, as if from perpetual worry. The sleeve of her red blouse was beautiful against his black jersey.

"I really am so grateful to you for letting me come tonight."

She reached out and touched his forearm.

He yanked back. The teapot he'd been holding crashed to the table, then to the concrete floor where it shattered, scattering fragments in all directions and splattering a few drops of hot tea on one of Lorna's stockinged feet. She exclaimed in sharp pain and raised her foot to soothe it, keeping her eyes on Yale.

Three or four emotions flashed across his face, ranging from surprise to disgust to concern. Lorna cringed, folding her arms across her breasts. She'd touched him before, upstairs, and he hadn't had such a violent reaction. He drew himself up, as if to recollect his dignity.

"I wasn't expecting you to touch me," he said stiffly. "Please accept my apology."

His manner was courtly and full of authority.

"Yes," she said, nodding. And then, "I'm sorry about your teapot."

"I'll get another one upstairs," he said.

He must be confused by his emotions, she guessed. She felt reassured. Maybe he just wasn't very experienced with women. Yale strode back across the room and went upstairs.

He had been in the kitchen five minutes when Lorna rose

quietly from her chair and followed his path, excited by the drama of the evening. She listened at the bottom of the stairs. The wind was blowing. She could hear the great gusts through the leaves of the trees. The sound came through the blocked-off side door to the basement. She would go up and help him with the tea, a way to reassure him over his awkwardness.

Since she was barefoot and the wind was howling, Yale didn't hear her enter the kitchen. She was partly hidden from view by the refrigerator. He had lifted the curtain from a birdcage and was talking to the occupant.

"Isabella, Isabella," he cooed in a high-pitched voice.

The bird chittered and ruffled her feathers and danced across the perch.

"Hel-lo, hel-lo," she said.

"Hel-lo," he replied in the same soprano intonation. "We have a great plan, you and I, don't we? We have everything mapped out to make it work like clockwork."

"Tick-tock," she said, only it really was the sound of a clock, not the words.

The crease in Yale's forehead was gone. His eyes were shining and loving. It was odd: his face looked nearly like a child's. Except for his mustache, he could have been a youth.

Yale reached his hand through the lifted cage gate, coaxed Isabella onto his forefinger, and gingerly drew her out into the room.

Lorna subliminally took in the scene. A big kitchen with wooden cabinets, their varnish darkened from age, and a linoleum floor with corners of tiles curling up here and there like sneering lips. Needs a woman's touch, she thought.

Isabella fluttered like a chorus-line belle, prancing along Yale's finger in her chartreuse costume, clucking and muttering.

"Polly wanna cracker? Cuckoo, cuckoo, cuckoo."

"Kinda talkative tonight, aren't you? Woke you up too quick, huh?"

He lifted her up close to his face and she nibbled his mustache, yanking on one whisker as if it were prime nesting material.

"Ouch," he said in mock pain.

A slow creaking, the sound of a door opening or closing,

edged its way into the kitchen. Lorna looked, but no door was moving. There wasn't any door. Then she realized that the sound was coming from Isabella. Lorna couldn't help it; she laughed even as she tried to squelch her noise.

Yale's head jerked up, his arm shuddered, and Isabella shot manically up into the air, heading first for the window, bashing herself against it, then pulsing around the room, her wings flapping as if they were feathered cymbals clashing. Lorna's blood surged, thumping in her throat. Isabella flew toward her and landed on her head. Lorna held very still, in her best nurse mode. Isabella instantly quieted down and began to tromp around in Lorna's thick hair.

"Don't move," Yale commanded, recovering his self-possession.

He walked steadily toward them. Lorna tilted her head downward as he approached.

In a sugary voice, he cooed, "Isabella, Isabella, don't be afraid. Here I am. Hop on my finger."

He was so close to Lorna. She could smell him. Every person has his special smell. Yale lifted his hand slowly to her head; Isabella backed off, then hopped onto his finger. Yale moved slowly across the kitchen back to the cage and set the bird inside, clicking the door closed, murmuring to her all the while.

Lorna could hear that the water in the kettle was on the verge of boiling.

"Why don't you go back downstairs and wait for me?" Yale said.

It was an order, not a question.

"Can I help you?" she asked, turning back halfway.

"No, I'll bring it."

She cautiously made her way back down. As she crossed the basement, she noticed the shards of glass from the teapot. She paused, looked around, and found a large push broom, like the kind used in school halls. With it she shoved the mess into a corner. She sat in one of the chairs Yale had put out, tugged her skirt down, and adjusted her face. She spotted Buford's polar bear on the table, and felt a bit of remorse that she'd forgotten her Bu for a while.

* * *

Yale set the new teapot in front of Lorna, then lifted it and poured her tea. His expression was controlled, his lips pressed tightly. She put three teaspoons of sugar in her cup and stirred loudly for half a minute while he poured his. He cleared his throat.

"I want to discuss my plan with you tonight." He paused. "I'm sorry, would you mind not stirring so loudly? The screeching bothers my ears."

Lorna timidly placed her spoon on the table.

"I want to fully explain my plan to you and I want you to listen very closely, because, although it's my plan, you are a very important player in it."

Lorna was flattered. She nodded, sat up straighter, thought about smoothing her blouse, decided not to.

"You know how important children are. Buford means everything to you: he is a way for you to be immortal. Through children, man lives on and on. Progeny are most important to us, and the most valuable things we give back to the world."

Lorna couldn't help the tear that crowded to the corner of her eye. She brushed it away with her hand. Maybe the tension was affecting her.

"Do you want a tissue?" he asked.

She shook her head, dabbing her cuff at the corners of her eyes.

"As I said, I have this plan. Would you like to help me?"

"You've been so kind to Buford. I owe you a lot."

She wanted to help him, especially if it meant she could be around him. Yale hadn't even touched his tea. He must be the kind of person who didn't eat when upset. She was just the opposite. Although he hadn't offered her any of the oatmeal cookies on the tray, she reached across for one. He didn't notice, but stood up to pace while he talked.

"You undoubtedly remember the night we froze Buford, I mean the night we saved him for you and posterity. I was very happy when I did that. Not only was it, as you say, a good, kind deed, but I knew that it was an important scientific experiment. For a year, I was pleased. Then I got to thinking. You see, I'd always planned to preserve myself in this capsule. In fact, it's written into my will that before my cousin, who is my heir, can get any of my money, he must have me cryogenically preserved in that capsule. A court would have to uphold my will."

He had strolled over to Buford's capsule and was affectionately stroking the silvery metal side. Lorna was halfway through her second cookie as his words sank in.

"But Buford!" she protested, the tide of panic returning. "You can't!"

The sound was muffled inside her full mouth.

"Can't!" Yale's voice was shockingly cold. He had switched again. "Who says I can't? Of course I can. It's my capsule, isn't it?"

He was looking at her, eyes wide open. She couldn't tell what color they were. They reflected deep red from the floor.

She gulped, then murmured, "My baby, my Bu."

"Don't worry, I've figured out the solution. I wanted to put myself in cryonic suspension to guarantee my immortality, of course. Ipso facto, if I can think of another way to achieve immortality, the problem is solved."

She didn't like him standing so close to Buford when he said these things. He could just swing open the capsule door and kill her baby. She compulsively ate another cookie, and offered them to him. He ignored the outstretched plate and she put it back on the table.

"Children are the answer. If I have children, it's a way to live forever! I'll be able to see my own future!"

His face was bright and he flung his arm out wide when he said "forever." Lorna caught his mood. Children—of course. Maybe what she had said to Buford was going to come true with no effort on her part: her baby would have a stepfather.

"Have you been married before?" she asked softly.

Yale looked startled that she had said anything. He paused, clearly calculating.

"Yes," he said, dragging out the lie.

"What happened?"

"Dead."

His answer seemed so final that she didn't dare ask more. Maybe he had to get used to a woman again slowly. It would be difficult. But she was a nurse. She was patient and understanding.

He paced, clearing his thoughts before proceeding.

"Now, there are several ways for me to have children," he continued. "If I want the best children, which of course I do, I must pick the mother or mothers carefully. This is where you come in."

Lorna felt proud.

"I need mothers that are healthy and young and strong. Do you know about the Nobel sperm banks in California?"

She had a cookie in her mouth and one in her hand. He waited for her answer. She shook her head.

"The Nobel sperm banks are where sperm from the smartest, the most brilliant and creative men are kept for women to use when they want a superior baby. Why can't I do the same thing right here? The greatest truths are simple. Geniuses borrow ideas and put them together in new and better ways. That's my solution. I hope you don't mind if I use the word 'sperm,' but this is a clinical matter and, as a nurse, you must deal with these things professionally. You have the girls at school. I have the sperm. Are you ready to help?"

Lorna was stunned. She'd stopped eating, and clutched to her bosom the little figures and the cross she'd laid on the table. The polar bear rolled off to the floor. Yale came very close to her, looking down as she held onto her statues.

"Will you do it?"

"What am I supposed to do?" she whispered.

"Are you stupid? I've just explained. Do I have to spell it all out again?"

She cowered and couldn't keep looking up at him. Her gaze was drawn back to the capsule. She set down the things she was holding, leaving her hand lying on the cross on the table.

"You will put my sperm in the girls I choose. School still runs for a few months, but I want to wait and start with the summer tennis camp. Those girls will be healthy. You work with the girls at tennis camp, don't you?"

"How did you know?"

"I'm not stupid. I saw the correspondence between the PE teacher and you. I know everything that transpires at school. Never forget it. Together we will devise a method to put my sperm inside the girls. No one will ever find out."

She started to talk, and choked. Her hand shaking, she took a sip of tea, and then whispered, "It's a sin."

"What's a sin about it?" he exploded. "They should be grateful! Not many girls get to have children from such a father. Of course, they won't know I'm the father. We'll keep that secret, at least for a while, maybe until the kids are grown and I'm a grandfather. Then I might leave the more promising ones some of my money."

"It's evil," she said.

She couldn't stop the words, though she covered her mouth the moment they were out. She watched his face. He was flabbergasted at her accusation.

"Me? Evil?"

She remembered his sweetness with Isabella, his kindness to Buford.

"What do you know about what's evil? Do you think it's evil for you to want Buford frozen so you can have him come back? No, you don't, do you? But most people would think you were evil. Just because this is for me, instead of you, you say it's evil."

"Why . . ."

"You're going to help—why what?"

Then she spoke quickly, fearing if she didn't hurry she wouldn't finish.

"Why can't you have a baby by me? I'd be happy to have your baby."

"You! A baby by you!"

His tone was heavy and sarcastic, stinging her like lime juice in a wound.

"You're neither young, nor healthy, nor intelligent. What's in it for me? I don't want to dilute my genes. Besides, you've already had your chance anyway."

She felt numb. Her fantasy had dissolved into ugliness.

"You're just afraid to be touched," she blurted out.

He stared.

"There is no point in randomness," he said. "It only makes sense if it's scientific."

"How do you think your mother had you?"

Yale's whole body went still. He moved deliberately toward her until he was bent over and his face was directly in front of hers. She was terrified. He grabbed her arm. He had no qualms now about touching her, hurting. She knew that the force of his grip was bruising her. Ernie used to bruise her that way.

"My mother has absolutely nothing to do with this. Do you *understand?* You are not ever allowed to mention her. Your lips, your mere thought, are dirt compared to that lady, so pure that you can't imagine such beauty and love."

He let her arm drop and walked away. He seemed to deflate a little, as if he remembered he should be polite. But then he puffed up his chest, planted himself in front of the capsule, and spun on his heel to face her.

"Are you or are you not going to cooperate with me?"

She was wringing her hands and no words would come out, though her mouth was shaped for them. He put his fingertips under the latch of the capsule's window.

"My alternative is to empty the capsule so I can be put in it. Buford won't survive. It won't take much, you know, to ruin his tiny, delicate organs."

Lorna slumped over the table, covering her whole face with her hands and moaning, "No, no, no. You can't. My baby."

She raised her head and leaned it back with her eyes shut, as if she were praying.

"Will you do it?"

She said nothing and kept her eyes closed. She had to do what he wanted. She couldn't live without Buford.

"Now, listen very carefully," he said, as if talking to a child or a near imbecile. "Two million people in the United States were conceived by artificial insemination. One in a hundred people in the whole world was so conceived. Have you got that? I said, have you got that?"

She nodded.

"The first artificial insemination of a woman ever was carried out in 1874. Surprising, isn't it?"

She nodded.

"That's a long, long time ago. Ninety-five percent of the meat industry is a result of artificial insemination. Now women's eggs can be frozen and kept in ova banks, just like those gifts of sperm that are frozen in the Nobel sperm banks. Isn't that wonderful?"

She nodded, and a tear rolled down her cheek.

"Someday women will be able to reproduce like termite queens. Scientists can already clone mice and leopard frogs. It's scientific, like Buford's future life. Do you understand all I'm saying? Sometimes we have to do unpleasant things to achieve a greater good."

His voice softened to just above a whisper.

"Sometimes we have to do things it's not in our nature to do. Mother, forgive me," he said, his voice as subdued as a prayer.

He drew a tiny steel scalpel from the top drawer of an old-fashioned oak file cabinet beneath the table. As he was shutting the drawer, she shifted her body and saw the glint of metal. Like a gun, she thought, suddenly profoundly terrified. His eyes, half-lidded, peered at her face.

"Are you ready to help science?"

A tear ran down the other cheek and she could hardly see.

"Put your hand up here flat on the table."

She wrung her hands together instead.

"I said, put it here."

She gingerly placed her left hand where he indicated. He pressed her wrist to the table. She gasped. His grip was so strong that she couldn't move. He took the scalpel and carefully, slowly, sliced off perhaps a sixteenth of an inch of her middle finger, as if removing the top of a soft-boiled egg. He released her arm. Pain flooded her finger. Blood oozed, then pooled on the table. She put her finger in her mouth. All the time she watched him. He was steely, as if controlled by a power outside himself.

"Are you willing? Say yes. Take your finger out of your mouth and say yes."

He held up the scalpel. Bloodied.

"Yes."

Her finger dripped. He crossed the room, opened a drawer, and laid down the tiny knife. He brought her a gauze bandage, gripped her wrist, and wrapped the gauze around her finger, taping it in place. She didn't want him to touch her. But he was firm and efficient.

Then she watched his face melt. Tears were swimming in his eyes. As soon as he finished and let go her hand, she pulled away, bent over to gather her statuettes and Buford's polar bear with her right hand, and put them back into the bag, then slipped it over her shoulder and, with her eyes still on Yale, edged over to Buford's capsule.

"My Buford," she said in a moan that almost became a wail. She patted the capsule. She tore herself away and walked warily toward the stairs. Yale rushed past her, and she flinched. He stopped at the top of the stairs and turned toward her, spreading his arms across the doorway. She looked up, terrified.

"I want you to say it one more time, so you don't forget."

He was not commanding this time, but almost begging.

"What?"

"You'll help me."

She saw his muscles bulging under the thin turtleneck. He looked huge.

"Yes."

"Yes, you'll help me."

"Yes, I'll help you."

Her finger was throbbing. He guided her down the hall to the door. From the porch the wind blew against her, and she had to push to get out. When she went past him, she tried to stay as far away as possible, but still could feel the heat of his body, could smell his sour, musky odor. It was raining lightly. The tiny drops mingled with her tears.

"I'll get in touch to arrange things," Yale said as she passed. "Thank you," he added softly.

The gentle gratitude shocked her. It was the same tone he had used when she arrived.

She fumbled her shoes on with her good hand, shoved her way out the gate onto the sidewalk, and turned down the hill. She could feel the rain soaking into the gauze, loosening it on her blood-soaked finger. Tears poured down her face.

Now, eight months after that terrible night at Yale's house, Lorna was in trouble, so much trouble. There was no way out. Yale had completely surrounded and trapped her. The memory of his alternating gentleness and violence still made her shake. She could never predict which person she would face, the Yale who sweet-talked a cockatiel and had tears of compassion for her pain, or the Yale who deliberately hurt her and ordered her to fulfill his will.

She had no doubt he would kill Buford, or her, if he

wanted. Yale had begun to chase her in her dreams; she knew that if she missed a step, he'd slice off her head. Awake, she consoled herself with the thought that she had no choice. She had saved Buford, and she had to save herself. He would kill her if she disobeyed him. She knew it even as she knew the sun would come up tomorrow.

CHAPTER THIRTEEN

Heads turned as Matt entered the cafeteria to examine the wall damaged by a flash electrical fire. He swept his index finger through the smoke soot on the stainless steel refrigerator door and examined the smudge.

"Looks like the fire was about ready to take off," he said, tapping the charred wood of a nearby cabinet.

"Yale Kaltmann sure can get it on," said the young school chef. "If he hadn't moved like greased lightning, we'd've been in a real situation."

His white chef's hat, with its popover crown, crouched on the top edge of his bushy eyebrows.

"Yeh, Kaltmann was here almost before I realized the fire had started. I smelled something. D'ya smell that? That's poison. He said it could poison people. I sniffed it but ignored it. I had the meat more in my nose, since I was stirring the tomato sauce."

Thursday: sloppy joes for lunch. Tomorrow the menu would be tuna casserole and Jell-O with marshmallows.

"Before I could say Jack Robinson, there was Kaltmann shouting, pointing the extinguisher in there. He tore off that access panel by the side of the fridge to get at the flames, but the foam spewed all over. My hamburger buns came out like they was frosted cupcakes. The fire stopped like he threw a wet dishrag on it. Fizzz. We all started coughing and laughing and slappin' him on the back. Then the fire engine arrived 'cause the smoke had set off the alarm.

"That guy may be antisocial but he wasn't shy with that fire," the chef concluded. "He moved like lightning: here, there, everywhere."

The recounting was extended by several other workers.

"Kaltmann oughta be a breaker." One young man whipped off his cook's hat and pranced around, holding a two-pound ketchup bottle like a fire extinguisher and pretending to spray fire foam into the Jell-O vat.

"He oughta get a condemnation."

"You mean commendation."

"Good idea," Matt said. Several of the women nodded, and Matt headed out to the hallway and back to his office. At this time of day, thirty minutes before school let out, Matt could swear the building seemed fuller than in the morning, about to split its seams like a giant reptile expanding inside its skin. It wasn't exactly that there was more noise now, although there was a steady, fidgeting hum. A head popped out of the boys' bathroom, peered around, saw him, and retreated. When the final bell rang, Miss Irwin's class always exploded first. Now, that was the kind of problem he should be coping with—Miss Irwin. Last week, for the third time in the past year, she had told her class that a relative of hers had passed on and had asked the students to bring in flowers for the deceased. Or there was Mr. Vaughan, who had locked a prankster in a wardrobe closet two weeks ago. Those were the normal issues a principal should be fretting about, not virgin pregnancies.

". . . oh, yes, Mrs. Johnson called again." Audrey was bringing him up to date. "She lit into me like a yellow jacket. Yelling. You'd think I'd called her bad names, she was screaming so loud. She said Tom Harper should be fired, said there were some people in town who would protect their girls even if the principal didn't care about them. I asked what people, and she said Squeeze Jarvis for one."

"Who's that?"

"I thought he was a pretty peculiar one to pick. He doesn't have a kid in school, but his brother Leon does. Squeeze used to be a wrestler. Anyway, I asked Mrs. Johnson what was bothering her about Mr. Harper. She said, 'Those classes, those filthy classes.' I tried to calm her, but I didn't suggest she call you back. Maybe she's just crazed because of the abortion and all."

"I'm beginning to feel kinda crazed myself. Will you ask Yale Kaltmann to come see me?"

Matt's knee was throbbing; he'd been standing on it too long. He'd had a problem with it ever since he was hit by some shrapnel while covering a guerrilla war in Central America. Maybe he should jog more often. He rolled his office chair back and propped his leg on the arm of the Naugahyde sofa.

He flipped open Yale Kaltmann's file folder, which Audrey had placed on his desk. One page with minimal information. Hired seventeen years ago. Forty-six years old. Address, 381 South Sycamore. That must be the old house, way off from any others, up on the small hill near the creek. A huge house, as Matt recalled. Always very neat and kept up, except that the paint on the windows was a memory and the side shingles were weathered like an abandoned fishing boat.

Blair sure couldn't write a story on Kaltmann and the fire from what was in this folder. Matt arose and stood gazing out his window, watching as a tractor as big as a tank, with giant plastic windscreens, roared down the street guided by a farmer standing to steer it. He turned, and started. Yale Kaltmann was standing silently just inside the office.

"Sorry," Matt apologized for jumping. "Didn't hear you come in. Audrey usually announces people."

"She's not there," Yale said.

He was wearing light gray overalls and had apparently come straight from some job, because he still had on his work apron with a dozen pockets all around just below the waist. Kaltmann was shorter than Matt, but he was fitter. Anyone who had to do physical work, especially holding his arms over his head so much in his wiring and other work, would naturally be strong through the shoulders. Matt strode the couple of feet across the small office, extending his hand to Kaltmann.

"Congratulations. I want you to know how grateful I am for your fast work in putting out the fire this morning. It could have caused a disaster if it had spread. I am glad I have people like you who are alert, quick, and competent."

"Anyone would've done the same thing, Mr. Chays," Yale said.

In his year as principal at Sand Ridge, Matt had talked to Yale Kaltmann numerous times, always on business and always briefly. Matt would consult with him on the operation of the furnace or the machinery in the kitchen. Matt had no complaints about the man's work, but he did note that Yale preferred to remain aloof from others in the school. Yale was one of those laconic workers who either figured words were excessive or who were timid before authority—Matt couldn't tell which. As maintenance engineer, he supervised one person who did most of the sweeping and fundamental cleaning inside the school, while Yale himself specialized in the more difficult, technical maintenance.

"A wire must've started the fire in the insulation at the back of the fridge," Yale said.

"Can't know when something like that will happen. The people in the kitchen say you moved like lightning, and that's what counts, how you act in a crisis. I wish there were some way we could reward you other than in words."

"Really, it wasn't that important," Yale said. "It was what anyone would do. I'll get the fridge fixed first thing tomorrow."

Yale's fingers fidgeted with a nail he had lifted out of one of his work apron pockets.

"I plan to call Blair Nelson and have him write an article for the *Oracle,* because the school could use some good PR. Problem is, I don't have much information on you here," Matt said, thumping the file folder on his desk with his knuckles. "Could Blair interview you?"

Yale was shaking his head before the question was completely out.

"No," he said calmly, watching Matt as if Matt were out to get him in some way, instead of reward him.

"The men in the kitchen were impressed. You know the Bible says you shouldn't hide your light under a bushel."

"What would the reporter have to know?"

"Where you got your electrician's training, and then some

111

personal information such as whether you're married, have children, that kind of thing—a human interest story."

Yale was shaking his head deliberately and spreading his hands in a resisting motion.

"How about if I ask you some questions and pass the information on to Blair? He wouldn't need much. Have a seat."

Yale accepted the offer, but perched on the edge of the molded plastic chair as if he'd get it dirty, although Matt noticed that even Yale's work apron hardly had a smudge on it. At that moment, Tobie stuck her head through the doorway and said, "Daddy." The final bell rang through the building and the rumble began: doors swinging, slamming, feet pounding, lockers clanging open and shut, shouting, running, sneakers screeching on the hall linoleum.

"I'm gonna go play ball," she said.

"But it looks like the sky is about to drop."

"You're just a Chicken Little," she teased. "I'll come home if it rains."

She twirled on her heel, scrunched her glasses up on her nose by pushing up the lower rim of the large frames with her right shoulder, and disappeared.

"My daughter."

Matt noticed that Yale's attention had turned wholly to Tobie while she was there. A little smile played at the corner of his thin lips.

"Fine little lady," Yale said, nodding.

"Sometimes I think she aspires to be Babe Ruth or Tarzan instead of a lady. A normal phase, I'm sure."

Yale cleared his throat and shifted in his chair.

"I guess I could answer some of your questions. I got my electrician's training first in the army. Studied refrigeration, too. After serving, I came back and went to Ohio State for a time, where I studied biology and some electronics."

Matt jotted notes. Born in Cleveland, grew up in Akron, came to Sand Ridge at age twenty-nine after leaving a job in a factory in Cleveland.

"Married?"

Silence filled with the sound of—what was it? Matt looked up. Yale was pulling at an adhesive bandage on his arm, causing a muted ripping sound, and sticking it down again. His lips were pursed.

"Can I not answer that?" he asked.

Matt shrugged and said, "Sure."

"I mean, I'll answer it for you, but I don't want it in a paper. You'll understand, won't you? I told Mrs. Ross that I was married, but in fact I never have been. See, I didn't want her to think there was any chance I might marry her. Women are like that, aren't they?"

"Lorna Ross?"

"She got divorced, you know, and then we got to be friends, but I didn't want her to get any ideas. If she sees it in the newspaper . . ."

"No problem," Matt said. "It's not necessary for the story. All I wanted was enough for Blair to write a nice article. It'll help. They're blaming me for these pregnancies; you probably saw something on it in the *Oracle*."

Suddenly Matt remembered his old journalist's trick: asking the low man on the totem pole could provide unexpected, and sometimes promising, leads. Yale was a bit strange and ostensibly out of touch with society, but he did have eyes and might know something.

"Parents are really getting upset. I'm wondering if you might have seen anything suspicious around the school grounds. You know how boys can be, and you get around the school a lot."

Yale peered down into the pockets of his work apron.

"I'll understand if you don't want to say anything, but I promise you that what you say will be just between us."

"There was one thing," Yale murmured.

Matt waited.

"A gang of boys used to meet. That is, I came across this bunch a couple of times. I haven't seen them since I surprised them once in the basement art closet. They might meet somewhere else. I think one of the boys was Nick Darien, you know him? Tall, tough, skinny fellow. Rough voice."

"What were they doing?"

"I dunno. They were all in a huddle. Once it looked to me like they were reading a magazine."

"You mean, like *Playboy?*"

Yale shrugged. "I doubt if it's serious. Another time I heard them discussing where they were going to meet. Maybe I shouldn't have told you. But I 'preciate what you said to me. I've done other things over the years here, but no principal ever thanked me before. Could be those boys are just doing the normal boy things."

Matt nodded.

"Even if this boys' group turns into something, no one will know how I got onto it. It's likely to be all innocent, but things are getting ugly around here. Tom Harper's in trouble. Anyway, I thank you for what you did in putting out the kitchen fire so fast."

They both stood. Matt stretched out his hand.

"I'm glad I can count on you."

"I'll help you keep the school open," Yale said.

Matt was surprised. But then, perhaps the whole town was talking about whether the school would stay in operation. Matt only nodded as Yale rushed to leave. Matt followed him through Audrey's office and watched him walk down the hall at a surprising clip.

CHAPTER FOURTEEN

Matt swiveled slowly in his old oak desk chair after he'd phoned Blair to tell him about Yale Kaltmann and the kitchen fire. The halls were quiet. Audrey had left. The overhead light in her office and the lights in the hall were on, but he liked the darkness in his office, muffling the day into night, helped by the clouds rolling in from the northeast over Lake Erie. It was dark now at five-thirty, even on clear days.

A pine tree listed at a forty-five-degree angle above the playing field. He should arrange to get it wired upright. He should be doing a lot of things: investigating the new copyright laws concerning the software the school board wanted him to purchase; lobbying the board for more computers for the seventh grade so Sand Ridge kids wouldn't drop behind Bay Village; seeking advice from Harper about the best brands of computers. Instead, what was he doing? Trying to delve into the psyches of the likes of Mrs. Johnson and Orville Molway.

He felt strung out from the day. "I'm bummin'" was the expression Tobie and her friends used for the feeling when things were going against them. But one element in the dismal gray of the twilight was incongruously soothing. A child traversed the far corner of the school grounds, scuffing his shoes through some leaves and sending a flock of migrating blackbirds up from the playing field in a folding wave and back down a few yards away, as if the weather were shaking out a lacy, diaphanous black sheet and replacing it. The leaves were off the tree branches, except for the dingy brown ones on the mulberry tree. In the backyard that abutted the school grounds, a single row of grapevines coiled about a trellis, reminding him of barbed wire on prison walls.

From the corner of his eye he saw a truck pull into the parking lot. He shifted to get a better view. There were two of them. Two of those elevated pickups, mudders, mostly for show or competition in four-wheel-drive rodeos. He could hear their rumbling engines through his window. Elevated way off their axles, they looked like metal dinosaurs. On one truck's elephantine tires, Matt could read "MUD SUCK-ERS." On the cab door of the other was written "Pickett's Linoleum: Laying It on Good and Thick." The slogan was flanked on either side by drawings of linoleum knives, their blades hooked like hawk beaks. Hector Pickett's shop was in Foley Township, just outside of Sand Ridge. His oldest daughter attended ninth grade at Sand Ridge Junior High. Matt had met only the mother, last year's secretary of the Parent-Teacher Association. Two men jumped out of the Pickett truck and three from the other. That ain't no "fat" walk, Matt thought as he watched the muscled gorilla walk of one of the men.

He could see them clearly because his office was fading into the evening dimness. He switched on his gooseneck lamp; the bulb popped and went dark. Shit. He'd get another one tomorrow. He turned to the windowsill to find his briefcase. Might as well head home.

The footsteps of the five men were ticking on the bare floor of the hall in the distance. A couple of them must be wearing cowboy boots, to judge from all the noise. Sounded like a radio show of *High Noon*. Peculiar how the senses are heightened when you're alone, Matt thought. The hall seemed extra long from the sound; the metal-lockered walls were sounding boards. School corridors were never built for

116

fine acoustics, although it wouldn't be such a bad idea, given the daily student din. Where were these guys going?

Matt turned from the window, examining each man as he crossed into the light. They each bulged through the door of Audrey's office as if pushed from behind, too big to enter like normal humans. The first one, who Matt instantly knew would be their spokesman, wore a garishly striped tie, as if he were the patriotic flag-bearer. The second one must be Hector Pickett; he wore a hooked knife sheath on his canvas belt. Two of the others, who wore camouflage khakis, were obviously related: similar bulgy eyes. One of them belonged to the gorilla walk; he had a razor nick with dried blood on his jaw. The last was short, about five two, and wore a blue leisure suit. All the men looked as if they had tried to tidy up or at least scrub their hands. Their movements alternated between bravado and hesitation. Feeding on raw group courage, they jammed into Matt's office before he could preempt them with his own move.

Backlit by the glow from the reception office, the five were nearly featureless. They hadn't touched him, but Matt felt as if he had been shoved back and a fist crunched up under his chin. The space was too cramped for so many egos.

"Gentlemen, what can I do for you?" Matt asked, trying to seize the initiative.

"Mr. Chays?" the man with the tie asked, lifting his tie with his thumb and smoothing it over his convex chest.

"That's correct."

"I'm Samuel Hersey."

He turned ponderously like a barrel and flattened his hand in the direction of each man as he named them: "Hector Pickett." Pickett stroked his hand over the linoleum knife case, perhaps out of habit.

"Leon Jarvis and his brother, Squeeze. This here's Storm Delbert," Hersey said, almost as an afterthought, remembering the short man to his immediate left. "We've come here on a friendly visit."

"In that case, gentlemen, may I invite you to have a seat?"

Storm Delbert turned, dropped his cigarette butt into the metal wastebasket at the end of the sofa, and headed for the near corner of the sofa with the determination of a baby bull. Just as he started to lower his thighs, he registered that none of the others had budged. He shifted back, smoothed out an imaginary wrinkle on his blue jacket, and pretended that it had never crossed his mind to sit down.

"We're not staying long. We just want to state our case real short, then leave," Hersey said.

Heads nodded. Squeeze shifted like a jerky rocking horse. Maybe Matt could sidetrack them on some point of personal vanity.

"I was watching you as you parked. Those mudders are pretty impressive. Are those the biggest tires they'll take?"

"I got some bigger ones at home," Storm blurted out. "They're so fat my truck can swim across rivers."

"No kidding?" Matt encouraged him.

"Storm," Leon Jarvis growled.

"We've come on behalf of ourselves and others to say we want Tom Harper fired," Hersey continued.

"I think we should talk about this," Matt said. "Perhaps you would like to flip that light switch behind you, Mr. Delbert."

Storm swiveled to comply, but Squeeze, at a nod from Leon, reached behind Hersey and put his hand on Storm's shoulder, immobilizing him as surely and calmly as if he had stung him with paralyzing poison.

"We just want to say our say. We pay our taxes. Our girls go to school here. There's no taxation without representation, and we want to tell you that if our girls aren't better protected, we'll take things into our own hands."

Hersey glanced around. They all nodded except Storm, who was still immobile under Squeeze's grip on his blue shoulder. "Amen," he murmured when Squeeze loosed his.

"You will read in the *Oracle* tomorrow that we have launched an investigation into the problem of the pregnancies," Matt said. "I'm just as worried as you are. After all, I have a daughter who is as vulnerable as any of the other girls. I fully intend to find the boys who are doing this."

"That's another thing, we come on behalf of the Sobo family," Hersey said. "They're law-abiding people and they don't want no trouble. That's why they didn't send a representative. They have more relatives they want to bring over from Hungary, so they want to lie low."

"I promise you, gentlemen, that I will do all in my power to get to the bottom of this. I think it is of great importance that we do not panic and make mistakes. If you would like to set up a meeting with me tomorrow, we could go over things more carefully."

"We don't need a meeting," Leon Jarvis said. "We want this thing taken care of. Harper. We don't want him teaching our kids. Parents are the ones who should teach sex stuff, not the school, 'specially not no citified Easterner."

"Mr. Harper does not deviate from the state-designated curriculum for biology," Matt said.

He felt ridiculous, uneasy with his bureaucratic line, talking toward the darkened figures whose emotions could only be judged by the tone of words and by large body movements.

"I don't think you understand," said Pickett.

"Yeh, we don't care if he's a deviate or not," said Leon.

Matt thought Squeeze's wrestler's neck rippled at the word "deviate."

"Mr. Harper is one of the finest teachers I know," Matt said.

"Then why is he telling jokes about boys pulling down their jeans? Ask him that," Hersey said triumphantly.

"That warn't in no state carricalum, I bet," Leon said.

"I do not in fact have the authority to fire any teacher. That can only be done by the school board," Matt said.

"We think you can do something about it," Leon said in a tighter voice. "We don't want our girls listening to that birds and bees stuff, not the way he teaches it, and none of that Darwin horseshit either."

There was a long silence.

"Well, that's it, isn't it?" Hersey turned to Pickett, who nodded and then whipped his head in a motion that meant "let's go."

There was no sense in replying. They turned and walked back through Audrey's office; Storm padded out first, then Leon. Squeeze filled the doorway momentarily, more like a receding train than a person. Cowboy footsteps echoed back down the corridor. There were no voices, only the steps, which seemed to vibrate in Matt's body. He watched, still in the dark, as they clambered into the trucks, Storm making a tiny run and a leap to get in. The trucks roared and backed. Pickett's headlights glinted off the first truck's chromed roll bar. They sped off.

An uneasy, ominous ambivalence crept into Matt's bones. What could one do when parents went over the verge of rationality? They hadn't even let him turn on the light. In a way, he felt raped, certainly invaded and mauled. Harper was the best teacher he had in the school, and these idiots were trying to get rid of him. He'd have to warn Harper. The more he considered it, the more incensed he grew. Clearly, if people were going to pin responsibility for these pregnancies on him, he would have to develop his own agenda. He would have to run the show, not have other people shoving him around.

CHAPTER FIFTEEN

Lorna sat staring out her office window. The narrow-slatted venetian blinds allowed the late October sunlight through, forming stripes like those on a prisoner's uniform across her face and arms. Outside on the ground, a giant woodpecker, with its herringbone feather suit and red cap, plunged its long beak into the earth again and again, as if trying to kill death itself.

Near her elbow, a jar was sitting on the windowsill in full sun to warm it up. The heat undoubtedly would kill some of the sperm, but that was better than putting frozen or ice-cold material into the teenagers and having them notice and maybe tell their parents. By now, she was used to the routine that Yale had forced her to establish to ensure that his strategy was not discovered. That didn't make her any less panicked right before she had to carry out another ordered impregnation.

The first time, early last June during the tennis camp, she'd thought she was going to faint. The morning before the girls were to come to her for their checkups, Yale had terrified her, locking her into her office and threatening that if she didn't carry out his wishes without a hitch, he would kill Buford.

"I'll take care of your baby" were his exact words, but the meaning was clear.

Then he'd pulled a narrow-necked flask out of a satchel. Later he used jars that looked like ones she'd seen in the science lab. She hated these jars intensely by now. Then, guided by her answers to his questions about how the girls would feel, he'd outlined a method for carrying out his obsession. He was relieved to learn that even a full pelvic exam could take as little as five minutes.

"Good, that will keep the other girls from being suspicious, if they don't spend really any more time with you."

When she told him that nurses were not allowed to perform full pelvic exams, he was silent for a moment, and then said, "Well, this is not a full exam. You are going to touch them as little as possible, and I rely on you to tell the girls in a fashion that will make them keep quiet."

Briefly she toyed with the idea that she could refuse. The whole thing disgusted her. She swallowed. Then he gave his warning that first time: "Remember Buford."

In fact, he managed to remind her every time exactly why she had to do what he said. This morning he had brought along his tiny scalpel to her office, pulled it out of his pocket, and proceeded to clean his fingernails with it, all the while telling her that he was growing dissatisfied with the way the operation was proceeding.

"Why?" Her voice came out in a squeak. She cleared her throat and said, "Why?" again more audibly.

"I think you should have a better ratio of successes to applications."

She sat silent. She thought the success rate was appallingly high. She was so terrified when he first made her do it that it didn't occur to her until later that she could have killed the sperm and then claimed he was infertile. Now that he knew he was fertile, he would certainly blame her if there was a falloff in pregnancies.

"And look what's happened with Evie Wagner," he accused.

She was amazed, dumbstruck at first.

"But you made me do it," she said finally.

"You chose her. Couldn't you tell she would be a bad bet, psychologically a liability?"

When Lorna had heard about Evie's suicide, she'd felt the same as when she first carried out Yale's orders—as if she was going to throw up. She didn't feel she'd actually helped kill somebody, probably because of the five months' gap between Evie's impregnation and her death. Lorna might have felt more responsible if Evie had died soon afterward. Sometimes she couldn't tell what she felt. She was numb. If she could just keep Buford alive and stay alive herself, that would be a mammoth achievement.

As Yale left this morning, he'd said in a loud, hissing whisper, "I want you to give my gift to two girls today. Got that? *Two.*"

His face was very close to hers. She could almost see his whole eyes. They looked dull, black and dull, as if there were little distinction between the pupil and the rest of the eye. She still couldn't see the full eye because of his overhanging lids.

From her seat at the window, she heard murmuring and giggling coming down the hall in her direction. The PE teacher sent over the girls five at a time, all day, until they'd all had health checks.

She rose from the chair, walked over to the radio, and chose a light rock station popular with the junior high kids. The girls burst into the outer room of her office, compressing through the narrowness of the doorway like notes being muted and released by a saxophone. Lorna had always managed well with the various generations of junior high girls. She listened well—for a grown-up. Unlike Miss Petit, the gym teacher, at least Mrs. Ross had been married and had a child, so the girls felt she spoke from experience when she answered their questions. Every autumn Miss Petit and Lorna were in charge of showing the film *How We Grow into Young Ladies* and answering the girls' questions about menstruation. More precisely, Lorna answered all the questions while Miss Petit ran the equipment. Lorna stressed that the point of menstruation was to enable women to have babies. Her role tended to make the girls like her, although they thought her a bit odd and lonely.

Lorna quickly checked to see that the water in the pan on the gas burner was simmering. Two long catheters were being sterilized in the water. She slid open the top drawer in the cabinet, set the jar inside, and checked that the other material Yale had provided was there.

She couldn't help smiling at the bubbliness of the girls in the next room, until she recalled her task and her depression returned. She forced herself into her nurse mode, a stance that enabled her to carry through her task. In addition to summoning the efficiency ingrained during her days of nurse's training, she blotted out her thoughts by recalling the night Buford had died in her arms. Only this strong emotion could overwhelm the powerful feeling of despair. She strode to the door of the waiting room.

"Hello, girls."

"Hello, Mrs. Ross," several said in unison.

"How come there are six of you?"

The girls giggled, and one of them pointed to two girls at the end of the sofa: identical twins, who clearly wouldn't be separated.

"You know from past experience the little speech I give you, but I'll give it again just in case you've forgotten or in case there is someone new."

The girls tittered, knowing that the topic was one that required discretion.

"Ever since you were little, in kindergarten or even before, all of you have been told that you don't let people touch your private parts. Isn't that so?"

One girl nodded.

"Sometimes, as we get older, doctors and nurses need to check out our bodies, to make sure everything is working the way it should be. That means we have to check out private places. This can be done very quickly. In fact, if any doctor ever takes too long in examining you, you should be suspicious.

"Today I am going to continue with our ongoing record of your posture. We want to make sure your spine is growing correctly. Then I will give you an eye exam, because if you can't see that cute boy across the room, how will you know if you have a crush on him?"

"You'll have to get close," said Hilda, a tall girl with glasses.

The others snickered, and Lorna smiled.

"As we grow up, it is necessary for us to open ourselves for examination to nurses and doctors. The examinations you have are very private. Part of becoming an adult is that we learn when not to talk about things that should remain private. When you become a full-grown woman, you will be examined regularly by a gynecologist, that is a woman's doctor. But now, while you are still young and your body is changing, we will monitor those changes just to make certain things are fine. When you are adult—and you are now young adults—you keep to yourself the exchanges you have with your doctor and nurse."

"You mean, I shouldn't tell my mother when she asks?"

"Yes, part of growing up is that you come to rely on yourselves, you separate from your parents gradually. This is a good and easy time to begin. If you have any questions about anything, I can answer them, or your family doctor can.

"Now, I think we're ready to begin. Does anybody want to be first?"

In the past, she had made a practice of letting the last girl she checked be the one who got Yale's "gift," on the theory that the last one was the shyest and least likely to talk about her examination to anybody.

"We will," the twins chorused.

"Okay, but I'll have to take you one at a time. Some of you remember that from last summer in tennis camp."

"How 'bout you, Rita, first?"

Her sister gently shoved her up from the sofa. Today Lorna wanted to get her obligation to Yale over fast. Maybe she should carry out the application on the first and the last in this group. Her head was throbbing with a dull ache.

"I don't wanna be first," Rita said.

"How 'bout you?" Lorna said to a girl she knew would be last if she hadn't picked on her.

Although Lorna had seen her before, the large, mousy-brown-haired girl was new in town and shy both about her body and about not knowing other girls in her classes. Apparently used to following orders, the girl rose and headed for the door to the examination room. Lorna closed the door to the waiting room. She walked to the other side of the room, turned up the volume of the radio, and closed the blinds.

"Now, Karen, the first thing we do is check your posture. To do that, you have to take off all your clothes, then stand here in front of this white sheet on the wall while I snap your picture. Actually it's not a picture, it's a silhouette. When it's developed, no one can tell who you are, can't tell your face. It's just a black and white silhouette. So the first thing you do is go behind that curtain, take off your clothes, and put on one of the long paper shirts you'll find stacked on the bench. Okay?"

Karen nodded shyly and pulled the curtain closed behind her. Lorna removed one catheter from the simmering water and turned off the flame. She attached the catheter to the bulb, inserted the tip into the jar, sucked the yellow-gray ooze into the narrow tube, and laid the whole thing in the drawer and closed it. She lifted a small hourglass from the second drawer and placed it on a table next to the patient's table. Karen stuck her head out from behind the curtain.

"Mrs. Ross?"

"Yes."

"Do I remove my panties, too?"

"Yes, honey."

A couple seconds later, Karen stepped out wearing the white paper shirt. After turning the lights low to improve the silhouette, Lorna helped the girl remove the shirt and showed her how to stand in front of the sheet. Her young body with breasts just barely blooming, pink aureoles so light, was incredibly sweet and made Lorna remember her own girlhood, now so long ago. Lorna walked behind the camera and clicked two pictures.

"Good, that was just fine. When you stand up straight, you're such a pretty girl. Now you can put your shirt back on and I want you to stand over here so we can test your eyesight."

Shy girls were always so relieved to put the shirt back on that anything else that followed seemed tame and almost unembarrassing. Even the part on the table.

After the eye exam, which Karen passed with flying

colors, Lorna said, "Now I want you to keep on the dress, but get up on this table and lie down on your back. Put your feet right here in these stirrups."

As she spoke, she lifted out the stirrups that Yale had made and attached to the table. Ordinarily they were kept folded and hidden beneath the edge.

"We're going to carry out a brief exam which will not hurt, just to make sure everything is going okay. Have your periods started yet?"

Karen nodded and said, "Five months ago."

"Does it hurt any when it comes?"

"A little bit."

"Have you tried doing some exercises, even walking?"

"No," Karen said softly.

"It can sometimes help."

Karen mounted the table as Lorna turned her back and put on some plastic gloves. Karen giggled a little. Lorna knew what it was. The posters on the ceiling were always a hit, partly because they were such a surprise. The girls never noticed them tacked on the ceiling until they were asked to lie on the table. One poster was of a lanky gorilla, carrying the slogan: "If you slump, your arms drag." The other was a close-up of a giant hippo, its mouth full of blunt teeth. "You don't have to floss every tooth—just the ones you want to keep," the inscription said.

"You like those?" Lorna asked.

"Yeah," Karen said timidly.

Lorna held out to the girl the hourglass, which had blue sand in it.

"Will you do me a favor and time me? I'm going to check you down here and I want you to turn this over. The sand runs from one side to the other in three minutes. I want you to tell me when it runs out. Okay?"

"Uh-huh."

Lorna opened the drawer, turned to the girl, and worked quickly, touching very lightly. No speculum was necessary because the catheter was no thicker than a very thin pencil.

"Now, this will pinch just a little," Lorna said.

No girl had ever really felt a pinch, but Lorna always said it so the girl was pleased when no pain was noticed. The mouth of the vagina was pink and healthy, the labia majora not large. Lorna, with gloves on both hands, spread the outer lips and checked the hymen to ensure that the hole was large enough for the catheter. Karen couldn't see Lorna at all since her knees were up and the paper dress blocked the view. Lorna reached for the catheter and, just before she inserted it, said, "How's the time on the hourglass?"

Karen looked at the hourglass as Lorna slid in the catheter and slowly squeezed the bulb on the end.

"Ummm," Karen said. "I think it's got a minute and a half to go yet."

"Good," Lorna said.

In, in, in. There are practically no nerves inside the vagina.

Slowly she withdrew the narrow tube.

"Did you feel any pinch?"

"No."

"Good, you're a model patient."

She quickly placed the catheter and bulb in the drawer, made certain the lid was screwed securely on the jar, and closed the drawer. She peeled off her gloves and dropped them in the wastebasket.

"Now what does the hourglass say?"

"It still has some."

"We beat it, then, didn't we? Now you can get up and put your clothes back on."

Karen swung her legs down and sat up. Lorna imagined the liquid sloshing inside her, though she knew that wasn't possible, for she didn't put so much in that a lot would leak out. Girls were used to excretions, but Lorna didn't want them to become alarmed by too much fluid. She'd once thought of giving out panty-liners, but decided that would draw attention.

Karen was a large girl. As she jumped off the table, Lorna realized she was approximately the same size as herself. Lorna was suddenly stabbed by the thought that Karen could have a baby. Lorna wanted another baby. Jealousy. That's what she felt, jealousy. But it was mixed, polluted with this awful nauseated feeling she had while carrying out her task for Yale. Jealousy and shame. It must be a sin, but she was trapped. Buford could be lost forever, if she didn't comply. She knew that as clearly as she knew she wanted another baby.

She placed the catheter in the small sink and poured the scalding water over it, then put it back in the drawer. Karen emerged dressed. With a quizzical look on her face, she held up her left little finger.

"Mrs. Ross."

Lorna turned around.

"Why does your fingerprint grow back the same after you burn your finger?"

Lorna held the girl's hand, examining the finger.

"I've noticed that, too. I don't know. I guess you'd have to ask your science teacher."

Lorna remembered the finger Yale had sliced. Her fingerprint had grown back the same. But she was a changed person after that. Suddenly, while holding the girl's hand, she knew what she would do. Her jealousy evaporated. Yale didn't control her completely. Maybe she wouldn't tell him right away, let him guess. But she was racing ahead of herself.

After Karen left, Lorna sped through the examinations of the remaining five girls. Speed was of the essence. The twins wanted to be checked together, but she refused. They were last. She was relieved. Now she didn't have to choose a second one for Yale. When the last twin rejoined the other in the hall, there were ten minutes before Miss Petit would send the next batch of girls.

Lorna quickly turned the key in the outer door, locking herself in. She returned to the examination room, stripped off her nurse's uniform and panties, removed the sterilized catheter from the pan, attached it to the bulb, and squeezed the bulb to take in as much of Yale's "gift" as the tube would hold.

She climbed onto the table, lay back, closed her eyes, and, by feel, inserted the catheter and slowly squeezed. Buford would like a brother or sister. He would. She knew he would. She lay there for five minutes thinking of Buford, thinking that at least Yale was handsome, thinking she'd taken power back into her hands. Then she dressed and prepared for the next batch of five girls. She washed out the jar with searing hot water from the faucet, wrapped it in a brown paper bag, and placed it in the wastebasket. That was the required signal to Yale that the deed was done.

CHAPTER SIXTEEN

In the morning, early, before anybody was awake in Sand Ridge, a shadowy figure in a stocking cap and with his neck swathed in a scarf that covered his lower face crossed the lawn next to the Chays house. It was quite dark. The man moved slowly. He knew there were no dogs here.

Matt's car was parked outside the garage. The figure approached the car from the north, behind the garage. He pulled a thin flashlight from his backpack. Perfect. A spotlight right on the hubcap. The light was one he'd ordered from the Serious Options catalogue. Paid to get the best.

He knelt and deftly removed one hubcap, making only the slightest scrunching sound. From his pack he pulled a lug wrench. He whirled one lug nut off, plopped it into his jacket pocket. Then another. The rest he loosened a little.

With the butt of his hand, he tapped the hubcap back into place. Not enough. Could he risk hammering it? Down the street, he suddenly heard the raucous engine of the town garbage truck. He waited, timing his blow to coincide with the screeching of the truck's brakes. The hubcap was tight.

As cautiously as he'd come, he left, circling south across a different lawn and away from the garbage men.

* * *

In times of turmoil, people try to act especially normal. Tobie and Matt were no exceptions.

Tobie knew her father often thought about Evie. But it was more complicated: he was worried about the whole school. Tobie had resolved to help out. She cooked supper before her dad came home; she washed laundry before the basket was full; she didn't tease him when he put the toilet paper on the roll upside down; she swept the porch more than it needed; she reported to her father on Squat's activities; she tried in general to be the perfect daughter.

She went bravely to the memorial service for Evie at Morton's Funeral Parlor. At first, sitting next to her father and gasping for breath amid the scent of thousands of blossoms, she tried to think of everything but Evie—of Squat's feeding program, of a new bird whistle she'd learned from Mr. Harper, of baseball. Finally she asked her father where the coffin was. Evie was there in that vase, he said, cremated. Evie was a quart of ashes. Tobie couldn't help herself: her throat clogged and she sobbed. Her father put his arm around her. She sensed his relief, as if she was crying for him, too.

Tobie had even offered to stay home from the slumber party tonight if Matt wanted. But he said no, she should go, he had to meet Niccole Epps for dinner. Tobie might as well spend the night at the party.

Matt sat in the car waiting for her, wondering if tardiness could be an inherited trait. Glenda had invariably been late to everything. Tobie was the same. God knew what she was doing in there. She didn't yet wear makeup, so it had to be something else. He swore she didn't start to get ready until she knew she was going to be fifteen minutes late.

A late wasp flitted around the inside of the car, buzzing only as it hit the canvas roof of the old convertible. Its burnt-brown legs dangled down, swinging at the joints. Reminded Matt of a war: a shell-shocked room in a decrepit hotel in Iraq where he and other reporters had been sitting around with some soldiers. Dozens of wasps zoomed around, bashing into the ceiling like helicopters. Every once in a while, a soldier would raise his AK47 rifle and blast one of the insects that had stopped on the ceiling. The shot shattered the plaster and expedited the breakdown of the hotel, the town, the society. The reporters, who had no guns, acted as if the soldiers were normal: sure, everybody shot wasps.

In the past three days, Matt's life hadn't quite been war, but neither had it been humdrum. A doctor's examination had found that Amber Smith was pregnant and a virgin. Turned out Blair Nelson was Amber's uncle. He had told Matt about the pregnancy and, like any good uncle with a model niece, refused to believe she could have had sex with anyone. Blair also told him that Katie Sobo was pregnant. Four girls were pregnant and all possibly virgins: Evie, Kim, Katie, and Amber. Matt calculated that there might be a fifth, since on Monday Orville Molway hadn't known about Amber but had been quoted as saying that there were four.

Matt racked his brain for some kind of reasonable explanation. But there was no logic to it. Each girl insisted that there was no contact with boys or men. To forestall parental criticism, Matt had circulated a memo among the staff saying that he was planning to call in a doctor from outside the town to consult with Nurse Ross and the rest of the school's staff about the situation. He did not want to imply that they were at fault, but he wanted to go on record, collect any information they might have, and show how seriously he took the problem. He hoped that the memo would scare whoever was causing the pregnancies and alert teachers to watch for unusual activities. Then he made sure that the memo was read in classes so that any boys who might be guilty would be intimidated by the implications of their activities.

On Wednesday Matt had begun to track down the suspicious clique of boys that Yale Kaltmann had mentioned. So far he'd gotten nowhere. But when Mayor Beachley called him threatening that some citizens were itching for a town meeting, Matt had extracted a promise that one of Beachley's sons would nose around Nick Darien, to determine where he hung out and with whom.

"You want to do more than complain?" Matt challenged Arnie, "Then get your kid to check out Darien and this bunch."

What was most worrying Matt, however, was Harper. Not Harper himself, but those screwballs who were set to run him out of town. Yesterday morning Harper had quietly walked into Matt's office before school and held his hand out with a broken chemistry vial in it. He set it on the edge of Matt's desk and sighed heavily. "The whole lab is smashed up," he said. Matt had followed Tom to the science lab. Bottles and vials were strewn across the counters and smashed. Bunsen burners were overturned. In the middle of the mess was a plastic model torso of a woman, the one used to teach students about human internal organs. Harper had not yet used the model, and was considering not using it at all after Matt had told him about the men in the mudders. The model had been tipped into one of the metal sinks. An axe was embedded in her maroon liver, with cracks radiating up and down the surrounding luridly colored organs. Chalked on the blackboard, in a crude, backward-slanting penmanship, was: "Vengeance is mine saith the Lord. Harper must go."

"If vengeance is the Lord's, why the hell are these guys preempting the Lord?"

"Guess they think they work for Him," Matt said.

Harper was quiet, but Matt knew that he was very disturbed.

Then he said, "Maybe it's time for me to dredge up the kiddies' smut magazines."

"Before you do anything, let's discuss it," Matt cautioned.

Because the class bell was about to ring, he and Harper had decided they would explain things as gently as possible to the children and move them into another room for the hour. Matt phoned Police Chief Leland, asked him to come investigate the vandalism and institute a round-the-clock patrol of the school grounds. Fingerprint dusting didn't immediately turn up anything. Leland was reluctant to detail his few police to a regular patrol of the school, but promised to "keep our eyes open." He thought it was probably just a prank.

Later, Harper had prepared to show slides to his biology class; the shades were pulled, the lights were out, and the children were raptly listening. As the first slide dropped from the cube into the machine, a bright light glared on the screen in the middle. The class gasped and tittered. Harper had removed the cube and found that someone had punctured a hole through the middle of all the slides. Then Harper's garter snake, which normally snoozed in a terrarium in the back of the lab, was found sliced up like sausage and neatly arranged in an S.

A terrible week. But Tobie had coped well. She'd cried at the funeral service for Evie, but that was healthy. Thank God she knew nothing about the other pregnancies. Matt didn't want her terrified. Wednesday, while cheerfully relating facts gleaned from her research on Squat, she'd asked him if he knew that frogs were traditionally used to test for pregnancy. He'd flinched but, fortunately, she was checking her note cards and didn't notice his expression. His apprehension at the prospect that she could mysteriously become pregnant was like a bruise on his brain.

CHAPTER SEVENTEEN

Tobie settled her overnight suitcase beneath her feet and tossed her sleeping bag and pillow into the backseat. In it she had packed two nightgowns, six pairs of earrings, her baseball glove, a book for sixteen-year-olds about a girl's first love, four of her favorite records, several lipsticks, eyeshadow, and rouge.

She was headed for the slumber party at Lisa Wade's, and her dad was going to see Niccole Epps after he let her off.

Miss Oops, she called her.

"Next time she comes to town, maybe you'd like to meet her," Matt said.

Tobie shrugged. She'd noticed that her father was growing his mustache, but she didn't mention that. When she was young she would have said something. It was embarrassing how ignorant you were when you were just a kid. Then you grew up and learned that whiskers are secondary sex characteristics for males.

The Wades lived eight miles out of Sand Ridge on the Green River. It was farm country. Most of the exhausted soybean bushes had already been plowed under. Rickety, weather-beaten barns, leaning toward oblivion, loomed next to tidy frame houses. The sun had disappeared around noon and the gloom of the long northern Ohio winter was settling into the deadening earth. The brightest colors were the oblong, orange mailboxes meant for the *Oracle*.

As Matt slowed to turn into the Wade driveway, Orville Molway braked his pickup before turning out. He had just dropped off Verity. He waved in passing.

"Look at that," said Tobie, craning her body around to peer after Orville's truck. "He's got a humongous rifle in a rack across the window. Scary!"

"Probably hunts."

"Hunts what?"

"Dunno, maybe deer, could be coons, rabbits, squirrels."

At the Wades' house, Tobie sprung open the car door. "Hey," Matt said, and she slid back across the seat to peck him on the cheek.

"I'll phone later tonight," he added.

She hopped out the door and flung it shut, dashing into the house. When you wanted kids to cling, they didn't, not even a little bit.

Matt would have to fix the clunk in the differential. Needed to tune the engine, too. He checked his watch after he let Tobie out of the car: a bit early to leave to meet Niccole in Cleveland. She'd called the school earlier to confirm and give him directions to her apartment; he'd nearly forgotten to bring the note with her instructions on it. He decided to drop by Harper's to see if he was tinkering on the old plum-colored MGA he'd bought last month. Matt himself had come to Sand Ridge with a much newer MG, but he'd had to trade it in on an American-made car or face community gossip about his lack of patriotism and concern for the local unemployed, thrown out of work by imported foreign cars.

Matt rounded the edge of Harper's brick apartment building into the parking lot at the back. He swerved and brought his car to a mock-screeching halt at a ninety-degree angle to the MG. Harper was lounging against the front fender.

"You need some lawn chairs . . . so you can sit out here and enjoy the parking lot?" Matt shouted.

Harper said nothing, stared into the distance. He was smoking. Looked like a joint. Come to think of it, that's the only thing Harper ever smoked. Damn, in public. Harper should remember that Sand Ridge wasn't the big city, where whiffs of grass were the norm on Friday nights. Matt quickly surveyed the surrounding buildings. Nobody around, and almost no windows looking onto the parking lot.

"Hey, whatcha doing?"

After a long drag, Harper said, "They're after me."

Matt switched off his engine and stuck his head out the window.

"Yeah? Who?"

"I got a phone call ten minutes ago. Man said, 'We're going to slow you down. Got that?' he said. 'To a stop, like you run into a concrete wall.' The guy laughed, hung up."

"We won't let them," Matt said.

"They've done it."

Matt swung open his door and stepped out, keeping his eyes riveted on Harper.

"Hey, man," he said in a friendly but concerned tone. "Don't you know this town won't tolerate a teacher who smokes grass?"

"D'you know how you can tell when you're stoned?"

"How?" Matt said, humoring him.

"You can't stop smiling," Harper said, grinning seraphically.

"I thought you had nothing to smile about."

"I want to live my life as a liquid, not a solid, not like concrete. The more liquid the better. What's the most liquid liquid?"

Matt couldn't help but smile as he gazed down at Harper slouching on the car. Suddenly he noticed that the MG was full of something and was sitting unusually low to the ground, tires bulging out at the sides. Gray covered the leather seats. The mahogany steering wheel had disappeared into it. He came closer and touched it. A shiver ran up his back.

"Stopped me pretty good, wouldn't you say?"

It was concrete. Poured inside the car like tapioca. Nearly set. The MG was ruined.

"How'd it happen?"

"Must've been somebody with a cement mixer truck. It'd be easy. Drive into the parking lot and slosh it in, like my car was a kid's sand bucket, drive off, nobody'd even notice who did it."

Harper flipped the butt of his joint onto the gravel, leaned over the MG, and wrote "R.I.P." in the hardening concrete right over what used to be the driver's seat.

"They're after me," he said, grinning like a loony and tapping his luxuriant dark mustache.

He stopped smiling as a new thought played over his face.

"I guess that means they're after you, too." He slurred the words.

"You just take care of yourself," Matt said, clapping Harper on the shoulder.

"Hey, how 'bout you give me a ride out to the sandstone quarry to see Archibald?"

"Now? It's getting dark. Who's Archibald?"

"He's this old guy lives out near the quarries. He gets samples and animals for me for my classes."

"Well, how 'bout some other time? Remember you're carless. How'd you get back?"

"Oh, yeah, right. Guess you're right," Harper said. "Hey, I'll see you," he added, moving off toward his apartment.

"Y'okay?"

"Sure," Harper said, waving.

The rolling of the wheels on the road was the only smoothness Matt felt. The rest in his mind was jagged as he mulled over the threats, the escalation of violence.

The cornstalks were stiffly silhouetted against the final rouged flare of the sunset. Bare trees twisted against the sky like maps of the human nervous system. Matt had gently escorted Harper back to his apartment, convinced himself that Harper was straight enough to talk to Chief Leland, opened windows to air out the apartment, and hidden the grass, then phoned the chief himself and stayed long enough to answer a few questions. Harper was quickly losing any incentive to stay in Sand Ridge, Matt realized. Threats, broken lab equipment, vandalized slides, now this. This concrete stuff must've been done by an adult. No way it could be carried out by a gang of youths.

Matt liked driving from Sand Ridge's sidewalk-rimmed streets, lit by cozy, amber living-room lights, into the narrow farm lanes, then onto the larger roads with center markings. Higher yet (the wider the road, the more elevated from life around it) he merged onto the divided, double-lane highway toward Cleveland and the newly fashionable Flats area along the Cuyahoga River. He cruised past a rusted muffler pipe that was deposited on the verge like a car turd. This curve was always dangerous for people who didn't know the road. There were skid marks and tire shreds. The thready rubber shards were numerous tonight. A large truck must've had a blowout.

As he sped past the Cleveland airport and the automobile assembly plant, Matt noticed that somebody had erected three gigantic white metal crosses next to the highway. A local church, no doubt. Niccole's words about the little white crosses along the highway that marked car-wreck fatalities rang through his head.

Civilization was so precarious; madness and violence bubbled barely beneath the surface, searching for an outlet, waiting for the emotions to take over. It was shocking, after all these centuries of education, that rationality could collapse with such ease in Sand Ridge. But what else could Matt do than what he'd already done?

When the shimmying in the wheel started, Matt thought he was imagining it. He looked hard at the road to see if new rumble bumps had been built into the pavement. He gripped the steering wheel more tightly. The shaking worsened. His adrenaline surged. Slow the car, but don't brake too hard.

God, it took forever to decelerate. The wheel was wallowing back and forth. A car was coming up too fast behind him. Pass, you fool, pass. He must've said it out loud. Couldn't the driver see his hazard flashers? The car zoomed around. Accidents happen so fast, but they go on forever. Tobie floated into his brain and hung there, Tobie holding the frog. He was down to eighteen miles an hour. A whir and loud bang. Amazed, he saw the right front tire fly off, bounce, and speed off the road like an out-of-control top. He grasped the steering wheel firmly. Mammoth blue sparks flashed up from where the fender and wheel drum struck the concrete like flints on steel. The car slewed around as the rear end overtook the front, but Matt steered with it, grinding to a halt on the shoulder of the highway.

He sat there, afraid to take his hands off the wheel. He was hot. His hair crawled on the back of his neck. His pulse was pounding in his ears. For half a minute he stayed calm. Then he began to shake, first in his elbows, then his wrists. When he wanted to get out of the car, his knees quavered. He crossed his arms over his chest and leaned his head against the steering wheel. First he thought of Niccole, he would be late, then of why the wheel might fly off; he could think of no reason. He didn't know how long he sat there before he heard a knocking on the window glass.

A face framed by a scruffy beard and wide-brimmed felt hat peered at him. The man's mouth moved. Matt couldn't hear him, but he studied his lips like a deaf person.

"You okay?" That must be what he'd said. "You all right in there?" Matt could just barely hear the words.

He rolled down the window, and the man in black, baggy overalls asked again. Must be Amish. This was quite far north of Holmes County to find an Amish farmer.

"My wheel came off," Matt said.

He heaved the door open, upward since the car was at a tilt off the shoulder. A yellow school bus boomed past on the center lane. Children were singing songs and waving out the windows. Where was the man's horse and black Amish wagon with its luminous orange triangle on the back? A small pickup truck was parked behind Matt's car. Probably not Amish, more likely Mennonite.

"I live a half mile away," the man said.

"Then you can phone for me," Matt said.

After reassuring Mr. Yoder that he was fine physically, Matt provided him with Niccole's phone number and the AAA number to order a tow truck.

"Probably bunged up the drum," Mr. Yoder said, leading Matt around the car to look.

Sure enough, the rim was chewed and bashed, the lugs twisted.

"Can't put a wheel back on that. You're lucky to be alive." Mr. Yoder spoke deliberately, intensifying the import of his words.

The Mennonite helped Matt set up an emergency flare on the edge of the highway behind the car to warn the oncoming traffic in the gloom. After Mr. Yoder pulled away in his pickup, Matt calculated that the soonest Niccole could arrive was in fifteen minutes. Enough time to look for the tire. He dug his flashlight out of the trunk and headed back down the road. He felt he was in a state of suspension, almost like amnesia, except that the accident was perfectly clear in his brain as he rehearsed the sequence of events to figure what had gone wrong. If the screws and bolts had been messed with, he'd know it was sabotage, because he'd tightened them himself last time he inspected the tires.

A sliver of now-gold sunset provided some visibility, but the day was dissolving. The wheel could have bounced in one of many directions. If he were a wheel, he thought, and had spun off in the direction he had seen, where would he have gone? A highway storage area for winter road salt lay a few yards down the hill. Maybe there. Matt surveyed the graveled yard, walked all the way around the giant tepee-igloo salt house, noting that the fan in the back was whirling in the stiff, cold breeze. He walked into the igloo, his flashlight shaft bobbing across the cavelike walls. He cast the light down. There, on a large mound of rough salt in the center of the building, sat the tire. A faint tread path was pressed through the salt. Extraordinarily, the hubcap still clung to the rim. Matt shifted the tire, wedged the flashlight into the salt hill to give him a fixed light, then nudged the screwdriver blade of his knife around the hubcap perimeter until the metal popped off. Three lug nuts dropped out.

A piece of paper was wadded inside. Matt removed it, sat down on the tire, and, holding the flashlight up with one hand, smoothed the paper over his knee with the other. A double page of slick paper from a magazine. Couldn't be. It was. The centerfold of a *Playboy:* a blond, naked nymphet. There was some writing in pen across her rosy hips. Matt held the flashlight closer. "You better," a scrawled word he couldn't quite decipher, "off." Along the girl's leg was printed "Or Tobys next." He tried to make out the scribbled word. "Lay." It must be "lay." "You better lay off. Or Tobys next." Didn't spell her name right.

He slumped down on the edge of the salt mountain and

propped his head in his hands. They *were* after him. Trying to scare him off. They must know that the dearest thing to him was Tobie. Shit, why did they have to involve her? She was perfectly innocent! So were Evie and the others. Suddenly he felt drained. The adrenaline had run out.

But the bolts. Only three. They—whoever they were— had removed two and left these loose. It was a miracle he'd been able to slow down before the wheel spun off, a miracle he was even alive.

He heard a crunching on the gravel. He turned, the beam of his flashlight whipping around and flashing through the igloo doorway like a beacon. Niccole, in delicate silhouette, stood in the archway. Her hair was in a braid down her back. He remembered the ring. How could she belong to someone else?

"Are you okay?"

That milky, deep voice.

"I'm okay. You okay?" he replied in singsong.

"How can you make jokes? I was so worried when that man called me, even though he said you were fine."

Matt lifted the wrist that was holding the flashlight. He couldn't explain, but he felt silly, giddy. He held the light just beneath his chin.

"Ohhh, don't." She moved toward him. The swish of her quick movement came with a lemony perfume. "Don't do that. It makes you look ghoulish."

Matt laughed.

"Are you really okay?" she insisted.

"Hey, I'm fine. A little shaken. It appears a band of sex-crazed boys are after me, or rather after Sand Ridge girls, and since I'm after them, they are after me."

"Huh?"

His senses were intensely heightened. Life was new again. He shone the light on her. She was wearing an electric-blue sweater and trousers. He'd forgotten that she was so small.

"You know that you are environmentally sound."

"I know, I know," she said in exasperation.

"You've heard that one, too?"

"Small is beautiful, right?"

"I guess you have."

"Look, you're in shock," she said.

"I am?"

"You are. I've brought you something."

She held out her hands and he locked the light beam on them. Carefully she peeled a stick of chewing gum like it was a banana. Gum, the kind she'd been chewing after her car was bombed at the abortion clinic.

"This will calm you."

"Peculiar medicine."

She held the stick to his mouth and he opened it. She folded it in, touching his lips lightly. God, she hardly touched him, but a yearning in him bloomed wildly. Maybe he *was* in shock.

"Come," she said. "Let's go to my apartment. I'll fix supper for you. You're in no condition to function in public."

"No?"

Light from the flashlight struck her head as he moved. The part in her hair was vivid, white and vulnerable, the color of her hair like flame. His senses must be exaggerating.

"No," she replied firmly. "Come on. Give me the flashlight."

He probably would have followed her into a deep fjord, if she led him there. He rubbed his lips with the back of his hand.

CHAPTER EIGHTEEN

Late that night when Niccole unbraided her thick, coppery
hair, Matt thought of Rapunzel who'd helped her lover up
into her tower by letting down her long tresses. She sat in
front of her wide window that overlooked the drawbridges
of the Cuyahoga River. On the ledge behind her, seagulls
flapped and muttered and shuffled their feathers like tarot
cards.

Before that, though, Niccole cooked an elegant spaghetti
dinner, with fresh pasta, basil from a friend's garden, and
hand-grated parmesan cheese.

She suggested that Matt remove his gum, "now that we
have real medicine available," and gave him a large glass of
bourbon. He'd gulped it, and it must've helped because he
forgot that his car was stuck at the gas station, where it had
been towed. All he could think of was the development of
his professional relationship with Niccole. Exerting great
willpower, he kept from touching her. Something she ex-
uded, a fanatic determination to be separate and in control
of herself, an atmosphere that was fanatic because it was
still new and not settled inside her, made him cautious.

For the first half of the first drink, he sat sprawled near the
floor in a canvas-covered beanbag chair and watched her
preparing a salad. The apartment was elegantly but sparsely

furnished like a Japanese house. The floor was covered with a straw mat. Over that three or four rugs were thrown atop each other. There were several beanbag chairs and a futon in an oak frame. A low enamel table surrounded by cushions was where they would eat.

He helped her peel the onions and garlic and chop them. In her car on the way to her apartment, he had told her about the pregnancies, about Harper. (Should he have told her about Harper? She might like Harper too much if she met him.) He told her about Augusta Johnson's neighbor, who'd informed Audrey that Kim had been carried out of the house by her father when she was taken to the abortion clinic—*carried out,* that must mean the girl was already in pain; maybe someone had already tried to help her abort, maybe this would be pertinent to Niccole's legal case. He reminded her about Orville's sermon Sunday; maybe she'd want to attend.

He was methodically and efficiently chopping the green peppers when she said, "You're not at all like Kevin."

He added the basil and celery and minced them together. The point of her going to Orville's sermon, he said, was that she could gain an idea of Augusta Johnson's world and why she might lie about Kim's abortion and then cover it up with a lawsuit. He wasn't saying that that was the case, but hearing Orville might give her some leads. Besides, he wanted her to think about becoming more involved in the issue of the pregnancies. He thought Kim's pregnancy was part of a pattern somehow, and he needed the help of a woman to interview the girls.

"Don't you want to know who Kevin is?"

Niccole put her hand on her hip in irritation; she was clutching a cleaver.

"Hey, you mustn't treat knives that way," Matt said, reaching over and gingerly removing the instrument from her hand.

"Don't you?"

"Gee, do I? Is Kevin your meter reader?"

She looked at him in astonishment and rolled her eyes.

"Your plastic surgeon?"

"With a nose like this?" she said, running her finger over its prominent curve.

"Your late dog?"

She laughed. "You're getting close."

"Not your husband!"

"Ex-boyfriend."

"I don't think I want to know." He grinned. "We are having only a *professional* relationship, right?"

She looked puzzled.

"The ring: you showed me your wedding band when we left Sobo's and said, 'Strictly business,' remember?"

She looked sheepish.

"I use that ring bit as protection when I don't know men well."

"I can't expect you not to have a past," Matt said. "In fact, I want you to have a fascinating past. I wouldn't want you to be so young that you had a void for a personality. Not to say that we have anything but a businesslike relationship, I hasten to add."

He paused. Her eyes avoided his as she measured out the pasta.

"So, tell me about Kevin."

Kevin was her boyfriend of five years who now lived in New York. They had met in California in college when she was working on her B.A. in history, a major for people who don't know what they're going to do. She'd broken up with Kevin two months ago, and he was still trying to persuade her to change her mind. He was a computer programmer who dabbled in computer rock music. The problem, or part of the problem, was that he wanted her to play a stereotypical female role. The straw that broke the proverbial camel's back was that he wouldn't cook or wash dishes; silly, right? she asked. But what era did he think he was living in, anyway?

"You're still pulling away from him and establishing yourself," Matt said.

She nodded. "I guess that's why I have to lay out my conditions right away."

Earlier she had changed into a soft, beige silk blouse that set off her rust hair and dark eyes. She was barefoot. One end of a long Indian paisley silk scarf hung down from her neck between her breasts; the other end flowed down her back. She'd looked up at him earnestly, and Matt's hand had reached out. He couldn't control it. He touched the edge of her scarf, then her shoulder. She shuddered very slightly. Then she'd averted her face and lightly put her hand on his, then moved away, out from under it.

"Hey, have I complained about your conditions?"

"No," she said in a half-quizzical tone. "I think you're over your shock from the car," she added, and laughed.

He was silent, then said, "I didn't mean to push."

"I can't expect you not to be normal," she said, "just like you can't expect me not to have a past."

He watched her closely. Was she turned off by his age? Compared to the way she popped around, up and down on the beanbags, flitting to her knees to set the low table, he felt like an aged mastodon. She probably wasn't one who thought gray hair was distinguished. Oh, well.

During the meal, he answered her questions about Sand Ridge and his job. She told him about growing up in a suburb of Dallas, practicing in college to lose her Texas accent. She said she'd had a million different kinds of jobs, including attendant at an isolation tank where people were closed into tanks partially filled with water and left to float in the dark for an hour to relax and meditate. Before her current legal aid job, she'd been a freelance indexer of books for several small California publishers.

"Makes you think a lot about the alphabet. Have you ever thought about the letter *x?*"

"Not much," Matt admitted with his mouth full.

"There's something illicit about an *x.* If you scan a page, the *x*'s stick out. Like in sex or relax. And if you take *z* . . . there's something bizarre about *z*'s."

Over dessert of blueberries with cream, Matt found himself talking about Tobie, his wife, his life as a journalist, first in Washington at the State Department and then covering various wars.

She smiled as she cleared away the last dishes and turned out the lights. They then sipped liqueur and watched reflections fracture and undulate across the river's surface.

"So covering bureaucrats is dull compared to being a junior high principal?"

"Yeah, I find it much more interesting to worry about kids who paint eyeballs on the outsides of their eyelids so they can close their eyes in class and the teacher won't know they're sleeping."

"I had in mind a principal worried about virgin pregnancies."

Matt winced. "It's sick, really sick. You know, I've been trying to work out the timing. The coroner said Evie was five months pregnant. That means she conceived in June. And you said Kim was three months pregnant? Now here it is the second week in November. Amber is two months, according to Blair. This boys' club Yale Kaltmann mentioned is the only thing I've got to go on so far. And I don't even know if it exists. Since the girls are virgins, the only thing I can think of is that these boys are, if you'll pardon my language, jerking off and finger fucking them, and the girls are too embarrassed to say anything."

Matt watched her expression carefully. She was attentive, as if calculating the facts and figures for a legal document. Successive waves of compassion, disgust, and anger played over her face.

"What do you think? Will you interview some of the girls? Would you come to Orville's sermon?"

"I'll think about it," she said.

She rose from her cushion, calling back from the bedroom that she was getting his sheets and towels. Suddenly he remembered Tobie. He searched for the phone and found it by following the cord into a kitchen cabinet. When he reached her, Tobie sounded speedy, her words tumbling over each other, and she babbled about makeup the girls were trying on and apple tarts. Was she really okay? he asked. Why was she breathless? She'd just jumped off an exercycle in the basement when he called, she told him.

"Now, you must remember to sleep tonight," he said.

She giggled.

"Watch my lips," he said with exaggerated enunciation. "Be sure to sleep tonight. Did you see that?"

"Okay, okay," she said.

She didn't even ask where he was, and when he said he'd be late because he'd had some trouble with the car, so tomorrow she should get a ride home, she didn't seem bothered.

"Watch my lips?" Niccole said, smiling, after he hung up.

"Yeah," Matt said, and carefully not moving his lips, he said through his teeth, "Watch my lips."

She laughed. "For a principal, you are unusually silly."

She yawned, stretched like a cat. "Do you want to sleep in the bedroom where it's dark in the morning, or here in the living room where the view is fabulous in the sunrise? I usually pick the view myself."

"View looks good even in the dark," he said. "I'll opt for here."

A cargo ship was passing, riding high and illuminated like an amusement park. Dark figures of sailors dashed about on the deck.

They spread the futons half a foot apart on the Navajo rug. While she was in the bathroom, Matt stripped down to his T-shirt and shorts. He listened to the water running in the shower. He felt like an aroused teenager, versed in the most exquisite, prolonged restraint of desire. She turned out the lights and padded back, stepping onto the futon, dropping to one side her robe, which covered a long blue nightdress, and sat down into a Buddha fold. She began unbraiding her hair, brushing it forward over her face and then back, so that it fell, like her silk scarf had, half down her front to just below her breasts and half down her back. Then she stretched out, pulled up the covers, and said "'Night."

"G'night," he said.

She slept on her right side and made the slightest of breathing sounds. He didn't know how long he watched her, the way she flung her arm over her head, the smooth curve of her hip swelling from her thin waist, her magnificent hair that flared out on the sheets.

When he woke up, she was watching him, sitting again with her legs intertwined, and licking some blueberries from the palm of her hand. The sun was pouring from behind the apartment building as cleanly as water. The view was wonderful, though not in the usual scenic sense, for not everybody likes relics of the industrial revolution and dock areas. Steel drawbridges, one painted bright blue, dotted the area like Erector Set toys. A barge was grunting along against the current, low in the water. Seagulls were circling and mewing over a tiny island upriver.

Matt lifted his body to lean on his elbow and rubbed his eyes. Hell, she certainly must've taken a good look at him while he was asleep, at all his gray and his crow's-feet. Oh, well, truth in advertising: he is as he appears, ten years older than she.

"Eight hours of sleep, what a waste, eh?" she said, braiding the tips of her hair in play.

"Yeah, it's really a pity that we have to waste two-thirds of the day awake."

They ate breakfast, black bread, cheese, and bananas. He showed her how, if you squeeze bananas coaxingly and gently, they split lengthwise into thirds. "Just amazing, Ripley," she said. Her face was lightly puffy around the eyes, but without her makeup she looked wonderful, more vulnerable. Another cargo boat plugged by, this one from Panama. She knew all the flags by now. The whistle blew on the ship, immediately followed by the buzzer of her intercom. She looked puzzled, checked her watch, then answered it.

"It's the postman, ma'am; you've got a package. I'll leave it down here."

She came back up the four flights of stairs lugging the package, humming snatches of some tune only she could have identified. She closed the door with a flick of her heel, strode over, and set the package, in a cardboard box a foot tall and about eight inches wide, in the center of the low table.

"It sounds funny."

"Like what?"

"It sloshes," she said, lifting it again and demonstrating. "Can't be flowers, too bad, I like flowers. Maybe it's a doll's waterbed."

"Why don't you find out?"

"It's pretty heavy."

He picked it up: about three pounds.

"Liquid, who would send me something liquid?"

She looked and found no return address.

"D'ya like suspense or something?"

"Not real suspense, but packages, yeah, that kind's okay."

"You can do it," he teased. "I'm sure you can."

She pulled a long knife out of the drawer and he warned her that he had sharpened it last night. She put the tip under the extra-tensile nylon packaging tape and slit across the top of the box, then across the other side, and then neatly down two adjacent sides, so they fell down like a flap. White Styrofoam packaging nodules in the shape of peanuts tumbled all over the table.

"Confetti!" she said, picking up a handful and tossing them in the air.

Matt shuffled the box off the table, leaving its contents there. She brushed off more Styrofoam until there was a clear quart jar standing in the middle of the table.

A putrid gray, curled object with purply edges floated in liquid in the jar, bumping on the bottom. They both leaned over to examine it. It was only two and a half inches long, its head abnormally large, its limbs coiled self-protectively, its eyes clammed shut. Formaldehyde fumes hit them. Niccole gasped and drew back.

"It's a fetus, isn't it?"

She turned and covered her mouth with both hands. Matt reached out to rotate the jar.

"Dog fetus," he said.

"How could they do that? Why did they send it to me? Who do you think did it? I feel sick."

To stop her sudden shaking, she sat down on a cushion and crossed her arms. Matt put his hand on her shoulder comfortingly.

"They're trying to scare you."

"They're succeeding."

"Wait, here's a note."

Matt pulled a sheet of folded paper from among the wrappings and handed it to Niccole. It was a standard page of typing paper. On it in black felt-tip pen was printed: "This fetus, a spaniel. Warning: Lay off. Don't help Mr. Chase."

She dropped the paper and they sat in silence for at least a minute.

"What are we going to do with it?"

"Call the police; it's evidence," Matt said slowly as he mused. "It's odd, you know, 'lay off,' that was the exact phrase used on the *Playboy* centerfold in my hubcap."

He paused, picked up the note.

"The same pen. How did these boys know I was going to ask you to help me? They spelled my name wrong, too."

Niccole now stood gazing out the window as if for solace. Matt picked up the jar gingerly, thinking about whether the police would check it for fingerprints. He carried it to the closet and set it on the floor. Then he walked over and stood next to her. The morning sun tipped the edges of her hair in gold. Her robe was disheveled, revealing the curves of her breasts at the top.

"I guess the decision has been made for me," she said, turning toward him. "Into the world of teenage girls and preachers. I'm scared."

Her dark eyes pulled him, inviting him, in conflict with her earlier words. He resisted, folded his arms and gazed far away into the mists wafting through the iron filigree arches of the drawbridges.

"I get angry when I'm scared."

Matt gazed down at her. He wished he did. He just got scared when he was scared.

CHAPTER NINETEEN

"Coon dogs," said Lisa.

She was explaining the eerie howling across the valley opposite the Wades' house.

"It's hunting season."

"Creepy," said Tobie.

"My dad says there's two kinds of coon barks," Verity said. "One for tracking and one for when the coon is treed."

Lisa was showing them her calico kittens. "Calicos are always girls," she told them. Standing in the garage door next to a bowl of milk, she called, "Kitty, kitty, kitty," in a falsetto warble.

It was an eerie confluence of events in the darkening yard: Lisa melodically summoning the cats, the coon dogs' hootings and howls weaving over each other. It made Tobie feel gloomy, and she told Verity about Evie's ashes. They sank into silence.

Suddenly, without warning, lights blazed on. The house was lit up like a monument or the city hall. Verity screamed and dropped to the grass. Tobie threw up her arm to avert the blinding glare. Enormous floodlights sunken into the ground at the corners of the house had flared into the night. One of the lights was directly at the three girls' feet, shining into their faces.

"It's okay," Lisa said. "They're just to keep hunters from shooting at the house by accident."

Tobie stepped out of the direct beam. "Verity, you okay?" she asked.

Verity was sobbing, sitting up and rocking a little.

"It's just a light. Whats'a matter?" Lisa said.

"Nothing, nothing, though I walk through the valley of the shadow . . ."

"Come on, Vare, let's go in." Tobie shivered.

Lisa, still standing directly in the light's beam, shrugged with theatrical exasperation, looking down at Verity.

Tobie put her hand on Verity's shoulder. She didn't try to move her. Verity was a strapping, big girl, and Tobie was strong, but much smaller. Finally Verity stumbled up, saying she was okay, okay. The floodlights reminded Tobie of a prison-yard scene in a movie. Across the river, the dogs were on a particularly long run, or maybe they'd chased their victim up a tree and were celebrating. They howled in chorus. Tobie was relieved to get inside and shut the door. Lisa locked it, double-locked it.

All the girls' sleeping bags had been tossed into the den as they arrived. When the first girl unrolled hers, it was a signal for others to stake out their territories. Suitcases and overnight bags were arranged like furniture. The jockeying always continued late into the night, the girls settling and resettling who was next to whom like a flock of fussy penguins, claiming an island and maneuvering around each other's nesting sites. Despite the occasional earsplitting stereo record, there was a subdued, shy fluidity about the party. Talk occurred among clumps of two, three, or four girls, who meandered around the house.

Amid this group of thirteen- and fourteen-year-olds, extraordinarily discreet about their bodies, self-conscious about developing breasts and burgeoning hips, Gloria stood out. Gloria was older, fifteen. Lisa had invited her, even though she didn't fit in, because she was her lab partner in biology. Tobie had heard that Gloria's mother was a lesbian. She couldn't figure out how lesbianism worked, technically. Rumor had it that Gloria did more than kiss boys. Tobie hadn't even done that. Except for doctors, nobody had seen Tobie naked since she was eight years old.

When Gloria stripped off her Prince T-shirt and stood in the den next to the pool table exposing her breasts, real breasts that drooped, news of the event spread fast through the house, and the girls collected.

"See, like this," Gloria said to Alice.

She pointed to her nipples, which were covered with circular, beige Band-Aids.

"Then you can go without a bra and it won't show."

"Yuck, bras," said the only other girl in the room who wore bras.

"I can't wait to wear one, a real one, not a training bra," said another girl.

"Doesn't it hurt to take them off?"

"Only a little."

Gloria slipped her fingernail under the edge and peeled the Band-Aid off. The crowd leaned forward. She stuck it back on so that her breasts again looked blank, like Orphan Annie cartoon eyes.

Jasper, Lisa's older sister, who'd been upstairs on the phone with her boyfriend, came up behind a cluster of girls in the den doorway.

"Tell them about finger fucking, Gloria. Tell them about blow jobs."

Her voice was acid. The young girls shifted, frightened.

"Jasper, you promised you'd stay upstairs or go to the Prossers' house," Lisa complained.

"I got a blow job last week," said Cheryl.

"Oh, yeah? Where?" asked Jasper.

"At Olga's beauty salon."

"You mean a blow dry," said another girl.

"Oh."

Gloria wriggled her T-shirt back on and picked up her pool cue.

"I'm pregnant," she said defiantly, glaring at Jasper.

"Who'd ya let do it to you? Rudy? Drew? Judson? Or was it all of them?"

"I'm a virgin."

Gloria hit a blue ball hard but not square; it hopped against the felt and bounced off the pool table.

"Oh, yeah, I hear virgin pregnancies are going around," Jasper said.

"Jasper, please," Lisa begged, pulling on her sister's arm.

The older girl turned on her heel, strode across the living room, walked out the front door, and slammed it.

"Well, don't just stand there staring like I'm some kinda freak. Haven't you ever heard of a girl getting pregnant?" Gloria demanded.

"Not our age."

"Wanna bet? What about Kim Johnson? She got an abortion. What about Katie Sobo? What about Evie? That's why she drownded herself."

Tobie thought Gloria was lying until she got to Evie. But what if she was right? How could Kim and Katie get pregnant?

"C'mon, Alice," Gloria said, shoving the balls into the triangular frame.

The girls were stunned into private thoughts. Here they'd been worrying about holding hands and kissing boys, while their friends were getting pregnant. Maybe. They drifted back into their small groups, still afraid to talk about the issues immediately. What if Kim really was pregnant? Was that why she hadn't come tonight?

Tobie propelled Cheryl, Penny, and Verity into the large combination dressing room/bathroom, where in front of a big, low mirror they experimented with makeup and earrings. They discussed a girl at school who had tweezed out all her eyebrows and drawn two arches in their place. She'd had to wear dark sunglasses for a while because her eyelids were swollen.

"She's a ho," said Penny, using the slang word derived from "whore," but much milder in meaning. "All she wants to do is flirt with boys."

"Her eyebrows washed off in the rain. I saw it," Cheryl said. "She was in the girls' room drawing them back on."

They all laughed, all except Verity. She sat on the pink vinyl seat next to the tub with her navy blue cardigan buttoned up to the top over a loose cotton dress.

"C'mon, Vare," Tobie said, and took her by the wrist. "Why don'tcha put on this eyeshadow. You look good in green."

Verity listlessly accepted the makeup stick and for a few

157

minutes leaned over the cabinet with the others, but her feigned interest dissolved and she slumped to the seat again.

"You look like Nurse Ross," Tobie said to Cheryl, who was contorting her lips in applying lipstick. "Remember that, Vare?"

Verity smiled. The two of them had surprised Nurse Ross in her office one day when she was standing in front of the mirror. She was performing chin exercises, contorting her lower face and making her lips change from a small circle to a scream, but with no sound. Then the nurse stretched her lips from one side to the other, like Popeye saying, "Psst," out of the side of his face. When they giggled, she was embarrassed and hastily explained that when women get older, their neck muscles sag. "I used to have a baby, you know," she said. The two of them didn't reply, uneasy that they had inadvertently peeled off her outer layer of presentability.

"I feel sorry for her," Penny said.

"Why doesn't she go with Mr. Kaltmann? I've seen them walking together," Cheryl said.

"He's kinda handsome."

"She's too fat."

"No, she's not."

"Do you know why Mr. Kaltmann always wears one sleeve buttoned down when the other one is rolled up?" Cheryl said. "He's got a tattoo. One day he was reaching up, putting in a light bulb in the hall in the basement, and I saw the edge of it sticking out. It was a woman. All I could see was her head; she had spikes out of it like the Statue of Liberty. I couldn't see the whole thing. He caught me staring and stuck his hand in his tool apron."

"There's nothing wrong with tattoos, my dad has a tattoo," Tobie said. "He got it in Saigon. It's a bluebird. He said it hurt a lot."

"I like Nurse Ross's hourglass," Cheryl said.

"Neat blue sand," Penny said, nodding. "I tried blue lipstick once."

"They don't make blue lipstick."

"Yes, they do. Or they did."

Tobie didn't remember any hourglass or blue sand in Nurse Ross's office, but she didn't say anything.

Cheryl moved close to the mirror, pulling her eyelid sideways to apply eyeliner. She didn't look at the others when she asked, "Did you feel anything when she examined inside of you?"

The question was addressed to the air. No one answered for a moment.

"Huh?" Cheryl said, looking at Penny in the mirror.

"Huh-uh," Penny said. "Besides, you're not supposed to talk about that."

"She said don't talk about it to your parents," Cheryl said. "Did you feel anything, Tobie?"

"No," Tobie said. "I don't think she examined me inside."

"Maybe she did and you didn't notice. I told my mother and she said good, she was glad the nurse was checking me out, what with all the promiscuity in girls younger and younger."

"Why didn't I get examined inside?" Tobie asked.

"Maybe she's doing spot checks," Cheryl said. "What about you, Verity, vegetable Verity, c'mon, try on this stuff, what about you, did she examine you?"

Verity roused herself, nervously.

"Yeah," she said.

She didn't want to talk about it. It was too embarrassing. She was more worried about how God could get in there and make her pregnant. God was everywhere, but you couldn't feel Him. He was like a ghost, but a special Holy Ghost. She'd always thought the only way to get pregnant was if a boy was involved. Adults lied. It was like Santa Claus. Only worse.

Maybe she'd get spot-checked next time, Tobie thought.

"I want some big dangly earrings," Penny said, "but my mother won't let me. She says I have to grow up more. Sometimes I think they never let you grow up. My mom says the same thing to my sister, wait till you grow up, and she's sixteen!"

The girls debated the merits and fashions of pierced earrings, and judged that more than three per ear was tacky.

"Did you know that your earlobes keep growing when you get older?"

"Oh, no!"

"And your nose! My mother told me."

"Oh no—se!"

They all giggled. Tobie turned and touched Verity's pug nose.

"There's hope yet," she kidded.

Verity took a deep breath and said very softly, "Did Evie kill herself because she was pregnant?"

Conversation stopped and the girls turned toward her.

"Maybe," Tobie said.

"She didn't have to do that, though," Cheryl said. "She coulda had an abortion. It doesn't hurt too much. That way she wouldn't have to have a caesarean and get a scar."

"My mom says when I turn sixteen I can have contraceptives if I want. She says that's better than getting pregnant."

"That's weird."

"It's not. It's sensible. She says so. She says one of her friends gave her daughter a dildo when she was sixteen."

Nobody else asked what that was, and Tobie wasn't about to.

"Do you know what a blow job is?" Cheryl asked.

Silence.

"Yeah, it's when you're kissing a boy and you blow a little in his ear," Tobie said. "I saw it in a movie."

"Stoopid. No, it's not," Penny said.

They all turned toward her expectantly.

"It's when a boy puts his whatchamacallit in a girl's mouth."

"What's that?"

"You know, his hangy-down thing."

"His penis," Tobie said, disdaining euphemism.

"In her mouth?!"

"That's disgusting! Ooooh. Gag."

"Why would anybody do that?"

"I bet only sluts do that."

"You made that up, Penny."

"No, she didn't."

Jasper had returned like a phantom. The younger girls started and pivoted to stare at her.

"A blow job is when a boy puts his penis in a girl's mouth and she makes him come and then she swallows it."

There was dead silence in the bathroom. Jasper turned

and walked back downstairs. The girls heard the front door slam again. They remained too shocked and embarrassed to look at each other. Lisa broke the mood when she called up the stairs, "Anybody want something to eat? There's a choice of popcorn, frozen apple tarts, ice cream, and potato chips." The girls in the bathroom laughed and sheepishly caught each other's eyes.

"Sure," said Cheryl, breaking up the group and heading downstairs.

Tobie was leaning over the big unabridged dictionary in Mr. Wade's study, looking up "dildo," when the phone rang. Thinking it could be her father calling early, she picked up the receiver on the desk. "Hello?"

"Hello." It was a boy's husky voice.

"Hello." Lisa had also answered the phone in the kitchen.

"Lisa?"

"Yes."

"A friend of yours suggested I get in touch with you. She said you were very friendly."

"Who was it?"

"I don't remember. Some girl I met at a party."

"Gee . . . well."

"Would you like to meet me?"

"I dunno. I guess."

"Can you tell me what you look like?"

"I'm medium height. Brunette hair."

"What's your figure like?"

Silence from Lisa.

"I mean, do you have big breasts?"

"Who are you?"

"Just a friend of your friend."

"You gotta tell me who you are."

"Do you ever want to have a baby?"

"Yes . . . well . . . no. Who are you?"

"We have lots of things that can make you happy. We can give you a baby. You want one?"

"Lisa," Tobie interrupted, "you oughta hang up."

"Yeah, bye," Lisa said.

"No, no, wait a minute, I just want to meet you."

"Hang up," Tobie said.

"Just wait where you are—we'll bring you something to make you very happy," the gruff voice said, panting and breathing hard between phrases.

Lisa hung up. Tobie did too and dashed downstairs. The kitchen was crowded with girls who had come to eat.

"Jeez, Lisa, why did you keep talking to him?" Tobie asked.

All the girls turned to listen, forcing Lisa and Tobie to relate the entire phone call.

"What should we do?" Lisa said.

"Go home?" asked one girl.

"I don't wanna go home."

"Maybe we should call someone."

"If we do that, they're going to make us break up the party."

"Look," said Gloria, "that scum, whoever he is, can't do anything. If we just stay locked in, nobody can reach us."

"Something can come in through the keyhole. That's the way the Devil operates," said one girl who was fond of reading horror books.

"That's dumb."

"I'm scared."

"They can't make us pregnant through a keyhole or anything like that."

"How do you know? How did Evie and Katie get pregnant?"

They all turned toward Gloria, who was dishing out some ice cream.

"What are you looking at me for? God, you all stare a lot."

"How did you get pregnant?"

"How should I know? I'm a virgin."

"Are you going to keep the baby?"

"Maybe I will, maybe I won't."

Verity started crying and collapsed again, this time onto the kitchen floor like a Raggedy Ann doll. The girls drew back, while Tobie knelt and asked what the matter was. She asked if she wanted them to call her parents. Verity sobbed, "No!" so vehemently that they were taken aback. Tobie urged her to lie down on her sleeping bag with lots of pillows. The girls discussed whether or not they should call an adult and inform them of the boy's phone call, already reverting to their confident, grown-up speech patterns. No one really wanted to end the party, so they decided that when Rutha Prosser came from next door and when Tobie's father phoned, they would say everything was fine.

By eleven o'clock, they had declared to the world that all was well, including Tobie's assurances to Matt. Then they carried out their tradition of smearing toothpaste over the first girl who fell asleep. Cheryl had dozed off in an easy chair next to the stereo. The word went out and the girls clustered around, whispering and giggling. Lisa administered the first smear all over Cheryl's shortie pajamas. But Cheryl didn't budge, so the next girl daubed her cheek with the vivid green, minty goo. She awoke with a start and a groan of acknowledgment of her dubious distinction, which was followed by laughter and hooting from the girls.

Amid the noise the doorbell suddenly rang; the house hushed. Nobody moved. Then a loud varoom, varoom from a motorcycle split the night air, receding down the Wades' driveway. Tobie rushed to the window, but the spotlights glared back at her, trapping the house so that nothing could be seen beyond the circle of light. After five minutes of debate Lisa opened the front door. A brown paper bag sat on a flagstone near the door, its top gathered and tied with a yellow ribbon from which hung a card.

Gloria picked it up and read out loud: "A baby from your loverboy."

"Who's it for?" Lisa asked nervously.

Gloria turned the card over and showed it to them: "To Tits." Tobie glanced at Gloria and looked away. Gloria untwined the ribbon from the bag's bunched top and opened it.

"Lisa, why don't you look?" she said, passing the bag to her hostess.

"I don't want to. It's not to me."

"You got that phone call."

"I don't care."

"Here, I'll do it," Tobie said.

Nothing was moving in the bag. It looked pink. She reached in and pulled out a naked baby doll of rubbery plastic. A pungent, sweetish odor came, too.

"P.U.," said Cheryl, holding her nose.

"Uuuuuugh," Tobie said, dropping the doll. "It's got gunk on it."

"What is it?"

"It's white."

"Stinks."

Gloria picked up the doll by a clean foot and sniffed it, while all the girls watched. She quickly and viciously flung it, head first, out over the sidewalk, through the glare of the spotlights, until it disappeared into the dark. They heard it land on the gravel of the driveway, its hard plastic head skittering and scraping to a stop.

"Why didja do that?"

"It's jism."

"What's that?"

"Comes out of a boy's thing."

Tobie bolted inside and dashed to the kitchen sink to scrub her hand, using the hottest possible water, detergent, and Ajax, till the palm of her hand hurt. Maybe that's how Evie'd got pregnant, why she killed herself. When Tobie came out of the kitchen, she made all the girls shut up about the doll. "I don't want to talk about it or hear about it." They turned out the lights and the house settled into whispers. Verity's sleeping bag was next to Tobie's. After the last light clicked off, Verity reached over and grasped Tobie's hand, the one that had touched the doll, holding it for a while in silence. Tobie felt better. It was like leprosy. In the Bible, no one would touch a leper. Except Jesus. Verity was a good friend.

CHAPTER TWENTY

One day Tobie left her baseball mitt in her locker and forgot to fasten the combination lock. Yale, who seldom let anything escape his attention, noticed the lock dangling open as he walked through the school hallway late in the evening. He knew it was Tobie's locker because he'd been watching her for a while now. He opened the door, discovered the mitt, and decided to borrow it for a little while. He took it home with him and carried it up to his bedroom, a garret in the top of the house. It fit right in. The color, a light red-ocher, was the same as a dozen or so carved wooden arms he had hanging around the room.

He'd bought the whittled arms from an estate sale at Yetter's Flea Market. He was occasionally called to Yetter's to repair the commercial meat freezer there. Each wooden arm started at the elbow and ended in a fist. Yale had hung them randomly from the dark-stained oak rafters of his room. The antique dealer said they'd belonged to a man who collected shamanic and witchcraft objects. Carved in various sizes, some were hung from leather thongs and some stood like small obelisks.

Yale knew exactly why the arms fascinated him. When he was in the army, and after those horrible guys had forced him to get his tattoo, he remembered a petty officer who'd talked about hands a lot. Hands are our great gifts from nature, he said. No other animal has hands as sensitive as a human being's. Hands make beautiful work. Without hands, our brains are useless blobs in our skulls, he said. True, the petty officer was trying to get the grunts to perform menial tasks. But the idea of the wondrousness of hands stuck with Yale.

Tobie's mitt was so well worn that the fingers easily folded down. He'd put the glove, palm up, on a bookshelf. A pine arm was suspended over it from a higher shelf.

As was his ritual, Yale turned the lights off. The blood-dark beech tree leaves outside the high window always clung to the tree all winter, blocking any view from the ground. Yale had chosen this side of the house for his room because of its seclusion.

He always performed the ritual standing. It was not done for pleasure, after all. And the more quickly the obligation was fulfilled, the better, as far as he was concerned. He liked best to carry out his duty when there was a storm. This night, rain poured against the windowpane, glazing it so his eyes felt unfocused. Winter was almost here; the temperature was barely above freezing. Heating the house made the air inside dry; his eyes felt hard-boiled and gritty. He'd had the furnace turned on for more than a month now. To save on his heating bill, only the vents in his bedroom and bath were open; the basement was warmed by the heat from the furnace and the freezer motors. He carried a small quartz heater with him to other rooms.

He turned on the tiny cassette recorder containing a tape of Johann Strauss Viennese waltzes. He could float away on those, like when he was a little boy listening to the waltz music waft beneath his mother's closed bedroom door.

He'd taken a couple of Erlenmeyer flasks with corks from the biology lab, but Yale found their necks too small. Instead he'd started using ordinary lab jars, each with a frosted patch to write on. He, of course, left the patch blank. He usually collected for a week or two before delivering it to Lorna. The jar, icy from the freezer in the basement, sat in a small Styrofoam box containing dry ice, the lid still screwed on. He'd checked the generator in the basement and all the other machines before he came upstairs. Even from here he could hear the reassuring hum of the motors.

He would return Tobie's mitt. He certainly wasn't a criminal. A criminal stole things permanently. His motives were only the highest. He'd begun to think about Tobie gradually after she'd stepped briefly into Mr. Chays's office that afternoon. What had really started him thinking was that Lorna was not doing things properly. He had left the choices to her, but now he realized that was a mistake. The woman was unsound. She didn't have the judgment to pick girls who would make stable mothers. Look at Evie. Killed herself. He felt very sorry for that. The girl's home life apparently was not conducive to emotional stability. Then there was Kim. He wasn't quite sure what had happened, but Lorna thought the mother had made Kim have an abortion. Now, what kind of love was that?

Just think, if his mother had had an abortion, he wouldn't even be alive. That was one reason he was pleased about Verity Molway. Her father definitely would not let Verity have an abortion. Yale felt odd about that newspaper article with the Reverend Orville claiming virgin births. Yale was proud of being the father, though he knew it was not a good idea for people to know. However sensible his position, somehow he knew they wouldn't see it his way. Someday, maybe he'd tell his children he was their father and they would be proud. Or maybe he'd leave them his money.

When he realized that Lorna was making mistakes, he decided he would have to take even more control. Tobie didn't have a mother to take care of her, but he thought she seemed to be a sensible young lady. There was no doubt that her father loved her a great deal. He liked Mr. Chays and wanted to avoid hurting him. Nothing and nobody must interfere with his plan. He didn't want to hurt Miss Epps either. Lucky he'd found out about her from that note on Mr. Chays's desk. No, not luck. He'd found it because he was meticulous and clever.

He just wanted them to be scared off the trail. If he could get Matt Chays investigating the gang of boys, that would be okay. Finding that mother spaniel freshly hit by a car was another lucky stroke. Took him a while to think out that plan. It should make Mr. Chays and her more suspicious of the boys.

Mr. Chays's memo to the staff about inviting in an outside doctor to inspect things with Lorna bothered Yale. He'd had one discussion with Lorna and told her how to avoid any problems if this should happen. He even thought up sample questions a doctor might ask her and made her practice the answers. He really had to take her in hand. She seemed more hysterical lately. He'd have to tell her exactly which girls to pick, since she had such bad judgment.

Yale especially liked this lyrical, slow waltz playing now. He looked at his beloved teddy bear that he had kept since his childhood. "Freddy the Phoo," he called him. The bear was so well loved that it was bald where the fur had been rubbed off its ears that had served as handles. Yale reached over and straightened the bear up from where it had fallen forward on its nose on the mattress.

He closed his eyes. He'd put on his rubber gloves to keep the Vaseline from getting on his hands. It usually took three sessions to provide enough so he could take the jar to Lorna. This was the third. He'd removed the lid from the jar. Frosty steam floated up from the dry ice. He opened his eyes and bent over to touch his face to Tobie's baseball mitt. He picked up the jar, closed his eyes again, and thought of eternity as an endless blur of clocks and calendars. He thought of small pink babies waving their perfectly formed fingers and toes in the air. The music was unbearably sweet and intense.

That was done. He turned on a light and held up the jar. Enough to take to Lorna. He put the lid on the jar, nestled it back into the dry ice, removed the rubber gloves, and took the box down to the freezer in the basement. Little puffs of mist squeezed from the corners of the box into the cold air with each step he took. For the past six months he'd felt so much younger, now that he knew he was going to be a father. His age no longer bothered him. When he was at home, he felt restored, felt like he had as a kid when time was so long and the summers were unending. Yale felt pleased at taking supervisory control of Lorna. His own precision and decisiveness were always reassuring to him.

After he'd replaced the jar in the upright freezer, he thumped the metal capsule merrily. He owed it all to Buford. Well, not all. After all, Buford had hardly thought up the idea.

"Tell your mother not to mess it up," he said out loud. "Hey, boy, we'll get you back alive someday. We will."

CHAPTER TWENTY-ONE

A smeary atmosphere enveloped Sand Ridge, like water thickened with a touch of cornstarch. Tobie had already dashed outside and back to report that worms were "sashaying around" on the sidewalks; they'd oozed up from the waterlogged soil to keep from drowning.

Matt poured his coffee extra strong, waiting for Tobie to bring up the topic of church. He'd decided he'd best forewarn her about Orville's sermon. "You gonna polish your shoes for church?" she asked.

Well, no, he didn't think anybody would notice his shoes. The sermon might be a bit strange today, he cautioned. Reverend Molway was going to say something about girls in Sand Ridge having babies but being virgins at the same time. Absorbed in pouring maple syrup onto her pancakes, Tobie concentrated her attention even more. She'd grown more shy lately about topics connected with sex. "That's not possible, is it?" she asked with a hint of panic. Matt reassured her that it wasn't.

"As for the Virgin Mary," he said, reading her thoughts, "I've taught you that every person must make up his own mind about what he believes in religion. You might come to a different conclusion than me. I don't even know if there is ever a final decision on this sort of thing. I mean, each day of our lives we show our moral, ethical, and theological beliefs."

"We're not saved, are we, you and me? Not born again?"

"Not by Reverend Molway's definition. You've been to a lot of different churches by now and you can see how many different ways there are to worship God."

"Do you believe in God, Daddy?"

"I think so."

"How could God let Evie die?"

"Honey, how to explain the existence of death and sin and evil has confounded the best minds in the world for centuries. I think if someone tells you they have the answer, you better watch out. The only answers I've been able to find are in the ways people live. And you know how complex even one person can be, right?"

She nodded and pursed her lips as she drenched a pancake bite.

"You're going to hear a lot of words today. I think we try to understand things by putting them into words, and sometimes we can get close to truth that way. Reverend Molway is going to explain things, and he may not be right."

"What's he explaining?"

Matt told her there were a number of peculiar cases of girls who were pregnant and who claimed to be virgins. He couldn't explain it himself yet, but there was no reason to be afraid. She knew how pregnancy happened, and maybe some of these other girls didn't and got themselves pregnant while playing around with boys.

"I won't let anybody touch me," she insisted, avoiding his eyes.

He sighed. Would this make her afraid of boys? Frankly, when he thought about it, he'd just as soon she not let anybody touch her at the moment.

Matt warmed up the car heater while waiting for Tobie, who was running late, as always. The mechanics had been able to fix the car's wheel quickly yesterday, a day early. When she finally bounced into her seat, the car was warm and Matt was drowsy, dreamily recalling his evening at Niccole's.

* * *

The Pillar of Salt Tabernacle of the Lord of Hosts was located back off the road on a vast, level field of dried and decapitated cornstalks. Orville's church and Sand Ridge's water tower shared the gravel road off the main highway. Matt pulled in under the spidery legs of the tower.

A loudspeaker was suspended high on a tower leg and music from the electric church organ was being piped through it into the parking lot. Orville prided himself on devising ways to bring more souls to the Lord. Fifty yards to the left of the church, the congregation had erected a gigantic billboard with a drawing of an open book and, in Day-Glo colors, the slogan "Got Questions? The Bible's Got Answers." The church itself was white clapboard, with tidy bushes and myrtle ground cover fringing the walls. The frame building seated about three hundred people, if they were willing to pack tightly together.

Everybody was trying to jam in. They tried to maintain proper Sunday decorum, but a manic undercurrent surged through the neatly dressed and carefully coiffed crowd; they pressed forward through the doors. It was easy to tell the regulars. They carried oversize leather Bibles, some with their names embossed on the cover in gold; the most devout had frayed bookmarker ribbon tails hanging from the bottoms of their books.

Inside the church, ushers passed out handshakes. Across the peach-colored carpet in a far corner of the lobby stood Lorna Ross, her palms cupped upward inside each other and her light blue sweater dipping gradually in front, in the manner that, twenty years ago, girls were told would make them look thinner.

From the auditorium, Verity waved at Tobie and wormed her way up the center aisle against the tide of people searching for seats. Matt spotted Blair (who even in church had a pencil behind his ear) and briefly chatted with him about the possibility of a town meeting. Tobie handed Verity half of her long, pop-pearl necklace, making sure she got some blue beads and some yellow ones. "Like the rosary," Tobie whispered. "Hail Mary, mother of God," and she loudly popped a pearl. The girls giggled. Before Verity returned to the place where her dad had told her to sit, she asked, "Will you always, always be my friend?"

"'Course I will. I gave you my necklace, didn't I?" Tobie said.

Matt and Tobie settled at one end of a pew three-quarters of the way back in the packed auditorium. Slowly, as if the pew were a laundry bag being stuffed from the other end, they were squished against each other. Tobie removed a hymnal from the rack and sat on it so she would feel less claustrophobic.

Hector Pickett was five people to the right in the pew ahead. An electric charge went through Matt at the memory of the *High Noon* threat of the five townsmen in his office. Pickett must know that Harper was still teaching.

The organist lunged back and forth across the keyboard, his bulbous tie swinging like a pendulum, his gestures growing increasingly flamboyant. In the middle of the platform was a white podium, shaped vaguely like a body. It represented Lot's wife, who was turned into a pillar of salt when she disobeyed God and looked back at the decadent and evil city of Sodom. Now her salt figure faced the congregation.

Matt checked his watch: fifteen minutes late. The congregation pulsed and murmured. A door opened on the platform, a hush swept from the front to the back of the auditorium, and Orville, dressed in a creamy white choir robe, strode across the platform to the podium. He thrust both his arms high over his head. The fanned sleeves fell about his elbows, exposing the blond fuzz along his arms. He raised his eyes upward. The rouged birthmark was visible across his cheek. The organ surged in a lumbering diapason of chords and faded. The congregation was silent.

"Hosanna. Hosanna. Hosanna. Oh, Lord of Hosts, Thou art the Lord Almighty, the God who led us out of the wilderness of yore, who sends Your angel, the sweet Gabriel, to us in every age and clime. You know every thought we think, we cannot hide from You, though we try. We shrink in the dark, hide behind doors, cover our sinful deeds, pretend we are good."

"Hear, oh hear," said a singsongy, deep voice from the front of the auditorium.

Orville looked surprised at the interruption, then said,

"That's right, sister, bear me up." He swept his arm in her direction.

"Let us sing. Hymn number 394. Lift your voices to the heavens in praise."

Orville swept his hands upward and the crowd rose. Matt turned slightly, surveying people. Yale Kaltmann, directly behind him, awkwardly stuck out his hand for Matt to shake. Then Yale lowered his hand to Tobie. She pretended to be busy singing the hymn, studying the hymnal. Yale shrugged for Matt's benefit, as if to say, "Don't worry," and patted Tobie on the head. She ducked and buried her face in the book, her blond hair falling forward and covering her face. Matt put his arm around her shoulders and she leaned against him, head bowed. Matt could remember when he was a kid being panicked in public, but, as a boy, he'd felt a compulsion to hide his shyness. At least girls were freer that way.

In the middle of the hymn, two trumpeters suddenly began to blow like the End was nigh. The congregation, which had been whispering and singing timidly, snapped alert, startled. Some people started clapping.

"That's better," Orville said when they sat down. "You know, the Lord says, 'Make a joyful noise unto me.' Noise—that means even those of you who can't sing can at least make a noise."

The crowd laughed.

"Let's all stand," Orville said.

Popping up and down gets the adrenaline going, or at least keeps people from drowsiness. Every kindergarten teacher knows that.

"Let's all raise our hands with our palms before our faces and spread our fingers."

Matt hated being manipulated, hated doing stupid things in crowds at the demand of pulpit pounders, politicians, comedians, or whoever. Made him sweat. He hoped to God Orville wouldn't start calling on people to do some demonstrative fool thing, or to give testimonials.

Tobie grinned up at her dad; she knew these things bugged him. Orville turned sideways and held up his hand. In profile, his turtle-beak upper lip was pronounced.

"Does everyone see their palm? The word 'palm' comes

from the Latin *palma,* meaning palm of the hand. We use the palm to shake hands, to express friendship. There is another palm. That's right, a palm tree leaf. It's shaped like the palm of the hand. As Christians and devout lovers of our Lord Jesus, the palm tree is an important symbol for us. When the followers of Jesus celebrated his coming into Jerusalem, the multitudes of people cut the fronds of palm trees and waved them and laid them in our Lord's path. I ask you now to take your hand, your palm, that spreads like a branch of a tree, that spreads like the wing of a sparrow— and we all know our Lord watches over the tiniest of sparrows, nothing, no one is inconsequential—now raise your palm to the Lord God Almighty and beg forgiveness for horrid sins so scarlet that the cardinal, our state bird, cannot match them."

Remarkable performance, Matt thought, without raising his hand. At that point, he spotted Niccole across the church and slightly to the rear of the hall. The frizzy tendrils of her hair were backlit, framing her face in an auburn aureole. She smiled at him, rotated her upheld hand, and bent the tips of her fingers ever so discreetly in a wave. His heart, or whatever it is that leaps, leaped. He lifted his hand just above his waist and dipped his fingers toward her.

Tobie whispered, "Who's that?"

"Miss Oops," he leaned over to murmur in her ear.

She shot him a sly, amused glance. Matt saw Shadrack down near the front, fidgeting next to his wilted mother. Verity sat to her right, caressing her necklace and occasionally slipping it between her lips. After the collection plates were passed, the sermon began. Very faint background organ music was playing. Orville waved it to silence.

"My father's name was Charles. Some people called him Chuck, although he hated that, because 'chuck' was also a word meaning to throw out. When I found that out, I used to get his goat by saying things like, 'Hey, Mom, give me the trash, I'm going to charles it.'"

The congregation roared.

"Like most kids, I didn't appreciate my father until he was gone. But we have to appreciate the Lord, our Father in heaven, or we will be beyond redemption. I am glad I was born poor, so that I could learn about true riches. I am glad I am a sinner, so I will listen to the Lord. We are all sinners. You're a sinner, and you're a sinner, you have to admit it, you have to admit your own degradation, wallow in muck. The stink of pig slop covered the prodigal son, and it covers you and me.

"Sin is becoming more and more acceptable in our degraded society. We see today a dreadful sin: the murdering of unborn human beings. Abortion, I even hate to say the word, is an abominable crime. Abortion is not a question of women really; it's a question of justice. Justice to the life destroyed.

"Who can persist and deny the Lord, then hope not to be turned into a rock, a stump, a pillar of salt? Let this podium remind you of the price we pay for accepting Satan's ways!"

He whacked his hand on the top of the podium, the blow reverberating through the microphone system. The volume and escalating speed of Orville's delivery increased the tension.

"We must not hide from sin—our own or others'. We must not cast stones at the sinner, for we are all sinners, but we must drive Satan out. We must admit our sins and strive to help others find Jesus. The Lord Jesus is forgiveness. Are there sinners among us?"

A strangled cry rose from the midst of the congregation. Heads pivoted, trying to locate the source.

"Who cries out to the Lord? Don't be afraid, come into the light."

Orville searched the audience, his robe flaring like wings from his outstretched arms.

Another wail. An arm thrust up, grasping for help, drowning.

"The Lord is full of forgiveness! Come unto his embrace!"

Augusta Johnson rose, trembling.

"Oh, Lord, forgive me. I have sinned a horrible sin."

Even as she swayed and wailed, her hands thrust upward in despair.

"I have sinned, I beg forgiveness," she moaned.

She tore her dress down the front. The ripping sound was tiny and rasping, but filled the sudden silence in the church. There was murmuring from outside the edifice, where people were trying to figure out what was happening. Mr.

Johnson stood, enormously embarrassed by his wife's behavior, and tried to close her spiky fur coat around her.

"The first step to redemption is admitting our sin. This poor woman humbles herself before Thee, oh Lord." Orville stretched out his berobed arm; tears ran down his cheeks. "Bring this humble woman, this sinner, forward."

Mr. Johnson was desperate to get his wife out of the limelight. He carefully steered her by the arm into the aisle. Like an athletic trainer, Orville talked the Johnsons down to the front and up onto the platform. It was obvious to the audience from the muffled argument that ensued between Mr. Johnson and Orville on the platform that Orville wanted Mrs. Johnson to speak to the congregation, to bare her soul. But Mr. Johnson gesticulated vehemently and refused, placing a hand firmly on his wife's bent back and forcing the weeping woman out the door at the back of the platform.

The congregation was abuzz. Matt caught Niccole's eye. She must realize that Mrs. Johnson had, for all intents and purposes, admitted that she'd tried to give Kim an abortion. That would mean the end of the lawsuit. Orville stepped back to the podium. When he raised his arms, a hush spread across the church. He was silent for a full minute, and nobody dared talk.

"Do not feel smug. We're all sinners. We do not let in the Lord, we refuse His signs and deny our responsibilities every day."

The organ began playing so that the music was only a hint.

"My ways are not your ways, He says. Remember what He did to Nebuchadnezzar. He caused him to grow feathers and claws because of his disobedience. Remember Melchisedec? In Hebrews we learn that Melchisedec had no mother and no father. How is this possible, you might say? In Luke 1:37, we have it, and I read to you the holy word: 'For with God nothing shall be impossible.' When did the Bible give us this law? Exactly as the angel Gabriel told Mary that she was pregnant, even though she had known no man.

"Throughout our human history God looks down on us. Usually He maintains a hands-off policy. But every once in a while, He shows pity, every once in a while He shows us His unbounding love, then He intervenes. We must learn that all

177

things are possible, if the Lord so wills. The Lord speaks to us now! Listen! He wills it that we know that a virgin girl can become pregnant."

"Wrong! That's wrong!"

Hector Pickett had sprung to his feet.

"It can't be. The cause is at the junior high school! If you teach children wrong, they will live wrong and do evil! You teach children Darwinism and about genes and tell them their ancestors are apes, they will sin. It's the school's fault."

Pickett whipped around, and all eyes followed his outstretched arm, pointing at Matt.

"He's in charge; it's his fault if it doesn't stop. He has the power!"

Pickett was screaming. His face flamed red.

Tobie reached over and put her small hand inside her dad's. He gazed down at her. Her glasses had slid down her nose and she shoved them back up. He squeezed her fingers reassuringly, then lifted his head. People craned their necks to look at them. Matt sat still, tried to relax, though his heart was racing. He noticed that Pickett didn't have his linoleum knife on his belt.

The next thing Matt noticed was the tidy, gray bun on the back of Audrey's head as his secretary rose and majestically turned. Pickett continued to rant, repeating his accusations, and the muttering of the congregation sounded like a flock of grackles settling down for the night. Matt could feel a blush rising up his neck. He was used to tight spots, but as a reporter he'd never been the focus of contention. He was unsure whether he should respond, but was inclined to sit still, let Orville take control. In his indecision, he glanced over at Niccole. Something hard to describe shone in her face, and he didn't know why, but it gave him courage to be calm.

"Stop," Audrey commanded, raising her manicured index finger, as if reprimanding a child.

Pickett slowly turned to see who'd spoken.

"What you say about Matthew Chays is wrong and you know it. It is not his fault this is happening. He's a good man and he's doing all that anyone could do."

"I think you're an interested party," Pickett sneered.

"We're all interested parties, especially Mr. Chays," she said austerely.

The congregation's whispering escalated into loud discussions, drowning out Pickett's response. Orville shouted over the noise, "A soft answer turneth away wrath."

Pickett, now standing oddly alone and silent as the debate swirled around him, looked down at his wife, pulled her up by the elbow, and with her pushed out to the end of the pew. As he fumed and huffed, shoving her ahead of him up the aisle toward the back door, several voices called out, "Way to go, Pickett," "Right on," and "Shame." Audrey sank into her seat; people surrounding her patted her shoulders in sympathy. The church was in an uproar.

Orville, who had been waving his arms for quiet, nodded to the organist to play the doxology loudly. The congregation automatically rose to its feet and stopped talking to sing. Then Orville asked them to be seated. They hushed. He cleared his throat, pausing for the apprehensive quiet to gnaw a bit in their minds.

"Oh Lord, we are all doubting Thomases, we are scum in our lack of faith, we deny the prophets and the visions and our Lord. Like Simon Peter, we deny and the rooster crows, we are miserable and ashamed, and yet we sin again. Why are we like that? Over and over again, the same sins. Open your Bibles to Hebrews 11."

Tobie peeked at Matt, who glanced down at her reassuringly. Oh, God, he thought, you've given me this wonderful, graceful child, with her quirky love of animals and life; please take care of her. Matt would rather die than have anything terrible happen to Tobie. He could understand why all these people were panicked. Their children were part of their very being. They wanted to believe that God was taking care of them.

"This whole chapter is about faith, and Jesus, today we need thy faith. I need a touch from Jesus. I need anointing in thy holy oil. The Bible says, 'Now faith is the substance of things hoped for, the evidence of things not seen . . . things which are seen were not made of things which do appear . . .'"

For Matt, the question was: would the town side with

179

Pickett and blame Matt, or would most of them believe Orville? It was illogical to think that sex education was to blame, but clearly Pickett had followers.

"By faith, Abraham . . ."

What was the truth? If Orville was right, maybe Sand Ridge would become a religious shrine, like cities in Europe where the Virgin Mary was reported to have appeared. If Pickett's view held, Matt might as well start packing his bags and look for a new job.

"Through faith also, Sara herself received strength to conceive seed, and was delivered of a child when she was past age . . ."

If the town panic spread, Matt figured parents would start pulling their children, or at least their girls, out of classes.

"By faith, Moses . . ."

In that case, he'd go to the state Department of Education and ask to have Christmas vacation start early. He could convince the board, surely, that the kids could fulfill the attendance days required by keeping school open through June, and that things needed to be sorted out right away.

"Then in verse thirty-two the Bible says, 'What shall I more say? For the time would fail for me to tell of Gedeon, and of Barak, and of Samson, and of Jephthae . . .' Yes, all things are possible through faith. By faith, Evie Wagner . . ."

A murmur rolled through the congregation.

"By faith, Evie Wagner," the woman down front said loudly in her bearing-up.

"If it was possible for Sara to have a child when she was old and for Elizabeth to bear John the Baptist after her time, for Melchisedec to have no father and no mother, all things are possible to God. They are possible, yes. I, too, didn't believe the word of God to me at first, but it is possible for our young girls, our pure and virgin young girls, to bear children.

"But we don't believe, and Evie Wagner was driven to kill herself, may her pristine soul rest in peace. Yes, brothers and sisters, by faith, Kim Johnson . . ."

The murmur swept over the people again.

"And her mother had no faith, and the child of the Lord was killed. Oh, Jesus, forgive us our deepest, darkest sins.

"By faith, Katie Sobo . . ."

The murmur turned into a roar that could be heard echoing outside. The Sobo family's strictness with Katie was well known. Heads turned to find them, but the Sobos weren't in the church. Orville raised his arms and silence fell. How many more could he list?

"By faith, Verity Molway . . ."

The congregation hushed, then exploded. Tobie gasped; her hand flew to her mouth in horror as she searched Matt's face for confirmation, reassurance, explanation. He couldn't imagine what was on his face, certainly no explanation and probably no reassurance. Tobie stood up to locate Verity. The congregation buzzed, shifting to see Wanda and Verity. Matt noticed that Shad's and Verity's heads were ducked, hiding their faces. Suddenly the sun burst forth, and the rays of light shafting through one skylight landed squarely on Verity. An "ahhh" of amazement swept across the auditorium.

"Yes, my very own daughter. You can see why I doubted the Lord, you can see that I had to pray and go back and pray again, till finally I had to believe."

No, just the opposite, Matt thought. If anything threw doubt on Orville's theory, it was that his daughter was one of those pregnant. There probably would be some who believed Orville, but it sure looked like Orville was trying to find a way to get himself off the hook. How could a preacher be seen having a sinful daughter? Matt believed Orville was sincere in his belief that Verity was a pregnant virgin, but the town was going sincerely crazy.

"Now I must ask if there are any more young girls who have been blessed. Don't be afraid. If you speak out, your 'nointing will be plain. God has been gracious to us, has given us life and breath and all things. Every once in a while God reaches down His holy hand and 'noints us specially. Is there anybody?"

Slowly from the left side came a ripple of movement and all heads turned. Gloria was standing with her head angelically bowed. Matt looked at Tobie, who glanced back at him skeptically. There was another wave of murmuring from the back. Everyone turned around, and there was Amber Smith, a truly exquisite-looking girl, who had been coaxed by her mother to stand up. Clearly Amber didn't want to; she kept trying to sit down again.

Tobie pulled on Matt's shoulder, and he leaned over. "Is it possible?" she asked.

"I don't think so," he said. "We'll talk about it."

"Are there any more?" Orville asked.

Please, God, please, whatever, make there be no more, Matt thought.

"Let us pray."

Most heads bowed.

"Oh, Jesus, let our young girls be vessels unto honor and sanctity, let them through the fruit of their wombs glorify Thee. The Good Book tells us that when Mary heard the prophecy of the angel Gabriel, she was troubled. So might we be troubled. But Gabriel's answer to our worry is, 'Fear not, for thou hast found favor with God.' Oh, Jesus, touch us. Amen. Let us sing, hymn number 254. And while you sing this hymn, I want you to raise your hosanna fan, raise your hand and praise the Lord."

The disturbed congregation sang, swaying their hands, some of them looking raptly inspired. Small children stood on the pews and danced, as if it were a game. A few people edged out of their pews to leave early. At the end of the hymn, Orville shouted, "Wait, wait. Now I want you to turn to the brothers and sisters around you and give them your hosanna; you are your brother's and your sister's keeper, give them your hand."

Tobie shook hands with the woman to her right and then, sheepishly, she turned back and stretched out her hand to Yale. Out of the corner of his eye, Matt saw that Yale was surprised. He bent solicitously toward Tobie. A shock of his black hair fell forward. The tattoo on his arm flashed its ditto-machine blue briefly as he stretched out his hand. He slipped quickly into the aisle afterward, holding the hand that Tobie had touched with his other, almost reverently.

While Matt was accosted from all sides by disturbed parents, Tobie squeezed past him and scurried toward Verity. She shyly took Verity's hand as they locked eyes. Tobie motioned the larger girl to lean over, and whispered in her ear. Breaking free from the parents and walking into the parking lot, Matt spotted Niccole as she slid into her car.

She lifted her sunglasses. Matt leaned down to her car window and said, "It's enough to make you give up church, isn't it?"

"You mean you'd charles it, just like that? Oh, ye of little faith."

"I'll call." He smiled and turned away, thinking it best not to draw too much attention to themselves, because he still intended to ask her to assist him.

Tobie came running across the parking lot as Matt walked toward their car. They exchanged glances, but didn't talk until they'd settled into their seats.

"What'd you say to Verity?"

She'd removed her necklace and laid it in her lap.

"I said I was her friend, just like she was mine at the slumber party."

Then she told him about the slumber party—well, she sort of told him. She sanitized it so as not to embarrass him. She didn't tell him about the meaning of blow job, or about Gloria's circular bandaids. But she did tell him about the boy's phone call and the doll in the paper sack that had "stuff from a boy's penis on it." She didn't say she was the one who'd touched it, though. "'Nointing." She wondered what "'nointing" really was.

Matt felt sick. Now he was sure. He had to find that gang of slimy bastards, and find them fast.

"You gonna play ball this afternoon?" he asked as they turned from the gravel road onto the highway.

"Nope."

She wound a strand of her long hair round and round her finger.

"Why not?"

"I don't want to. Besides, I lost my baseball mitt."

CHAPTER TWENTY-TWO

The earth froze hard in a solid, deep cold that was unusual for the second week in December. Birds huddled by the dozens on chimneys, toasting their featherless feet. Across from the Café Rififi, which was attached to the Good Dough Bakery, the willow tree in the park had lost its last crescent leaves; the hair-limber branches hung down, anemically yellow.

Niccole wore her heaviest wool slacks, a turtleneck sweater, a knit cap, and her lamb's-wool coat, but the damp cold still seeped into her bones. Sitting on a wrought-iron chair at a marble-topped table in the café, she waited for Lorna Ross. Out the glass wall, she could see ghostly stains from leaves that had been smashed onto the sidewalk. Niccole coddled a cup of cocoa between her hands. She'd removed her coat, but her cap was still pulled over her ears, her coppery hair drawn back at the nape of her neck.

Café Rififi was Sand Ridge's attempt at bohemia. Its walls were entirely plastered with mirrors, which reflected every angle of a gigantic schefflera plant with waxy leaves that overhung the surrounding tables from a carved sandstone pedestal in the center of the room. The café served tea, coffee, cakes, pies, and its claim to fame, apricot eclairs. A

Tunisian birdcage, white with blue trim, dangled from the ceiling in the back corner near the refrigerated pastry case. In the cage, cerulean parakeets stroked each other's beaks and groomed their toenail cuticles.

Matt Chays had suggested that Niccole start her interviews with the school nurse. He'd arranged to pay her a minimal fee out of his discretionary fund. On the Monday after Reverend Orville's sermon, Mrs. Johnson had dropped her suit against the abortion clinic, but Niccole's anger over the threat she'd received, and her promise to help Matt, had brought her back to Sand Ridge. Besides, she was curious about what would happen when the town discovered the boys who'd caused the pregnancies. She had convinced her boss at the law firm that he should let her off for half days several times a week to explore the peculiar occurrences in Sand Ridge. He was finally swayed by her argument that future legal actions would probably develop.

The glass front door of the café whooshed open, shifting the sweetened air like incense clouds. Two women strolled through, chattering. They glanced at Niccole and headed toward a table in the back. Good. Niccole had chosen this place in the front alcove that jutted out onto the sidewalk so that Mrs. Ross would not feel anyone was listening to their conversation. The alcove was colder than the rest of the café. Niccole lifted her coat from the chair onto her shoulders.

When Lorna Ross entered the café, she held something in her upturned hand, making it difficult for her to open the door. She looked around uncertainly. Niccole, recognizing her from Matt's description, waved and nodded. Lorna's nose was luminous from the cold, her large hands chapped and red. A "sad sack," that's what Niccole thought when she saw her. Except Lorna wasn't baggy. Rather, she was vigorously girdled. Her midriff and bosom looked rigid as machinery. She seemed repressed, like she might fall apart if it weren't for the corseting beneath her blouse and slacks.

"You Ms. Epps?" When Niccole nodded, Lorna sank into the other chair at the table.

"You must be freezing."

Lorna shook her head.

"I was when I came in. You must be."

Lorna shook her head again. She held her hand on the table, opened her fingers, and examined the rock she held.

"Blue," she said.

Niccole looked puzzled.

"Sandstone in the deepest part of the quarry is bluer. A man at the quarry told me the rock slices like cheese before the air hits it."

She stopped and slyly looked at Niccole, as if only then realizing she was talking to someone.

"You the woman Mr. Chays says I have to talk to?"

"I'm Niccole Epps. You don't have to talk to me, I mean, I don't want you to think you're forced. But it would help us with these girls, you know, like Evie. You went to the quarry?"

Lorna clunked the sandstone on the marble tabletop and said nothing for a long time. Niccole sipped the last of her cocoa and brushed the chocolate mustache off her upper lip.

"I don't know anything about the girls," Lorna said.

"No, you know what we all know, but I hope that by asking questions of people who have contact with the girls, we may be able to come up with some clues as to how this could be happening. Mr. Chays said that you were there when Amber Smith got morning sickness."

Niccole paused. It was going too fast. Lorna Ross needed to be set more at ease. She was nervous with Niccole's seeming authority. Niccole asked her if she wouldn't like something hot to drink. No. Cake? No. Niccole glanced over to check the menu chalked on a blackboard beneath the schefflera plant. Apricot eclair? No. Jeez, how could she relax this woman? As if to help her out in her discomfort, Lorna reached into the voluminous pocket of her coat and pulled out a piece of knitting. A child's mitten.

"I was there. I was the one Amber Smith told. I'm the school nurse, that's why she came to me."

"Mrs. Ross, let me explain: I'm not singling you out. Mr. Chays thinks you are doing a fine job. I'm going to interview lots of people around the school, including lots of girls. I needed to start somewhere, and since you are a responsible person who has dealt with the kids, it seemed logical to consult with you. I'm just asking routine questions."

Lorna's chapped fingers worked the yarn slowly. She knitted in the European manner, throwing the yarn over the needle with the left hand instead of the right index finger. She nodded.

"Did Amber Smith ever mention any boys to you? I mean, did she give any hint that she liked any particular boys?"

"I didn't ask. Sometimes I hear the girls talking about boys, but I don't pay much attention."

When the waitress came to the table, Niccole finally convinced Lorna to accept a pecan cinnamon bun from the pastry wagon. Then Niccole tried another tack, asking Lorna to explain what her job required. Knitting doggedly and only occasionally raising her eyes, the nurse explained a few of her procedures, then switched tracks to tell how once a year she gave a lecture to the fifth- and sixth-grade girls about menstruation. And if their period should start when they were away from home and had no sanitary pads . . . Niccole was frustrated by Lorna's straying from the subject. She seemed foggy, distracted.

The door of the café sucked open, and a mother with a preschool daughter walked across to the pastry counter. Niccole started to steer Lorna's conversation back to something more germane by asking for a description of Lorna's examination procedures for the junior high girls' health. But Lorna wasn't listening. Her attention was riveted on the mother and daughter. Lavishing them with adoration, was the way that Niccole described it to Matt later.

Lorna picked up the blue sandstone and held it tightly. She was oblivious to Niccole. The mother bought a loaf of bread and turned to leave, reaching back to yank at her daughter's arm to drag her from the café. The two disappeared down the sidewalk. Lorna let out a huge sigh, and then remembered Niccole.

"Did you ever have a baby?"

Although she was addressing Niccole, Lorna seemed lost inside herself.

"No. My mother is always pestering me to have one, but I don't want one yet. They put a crimp in your style, that is, if you want to go to law school."

"You're a lawyer, you help people in trouble?" Lorna asked slowly.

"No, I work in a law firm and I'm studying to become a lawyer. Why?"

"Oh, nothing, I just have a friend . . ."

The sentence faded, and Lorna stared out the window.

"I had a baby boy," she said. "He would be ten now. He passed on. But someday . . ."

Again the sentence faded. She spread the half mitten out on the table to inspect the evenness of the rows, then dropped the knitting in her lap to take a bite of the cinnamon bun.

"I'm sorry, I didn't know," Niccole said softly.

"I think everyone should have a baby."

Lorna played with a half of a pecan on the sweet roll, shoving it into the caramel icing with her fingers. Niccole had a sickly feeling; the pecan reminded her of a tiny brain. She felt her gorge rise. Lorna pried the nut out of the icing and set it on the plate. Its two lobes were convoluted and shriveled.

"I'd like to be pregnant again."

This aimless talk was no help at all to Niccole's research. She doubted that she could get Lorna to say anything useful, no matter how long she humored her.

"Well, you could, you're not very old, are you married?"

Lorna ate the nut.

"I am getting old."

She ran her index finger under her chin to show her sagging muscles.

"But I don't care if I'm married or not. I just want a baby."

The yearning in her voice was excruciating.

"Look, you're not old. I was thinking the other day I should get a nose lift."

Niccole smiled, wanting to lighten the mood. She was getting nowhere as Lorna sank into her gloom.

"You know, you can have the tip of your nose bobbed. Your nose grows longer and tips downward as you get older."

Lorna looked at her as if she were mad.

Hell, this woman has no sense of humor, Niccole thought. Better just to ask her right out.

"Do you have any ideas on who could be causing the pregnancies?"

Lorna glanced at her for a fleeting second. Niccole could have sworn the nurse's eyes were terrified, but Lorna cast them down quickly and picked up her knitting again.

"It's all so horrible," Niccole said quickly, to assuage the harshness of her question. "Whoever is doing it deserves to be fully punished."

"Mr. Kaltmann says he told Mr. Chays there was a bunch of boys—"

At that moment, the door of the café flung open and there was a clackety of running feet. A little boy virtually fell into the café, then sprang back, holding open the door and shouting, "I beat-cha, I beat-cha!" He looked about ten years old. A girl dashed up behind him, her long blond hair floating out behind. Niccole recognized her as Matt Chays's daughter from seeing them together in church. Both children were out of breath. Tobie came through the door and immediately realized they were creating a ruckus.

"Gavin, close the door," Tobie instructed with a frown and moved him away from it. "Why must you follow me everywhere? You're like a shadow," she added, as a way of explaining to any listeners that she was not really responsible for this pest.

Then she turned to survey the café, looking to the back first, then spotting Niccole and Mrs. Ross. Still breathing heavily, she approached their table.

"Are you Miss Epps?" she asked politely.

"I am. You must be Tobie."

"You know my name?"

"Sure, your father told me."

Out of the corner of her eye Niccole saw Gavin precariously stretch across a table. She sprang up, reaching to stop him just before he knocked off the ashtray.

"Whew!" she said, lifting him bodily off the chair.

He followed her like a puppy as she returned to the table.

"Gee. You're short," he said. "Are you grown-up?"

"I think so," Niccole said.

"You're shorter than Tobie. Why are you so short?" he asked.

"Because I'm from Texas."

"Are people short in Texas?"

"No, they're tall."

Gavin looked baffled.

"They need me to bring down the average, so they don't get swelled heads just because they're big and strong."

When Niccole turned back to her, Tobie was momentarily flustered, then remembered her sober mission.

"My dad asked me to come tell you that he won't be able to meet you tonight. He's very busy, but he'll call you this evening."

"I hope everything's okay," Niccole said.

Tobie shook her head.

"What's wrong?" Niccole asked, touching Tobie's arm lightly.

"Cheryl," Tobie said, her voice barely audible.

"Cheryl who?" Niccole said.

"She killed herself in the garage."

Tobie's eyes were fixed and large, her hand clamped half over her mouth.

"Why did she do that?" Niccole asked, a sickly feeling settling in the pit of her stomach.

A half-gasp, half-moan came from Lorna. The nurse had dropped the mitten she was knitting and was rocking back and forth holding herself in her arms.

Then everything happened so quickly. Niccole looked over to where Gavin was examining the mirrors glued onto the walls. His fingers were tucked behind the corner of a foot-square mirror panel. Lorna's panicked face was reflected in that particular square. Suddenly her face slid off the wall.

"No, watch out!" Niccole shouted.

Too late. The glass smashed on the tile floor with an enormous crash. As Niccole leaped up to make sure Gavin was not hurt, Lorna grabbed her coat, left her knitting where it fell, and disappeared out the café door, moving surprisingly quickly. Niccole knelt down to examine Gavin's hands as he waved them about. He was unscathed, grinning uncertainly at the chaos he'd caused.

CHAPTER TWENTY-THREE

Steering around the corner onto Ivy Avenue, Matt berated himself for blurting out Cheryl's name on the phone so that Tobie'd heard. He should've been more careful. All he needed now was a rash of teen suicides. Evie, now Cheryl.

Four fire engines were crammed onto the street and into two adjoining driveways. A squad car blocked regular traffic. Fire hoses wormed across the lawns from the hydrant at the corner. Firemen were tromping around disconnecting the hoses and standing in groups talking and shaking their heads.

Matt parked, got out of his car with a feeling of doom in his throat, and jogged through a rose bed, around a pond, past several houses and up to the gravel driveway to the Mulls' white frame house.

The garage was charred, still smoldering. Chief Leland and a knot of policemen were milling in front of it as the remaining fire hose was used to soak a smoking wall. Neighbors clustered in murmuring clumps at varied distances from the ruins. Matt heard several people say his name as he strode toward the garage. The police and firemen parted for him. He stopped next to the few still active firemen, next to where the garage door had been.

The roof beams, in some places gray as barbecue briquettes, had caved in. Some of the debris had been pushed aside.

Seeing but avoiding what he saw at the center, Matt noticed peripheral things—shovels in a stack where they'd fallen over, their handles charred, a wheelbarrow with its plastic wheel melted to the concrete floor, a blackened lawn mower in the corner, aluminum garbage cans in an orderly row. His mind didn't want to accept what was before him. A three-gallon gasoline can for the mower stood next to her, a patch of red paint still visible on its side.

The stench of burnt flesh pervaded the smoking, dripping ruins of the garage. Matt knew that smell from Vietnam. He covered his nose. He felt as if he'd throw up.

Cheryl's body, what was left of it, was crumpled next to the gasoline can. Her outstretched arm balanced over its handle. Her face, the flesh burned off, looked toward him. Her mouth was open as if in a scream.

He covered his eyes with his hands, lowered his head, then raised it again and ran his fingers through his hair. He turned to look around him. People were watching, hushed.

One woman beside the garage began saying in a crazy, high voice, "Let me comfort you, let me help you."

The woman she addressed stood silent, staring straight at the contorted, charred body. She stared at it, but looked right through it at the same time. The hysterical woman put her arms around the other.

"Don't look at her," she pleaded. "Turn away."

She tried to force the woman to turn around, exerting all the force of her small body. But the other woman was fixed like a concrete block.

The pimply-faced young cop who'd been in the quarry approached Matt with a respectful "Hello, Mr. Chays," then faded away as he was replaced by Chief Leland.

"It's awful," Leland said, shaking his head and jowls.

Matt surveyed the crowd, which was increasing rapidly.

"You gonna get the body outta here?" he asked Leland.

"Oh, yeah. Hey," he called to the retreating back of the young cop. "Wouldja go phone Harry?"

"It's okay, the coroner's been called. He'll be here any minute," said Jock Stark, Leland's sidekick.

"Matt," Leland said, "do you think you could get Mrs.

Mull back inside her house? This'll not be too pleasant to watch."

"Is that her?" Matt asked, nodding.

"Yeah, she's been standing there the whole time the guys were pouring water on the fire. Didn't move. Didn't cry or nothin'. Like a statue."

Matt deliberately surveyed the scene. Almost everybody was watching him now. He noticed Blair just arriving. He must've been out of town to be this late.

Matt walked over to the motionless woman.

"Hello, Mrs. Mull. I'm Matthew Chays."

She continued staring, but her eyelids fluttered.

"Mrs. Mull, I'm very thirsty. I wonder if I might have something to drink. Maybe a cup of coffee?"

"Thirsty?" she murmured.

She turned slightly, tearing her eyes away from the horrible vision of her daughter.

"Yes," Matt said, relieved that he'd disconnected her from the scene. "Anything would do."

"Come, I'll get you something," she said.

Matt put his hand under her elbow and guided her back to the side entrance of her house and into the kitchen. She walked in a daze. The semihysterical woman dogged their footsteps, and two other women followed. Once in the kitchen, Mrs. Mull headed for the stove to fill the coffeepot. Matt said one of the other women could do it; why didn't she sit right down at the table? She was probably in shock, he said, it would be good if she sat down.

She acquiesced, sinking onto the cushioned colonial-style chair with a moan. The TV on the cabinet was blaring out, a talk show about women who refused to extricate themselves from miserable marriages. Matt pointed to the set and one of the women snapped it off. He pulled out another chair and sat down.

"Mrs. Mull, I know this is very painful, but do you know why Cheryl did this?"

"I love her. Why did she do this? I told her I didn't care if . . ."

Mrs. Mull rubbed her hand across her eyes. Matt heard a man's voice in the hallway. He was on the phone, asking for the whereabouts of Mr. Mull. Telling some company that, yes, it was an emergency; even if he was a salesman, they must know where he was.

"It's Norm's fault! He always was mean to that child," said the semihysterical woman in her piercing soprano. "That's Mr. Mull," she added when Matt looked at her.

"Now, Lizzie," chided another woman.

"It's true, you know it's true," Lizzie defended herself. "It's 'cause he made her do amniocentesis and she found out the baby was deformed. That's why she did it."

"I woulda raised the baby no matter what," Mrs. Mull murmured. "I told her I didn't mind. But Norm, he . . ."

"See?" Lizzie said, sticking her chin out self-righteously. "What'd I tell you?"

"It was the TV," Mrs. Mull said. "She saw that man burn himself up."

Matt had seen it too. On the news the previous night, a Korean student had poured gasoline over himself, lit it, and burned himself to death. It was the kind of footage TV people seemed to love—live deaths.

Mrs. Mull picked up a cup that sat in a saucer on the table.

"Do you want something to drink?" one of the other women asked her solicitously.

She raised it slowly, examined it, and threw it hard across the room against the TV screen. The purplish glass of the screen crashed, then tinkled, as bits continued to fall. Even Lizzie was left speechless for a few seconds. Then she screamed.

"For Christ's sake," said one of the other women. "Lizzie, shut up."

At that moment, finally, Diane Mull collapsed. She started sobbing and moaning. Now the women knew what to do. They hovered over her, then urged her into the living room to lie on the sofa. On the way past the kitchen window, she turned to look out, but one friend yanked the curtain to close off the scene of the plastic body bag being lifted onto a hospital stretcher.

CHAPTER TWENTY-FOUR

Yale was standing near the top of his ladder thinking about twins. Not twins he might father, though that would be wonderful. Rather, two girls were "twinned" in his mind: Cheryl Mull and Penny Peters. Cheryl because she was dead. And Penny because he'd learned something disturbing about her from Lorna Ross.

Earlier this morning when Yale opened the newspaper and read the story on Cheryl's death, a peculiar thrill of secrecy and complicity had shot through his body. Cheryl's death was disgusting. But, in a way, she'd done the right thing. He didn't want to have a deformed child any more than she did. Maybe there was some other way she could have gotten rid of it, but her parents were probably being difficult.

An hour ago when Yale'd dropped by Lorna's office before the kids started to show up for school, her eyes were all red and bloodshot.

"What's wrong?"

She'd looked up dumbly from where she was sitting. She wasn't very bright, he thought. That was good, because she couldn't think too much for herself. She was easy for him to control.

"What's the problem?"

He'd spoken rather harshly since it seemed to have a calming effect on her. She was quite an unstable personality.

"What if Penny does what Cheryl did?"

"Penny? Penny Peters?"

Her silence meant assent.

"Why should she?"

Lorna sniffed and blew her nose on a hanky she pulled out of her sweater sleeve.

"She said her family has a history of insanity and she's worried her baby might be crazy."

"When did she tell you that?" he asked, alarmed and angry.

"The other day. It would be terrible if she killed herself, too," she said, choking.

She's making up something to worry about, Yale thought.

"Did she say anything that makes you think she would?"

"Her family is worried about her baby," Lorna said, not looking at him. "She said she'd rather die than have an insane child."

So now Cheryl and Penny were twinned in Yale's mind. Yale had to admit that he had the same feeling Penny did. His mind had been throbbing ever since with a single thought: stop it, stop it.

Maybe Penny could have a miscarriage. He'd think of something. The best thing was to await the flow of events, then move things in the direction he wanted. He vividly remembered the scene from *Gone with the Wind* where Scarlett O'Hara had a miscarriage because she'd lunged for Rhett at the top of a flight of stairs, missed, and fallen all the way down.

High on his ladder where he was replacing light bulbs, Yale felt godlike, looking down as the remaining children dashed up and down the main stairway to their classes after the bell.

One boy took the stairs two at a time up to the landing where Yale was, then three at a time on up to the second floor.

Then he saw Penny—as if he'd willed her into his presence. She was clutching her backpack in front of her, running down from the second floor. He rapidly descended the ladder. No one else was around. She didn't take any notice of him.

She stepped on the next-to-last step and spun her body around to head down the second flight of stairs. He lifted the ladder and swung it in front of her. She raised her head, her eyes tangling with his in surprise and fear. A miscarriage was all that he wanted. She would think it was an accident.

She screamed, just like Scarlett. She bumped and screamed. First headfirst. Then her body shifted sideways. The stairs were long and tall and wide. Yale felt like everything was in slow motion. All he could hear, aside from the screams, was the pounding of his own blood, which no longer seemed to be in his heart but only in his head.

She stopped with a loud thunk. She'd hit one of the iron balusters. She was silent. Curled around like an embryo, she lay with her head higher than her feet.

Yale set down his ladder and hurried down to examine her. He'd look like the one to find her first. When she came to, maybe she'd forget what had happened. Certain things you couldn't have control over, but they could be worked into the plan.

The boy who'd recently run up the stairs now came skipping down, probably to request a late slip from the office. At the landing he slowed down. He approached Penny and Yale cautiously, instantly afraid.

"What happened?" he blurted out.

"She fell. Run to the principal's office and tell him to call an ambulance," Yale said, almost shouting.

Nervous energy flooded through his body. His blood was still throbbing, but he was in control.

"Go. Fast!" Yale ordered. "Tell Mr. Chays it's an emergency."

The boy, desperate to get away from the scene, leaped on down the stairs four at a time, breathing hard.

Yale gazed at Penny's pale face. It was sweet. When she came to, she'd only remember it was an accident. Her left hand, with irridescent purple nail polish, rested limply on her breast. The halls were quiet except for the boy's footsteps. Yale became aware of the drone of the public address system. He could hear Mr. Chays's deep voice.

". . . tragic. We've all known too much tragedy recently," Matt was saying.

He'd just delivered the announcement of Cheryl's death.

"If any of you feel disturbed and have no one to talk to, please don't bottle up your feelings. You can walk into Mrs. Grenell's office at any time. She's your guidance counselor. Or you can come in and talk to me. How we meet sorrow in our lives is important. This is a very hard time for us all."

Suddenly he was interrupted by a voice shouting, a young boy's voice. "It's an emergency!" he shouted, his voice cracking. "Emergency. Penny's fallen on the steps. She's not moving!"

Oh, God. Shit. Matt realized the whole thing was blaring all over the school through the microphone. He clicked it off.

"Now, what is this?"

He put his hand on the boy's shoulder, trying to calm him.

"She's hurt," he said.

"Show me."

The boy whirled around and ran back out of Audrey's office.

"Call the ambulance," Matt shouted back to Audrey as he followed.

Penny Peters was lying curved on the steps, her purple backpack fallen below her feet like the dot on a question mark. Yale Kaltmann was down on one knee looking at her. His ladder was up on the landing.

Matt couldn't believe this streak of horrible occurrences. At least this was a straightforward accident. He felt guilty for thinking such a thing, but he couldn't suppress it. Penny wasn't moving or groaning. Matt ran up to the stairs. Yale stood up as he approached.

"Is she hurt bad?" Matt demanded.

Yale could tell that Matt wasn't thinking about him at all. He didn't even look suspicious. Would he have to tell him he was involved? When she came to, what would she say?

"I don't know," Yale said. "Maybe we should move her down off the stairs and make her more comfortable."

Matt sank to her side, picked up her wrist, and placed his fingers across it.

He couldn't feel a pulse. Her eyes were closed. He felt for

her pulse in her throat. Nothing. Her forehead was reddish and swelling.

"How did this happen?"

"She fell," Yale said.

"How?"

"I don't know. I was putting in a light bulb. I had just taken down my ladder when she came around the corner and stumbled and fell. My back was to her. When I turned, she was falling and screaming. She hit her head there," he said, touching the iron post.

"How long ago was all this?"

"I don't know. Maybe three minutes now. The boy came down and I told him to go tell you."

Matt felt her wrist again. Please, God, let her live. It might be too late to pray. His heart felt like lead.

"Let's move her," he said.

Yale walked down a few steps to her feet and they carried her down the last few stairs to the floor. On his knees leaning over her, Matt unbuttoned his cardigan, removed it, rolled it up, and gently placed it under her head.

He bent, opened her mouth, pulled out her tongue, and began mouth-to-mouth resuscitation, breathing in a few times. No response. Still no pulse; he decided he'd better concentrate on restarting her heart. He moved back, set the heel of his hand beneath her sternum, and pushed hard. He kept up the cardiopulmonary resuscitation for thirty seconds, then reverted to mouth-to-mouth, then back again.

While Matt was trying to revive Penny, Yale looked on, feeling a bit useless. But mostly he was relieved. It looked like she was dead. He wouldn't have to worry about what she'd say.

He'd killed her. He felt strange and powerful.

Children were slowly gathering, as silently as snow, creeping down from the second floor and flowing toward the stairway on the first, but keeping a terrified distance.

Audrey emerged from the office and began instructing the teachers to shepherd their children back to classes.

Yale watched Audrey for a minute; then he walked up to the stairway landing and, stretching out his arms, said, "Now, go back to your classes, children. Mr. Chays is taking care of things."

They shuffled reluctantly up the stairs and out of sight. By the time he returned to the scene, the paramedics were racing down the hall toward them. Matt stood up as they took over.

They repeated his actions, felt for Penny's pulse, looked into her eyes, tried both mouth-to-mouth and CPR. They roughly rolled her onto the stretcher, snapped down its wheels, and sped her out to the ambulance. Matt ran after them, then slowed and stopped. The siren began to wail even before the ambulance pulled away from the school.

Yale had followed Matt partway down the hall and was at the door when he turned back into the building. Behind him Audrey stood, her arm around a sobbing Lorna.

"It's terrible, yes," Audrey said, patting the nurse's shoulder.

"Thank you for your help," Matt said to Yale as he passed him.

"Mr. Chays," Audrey said.

He nodded.

"Mrs. Ross says that Penny told her she was pregnant."

"Oh, no!" Matt said, and clutched his forehead.

"When did she tell you this?"

Lorna's tears were coursing down her cheeks. She didn't bother to wipe them.

"Last week."

"Last week! Why didn't you tell me?"

Lorna choked, sobbing so uncontrollably that she couldn't answer.

The nurse clung to Audrey. Matt offered her his handkerchief.

"There, there, this is hard for all of us."

Lorna kept sobbing helplessly. Audrey shrugged, took the nurse by the shoulders, and steered her down the hall toward her office.

"Here, let me take her," Yale offered.

Lorna shrank back with a feeble, odd sound, clutching Audrey's arms.

"It's okay," Audrey said to Yale. "It's better if a woman does this."

Matt watched the small drama; then his thoughts shifted. Penny's parents had to be called.

Should he tell them Penny was dead? Maybe there'd be a miracle. Maybe the paramedics would revive her. He dialed, got Mrs. Peters, and quickly told her that her daughter had been injured in a fall down the stairs and was now on the way to the hospital.

As he said bleakly to her, "I'm sorry," he had visions of more and more phone calls, announcements of disaster. He couldn't allow it. He made his decision at that instant: he didn't care who yelled at him—Arnie Beachley, Pickett, employees, parents—he was closing the school early for Christmas, and he'd keep it closed until normality could be restored.

CHAPTER TWENTY-FIVE

Matt was running, running, running, looking for the man he sought to kill. It was dark, blue-black. The wind was blowing. He was cold. He was on his way to a funeral, two funerals. A mother was sobbing somewhere. He was thrashing, throwing the blankets about. He woke up. He was cold, in a cold sweat. He sat up in bed and rubbed his hands on his arms.

It was 2 AM. Matt climbed out of bed, padded over to the window, and drew back the curtain. The tree outside was blowing wildly, its topmost branches bobbing like flotsam on a violent ocean.

"Gotta get Tobie out of town," he said out loud.

He wanted her to miss the funerals for Cheryl and for Penny. He would send her off to Nana and Grandpa in California for the Christmas vacation. He wrapped his flannel robe around him and walked slowly down the stairs so Tobie wouldn't hear the floor creak from her room. He called the toll-free numbers for several airlines until he found one that he could book for tomorrow noon to Oakland.

The next morning after he'd put Tobie on the plane, he headed back to his office. Most of the teachers had cleared out before noon. A few were still puttering around, taking artwork off walls and helping to check that all the student lockers had been emptied.

Matt phoned to postpone the medical doctor's investigation that he had previously arranged to take place this week. Arnie Beachley's son appeared timorously at Matt's door while Audrey was temporarily out of her office. He'd forgotten that he had asked the kid to come to his office today so he could quiz him on the boys' club. But Matt's questioning was to no avail. Did he know what the club was all about? The skinny boy was sitting on a straight-backed chair with his legs crossed. His top leg bounced like crazy. Matt reached over, placed his hand on the knee, and the boy leaped in alarm. Yeah, well, he thought he could guess what the club was about, the boy said. "And those jerks are all going to go blind, or have their things drop off," he said, "according to my dad." He'd never been to a meeting, he claimed, but had heard about it from a friend whose name he couldn't remember at that moment. Matt decided it was hopeless and let him go.

That evening, ten minutes after Audrey had left for home, the coroner, Harry Cornell, phoned. Penny's death had been caused by the blow to her head; her heart must've stopped shortly after that. He had only one question. She'd sustained a bruise of two parallel marks about four inches long on her thigh just above her knee. It was nowhere near any of the other bruises caused by the fall, and he wondered if Matt might be able to explain it.

Matt told Cornell he'd question Yale Kaltmann and call him back. Then Matt phoned Yale's office and asked him to come see him. When the engineer arrived, Matt was on the phone, so he waved him to sit on the sofa. But when he hung up, Yale was still standing, looking for all the world like a nervous schoolboy. Matt usually forgot he was a boss to his employees until something like this happened, and he had to remind himself that from Yale's perspective, Matt was the person who could fire him.

Yale said he couldn't guess how this bruise could be different from the others. He hadn't seen her fall, he said, but only heard her, and when he'd turned around she was hitting the iron bar in the middle of the stairway.

Yale's forehead was red and he paced as he answered, watching Matt closely. Matt had the incongruously amusing impression that Yale was acting like someone he'd seen in a TV courtroom drama.

After Matt thanked Yale and told him that was all he needed to know, the man stopped pacing, but didn't leave.

"Is there something else?"

"Yes, sir," Yale said, and paused. "When are you going to reopen the school?"

"I don't know, why?"

"Well, sir, I just wanted to say I'd stand behind you. It's good to open it. Otherwise people will think you're weak."

Maybe Yale was worried about not getting paid if the school was closed.

"The union'll make sure you keep getting your salary," Matt said.

"It's not the money," Yale replied.

"No, I didn't mean that money was the most important thing," Matt said, sighing. Everybody had a different angle on why the school should be closed or open.

"I'll just have to wait and see," he added. "I appreciate your concern and your offer to be of help."

Yale turned to leave.

"Oh, yeah, one more thing," Matt said. "I talked to a kid about the boys' club. He wasn't much help. Sounds like nothing significant to me. They've probably stopped meeting, with Christmas coming and school out."

Yale didn't say anything.

"But thanks for the tip, and if you see anything you'll let me know, won't you?"

Yale nodded and left.

Odd duck, Matt thought, then dismissed the man from his mind as he drove over to see what Harper was doing.

Turned out he was preparing to leave for Christmas in Boston. He'd just that day received a bottle of skunk oil deposited in his post office box.

"Lucky I'm used to opening jars of peculiar chemicals," Harper said. "The stench was so shocking that I nearly dropped it and smashed it all over the post office floor. The Christian creationists . . . I don't think Jesus would approve of skunk oil as a weapon."

He rubbed one index finger across the other as if saying "naughty, naughty" to a child. Harper had refused to move his concrete-laden MG from the parking lot behind his apartment building. A couple of hubcaps and the rearview mirror had been stolen, but otherwise it sat in very solid splendor. He called it his statue to bigotry.

Harper left that day, and Matt took Niccole to the airport the next day for three weeks in Texas with her parents. It had been bitterly cold for a week. If this kept up, ice fishing on Lake Erie would be great when she got back, he told her. She said she'd never been ice fishing and would like that.

"It's a date," he said.

She lightly touched his hand that rested on the gearshift as she slid out the door with her small suitcase and disappeared into Hopkins airport.

Then Matt settled in for the loneliest three weeks he'd had in years. But at least no girls were getting pregnant mysteriously. Or rather, if they were, he and the school couldn't be blamed. By closing the school, he had temporarily eliminated it as the common denominator for all the pregnancies. That was a blessing at a blessed time of year. After New Year's, he'd consider reopening it.

CHAPTER TWENTY-SIX

Matt greeted Audrey and Lorna as he walked through to his office on the day after New Year's. They were discussing a piece of knitting Lorna had set on Audrey's desk. He closed his door behind him.

Matt sat down at his desk, leaned back, and swung his chair around. He picked up a stack of pink phone message slips and flipped through them. He pulled one out. Niccole had phoned from Texas and left a message with Audrey. The pink slip said: "Saturday noon at Nord Dock in Carlton. Shall I bring worms? Where do I get worms?" He smiled, crumpled the paper softly, and tossed it in the wastebasket. He'd call her later.

Suddenly the door whacked open, hitting the end of the sofa. Arnie Beachley charged in.

"Chays, why the fuck are you keeping the school closed? I tried calling you all day yesterday when I heard about it."

"Look, Arnie, I don't like it any better than you that I have to close the school. If there were a superintendent, she'd have the responsibility. As you know, Hilda Barnes quit when she got sick. But if I have to keep the school shut for the rest of the school year, I will."

"You can't do that! My kid's in ninth grade. He's got to

get into high school next year to play football. He can't do that if you close the friggin' school."

"If you had a girl, you might be happy that the school is closed," Matt said, his voice cold, controlled.

"You're saying I don't care about the town's students!" Arnie spluttered, growing red in the face.

"I didn't say that. But I'm getting plenty of pressure from parents of the girls to do something, and this is all I can do now."

"I order you to open the school!"

"You can't."

"What do you mean I can't? I'm the mayor."

"Precisely. The school board makes that decision."

"Yeah, well, I was talking to Sam yesterday and he feels the way I do."

"Speaking of . . ." Matt saw the florid, fat face of Sam Garland come through Audrey's door, his body blimping along behind it.

Then followed an exchange that Matt imagined in comic terms because of the two men's faces: Arnie, with his minimal chin, talking furiously, his mouth pumping, and Sam, who had a flabby, turkey-wattle chin, gobbling and clucking. Conversation between chins, Matt dubbed it in his mind; reluctantly he forced himself to focus on what the men were saying.

Arnie was asking Sam didn't he think the school board should reopen the school immediately. Sam, whose son was on the basketball team, said absolutely yes. Another parent with no daughter, and no empathy. Selfish sons-o'-bitches.

"Look, Sam, when is your next board meeting?" Matt asked.

"Next Monday," Sam said.

"Fine, Monday the school board should decide on the question. Open it up for discussion. The whole town can come."

"That's a week away!" Arnie said.

"I cleared my decision to close for this week with the state's Department of Education. They agreed that closing the school could help ease the tension and give us time to find out what's happening."

"You should ease tension by carrying on as usual," Arnie said.

"We were trying to do that before Christmas, when it seemed like every other day another girl was pregnant. And then two girls died. You can't call that business as usual."

"Well, you can't just keep the school closed on your own," Sam said.

"You're right, absolutely right." Matt sighed.

Didn't he have any supporters? Where were the parents of all the girls? Before Christmas, at least a third of the girls at the junior high were being kept home. Why didn't people who backed him speak up?

Matt could see into Audrey's office; the phone kept ringing, the buttons lit up all the way across the panel. Audrey was alone now, answering the calls. Not one friendly call among the lot, he bet. He rose from his chair, solid, decisive.

"I've had it. Had it up to here with all this bullshit," he said, drawing his hand across his throat like a knife.

"Hey," Arnie said patronizingly.

"Hey, crap. All you guys can do is beef and not provide any creative suggestions. You call your meeting, but now let me get to work. I have a million other things to do. Other people have their complaints and, meanwhile, I need to try to solve some of the problems around here that have been piling up."

The two men backed up as Matt loomed toward them. Then Sam turned to Arnie and bustled him out the door. Arnie was muttering something about heat in the kitchen. Sam said, "We can play hardball, too."

Matt shut his door, this time with a slam. What the hell was he going to do? These jerks had set his blood boiling, and he desperately wanted to take some action.

If Arnie and Sam organized for the meeting, and he was sure they would, he'd have to develop some strategy. But what? The frustration was debilitating. Maybe he should have people take lie detector tests. But who? The boys? The teachers? Who knew, maybe some sick parent was doing this. But how? He just couldn't imagine the technique used to entice these girls to have sex.

Matt sat down at his desk, picked up the other phone message slips, and got angry again. He gazed across the playing field, which, on a regular day, would have been full at that moment. The between-class bells had kept ringing all morning. He'd forgotten to have them turned off before Christmas. He ought to ask Yale Kaltmann to disconnect them. It was too melancholy to be reminded constantly of the children who should be romping through the school without a care in the world, or at least without adult-weight cares on their shoulders. Irritated still, he bolted up and out the door to find Kaltmann.

As he headed down the hall, the tiniest mustard seed of an idea occurred to him. Maybe he could set himself up as a target to smoke out the bastards who were doing this. He'd have to think about that, about how to do it.

Lorna was in her office pacing. No, not quite pacing, really. Fidgeting. Whenever she heard footsteps down the hallway, she would jump up, go through the waiting room and put her head around the doorjamb to see who was there. She wanted it to be Yale.

She'd come to school today because she had nothing else to do. During vacations she was at loose ends. When the school had been closed early at Christmas three weeks ago, she'd taken a bus to Toledo to be with her parents for a while. But that only made her feel worse. Her brothers and sisters were there with their kids and, rather than the children making her happy, they exposed her own loneliness. She was upset at how the grown-ups took their children so for granted, didn't value them and know how lucky they were. She left for Sand Ridge a day earlier than she'd planned, brooding and growing sullen—so much so that even her nephews and nieces had started calling her a sourpuss.

Back in her little apartment above the bakery, she knitted, took walks, and waited and waited for her period not to come. On day twenty-six she began taking her temperature. It was high, as it should be. Then on day thirty it began to fall, but she didn't believe it. On the graph she plotted it higher than it was. Must be some fault in the thermometer, surely. She had to be pregnant. She just had to be. On day thirty-three, quite late, it came. She wasn't going to be a mother after all.

Oh, Buford, poor Bu, he had so wanted a brother or sister. That, she told herself at first, was why she'd tried to become pregnant. But late one night as she was preparing for bed, she caught herself thinking that Bu was dead, really dead, not just temporarily frozen.

"No," she said out loud.

Over three or four days, she could think of nothing else but that Buford was dead. She rehearsed everything, even the tiniest details. The mirror that had fallen off the wall in Café Rififi when that little boy was playing with it. She was superstitious. That was one reason she liked going to Sister Rosalyn's seances. She got to thinking about that, thinking that seances are really for the dead. She visited Sister Rosalyn and asked her if she talked only to the dead. The woman wouldn't say so directly. Did she think Lorna was dumb and wouldn't know she had evaded her question?

As she gradually became convinced that Bu was dead, she broke down. She relived that night again and again. In her mind, the curtain blew out and blew out and blew out. She wanted to scream. She sobbed. Finally, she plunged into her true mourning for her beloved baby Buford. She thought about the meaning of the words "rest in peace." Poor Bu, with her talking to him in the seances, he hadn't been able to rest in peace.

As the mourning lessened in intensity—although it remained a dull, raw emotion—Lorna began to realize that she wanted to have another baby to take the place of Bu. She needed to continue to live. She grew even more obsessed with becoming pregnant. She felt at loose ends.

The newspaper story last Friday, saying the junior high school was going to stay closed for another week, left her feeling more adrift. She'd seen Verity Molway in church yesterday. She'd gone early, worn her white leather gloves and her hat. She deliberately settled herself in the Molways' usual pew.

Wanda entered with her children, shushing Shad, who was vehemently refusing to sit next to his sister. Wanda made them sit on either side of her. Verity was on Lorna's side, only a yard away. She was big, gloriously big. Lorna's belly ached to be like that. Afterward, as Wanda and Shad were leaving the pew, Lorna had reached over and touched Verity's arm and said hello. The girl grimaced.

"You must be very happy," Lorna said.

Verity shrugged.

"Being a mother is wonderful," Lorna said.

With tears in her eyes, Verity burst out, "Oh, Mrs. Ross, I don't want a baby!"

After that, Lorna was more convinced than before that she should have Yale's baby. She was an experienced, dedicated mother. She had the right attitude. Verity and her baby were to be pitied.

Loud footsteps in the distance penetrated her day-dreaming. Lorna jumped up from her desk, rushed to the door. It wasn't Yale, but a teacher far down the hall. But Yale was there, silently striding away from her on crepe-soled shoes. She felt hot.

"Mr. Kaltmann," she called out.

He didn't hear her. She cleared her throat, took a deep breath, and called again. This time he turned, his soles squeaking slightly.

"I need you," she said.

She was so terrified in his presence that she had to hold one hand with the other to keep from shaking. Yale crossed the hall and stood just outside her door. She had drawn back into the waiting room, like a lure. Yale didn't enter.

"Come in," she said.

Then, when she realized he wasn't going to, she lowered her voice almost to a whisper.

"I need some oil on the stirrups. They squeak when I move them."

He looked down at her, sensing duplicity but not knowing what she could want.

"I'll get the oilcan."

He turned and disappeared from her view. A few minutes later he returned, startling Lorna by appearing silently. The huge oilcan had a thin, foot-long spout.

"Which one?" Yale demanded, moving toward the examination table.

"Uh, I don't remember."

Lorna hovered around him as Yale pulled out one stirrup and moved it up and down. Silent. He tried the other. There was the very slightest of squeaks.

"That one."

"Not exactly deafening," he said.

She shrugged coyly.

"I saw Verity yesterday. In church."

He looked at her coldly. She could tell he was wondering why, really, she had wanted him to come in here. She was nervous. He probably thought she was going to ask to see Buford.

"She was very happy. She said she was. Just like me when I had my Buford."

Yale said nothing, fiddling with the stirrup.

"The baby is due February seventeenth."

"Did she say that?" he asked gruffly, but Lorna thought he sounded pleased.

"No, I figured it out. When do you want me to do some girls again?"

She was asking to do it again? Yale couldn't conceal his suspicion.

"Why? You aren't seeing any girls. Are you?"

"Well, yeah, a few are coming in to swim this week," she said softly, looking down instinctively so he couldn't see her eyes while she lied.

"Next week, maybe," he said.

"The school may not be open next week."

"What do you mean?"

There was a new, threatening edge in his voice.

"I heard Mr. Chays say that in his office this morning when I was talking to Audrey."

"What exactly did he say?"

Yale moved toward her. She shifted back, away from him. Both stirrups stuck up above the table.

"He said . . . he said . . . I think he said he'd close the school for a year if it would stop . . ."

Her voice trailed off.

"Hello," a man's voice boomed out, rolling in from the outer door of the waiting room.

"It's Mr. Chays," Lorna gasped.

"Quick, go delay him," Yale hissed.

She paused.

"You're in this as much as I am," he spat out.

Lorna whirled and ran out to the other room as Yale moved toward the stirrups to turn them down beneath the edge of the table.

"Mrs. Ross, have you seen Mr. Kaltmann? Downstairs they said I might find him here."

"Yes, he's fixing . . ."

She paused. Oh, God, what?

"He's fixing the venetian blinds."

She had virtually thrown her body in Mr. Chays's way, but he was bigger than she was and, since she was not used to stopping anyone in higher authority, she quickly melted backward as Matt leaned to peer into his office.

Yale didn't look like he was repairing the venetian blinds. He was standing in front of one corner of the examining table, his hand behind him as if he was leaning on it. Well, Matt didn't want to embarrass him. If Yale and Lorna had something between them, he didn't want them to think that he minded. He remembered Yale wanting to hide from Lorna that he had lied to her about being married. In retrospect, maybe there was something more complex between these two.

"Mr. Kaltmann," Matt said, "I was hoping you would find time today to turn off the bell system. I think we can do without them while the school is closed. Is that possible?"

Yale appeared nervous.

"I realize you may not be able to find time today. Tomorrow would be okay, too," Matt said hastily, trying to fill in around Yale's uneasiness.

"How long is the school going to be closed?"

Yale leaned backward as he spoke and Lorna simultaneously shoved a stapler off her desk, causing Matt to bend over to retrieve it. Yale quickly and inconspicuously folded the stirrup beneath the table behind his back, then moved away from it.

"I've said a week." Matt sighed.

"Only a week?"

"Well, I'd like to close it longer, but I think I'd have a riot on my hands. I'm going to try, anyway."

"You can't do that."

The urgency in Yale's voice surprised Matt. Of course, they were all concerned about their jobs and pay.

"Don't worry, you won't lose any salary, I'll see to that. Besides just about everybody seems against me on this, so I'll probably lose."

"So maybe a week?" Yale wanted reassurance.

"A week," Matt said. "It can't be too hard to disconnect the bell system, can it?"

"Oh, no, sir, no problem at all. I'll do it today."

Yale was visibly relieved.

"Good, thanks."

Matt turned to go.

"But I'm going to try to close it longer. I've got to try, don't you agree, Mrs. Ross? This horrible stuff can't go on."

Lorna, surprised that he had addressed her, nodded yes. But she didn't feel yes at all. She couldn't carry out her plan if the school was shut. She never thought she would be on the same side as Yale. Despicable idea. But she had other reasons than his, higher reasons.

"Thanks," Matt said to both of them. "Thanks for supporting me. We'll all make it through this."

He turned and left.

"Damn!"

Lorna was shocked to see that Yale's face was contorted and angry. There was a red stripe about an inch wide right down the center of his forehead, exactly where a major artery flowed. Otherwise his skin was white, but there the surface was inflamed from his fury.

"He can't do this. I don't want to hurt him."

Suddenly he remembered Lorna was there.

"I'm not violent. I don't want to hurt anyone."

Lorna cringed toward the waiting room, hoping Yale would follow her out. He brushed past her through the door, then spun around, shoes screeching.

"We're in this together—don't forget."

An icy terror shot up her back. His voice was low and he seemed to be crouching over her like a lion, ready to rip her apart. Then he was gone silently down the hall.

She slumped down on a chair in the waiting room. Failure, utter failure. Yale was suspicious of her, and anyway she'd have no sperm in time for this month if Mr. Chays won and kept the school closed. She got up wearily to move to her office chair. She was so alone. If there were only someone to talk to.

A tiny puddle of yellowy oil lay on the floor immediately below the end of the patient table. Lorna took a tissue from the sleeve of her sweater and wiped it up. A wave of jealousy over Verity blotted out her despair. She picked up her knitting from a basket on the floor at the far corner of her desk and began to purl automatically for a whole row until she realized that was wrong and she had to rip it out.

CHAPTER TWENTY-SEVEN

Yale had been out on the lake for well over two hours, cruising and waiting for Matt and Niccole to get situated. He'd seen their cars arrive and park, then the two figures disappear behind the breakwater. The wind of the Alberta Clipper moving down from Canada had long ago numbed his face even though he wore two face masks. It had been six years since he'd been on the ice, six years until yesterday, that is, when he spent the day boning up on his technique.

Yesterday he had hitched his electric-blue DN iceboat to the back of his van and driven out to the lake to practice. Six years away from boating had made him rusty. He was pleased, however, to find that he remembered it quickly. He pushed the boat out from the shore till the ice was almost as smooth as a mirror, faster and faster to get momentum, and then leaped aboard. The exhilaration came back.

He practiced with a woolen muffler, throwing the plaid scarf out on the ice and then scudding away from it, turning, and zooming back, aiming at it. It took a while to get his reflexes and timing just right. He played the wind fast and gracefully. He hotdogged some, hiking, or tipping up on one blade. What a beautiful instrument this was. Compared to a sailboat, an iceboat had a superior lift-to-drag ratio. A sailboat couldn't go much faster than the wind, but an iceboat could speed three to five times faster. The sensation was almost one of flying..Yale had polished the sides of his runner plates to keep the light snow on the ice from sticking.

Yale's irritation over the school being closed was fueled by his growing obsession with becoming a father again, especially after the deaths of Cheryl and Penny. His determination took shape in the iceboat plan after he'd sorted through Mr. Chays's phone message slips in the trash and found the one from Niccole saying where they were to meet for fishing and at what time.

He figured that if Mr. Chays was out of the picture, the school board would have to appoint an acting principal. The pressure to keep the school open would force Chays's stand-in to cave in. Yale didn't want to hurt Mr. Chays. He liked him. Besides, he was Tobie's father. If he could just be hospitalized for a while, so that he needed a substitute, it would solve Yale's problem. When Yale practiced, he aimed for the extremities of the six-foot-long scarf, imagining it was a leg.

It was almost a year since he'd first thought of his strategy for achieving immortality. What a lot he'd accomplished in that time! But he was a perfectionist. He wasn't satisfied. Lorna had screwed up with too many girls, making bad picks. He was now determined to direct her in every detail, to add to his family. But he couldn't do it if the school was closed. That thought haunted him.

He was spurred on by the anticipation of becoming a father for the first time. Early in the week when Lorna had named a date for Verity's lying-in, an unexpected thrill had shot through Yale's body. It was a thrill he'd repeated many times afterward, by thinking about a tiny baby, his baby, coming into the world.

At the thought of holding his baby in his arms, Yale laughed into the blustery wind. The air was cold on his teeth and hurt. He was goaded on by the pain. He considered endurance of pain the sign of an athlete. The wind was perfect for his purposes, good for speed, as it built toward a winter storm that was predicted for that night.

When he tacked across in front of the outer dike and

finally spotted Matt and Niccole in the cove, he calmed down. His mission was clear.

The heart of a hidden, camouflaged animal slows down when the beast is frightened. In contrast, the heart of an uncamouflaged animal, like man, surges faster when the mind is terrified. Matt remembered Tobie reading that to him from one of her many animal books.

But his heart, as he was driving to meet Niccole on the shore of Lake Erie, was doing something quite different. Flip-flops, as if it were on a trampoline. He was embarrassed by his anticipation. He felt like a teenager, and tried to calm himself with deep breaths.

Matt swung his car into the parking lot and lodged it ten yards from the only other vehicle there, a big station wagon with lots of fishing gear in the rear end. He was fifteen minutes early. He turned on the radio to hear the local news headlines. The fourth item was about Sand Ridge. "The school board will meet with citizens of Sand Ridge Monday to deal with the horror that has been tearing the town apart and—" He snapped it off.

The gigantic, charcoal gray boulders of a man-made dike jutted out from beneath the parking lot. It curved in a broad, parenthetic swoop around the large cove; Matt could see two figures at a great distance out on the ice. The dark of the rocks was capped and softened by last night's snow. Everything looked marbled. Clouds above the dike mimicked the shape of the boulders, but were reverse in color, like a film negative.

He stepped out of the car to survey the cove. It would be best to go out into the middle of the ice, far enough out to increase the chances of catching something. The two men in the distance had caught a fish. One of them strode over to the other, who was hoisting his rod. Matt could see them pull the fish up, its scales shining from far off as it thrashed, hanging on the line. When Niccole's small, white Pontiac, which she'd bought after her old car was bombed at the abortion clinic, turned in between the entrance pillars to the parking lot, Matt waved and then motioned her down toward his car, guiding her in with an exaggerated parking lot attendant's gesture. As she nosed her car in next to him, he made a grand bow in front of her opened window.

"Madame, your parking place. I mean, mademoiselle."

"I wonder what the French for Ms. is?"

"Hmmm," was the best he could muster in reply.

He circled behind her car to open the passenger door and slid in next to her.

"Hi."

"I hope I'm not late," she said.

"Right on time."

"So, is this a good fishing day?"

"About perfect, I'd say. See those two people way down there? I just saw them pull up a pretty-good-sized one. I assume you like to eat fish?"

"Oh, yes, especially fish cheeks."

"You, too?"

"Usually I gross people out when I say that," she said.

"Fish cheeks are one of the great culinary delicacies of the ancient and modern world," he said, and added, "I see you know how to dress for the weather."

She wore a tricolor down parka with chartreuse, blue-green, and rose triangles slashing across it.

"I've learned. I wear so many pairs of long underwear and other things that I can hardly cross my legs and I walk like a fat lady."

Matt's eyes went down to her shoes. Niccole followed his glance. She had on moccasins.

"My boots are right back here."

She reached over into the backseat and pulled them up from the floor.

"There's only one thing you're missing," Matt said. "And I brought one of Tobie's for you."

"What's that?"

"A face stocking. The wind is very cold out there; it'll burn your skin if you're not protected. The only problem is it's orange and will clash with your parka."

"Hey, guess I'd better go home," she teased. "Now, tell me how you do this ice fishing."

"Tell you what, let's just do it. Get your boots on and then come over to my car, and we'll lug the gear out."

Niccole stood with her arms stuck out like a clothesline pole while Matt draped her with things to carry. A couple of fold-up canvas stools over her left shoulder, a small backpack with a thermos and munchies on the right shoulder, and an empty white plastic bucket in her hand. He carried four stumpy fishing poles, a tackle box, an auger, a bucket of minnows, and a small kerosene heater built for use outdoors.

Clanking along, they headed toward the area of the lake enclosed by the dike, picking their way over the giant boulders. In the distance a train, what used to be the New York Central and was now Conrail, hooted.

"Is the ice thick enough?" Niccole asked.

"Oh, yes. It's been frozen since mid-December."

"The Cuyahoga River was frozen for a while, but they keep breaking it up with little icebreakers. I watch them outside my apartment. It's funny to think of the Cuyahoga frozen after you know that it's most famous for catching fire."

"Lake Erie's frozen about two miles out."

"Then I feel safe."

"You've heard of Kelly's Island?"

"Uh-huh."

"That's a mile out, and the residents cross over to the mainland on snowmobiles, even drive cars over. Now and then someone miscalculates, though, and loses a truck or something."

"Hey, did you read this sign you just passed?"

Niccole paused in front of it and read out loud: "State and local health departments advise against the eating of fish caught in this area."

"Out of date," Matt said. "The lake was declared totally safe a year ago. They just haven't taken down the sign yet."

"Anyway, maybe we won't catch anything."

Matt charged right out on the ice, but Niccole slowed down at the edge. She gingerly stepped on it and nudged along to get a feel for her footing. She stopped and bent over.

"Listen," she said.

Matt stopped and came back to stand next to her.

"It sounds like it's tickling under the ice," she said of the sloshing water. "And, oh, look at the tiny frozen perch."

She walked a little farther on, bent over.

"Minnows, frozen. It's like one of those practical-joke ice cubes with a fly in it."

Matt felt his spirits lifting, as if the great hand of God had smoothed out the stress on his forehead. Seagulls were mewing and drifting overhead. He led Niccole about a hundred fifty yards out from the shore into the middle of the cove, and said, "How about here?" She agreed, and they unloaded.

"Who taught you to ice fish?"

"I first did it when I spent a winter in Holland," he said. "But it was really Harper who taught me about the fishing techniques he'd learned in New Hampshire. In fact, this is his."

Matt took the hand auger and began drilling a six-inch-wide hole, slowly chewing the ice and screwing into it.

"I figure we'll cut two holes a distance apart, and then we can each watch one of them."

Niccole unfolded the canvas seats and sat observing, her chin in her hand as she leaned on her knee. It reminded him of how Tobie followed him around and watched him working on projects around the house.

"What kind of bird is that? It's huge."

Matt stopped drilling and turned to look where she pointed.

"A harbinger."

"Harbinger? There's no such bird," she said, smiling.

"Oh, yes, they come before spring or, in this case, before good things happen."

"Right. You know, you're very silly."

"Yeah, guess I'd better get serious."

"No, I like it."

Matt finished drilling the first hole.

"Now, what do you think. About five yards apart? That way we can sit here in the middle and watch the lines."

They set up the poles in the first hole and then began work on the second.

"What are those? They couldn't be sailboats."

Niccole pointed out beyond the dike, where the tips of brightly colored sails flitted along.

"Iceboats," Matt said.

"Good day for it," Niccole said, her voice whipped off her lips by the rising wind.

"Yeah, guess we're too far from the dike for it to block the wind."

The cove was formed by three breakwaters. The first extended out from the parking lot, curving from left to right, ending directly in front of Matt and Niccole as they looked north across the lake. Another dike curved around from the right, pointed toward the first, and left a gap fifty yards wide as an entrance to the cove. Farther out, a straight breakwater shielded the gap to keep out the waves from the lake, but allowing boats to come around either of its ends to enter the cove.

Matt drilled the second hole and baited Niccole's two hooks; she lowered the lines into the lake and then propped up the poles. She put the canvas chairs back to back like bookends and for a while they sat that way, but their weights were unequal. They turned themselves sideways so they could talk, gaze around, and watch the poles at the same time. They had put on their face stockings and their voices were slightly muffled through the cloth.

Matt told her that iceboats originated in the seventeenth century among the Dutch, who used large ones to move cargo. The Dutch had introduced them into the Hudson valley, where iceboating became a sport of the landed gentry. FDR'd had a boat named *Icicle.*

"Those things are goddamn fast," he said. "They've been known to exceed a hundred forty miles per hour."

"That's fast."

"Yeah, but that's only the skeeters. Most of them, like those over there, are DN-class boats."

"DN?"

"Named after the *Detroit News,* where in the late thirties somebody figured out that if you used epoxy instead of metal fasteners, you could build a really light hull."

"They're nice, aren't they?" she said, gazing dreamily lakeward. "Each one is like half a butterfly."

Niccole told Matt more about her vacation. Little things. Her nephew, she'd discovered, was a sleepwalker; it was pretty unnerving to see a child walking around with his eyes wide open, focusing on nothing but his own dreams. She told Matt about hearing on TV the day after Christmas that somebody had bombed an abortion clinic in Oklahoma.

"They left a message at the site that they did it as a birthday present for Christ. Disgusting, no?"

During the next half hour, they caught two walleyes in succession, then a large perch, then a carp, which Matt threw back because they feed on the dirty bottom of the lake.

When Niccole removed her face stocking and took a swig of cocoa from the thermos, it felt refreshing to shake out her hair. They stood up and walked over to check their respective poles. Matt, who was patrolling the hole closer to land, turned and saw a DN with a white and yellow sail glide in front of the far breakwater, then turn into the cove. It began to pick up speed, heading straight at them.

He expected the craft to tack again, but though it swerved a bit, it continued at them, moving faster and faster. It must be out of control. Matt's heart was thundering in his throat. There wasn't much time. Maybe there wasn't enough time. Niccole's back was toward the boat.

He screamed, "Hey! Watch out! Get out of the way!"

Yale was too far away to see their features. Their great difference in height marked them, and the bright parka meant one of the figures was a woman.

He pulled in his sail and turned the boat to head into the cove, pointing at the remote figures. He raked the mast back to build up speed. It was good. He gently coddled the tiller in his palm. Faster, faster. About thirty miles an hour. He swung the tiller so that the boat lurched and looked out of control. He whipped it back. Anyone watching might think he was drunk or had had an epileptic fit or some lapse in control. As he began his run, his adrenaline surged. He told himself to remain calm and cool. But he could feel his forehead was hot.

The wind numbed his face muscles even through his two stocking masks. Forty miles an hour. Fifty. The steel runners spewed frosty splinters into his face, nicking his eyelids and forcing him to squint.

The hiss of the runners on the ice was music to him. As he sped into the cove, the surface grew rougher. The boat vibrated when it hit abrasions and small craters.

He whipped the boat drunkenly again, then zeroed in on them. Niccole was in a direct line with his most accurate approach to Mr. Chays. Yale didn't want to do anything to Niccole. Jesus, why didn't she move? She was looking the other way.

He yelled. It was an unspellable scream. A listener might have been forgiven for thinking it was a victory cry. Actually, it was a primitive alarm. Yale didn't want to hit Niccole.

CHAPTER TWENTY-EIGHT

Niccole removed her glove so that she could use her fingers better, and pulled up one of the fishing lines to see that the bait was still intact on the hook. Just as the minnow emerged from the water, she heard Matt shout.

She turned her head, though her body was still bent over. Matt was pointing at something behind her and screaming. She couldn't hear what he was saying because the wind was blowing toward him.

She jerked upright and whirled around, yanking the string out of the water. An iceboat was slamming toward her at high speed. It was aimed straight at her, its sail bent back at an extreme angle. She thought the man on the boat shouted. She wasn't sure. She tried to fling herself away from the path of the boat, but her feet slipped, and she tried to break her fall with her ungloved hand. Her pants caught on an ice outcropping and tore. She ended up on her back, her hair splayed out on the ice.

The blades hissed on the ice, and she could hear the impact as they struck small holes and ridges. The near runner looked as if it would hit her in the head. She turned her face away. There was a yank on her hair. She heard the creaks and groans of the rigging. Then it was past.

She lifted her head. The runner blade had neatly sliced

through her hair. Five inches of it lay on the ice, arrayed in a foot-wide swath. It looked like decorations for hundreds of fishermen's flies.

The bait bucket with the minnows spun around like a whirligig, spewing tiny silvery fish outward in a wheel. She twisted her body around to see where the boat had gone, lifting herself to her elbow. The iceboat was headed for Matt.

He stood transfixed. He couldn't tell if Niccole was all right, and he numbly understood that the iceboat was now pointed right at him. He saw the smokestacks in faraway Carlton, airplane warning lights on them flicking through the dismal gray haze and clouds.

When he'd first seen the boat, he'd ripped his face stocking up off his head and flung it away. The boat smacked the canvas stools that stood between the holes and they skidded off to either side. Matt had the same disembodied feeling as when the wheel came off his car. The thought— clear, sharp, and brief—flooded over him that everything had become so sinister since the events at school had begun.

He bent down for the three-foot-long auger lying at his feet. It was his only available weapon. He lifted it, gripping the handle with both hands, swung it around his head, and pitched it with all his strength across the trajectory of the oncoming boat. As he let it go, he had a fantasy that it was a boomerang and would come back to him. It crashed to the ice and skittered along. The front steering runner smashed into it, spinning it away. The boat wobbled, lurched, and veered to one side of Matt.

The boat sped on; it had sliced in half one of the walleyes they'd caught. Blood was splattered on the thermos. Matt could see the man hunched over, straining to control the boat. He had no face. Or rather, he had on a face stocking. The boat rammed on, lurching unevenly because of the auger's damage to its steering. Then it slowed down, slewed around, and arced away from them back out to the lake, quickly picking up speed.

Matt felt breathless, his forearms inert, his muscles tingling. He turned and ran toward Niccole. She stood up.

"You okay?" he asked.

"Well, I wouldn't go that far." She smiled, relieved that they both were apparently intact.

"No, really, are you hurt anywhere? How's your head? No concussion? That was quite a fall."

"No." She shook her head. "How 'bout you?"

"Look," he said.

He reached over to her arm and her eyes followed his hand.

"Careful, don't move," he commanded.

He slowly extracted a fishhook from deep in the sleeve of her parka.

"I've had a hook cut out of me once," he said. "Not pleasant."

He threw it on the ice. Then he noticed that Niccole was shaking, her legs wobbly.

"Hey," he said softly, and pulled her toward him.

She melted against his chest, grateful for support.

"I guess I need some gum," she murmured.

"He sure was out of control. I wonder if he had some kind of seizure," Matt said.

"Out of control? Looked to me like he was aiming for us."

"You're more of a conspiratorialist than me," he teased.

"You trying to say I'm crazy, emotional, a woman, is that what?" she said angrily, pulling back, but he was firm and insisted on still holding her.

"No, no, hey, I was only teasing."

She softened.

"The trouble with you, Matthew Chays, is you're too nice. You're not suspicious enough."

"How close did he come to you?" Matt asked. "For a minute, I thought he was going to hit you."

"Close," she said.

She lifted the edges of her hair and pulled them to the side of her head so she could see them, too.

"He cut about five inches off. There it is."

She pointed to the hair spread on the ice, some of it blowing away with the wind.

"Jeez, no wonder you're shaking."

Matt looked toward the shore and saw the trees bending

violently in the wind. A squall was moving in fast. They'd better get home. He felt tired, exhausted after the adrenaline rush.

They swept the minnows into the water in the hole and gathered up the poles and bucket. Matt reached over and, with his broad hand, bunched up the cut-off hair and stuffed it into his jacket pocket. Niccole looked at him quizzically.

"The evidence," he said.

"More evidence," Niccole said, pointing to the sliced fish. "Shall we take it?"

"Sure. We'll eat that evidence."

Matt slid the fish into the trunk on top of some newspapers he'd brought along. It began to snow frenziedly.

"Huge conglomerations," Niccole said, catching three flakes on her glove.

"Multinationals, formed in leveraged takeovers high in the sky."

"Economics of weather," she replied, smiling.

It was a relief to smile, even if they were forcing their spirits up, hoping by artificial cheerfulness to retake control.

"Guess we have to drive in separate cars," she said regretfully.

"Unless you want to leave yours here?"

"No, that's dumb. I'll follow you. Don't lose me," she said.

"I'll take back roads. They'll be faster. The snow hasn't started to stick too much yet."

As they steered south, the snow thickened. Niccole memorized Matt's taillights. She only lost him once, when he zoomed through a traffic light that she missed; but he pulled to the verge and waited till she caught up.

The wind grew wilder. Traffic lights danced and bobbed on the cables strung across intersections. Niccole empathized and felt airsick. Dumb, empathizing with inanimate objects.

Trailing Matt's navy blue car, she felt secure. Suddenly she realized—why hadn't she thought of it before?—that Matt might have just saved her life. The boat still could've missed her, even if she hadn't moved. But she wouldn't have even known it was coming if he hadn't yelled. Now she felt attached to him by these few intense moments, no matter how far apart their lives should split in the future.

Why did she feel so safe and secure with him? He seemed so solid. She'd always thought people had to be kooky in some way or they would be snoring bores. An outlook adopted from Kevin, no doubt. God, no, Matt wasn't flaky; he was *soooo* responsible. But he wasn't boring. She liked his quiet quirks and humor.

Peculiar that she felt safe with him. Here he was walking around in the strangest imaginable situation with young girls falling pregnant, accused of responsibility in some way and not knowing what the hell to do about it. What was safe and secure about that?

A year ago she and Kevin had made love for the last time and split like atoms. She'd been abstinent since then, had not found any man she wanted. Maybe she was getting particular. Two months ago, shortly after she'd met Matt, she'd surprised herself by digging out her old birth control pills and starting to take them again. It wasn't that she planned to have sex. In fact, she could have made love with Matt in December, but she wasn't emotionally ready. She didn't think they would tonight. At the most, they might cuddle. The day had been too traumatic.

Who was she fooling? She knew it was coming, thundering down on them. She knew she would resist it. That intensified things, the way simultaneously resisting and giving in to an orgasm made it more brilliant. Actually, she was shy about sex with a new man. It might flop, like a storm could suddenly fizzle or be blown away to kingdom come. Where was kingdom come?

Holyfuckinshit, his eyes were tired. Matt squinted into the rearview mirror, trying to see Niccole's car in the blizzard. Obscure, like picking her shape out from among the folds of the sheets in a bed. Why was he thinking of her in bed? Perhaps his scrape with death had turned his mind to other elemental experiences, sex, for reaffirmation of life.

He pulled over and waited for her to catch up. He nosed back in front of her as her car appeared slowly out of the blanketing snow. He removed his hat and gloves as the car heated up. Like people in bubbles, they moved close to each other but didn't touch. She was thinking her own thoughts, he his. He wondered if their thoughts mingled somewhere between her car and his. Would she start to think about sex, now that he was? Of course, he'd been this way almost since he'd met her. And the better he knew her, the worse it was. It wasn't just her body he wanted. But then, he wasn't into pursuing women just for sex. He couldn't understand how men could do that. It seemed like a waste of time.

Her car pulled up close behind his at a light. Her hair floated around her shoulders. He wanted to observe more of her reactions to things; he liked watching how she accepted or criticized people and ideas and emotions. Some women were too gullible. She seemed to err in the other direction. But that meant he would have won more if she came to trust him.

He pulled into the driveway and drove up to the back door, so that the car trunk was parallel to it. She spun in behind him.

"You can't drive to Cleveland in this," he said.

"Not unless I leave now."

He raised his eyebrows, pursed his lips, and looked down at her with his head cocked.

"I won't. I'm ravenous."

They carried the fish and all the equipment into the basement, where Matt began to scale the fish in the deep sink.

"Okay if we eat the walleyes and I save the perch for Tobie tomorrow?"

"Sure. What can I do?"

He suggested that she find a couple of potatoes in the kitchen. While they baked in the oven, she could take a shower. He'd fix the fish and build a fire.

"Sounds great. I reek."

After her shower, she called down to him as he knelt in front of the fireplace, making twists of paper to ignite the fire.

"Yoo-hoo, Matt. Matt."

He loved to hear her call his name, as if it were a touch, as if it made him more real. The local weatherman on the television was blasting out into the living room, so Matt hadn't heard her at first. She had ventured partway down the stairs wrapped in a towel.

"Yoo-hoo?" he said, looking up.

"Do you have anything I could wear? I can't bear to put those fishy clothes back on."

He jumped up, saying, "Sure," and moved so quickly to the stairs that, in surprise, she let loose an edge of her towel as she turned. She had an exquisite ass. Big dimples on each side. Like those smooth concavities on Dimple scotch bottles. She grabbed the towel around her.

He handed his Black Watch plaid nightshirt to her through the crack of the door. Then she asked for another towel for her hair. He was certain Tobie had taken her hair dryer to California. That was okay, she said, she'd dry her hair by the fire. He took his shower and also put on a nightshirt, which, on him, was much shorter, coming to his knees, whereas the one she wore skimmed the floor.

They prepared dinner, broiling the fish with tomatoes, onions, and lots of oregano and basil, fixing a salad, and, all the while, having drinks. She had a bourbon. He had a scotch from the Dimple scotch bottle. They sat near the fire, using two footstools for tables. Occasionally Niccole switched her position to dry a different section of her hair. They exchanged places so she could dry the opposite side.

"I've always wanted a blunt cut," she said. "But this one was a bit too."

During dinner, Matt asked her a million questions. Not about her boyfriends or love life, but about Berkeley, student activism during her time there, where she'd lived in San Francisco. What was her best university course? Modern novel. Second best? Botany. What other jobs had she had besides the isolation tank and the indexer ones? Assembling chandeliers and being a model of shoes in a Dallas department store. He asked about her childhood, about music lessons. Piano. Ballet lessons.

On and on. Meanwhile, they devoured the food, making a small drama of eating the fish cheeks simultaneously and with a flourish.

"You're amazing," she said.

"You don't like how I eat my fish?"

"No, for asking so many questions. I've never had a man do that and actually be interested in what I have to say."

"That's appalling."

"What's appalling?"

"Appalling that no other man has done it. You're an interesting woman."

"Yeah, well, you're pretty unusual."

"How sexist am I?"

"The fact you could ask that, instead of insisting you're not sexist, speaks volumes."

"Well, a man claiming he's not sexist would be like a white insisting he's not racist, wouldn't it?"

"Exactly."

"I try not to be sexist in raising Tobie, but sometimes it's tough. She plays on the boy's softball team. That was okay to begin with, but now I'm worried."

"Common sense, given what's happening here."

"I worry she'll be maladjusted because she has no mother, and also because of all this stuff going on. I try to let her know she can do or be anything she wants in life—an astronaut, an artist, a veterinarian, a ditchdigger, whatever."

"You didn't say house spouse."

"I don't want her to marry a house. No, seriously, she can do that, too. But how do you raise a child to be totally free? How did you get as free as you are?"

"I'm not as much as I should be. Oh, I don't know. Reading, experience, age has a lot to do with it. People have always tried to pat me on the head, but I'm pretty prickly. Temperament plays a big part. But I think you're doing a fine job with Tobie, from the little I've seen."

The neck of her nightshirt gaped, and since it was too big for her, the V of it dipped low. The curve of her right breast caught his attention. He closed his eyes so he could stand it.

"What's wrong?"

"Wrong?" His eyes flashed open.

"You had your eyes shut."

"The view down your neck . . ."

Her hand shot up. He reached out and took it, pressing his over hers against her breast. She melted and moved toward where he sat on the floor, leaning against the sofa. Their bodies met. She kissed him on the neck. She said his name against his throat, and he knew he was doing the right thing.

"Are you sure?" he asked anyway.

"Very."

She straddled him, folding the nightshirt beneath herself demurely. She put her elbows up on his shoulders, then stroked her fingers up the sides of his face, extending the gesture and bending gracefully backward, her whole body committed to the soft arch. She leaned back over him, traced his eyebrows, the line of his nose, and his mouth before kissing it lightly, then less so, then more.

The floodgates opened. There were no more sentences. Only run-on words and thoughts and run-on arms and legs and breaths shared in and out when she rose onto her knees and pulled the nightshirt over her head, turned and raised his to his waist, and slowly, tantalizingly lowered herself onto him, blurring the whole room, the house, the night into bliss.

In the middle of the night, snow fell off a section of the roof in a slow, trundling moan that grew to a roar. Niccole sat up on the mattresses they had laid on the floor in front of the fireplace.

"What was that?"

He woke instantly, reached for her, and felt her fear.

"Snow on the roof."

He shifted to place a log on the embers. There was a sudden flare as the dry bark caught.

He leaned over her, placing his palms in the sculpted places of her bottom. His eyes roamed over her whole body. It was amazing. Her perfectly shaped pubic triangle consisted of black hair, totally unexpected for a redhead.

"It's not dyed," she said.

"Incredible. I like surprises," he said.

Her body molded against his, moving with his as close as a shadow.

The next morning as she was leaving, he said, "When will I see you?"

"Let's be loose," she said.

"How loose?"

"I don't know. I have to wait and think."

"And feel," he said.

"Funny you should say that."

"I have an intuition."

"You're not allowed," she teased. "What is it?"

"That we're going to have a fight."

"Tell me when and I'll bring my boxing gloves."

He bent over and kissed her through the window of her car, touching her breast with his left hand. She held his lower lip firmly between her lips, pulling it, wanting to keep his kiss. Then she let go.

CHAPTER TWENTY-NINE

For Tobie's homecoming Sunday afternoon, Matt bought a minute, red, portable radio with earplugs. She'd been begging for one for six months. He fixed their favorite pizza dough, with onion juice in it, and prepared pesto to spread on it with fresh parmesan cheese. He'd frozen the perch for another day.

Homecomings. They'd shared so many in her thirteen years. He had traveled constantly as a roving correspondent when she was little. "Cominghomes," she'd called them once when she was five. The name stuck for five years. After the movie *E.T.* came out, she used to greet him with an outreached index finger, mournfully intoning "home." He had to touch his finger to hers before she would let him do anything else. "Heart-in-the-throat times," she later dubbed departures and homecomings.

The moment he saw her come through the gate off the plane, his heart was in his throat. She'd lost weight. Not just a few pounds. A lot. She probably weighed seventy pounds, he calculated. Fifteen pounds less than when she left.

He pulled her into his arms and hugged her, giving her a kiss on the cheek.

"Hi," he said.

"How d'ya like my tan? See, I'm blending all the freckles together."

"Pretty good for the middle of the winter. But there's not much under it for the tan to stick to."

She looked sheepish.

"Nana said you would be surprised."

Surprised! He felt like crying. So he hugged her again. She started crying.

"What's wrong?"

"Nothing," she said, running the sleeve of her Disneyland sweatshirt under her nose.

"No?"

"When you hug me too long it makes me cry," she said, sniffing.

As a principal, he'd heard a lot from the counselors about anorexia and bulimia. It would make sense, if she'd stressed out over all the pregnancies and deaths.

"You have to eat or I won't have anything to hug."

They both had watery eyes. Hers looked extra large and limpid. He could feel her shoulder blades through her sweatshirt.

"I couldn't bear not having you to hug," he added.

He lifted her night case from her hands as they headed toward the luggage carousels.

"Want an ice cream?" he asked as they neared the airport concessions.

"I'm not hungry," she said, squinching her face.

"Well, you gotta eat pizza when we get home, because I made it special for you."

She didn't say she would.

"Nana sent you some artichokes and oranges and figs. I picked the oranges myself off their tree. And at the airport in San Francisco, we bought some sourdough bread."

"Sounds like a grocery store coming down that conveyor belt."

Matt was peering at the emerging luggage when Tobie said something he didn't hear at first. Something about her period being late.

"What?"

She whispered. "I said, my period is six weeks late."

Her words fell on him like molten metal. Burned into him. He felt as if he'd been violated.

"Daddy, I didn't do anything."

"Honey, I'm sure. You know I believe you. First of all, it's possible you're not pregnant. We'll go to a doctor right away—tomorrow. Second, even if you are, you know that it makes no difference in my love for you."

"I didn't do anything," she murmured over and over.

"I know, I know." He stroked her head, which she held down.

"Daddy?"

"Uh-hunh."

"D'you think when I touched that gunk on that doll . . . could that make me pregnant?"

"You washed it right off, didn't you?"

She nodded, sniffled, and looked up at him.

"There's no way that could make you pregnant."

No wonder she'd lost all that weight. She was probably subconsciously trying to starve herself, so she wouldn't have hips or become a woman capable of being pregnant.

On the way home, she didn't inquire about the animals, so he told her. Sam Houston had taken to chewing on Matt's earlobe a little too eagerly. They might have to release him to squirreldom in the spring. Tobie didn't protest. The guppies had produced a whole squadron of babies sleek as new submarines.

She didn't race around the house as she usually did to see what had changed. She didn't take the steps two at a time going upstairs. She didn't check her pets in the basement. Matt let her roam around in her room for a while alone.

"Tobie, Tobie," rang through the house.

She came to the edge of the stairs.

"Did you call?"

"No, not me."

"Then who?"

"Come see."

She descended the stairs holding the little red radio. "Thank you, Daddy. I know you're trying to make me feel better."

"Tobie, Tobie."

237

She followed the sound of her name into the dining room. Wig cocked his topknot and looked at her comprehensively with an amber eye and said, "Tobie."

"You taught him my name."

She looked wistful. Hell, who knew what she was thinking? Maybe she was thinking of naming a baby. At least, that's what popped into Matt's brain.

"Pizza?"

"I'm still not very hungry," she complained.

"Well, I'm ravenous, and I guess I'll just have to force-feed you."

She flopped down into a dining room chair and burst into tears. He dug into his pants pocket for his handkerchief, dabbed her cheeks, and left it in her hand. She used to like using his handkerchief.

"Maybe we should talk about your doctor's appointment," he said as gently as he could.

"I don't want to go."

"I can understand that you wouldn't want to, but, honey, you've got to find out."

"I don't want to find out."

She wasn't belligerent. Rather, she seemed listless. When he'd seen how much weight she'd lost, he thought he might have trouble getting her to eat. He hadn't dreamed she would flatly refuse to go to the doctor.

"Everybody'll find out," she said.

"No, they won't. There's such a thing as doctor/patient confidentiality. The doctor is bound by his professional ethics not to say what goes on between him and his patient."

She said nothing, but he could tell she was skeptical.

"What if I want an abortion?"

She blurted it out, and flashed him a defiant look.

He paused, then said, "We'll cross that bridge when we get to it. First you need to find out if you're even pregnant."

"That means you don't want me to. That's what 'cross the bridge when we get to it' always means."

"No, it doesn't."

She kept her head lowered.

"Look," he said, "I'm going to toss the pizza dough. Do you think you could help with the salad?"

He prodded her into eating one slice of pizza and a

helping of salad, meanwhile asking her questions about what she'd done in California. Went to Muscle Beach, for one thing. What was there? She wouldn't elaborate beyond men in tiny bathing suits. She made a face of distaste. So much of teenagers' language is body language, he thought. However, there was this place with fantastic skateboarders, she said. The boys did really dangerous things. Flips. Rode up and down the sides of swimming pools. Scary.

As they were saying good night, he said, "I'm really glad you're home. I missed you."

"Yeah, me, too," she said, smiling grimly. She hesitated and said, "Are there any new girls pregnant?"

"No."

He'd already told her about the school board meeting tomorrow night, and that it would determine if and when school reopened.

"Do you want it open, Daddy?"

"No, I want it shut until we get to the bottom of this. Do you want it open?"

"No. I'm scared."

"I know, honey."

"I'm all alone. I mean, it's my body and it's happening only to me and you can't help me."

"It is happening to your body. If it is. You know, we don't know it is."

She turned to go into her room. He reached out and pulled her to him and held her.

"Tobie, you know I love you, I'll do anything I can to help you."

"I know."

She pulled out of his arms, afraid she'd start crying again, and dashed into the room, saying "G'night," and slowly but determinedly shut the door.

Matt trudged downstairs and plunked down on the sofa. Tears welled up in his eyes and he wiped them away.

"Shit."

What could he do? Clearly she wouldn't open up and talk to him. It was too difficult. It pained him so much. This child he loved more than himself. This child was a woman, he had to tell himself. If he could only take on her burden. He'd die for Tobie if he had to.

Maybe she would talk to a woman. Audrey? Somehow he didn't think so. Tobie was concerned about other people in the town knowing. Niccole. Why not Niccole?

He waited until he figured Tobie was asleep, then phoned Niccole at her apartment. She said she'd take the morning off and thought there'd be no problem if she made up the time later. Matt told her he thought Tobie might open up to her, that Tobie wouldn't know that Niccole knew she might be pregnant.

"So, what am I supposed to do?"

"I think you can get her to tell you, and then try to encourage her to get tested."

"Right."

"How are you?" he asked.

"I think I'm going to have to get a new hairdo, what with the fact he ran over my hair at an angle. Maybe I'll get it cut real short."

"Oh, no."

"You want to vote, huh?"

"One vote for not too short."

"Since you grew your mustache for me, I guess I can have my hair cut to your specifications."

"My body still remembers yesterday," he said.

"Ditto."

They paused, and simultaneously said, "So?"

And then said good-bye.

The next morning at ten o'clock, Niccole knocked on the door. She lifted the brass knocker and let it drop against the door twice. Still no reply. Matt had said he'd be at his office but that Tobie would be home. She turned the knob and opened the unlocked door. It creaked as in a horror movie.

"Anybody home?"

She walked through the living and dining rooms into the kitchen. She set her bag on a chair. The basement door was ajar and the basement light was on.

"Yoo-hoo, Matt, is anybody here?"

She clomped down the stairs, deliberately making a lot of noise.

"Matt."

Tobie turned from bending over an animal cage as Niccole stepped onto the basement floor.

"Oh, hi, I was looking for your father. Welcome home."

"Hi. He's at his office."

"Oh, yes, of course."

She looked down into the cage. A chameleon was lying on a swatch of green Astroturf. He was turning green.

"Abracadabra's adjusting," Tobie said.

"To your being home?"

"That, too," Tobie said, soberly and with a hint of suspicion.

"How are you? You look like you lost a lot of weight."

"Um-huh."

"I hope you gain it back."

"Why?"

She was curious that Niccole talked to her as if she weren't a child. She seemed blunt without being rude. She didn't take the attitude that she knew Tobie better than Tobie knew herself. But maybe her father had asked Niccole here to get her to take the test.

"You looked prettier, healthier with more weight. This way you look like a cadaver."

"A dead body?"

"Yeah."

Niccole reached in and stroked the garter snake, wrapping him around her wrist like a bracelet. Tobie watched, grudgingly approving the fact that Niccole wasn't squeamish about snakes.

"I'm thirsty," Niccole said. "D'you think before I go over to your father's office I could make myself some tea?"

"Oh, yeah, sure."

Niccole found cups, sugar, and milk, then called down to the basement to ask where the tea was. Tobie, whose cautiousness was in a tug-of-war with her curiosity, went upstairs and showed Niccole how her father made tea from leaves in a Japanese pot.

"Are you still interviewing people?" Tobie asked.

"No, I did all I could and nothing really was conclusive or even very useful. But maybe I should interview some of the boys at school. Dunno, I'll have to think about that. What do you think?"

241

Tobie shrugged.

"Did you do anything exciting in California?"

"Sort of."

Niccole waited, munching some cookies Tobie had unearthed.

"I went to Muscle Beach."

"That's awful, isn't it?" Niccole said, making a face.

Tobie nodded in agreement.

"I don't like all those muscles," Niccole continued. "Frightening. Men think they can do everything because they are so strong. They parade around like peacocks."

"I hated it," Tobie said. "It gave me nightmares."

No kidding, thought Niccole, especially in her state of mind.

"I've always wanted to take karate, so I could be strong and no man could take me. In karate, you use your intelligence to defeat bulk."

Tobie looked interested. She helped herself to a cookie, nibbling on it.

"I should just do it. Would you like to take karate lessons with me?"

What am I doing? Niccole thought. This was not only a commitment to Tobie but to Matt as well. Did she really mean to do this?

But Tobie didn't say yes.

"Maybe . . . maybe not," she said, then paused. "I want to beat up men," she added fiercely.

"Yeah?"

"I haven't told my dad this, but I was walking back to my friend's house from Muscle Beach. There were a lot of people around on the sidewalks. The sun was going down, but it wasn't dark yet. I couldn't believe it. I was just walking along."

She stopped as if that were the end.

"And then what?"

"Then, this man who was coming toward me reached out and . . ." Tobie lowered her head. "I don't know if I should tell you."

Niccole said nothing.

"Well, he took his hand and ran it around my breast in a

circle. It was awful. Then he just kept walking. I felt it. I can still feel it."

Tobie shuddered.

"I know, I've had things like that happen to me."

"You have?"

"Every woman has."

Tobie's eyes were wide.

"I keep having nightmares about it," she said.

"That's why it's a good idea to learn karate."

Tobie took a vast breath up from her toes. But she wouldn't commit herself, at least not yet. Even if her father had sent Niccole here, maybe she should talk to her. Maybe she should test her reaction.

"You know what else?"

Niccole shook her head.

"I'm pregnant."

Niccole paused, studying Tobie's pretty, thin face.

"Are you sure? Have you been tested?"

"My period is late."

"That can happen when you're young and menstruation has just started, and especially if you don't eat enough. You should go for a test to be sure."

"What if I want an abortion?" Tobie said defiantly.

"If it comes to that, I'll discuss it with you if you want. You see, I think it's your decision. I don't know if your father would agree with me, but that's the way I look at it."

"Me, too."

Tobie was watching Niccole's face closely. She saw her take a very deep breath, compress her lips as if resolving something.

"When I was a little older than you, eighteen, when I was eighteen, I had an abortion."

Tobie looked amazed. She didn't know what to say.

"It was a mistake I made. Now, I know it's not the same with you. If you're pregnant, it's nothing you did. But, well, I just want you to know that maybe I can help you a little if it should come to that."

"Does my dad know?"

"About the abortion?"

Tobie nodded.

"No," Niccole said softly, looking long into Tobie's eyes.

Tobie braided her arms behind her back and pondered. There were five or ten seconds of silence.

"Okay," Tobie said.

Niccole looked mystified.

"Okay, I'll go."

"That's good," Niccole said quietly. "If you want, you could take the sample in to the Lambert County hospital. That way no one at the clinic in Sand Ridge would know the result."

"Really?"

"Uh-huh."

"I'll tell my dad that. He was really upset last night. Are you and him in cahoots? I mean, did he tell you to come here and talk to me?"

"He loves you a lot."

"That means he did."

Niccole nodded and smiled.

Again Tobie's face shone with amazement that Niccole was so up-front.

"There's nothing more important to your dad than you."

"I know. But sometimes it helps to talk to a woman."

"That's true. Anytime you want to talk to me, just call."

Niccole pulled a business card out of her handbag. Tobie read it carefully and admiringly.

"Will you?"

"I will," Tobie said, and smiled, the most beautiful, innocent girl smile.

"In karate, do you break phone books with your hand?" she asked.

"I dunno, but I guess we can find out."

CHAPTER THIRTY

The school board usually met in a small room at the high school, but tonight the crowd was expected to be so big that the magnificent, hundred-year-old, brick city hall, which was not used even for city council meetings because of heating costs, had been warmed up for the occasion.

The room was three-quarters full ten minutes before the scheduled start of the meeting. A murmuring rolled around the room the way a millipede's feet coalesce and flow along the length of its body.

Matt had thought he would know by now whether Tobie was pregnant, but the possibility was still hanging over him. Both Niccole and Tobie had recounted their versions of how Tobie'd agreed to go take the test tomorrow. He was relieved, but afraid he couldn't focus on the meeting.

He had to. When he walked into the room, a hush seemed to follow him like a shadow. People were extremely aware that he was likely to be the focus of the meeting.

"Saw ya on TV," said one man, who clapped him on the shoulder.

He didn't say he approved, Matt noted. Matt spotted Harper across the room. He decided to avoid him and sit next to somebody he didn't know well, so he could keep a clear brain and assess the political flow unimpeded. He picked a place about halfway back on the far side of the room next to a man he had seen on the streets but didn't know. The man nodded as Matt seated himself.

The room filled up fast; then people began stuffing themselves into corners and sitting in the aisles. The recessed ceiling lights shone down and made giant polka dots on the audience. Matt was directly under one, the heat pulsing over him. A technician uncoiled cords from the table mikes along one wall and out the door to a loudspeaker system in the hall.

Immediately opposite him on the right side of the room, Matt noted, there was a conglomeration of Keep-the-School-Openers, including Arnie Beachley, and next to him Sam Hersey, Hector Pickett, and the troupe that had visited Matt in his office before Christmas. None of the parents of the dead girls were there. A meeting could do nothing for them; their agony was permanent.

On the outer edge of Arnie's group was a small man with dark, wavy hair who looked Eastern European. Could that be a member of the Sobo family? Matt bet all the school's teachers were present, as were a fair number of other employees, including Yale Kaltmann, who stood with his arms folded at the rear of the room near the door into the hall. He seemed detached, his eyes shifting over the crowd. Matt wondered if Yale was still worried about his job should the school remain shut.

Dorothy Mattingly thumped the gavel on its block of wood. The crowd noise swelled, and then a loud "S-h-h-h-h" snaked around the room and out into the hallway. She stood on the dais looming over the crowd, pounding them into an enormous silence. It was the only pure silence of the evening.

"We will begin." She spoke like someone who could stifle a mutiny. Matt felt satisfied she could control the situation.

"First, there will be public discussion, limited to two hours. Following the public session, the school board will adjourn to an adjacent room and vote on the proposition before it that the junior high school be reopened. So that every point of view can be heard in the public session, each person may talk for only three minutes."

She held up a small brass clock.

"This timer will chime when the three minutes are up. I'll restart it when a new person begins to speak."

Hector Pickett had already attached himself to the far right microphone. He thumped it twice, and said, "Testing, testing. Madam Chairman, I'd like to talk about Mr. Tom Harper and the fact that Matt Chays refuses—"

"Wait!" Miss Mattingly, who was still standing, boomed down on him like a Wagnerian opera singer. He stopped cold. "I haven't yet finished," she said.

At first he stood there with his hip petulantly aslant, but when Sam Hersey leaned over and told him something, Pickett straightened up and stood more respectfully.

"I have a statement I want to read about the facts in this case."

TV klieg lights flashed on, causing the audience to shift and murmur. Miss Mattingly carried on like a seasoned news anchorwoman.

"We, your school board, have, to the best of our ability, determined that at least six girls have become pregnant at Sand Ridge Junior High. In each case, there is no rational explanation for the pregnancy, each girl claiming never to have had relations with a male. We therefore have called this meeting to air what has become a major public problem and one that we all want to solve as quickly as we can. This evening the board will consider a proposal to reopen Sand Ridge Junior High immediately. We're seeking public comment on this proposed action."

Orville was waving his hand in a broad arc at the back of the room, where he towered over everyone else.

"Oh, yes," Miss Mattingly added, her eye catching Orville's red face and alarmed arm, "we claim there is no rational explanation for the pregnancies. There are some, however, who have a religious explanation."

Orville lowered his hand and appeared reasonably content. He knew he would never convince the town at large of his revelation, since prophets were always persecuted.

When he looked back at Orville, Matt spotted Niccole squeezing her way into the room. He felt a surge inside him, warm and pleasant as a blush.

"And now we will begin," Miss Mattingly said imperiously.

"TV! TV! Turn off the TV cameras!"

The voice shouted from the left side. Matt didn't know the man. The school board had to allow the press, Miss Mattingly said, because this was a public meeting.

Finally, Hector Pickett and his Greek chorus of supporters could begin. His harangue was almost identical to the tirade by Sam Hersey in Matt's office. The problem of promiscuity, he said, was rooted in the education that children received in a secular humanist environment.

In a well-orchestrated tirade, punctuated by clapping and much body-shifting in creaking chairs from his backers, Pickett ran through his litany against Harper and Darwin. He was launched well into the middle of his speech when the melodic chimes from Dorothy Mattingly's timer went off. Pickett talked faster and louder, rushing to some end he had in mind, but he got lost on the way when people in the lines behind the microphones shouted, "Time, time!"

Thank God for the timer, Matt thought. When Pickett sat down to great applause from the right of the room, his buddies, now apparently including Arnie Beachley, began stamping their shoes on the wooden floor, setting chairs around them to vibrating. "Harper, Harper, Harper," they chanted.

Dorothy Mattingly raised her beringed right hand and a tittering hush fell over the room.

"For the sake of rebuttal, I think we should allow Tom Harper to put his case, if he would like."

Tom rose calmly from his chair and slowly wended his way to the microphone on the left, opposite the fundamentalist fire-breathers. With great poise, he stood before his attackers. He was dashing and foreign to most of the audience, his slight Boston accent in contrast to the broad Ohio drawl that often verged on Appalachian Mountain twang. After meticulously recounting how his science lab at school had been vandalized and how his MG had been poured full of concrete, he said, "Go and take a look at it. It's in the parking lot at my house.

"Maybe you'd like to mount it on a pedestal as a statue to vigilantism and put it in the town square. I'll leave it for you. Since it appears half the town is crying for my resignation, claiming that teaching the state curriculum could impregnate girls, I will oblige. Ask yourself after I'm gone, 'Did Tom Harper's going solve the problem?' Ask yourself, 'Do we want censorship in our schools?' I regret leaving."

He ended on a quiet note, the audience hanging on his words. A half second after he finished, Pickett and Leon and Storm Jarvis and others rose to their feet, cheering and poking their fists into the air.

Matt hadn't thought Harper would do anything like this. After it was all over, he would invite him back to teach—if he would want to return. Harper caught his eye on the way back to his seat, and Matt nodded, approving Harper's comportment, not his resignation.

Matt didn't notice exactly how the next speaker, a woman with ratted hair and rhinestones on her glasses frames, slid into yet another topic not directly related to the issue at hand: abortion.

If any of the speakers following her had intended to talk of something else, by the time they reached the microphone they too ended up ranting and raving either for or against abortion.

"You're killing people. A newly fertilized egg is as much a person as a teenager."

"Where do you draw the line when a person comes into being?"

"Abstinence before marriage and fidelity in marriage, that's the solution to our problem," said a man who claimed he had the biggest family in town and had lived in Sand Ridge for fifty-seven years.

Finally, a man who didn't know what to do with his hands, who put them in his pockets and rattled his money and keys, said, "Those babies have no father, y'know what I mean? They have no father. They don't know who it is, d'ya know what I mean? That means they don't have any identity. They're illegitimate. We gotta find out who the father or fathers is, that's what."

Someone shouted from the hallway: "Pass out contraceptives. Give the girls contraceptives."

By now the pitch of emotion in the room was at fever level. The last outbreak upset just about everybody: girls' parents, boys' parents, fundamentalists—but not the principal. Matt thought it was the most sensible thing he'd heard all evening.

Everyone was sweating. There were no windows to open, since they had been permanently fastened shut to preserve the historical facade of the building. Matt noticed that Niccole had rolled her hair off her neck onto the top of her head.

The short, dark man stood passively before the microphone. He began slowly in heavily accented English.

"I know America is nation of laws. My niece is Katie Sobo."

He clearly couldn't bring himself to say that she was one of the mysteriously pregnant girls, leaving it for people to know or surmise.

"We are very close family. When someone is hurt, we get together, we teamwork, is that how you say it? Yes, we teamwork together. We are talking to lawyers. We might suit the school. We don't want to say yes yet, but we're thinking on it."

He turned around and went back to his seat. The audience had gradually become very sober, struggling to understand his accented words. A lawsuit was a serious thing in Sand Ridge.

"If someone sues the school, that means the taxpayers will have to pay if the plaintiff or plaintiffs win," said Dorothy Mattingly, whose late father, everybody knew, had been a lawyer. "I would like to suggest that we try to wrap up these proceedings with a statement from the school's principal, Matthew Chays, who, as most of you know, believes we should close Sand Ridge Junior High," she added.

Matt sat for a moment before rising, wondering what to say. On his way to the podium, he could think only of Tobie.

"Our children are having children, and we can't explain it," Matt began. "Some of our children are dying." An awful hush fell over the room. "Last fall when all this started, we didn't realize at first that there seemed to be a pattern. We haven't been able to get any strong clue as to the perpetrators of these terrible events that are tearing our town apart.

"I have done several things and would like to list them. I've contracted an outside legal expert to interview the girls involved. I have been in constant touch with the state's

Department of Education, seeking their advice. As most of you know, superintendents decide when to close schools. I'm having to operate alone because Hilda Barnes resigned last month, so I report to the state regularly. I have arranged for an outside doctor who will come in and consult with our school nurse, Lorna Ross, on the matter.

"As you can see, what we've been able to do has been feeble. We have become very frustrated. Since so many people feel that this is all somehow happening at the school, I have advocated keeping the school closed."

Arnie Beachley started cracking his knuckles. He was sitting a row away from where Matt was standing. He popped them again and again, like castanets.

"Mr. Sobo's statement that he might sue gives you some idea of the legal implications for all of us, the taxpayers. Some people have suggested that we give lie detector tests. But I ask, 'To whom?' To random boys, to girls, to teachers? Isn't there a question of invasion of privacy? I don't think lie detector tests would help.

"I do have some recommendations. If the board votes to open the school, I would suggest that we consider busing the girls to other schools in the area."

A murmur went round the room.

"Or maybe you want to think of having mothers serve as monitors in the school. I'm not real sure what they'd monitor, but maybe their presence would have a dampening effect on the perpetrators."

An even louder murmur rolled all around him. He looked at Arnie, who was holding what chin he had in his palm. The mayor's eyes were blazing, heated by the boiling fury within. Just waiting to spill over, Matt figured.

"There's a teacher at our school who over a short period of time confiscated illicit and pornographic magazines from boys in his classes. He had each boy sign his name to the magazine before he took it. There were a surprising number of boys involved. I am therefore exploring the possibility of a ring of boys or a gang who somehow are doing this. It's not a strong lead, but it's the only one I've got."

Arnie leaped out of his seat, shaking with rage.

"You just want to keep the school closed because you have a girl!"

He worked his arms furiously for a moment, then sat down.

"Someone else could just as easily say that you want it open because you have sons," Matt said calmly. "I think we shouldn't go accusing each other. It will not solve the problem.

"I assure you here, before all of you, that if the board votes to keep the school open, my daughter Tobie will attend classes."

A hum of talk, approving his statement, swept the room.

"The main issue is not whether the school is open or shut; the goal must be to find the contemptible person or persons who are doing this. However, I believe that the school should be kept closed until we find the criminal. The way this is tearing our town apart is devastating. We're all living in terror that it will happen to a daughter, a friend next.

"What difference if a child should miss a semester of school? This is minor compared to a child having her life ruined. Life is more important than a mere semester of school."

As Matt turned to return to his seat, Arnie jumped up again and reached for the mike, snatching it from the podium hook.

"Semester!" he screamed. "A semester is a long time in the life of a kid. It determines their future. You can't punish everyone for the carelessness of a few girls!"

Miss Mattingly was pounding her gavel to no avail. The room raged out of control, with men and women standing up shouting at each other. Society seemed to have come completely unglued.

Someone began passing the microphone around, because the next thing Matt heard, as he lowered himself into his seat, was a woman saying: "I heard last week there was a man in town who was buying babies. Is that true?"

Noise and chaos. A man grabbed the mike and said, "We should live by the Ten Commandments, then we wouldn't have this problem. Every minute somewhere in the world there is someone breaking the Ten Commandments. That's what's wrong with our world." Miss Mattingly kept pounding, calling, "Order," into the din. Another man: "Bottom barrel people, that's the kind that would do this. Anytime a person uses kids to their own ends, that's Communism."

"You can't go behind parents' backs and have contraceptives," shouted a woman. "That promotes lust and looseness."

"More than in the heart," said a man.

"What's more than in the heart?" the woman asked.

"Lust."

"AIDS, that's the real problem, when are we going to deal wi—"

Someone sitting next to that speaker pulled him down into his seat. Dorothy Mattingly, who'd been pounding the gavel for minutes, whispered to the board member next to her, who passed a message on down the table. People stranded in the hallway were jumping up and down like pogo sticks and leaning around each other in efforts to see what was going on in the room.

Finally, a technician had the presence of mind to turn off the audience microphones. After they went dead, Dorothy hammered the crowd almost to quiet. The meeting had gone on for two and a half hours already.

Miss Mattingly announced that the board would adjourn to consult in executive session and would then return to vote in compliance with the "sunshine" laws. As the five board members scraped their chairs back from the table and disappeared into a back room, the crowd erupted into a loud buzz. The man next to Matt turned to him and muttered, "Good speech," but there was not much enthusiasm in his voice. Some people stood and stretched.

The air in the room was stifling. The smalls of men's backs were wet with sweat. People were mopping beads of perspiration off their foreheads. Matt's eyelids were tired, lead-heavy. He wanted to talk to Niccole, but they had agreed on the phone earlier in the day not to speak to each other at the meeting.

He didn't feel much sympathy for his position among the crowd. Shit, where were the parents of the girls? Too humiliated or too scared to come out? Everybody sat there, awaiting the board's return, the crowd growing louder and more upset.

When the board members emerged after a half hour's deliberation, the room fell quiet, pulsing with heat. Close the school, close the school, Matt thought over and over, as if to hex the board. He could almost hear Dorothy saying, "The school will stay closed," but that was an aural mirage.

Slowly each member cast his or her vote, the outcome hanging to the last: the vote was three to two to reopen the school.

Matt sat up straighter. His heart sank. He stood up and said in a low, steady voice, "Tomorrow morning the school will be open."

The crowd went wild, or at least it seemed that way to Matt. As he moved to the door, people cleared a path for him. After he had held Niccole's eyes with his for a moment, and just before he exited, he glanced over at the Picket crowd. Arnie's face was as rosy as a rooster's wattles, flushed with excitement.

Yale Kaltmann was standing there. Squeeze, the hulkman, spotted Yale as he looked around for another person to celebrate with. He must've said, "Gimme five," or maybe it was an instinctive reaction for them, because the two men clapped hands in the sportsmen's winning gesture. Yale looked abashed but pleased. Then Squeeze gave a jubilant whoop and patted Yale on the bottom, the way football jocks approve a victory. Male bonding, Matt thought.

CHAPTER THIRTY-ONE

Tobie strapped herself into the car for the drive to the hospital. She was so listless and droopy that Matt imagined she couldn't sit upright without the seat belt holding her up.

She gingerly set her backpack on the floor, making sure the bottle inside was upright, wedging it between her feet to hold it steady. They didn't talk. There was no point in asking her how she felt; he knew she felt lousy. Her whole future must seem to her to be hanging in the balance. Her thighs were so narrow now that the seat looked huge in comparison. He just wanted to see her eat heartily again.

She was ushered from the waiting room through the door into a technician's office where she handed over the bottle, withdrawing it reluctantly from the bag. Matt had been allowed to go with her because she was under fourteen. Then they were both told they'd have to sit in the waiting room until the test results were ready.

The room was crowded with females of various ages and three or four children with their mothers. Matt was the only man. The round-backed chairs with low arms were arranged shoulder-to-shoulder around the perimeter of the room. Tobie picked a chair and flopped into it, kicking her empty backpack as she dangled it down. Matt sat next to her, placing his arm around her. She shucked him off, obviously feeling isolated and vulnerable. She wouldn't look at him.

He couldn't say anything to her. Everybody in the room would hear him. The room was gloomy; its dirty, olive, cut-nylon carpet was as dark as the walnut paneling. A fluorescent light bulb ran across the ceiling, the bluish light making people look anemic. A plastic ficus with dusty joints "grew" to his right next to a table with magazines on it.

An enormously pregnant woman entered the waiting room, found a chair, groaned, and held her back as she lowered herself heavily onto the seat.

"Twins," she said to no one in particular.

Murmurs of sympathy ran around the room.

Matt noticed Tobie looking at a large poster on the wall at the end of the room, a picture of a pretty young girl who was very pregnant and not looking too happy about it. The print said: "Girls have to be smarter than boys—they're the ones who get pregnant." Then Tobie stared away, the kind of stare that's not bored but seeks refuge in stillness.

Matt perused the magazines on the table for the same reason he read cereal boxes—because they were there. Interspersed with *Cleveland Life* and several news-magazines were a couple of pamphlets called "The Wet Set," about baby care, and two magazines called *Mom-to-Be*. Or not to be, he prayed. God, if he only knew how to pray, really, so it worked. How could God want a girl like Tobie to be served with misery? Please, God, he begged.

He thought of the night Tobie was born. The lobby in the hospital in San Francisco had been nothing like this. When Matt first held his daughter, he had been terrified that he would drop her. She was beautiful. She really was. Even then she was scrawny. Scrawny and beautiful.

He turned to look at her now. Tobie felt him through her stare and slowly pulled into focus on him. She pressed her lips together and raised her eyebrows, signaling frustration at the waiting. At that moment, a nurse emerged and called her name. Tobie jumped, and Matt put his hand on her shoulder for reassurance.

The nurse in the small office was filling out forms as Matt and Tobie entered. She looked up and smiled, then glanced back down to locate the name.

"Tobie," she said.

Tobie's hands were twisting in each other.

"According to our tests—" The phone rang. The nurse lifted her index finger in a motion of waiting.

Tobie gasped, and Matt put his arm around her shoulder. Her eyes stayed glued on the nurse's face. She barely felt her father's touch.

"Can you hold on?" the nurse said to the phone, pushed the "hold" button, and placed the receiver on the desk. "According to our tests," she began again, "you are not pregnant."

Tobie's breath rushed out in great relief. Slowly a tear squeezed onto her right cheek. She turned to her father. She wanted him to hug her. She flung her arms around him and held on.

"It's okay, it's okay," he murmured.

"Pretty rad, huh?" she said, smiling the most impish smile.

Then her face sobered and was tinged with awe at her reprieve from a horrible fate. At the same instant, they both realized the nurse was watching them.

"Now, Tobie, I'm glad you're happy with this outcome." She held out a small booklet to Tobie.

"I would be happy to discuss with you—with or without your father—the question of contraceptives."

Matt was shocked. Tobie was so ecstatic, though, that he figured what the nurse said had scarcely registered.

"She's not interested," he said.

"Tobie, is that right?"

"I guess so," she said. "Daddy, guess what?"

"What?"

"I'm hungry!"

"There's only one cure for that."

The nurse studied them carefully. Matt noticed that her face suddenly changed; a look of recognition came into her eyes.

"Aren't you the principal? Yes, that principal over at Sand Ridge? I saw you on TV."

As the implications sank in, she looked at Tobie.

"Oh, I see," she said. "Well, I am very happy for you, for us all."

"Let's go." Tobie whipped her backpack over her right shoulder.

Matt followed her out, nodding good-bye to the nurse and thanking her.

Tobie insisted that they stop at the first hamburger joint they saw. She ate a giant burger with "the works" and a large chocolate milk shake. Her chocolate mustache was wonderful to Matt. She laughed and licked it off. She exaggerated the chattering of her teeth.

"Only nuts have milk shakes in the middle of winter," Matt teased her.

Intricate layers of ice had built up on the outside of the restaurant window. The lacy frost looked like it had been deposited over time, like geological encrustations of the earth. Tobie breathed on the window, fogging it over, and then with a spare straw she wrote "Yippee" in the condensation.

As she finished writing the word, her face went still. The expression in her eyes was complex. As if she were suddenly an adult. Oh, he didn't want her to grow up.

"You okay?" he asked.

She nodded.

"It was so awful," she whispered.

"I know," he replied, stroking his hand once over her hair.

"If I'd been pregnant, would you have let me have an abortion if I wanted?"

Matt sighed deeply.

"It would have been hard," he said. "In the end, I probably would allow whatever you wanted. I mean, it is your body, and one person, even a father, shouldn't control another."

Her eyes glowed as she watched him.

"Verity," she suddenly said, as if it were a normal topic of conversation. "Maybe I can visit Verity. She must be big. But not as big as that woman with twins. I could tell her."

"I don't know that that would be such a good idea," Matt said.

"Why not?"

"Well, think about it. If you were Verity and pregnant, would you want someone coming to you and telling you that they thought they were pregnant and were happy to find they weren't?"

"Oh."

"It would be fine to visit her, I mean, I think that's a fine idea, but you have to think of her feelings."

"I guess I'm just too happy."

She was floating. Life was a lark again. God, how Matt loved her, and how he couldn't bear to see anything bad happen to her. She plunked a handful of free lollipops into her backpack and stuck one in her mouth.

He drove straight to the junior high and parked. At the school door, she said, "Daddy, I'm so happy."

It was difficult to understand all the words with her sucker in her mouth, and he laughed.

Several hours later, right before lunch, Tobie walked into Audrey's office to check if her dad was in. When Audrey said he was, Tobie knocked jauntily on his closed door to the rhythm of "Shave and a haircut, two bits." She felt like she was going to explode with the news and put her hand over her mouth to keep it in.

The worst part of thinking she was pregnant for the last month had been that she was letting down her dad. She wasn't glued to him, as she used to be when she was a little girl. Back then she used to follow him around when he gardened and couldn't bear to be in bed in the morning after he got up because she might miss something. She wasn't like that anymore, but she did like to please him. He was better than most dads. He was handsome. He was adventurous, or at least he used to be. Now he had to restrict himself for her sake, until she was grown up.

He smiled when she stuck her head around the door. She flitted across the room toward him. She usually felt awkward when she came to see him in his office. Being the principal's daughter was a real pain sometimes, and she didn't like to make it worse by visiting him publicly. She just wanted to be normal, like the other kids.

"Guess what?"

"Can't possibly."

She cupped her hand around her mouth and leaned over to whisper in his ear.

"My period came."

"That's terrific." He squeezed her, his face radiant. "You were just uptight."

"Whaddaya mean?" she asked, as he fondly put a lock of her hair behind her ear.

"Our bodies are very sensitive machines. If we're tense, our functions are affected. That must've been what happened to you. Your body was just responding to tension signals in your brain."

She beamed, leaning back against his strong hold and placing her hand on the silky hair of his forearms. His hair used to be sort of alarming to her. But now that she'd grown up, she liked it.

"I expect you to eat lunch like a horse," he said.

She giggled.

"Like a famished girl, then."

She turned and dashed to the door, wheeling and waving and grinning as if she'd never stop.

CHAPTER THIRTY-TWO

Thomas Holden Harper, aged twenty-seven, you've come to a pretty pass, he thought. Sounded like something his father would say: pretty pass.

Harper sat with his feet propped on the corner of his desk in his lab. He was wearing running shoes and faded jeans, real faded jeans, not pre-faded jeans. No point in dressing up today. He had a low-level headache smack between his eyeballs. Came from last night's dope.

He'd quit his job yesterday and didn't know where the next one was coming from. He was packing up his stuff, clearing out his desk, plopping belongings into the two cardboard boxes on the floor. He'd have to think what to do about a lab equipment inventory. Ever since the Christian vigilantes had smashed up his plastic organ model and numerous bottles and glasses, he hadn't had an accurate count of test tubes and the like. It wasn't his problem anymore, but he'd need a good recommendation for his next job.

Maybe his resignation would make Matt's plight a little easier. Besides, he could go back to Boston and see Sarah, see if he wanted to marry her. If this madness, these idiot pregnancies were resolved, maybe he'd come back to Sand Ridge. That's what Matt had suggested when he'd walked over to see him last evening after the school board meeting. But he didn't feel very good about this town that had just run him out.

Harper had been sitting on his dilapidated sofa, smoking his first joint of the year, when Matt arrived. Sarah's picture sat on a shelf on the wall right above the sofa. Harper'd told Matt about Sarah before. But not much.

"Maybe I'll bring her," Harper said, nodding at the photo.

"Great. Small towns are tough if you're single," Matt said.

Harper stroked his goatee with his free hand. "Maybe she'll make me acceptable around here. How's yours?"

Their eyes met, and although they'd never discussed Niccole, Matt said, "Yup, you guessed. She's like . . . I don't know what . . . like . . . I give up. The problem is, she's into a career and hanging loose. But maybe that's what I want to do, too, hang loose."

"I doubt it."

"Me, too."

"Sarah does belly dancing. Did I ever tell you that?"

Matt shook his head.

"Not for money in her G-string or anything like that. She goes to a class for exercise. In fact, I'm the only man who's seen her do it. She does it like a sweet vamp, if there can be such a thing."

He took another drag.

"She's got the daintiest navel. An outie."

Matt laughed, and Harper grinned.

"So, bring her back," Matt said.

"You won't get to see her navel."

"Hey," Matt drawled, putting up both his hands in protest at the suggestion.

Harper felt sad about leaving Matt. It wasn't often that you ran into someone who was totally sympatico, the human equivalent of his dead MGA. He'd noticed the other day that someone had tried to scratch out the R.I.P. he'd etched in the concrete. He sure wasn't going to pay to move the car. He'd taken out the engine and sold it. The town could take care of the rest. He'd bought a new hatchback, which he'd drive to Boston in about a week.

As the bells rang, ending the morning's second class period, the frantic clamor of students' feet seeped into the lab. Harper had taped a sign on the closed lab door instructing all science students to report to study hall until further notice. He felt a pang of nostalgia for the bustle and patter of the kids. It was all around him, but he was already gone.

The halls quieted. He opened the door and stuck his head out. Empty. He hadn't been here long, but damn, he'd gotten to like these kids and this place. Except for a few jerks like Pickett and his gang. The doors were all closed as he walked down the hall. The scooching of chairs and general sounds of settling in were in the background. He started down the stairs. Down half a level, a ladder stood on the landing beneath a light fixture on the wall. Nobody was near it. Kaltmann must've left it there. It reminded Harper of the day in December when Penny had fallen down the stairs. If he remembered correctly, she'd fallen from the other side. It seemed so unfair she should've died. Matt had told him about the coroner's report. About two unusual bruise lines across her leg, three or four inches apart.

He stood next to the ladder. It was a "commercial duty stepladder," the faded label said, its stringers made of thick aluminum I beams, about four inches wide. He moved closer to the ladder, held up his hand to measure across the closest beam.

Suddenly he was aware that Yale had come up behind him, was watching. Harper turned. Yale's face was flushed and twisted.

"Oh, hi," Harper said.

Yale grunted.

"I was thinking about Penny. This was where she fell, wasn't it? You were there?"

"From the other side," Yale said, waving his arm: flash of blue tattoo.

"You had your ladder here then, too?"

"These bulbs burn out all the time."

Yale's eyes were glued to Harper's face.

"You know about the bruises on Penny's leg?"

"No, what bruises?"

Funny, Harper thought he specifically remembered Matt saying he'd queried Yale about it.

"She didn't fall over your ladder, did she?"

"Nope. I don't know about any bruises."

Yale's hooded eyes seemed to Harper to glaze over. Strange guy, really strange; maybe psycho-something-or-other. Harper measured him with his eyes. About his height, but twenty pounds heavier. Looked solid, even though he was probably fifteen years older than Harper.

"That was awful, that day."

"Yeah."

They stared at each other.

"Well," said Harper, suddenly wanting to get away, "I think you ought to write to the light bulb companies and get them to make longer-life bulbs. I think they can probably invent bulbs that never wear out, just like I think they can probably manufacture ladies' nylons that never run."

"They've got long-life bulbs. But the school would rather pay me to climb this ladder than pay for expensive bulbs." Yale moved his ladder to the proper place for reaching the sconce. He pulled a bulb from his overalls pocket and deliberately climbed up as Harper went on down the stairs.

Harper crossed the landing and descended on the opposite side, where Penny had lain. Near the bottom, he glanced back. Yale was crossing the landing to go back upstairs. He walked bowlegged, as if his genitals were gigantic, Harper thought.

Harper turned and strolled to the end of the hall and gazed out the window across the playing fields. His nostalgia returned, interwoven with his puzzling over the twin bruises. The clouds were piling up dark over the football field. A big storm was predicted, one of those that dumped tons of white snow like soapsuds and blotted out the earth. He'd have to make sure the weather was good when he took off for Boston. He turned from the window and started back down the hall.

To his right, with his peripheral vision, he noticed that the door on a student's locker was ajar. He walked into the alcove and, as he shut it, Lorna Ross leaned out the door to her reception room.

Surprised that someone was there, she started and mumbled hello. She was a cowed person, Harper thought. Her shoulders slumped like the proverbial postman's shoulders.

Aspirin. She undoubtedly had a bottle of aspirin. She answered yes to his query, and Harper followed her through the reception room into her office. Just through the second door, she turned toward him and hesitated.

"I'm sorry you're leaving," she said.

"Me, too."

She seemed intimidated that she'd spoken, but sincere.

"I'm sure you didn't have anything to do with the girls."

It was an odd thing for her to say.

"You never know," he joked.

She looked panicked, twitchy like a rabbit. She smoothed her uniform over her bosom. Turning, she opened a white enameled cabinet near the sink. Harper waited by the door, leaning on the jamb casually. On her desk, to his right, were stacks of children's charts. His eye caught sight of a red silk carnation stuck in an Erlenmeyer flask like the ones from the lab. Clever vase. As the metal door of the cabinet swung open, Harper spotted four or five glass jars that looked like ones from his lab.

"Where'd you get those?"

Lorna turned to see where he was looking.

"Oh, uh . . ."

She grabbed the bottle of aspirin and shut the door.

"They look exactly like my lab jars, with the frosty patch where you can write on them."

"Mr. Kaltmann gave them to me. He's . . . he's a scientist. He buys them . . . I guess."

Lorna was so nervous that the tablets were rattling in the plastic bottle. She was pale. Harper reached out to help her take the lid off the bottle. He tipped it, shook three pills into his left palm, recapped the bottle, and handed it back.

"Thanks," he said, dipping his head a little and trying to look into her eyes, which she kept lowered. "I'll remember this," he said lightly, and turned to leave.

As he spun out the reception room door, Yale brushed past him; no eye contact, no acknowledgment of his existence. He smelled faintly of lubricating grease. Harper turned into the hall. The door to Lorna's inner office slammed shut, but he heard Yale's voice.

"What did he want?" Yale's attempt to soften his voice made it come out hissing but clear.

Harper couldn't hear Lorna's answer. He walked on down the hall, going slower and slower. He stopped at the water fountain, gulped some water, and swallowed the aspirin. If the door was still shut, he could go back and listen. He pivoted and moved silently back.

"I can't wait any longer."

Yale's harsh voice.

"I don't want to. Not her."

Lorna sounded panicked, or in pain.

"I don't care whether you want to or not."

"Mr. Chays will find out."

"He hasn't yet and he won't. Let me take care of that. I want it done soon. I'll bring you a new jar tomorrow."

Harper's body flooded with adrenaline. He'd better split fast. He couldn't tell when Yale might exit. He whirled out the door, moving slowly and quietly at first, then broke into a sprint. Had to get out of sight if Yale came out into the hall. His heart was pumping. His mind was thundering: "Chays will find out," "new jar tomorrow." Was his imagination running away with him? If this was evidence, it was only circumstantial and intuitive.

He glanced back over his shoulder. No one yet. Matt's office coming up. He dodged around the door and came to a halt, breathing hard. Audrey looked up, unflappable, from her desk. She must have seen every possible crisis come through that door. He panted as she smiled.

"Matt here?"

"He won't be back till two o'clock."

Harper whipped his wrist up. Twelve-oh-five.

"Guess I'll catch him later, then."

It was good that Lorna was so dense, Yale thought. He'd just gotten her to tell him that Harper had noticed the jars in her cabinet, that he'd even noted that they were like the ones in the lab. Of course, Lorna had tried to cover up by explaining to Harper that Yale bought the jars. That was unusually quick thinking on her part, especially given how dense she was. Of course, she was wrong: he'd stolen them, one by one, from Harper's lab supplies.

Maybe Harper hadn't guessed anything, but Yale was increasingly sure that he couldn't chance it. Something had to be done. Be cool, he told himself. Be flexible. Be creative. As he lectured himself to calmness, he looked out Lorna's window.

Harper was getting into his car in the parking lot. A little electric-blue hatchback. Yale'd have to act fast.

"You heard what I said earlier. And I want it done as soon as possible. I've got to go now. Got to go to the lumberyard and buy some boards for a new kitchen table."

He said the latter very deliberately, although his heart was racing: he knew he had to follow Harper fast. But he wanted Lorna to hear the lumberyard bit, so she'd vouch for his alibi later, if need be.

She sat limply by the table. He slowly walked over to her door. Once he'd shut the door behind him, he began to run. He turned left, ran out the end hall door and along the front of the building, down through the basement door on the side. He raced into his office, grabbed his heavy coat, and sprinted to the back basement door that opened onto the parking lot.

Harper was just turning out of the parking lot, going north, when Yale emerged.

Yale had never gotten to his van faster and started it more smoothly than he did now. When he turned north, he spotted Harper up ahead—good thing the hatchback was such a bright color. Yale made himself breathe deeply four times. Calm. Cool. His life depended on it. Of that he was suddenly sure.

Harper knew too much. Yale didn't know exactly what he'd figured out. But, like himself, Harper was a scientist. That meant he knew how to reason, and his visit to Lorna's office couldn't have been a coincidence.

Yale followed at a judicious distance for a mile or so, and it became clear that Harper was going to the quarry area. The traffic thinned out as they approached one of the quarry turnoffs, and Yale dropped back even farther so Harper wouldn't notice the van behind him.

Harper turned in through the fence around one of the

huge pits, into the parking lot. Yale drove on past, slowed the van, and watched Harper's car through a patch of trees. Harper parked near the derrick at the edge of the pit. He got out and walked across the parking lot to a shack on the west side.

Yale backed up his van, hid it on a side road in the woods, and pulled some winter gloves out of the pile of equipment in the back of the van. He climbed out and took the short trek through the woods. On the way, he watched the frozen ground carefully, not only to avoid a misstep. He bent over several times to pull up sandstone rocks. Finally he found one shaped like a brick, with sharp edges. He brushed off the snow and dirt and carried it along in his left hand.

Yale slipped into the derrick shelter near Harper's car. He pulled the parka's hood over his head. Harper'd have to come back to his car. What the hell could he be doing in that shack? Somebody'd have to be a nut to live there.

Harper figured that the two hours before Matt returned to his office would give him time to drive out to the quarry and say good-bye to Archibald. Harper always called him Mr. Archibald. He had no idea whether that was his first name or his last, or if he had any other.

Archibald lived in a shack beside one of the parking lots near the North Ohio Building-Stone Factory. The company paid him a pittance to act as a guard, and they let him live in the old workers' warm-up shack. Archibald would probably have lived there whether he was paid or not.

Harper had gotten to know him when he came out to the quarries collecting water samples for his classes. He always returned his water samples to where he'd collected them, out of respect for the environment. He'd crossed paths with Archibald fairly often. Occasionally the old man—he was one of those men whose age was impossible to tell—saved samples or natural oddities or animals for Harper. The late, great, chopped-up garter snake had been an Archibald gift. Archibald lived in his own world here, oblivious to the town's and the world's news, since he only read newspapers when they strayed his way. He was more interested in his immediate surroundings and in his bourbon.

Harper had dug an old bird whistle out of his desk to take to Archibald as a parting gift. He felt in his pocket for the whistle as he crossed the parking lot, running his thumb over its smooth, carved belly. When he came back next fall—if he did—he'd take his kids out to the quarries for a field trip. It'd make a great hands-on geology lesson. He could tell them about the sand laid down millions of years ago, how it turned into boulders with such a high silica content that it was used in steel furnaces: stone without fractures, harder than bricks. He wouldn't take them to this particular pit, because Evie had died here, but there were lots of others.

Harper knocked on Archibald's wooden door. The old guy had patched the shack incrementally, with aluminum siding on the north and with slate and asphalt shingles on the roof. For most people it still would have been cold, but wearing a few sweaters and with the heater running, Archibald never seemed to notice the temperature.

Harper pounded harder. Still no answer. A radio inside was blaring out country and western music. He turned the doorknob and swung the door open. He stepped inside quickly to keep the warm air in. The place was heated by a gas stove attached to a propane canister. The old man had insulated the weather end of the shack with fiberglass strips he'd found thrown away on a building site. He'd pasted magazine pages over the walls, mostly slick paper pin-up nudes, and some mountain scenery.

Archibald lay on his bed. When the gust of arctic air whipped in with Harper, the old guy sat up.

"Whuh?" he said.

"It's only me, Harper."

"Harp," Archibald said, grinning.

"Hey, old buddy, how are you?" Harper asked, patting him on the shoulder.

"I mus' apol'gize," Archibald said, slurring his words.

"A bit much to drink, eh?"

"Yeah, I don't do it in the summer, y'know. But it helps the blood in winter. 'S gonna snow a whole shitload this afternoon."

"Yeah, I heard. I've just come to say good-bye."

"G'bye? You can't leave. Jus' like that."

"I'll probably be back. I quit my job. Trouble with some Christians."

"Christians, bah," Archibald said with a put-down hand gesture. "They don' know what it means, most of 'em."

"They don't like the way I teach."

"They don' know nothin'. You're a fine teacher. That book you gave me, over there, on birds, I'm readin' it. Last Saturday I found me two screech owls. I looked 'em up in there."

Archibald's relative lucidity suddenly dissolved.

"I'm sorry," he said as he slumped sweetly as a baby back onto the bed.

Harper unfolded a blanket at the foot of the bed and pulled it over him. He looked around for something to write on. A partially used school exercise book lay on the table. Harper pulled out a page and wrote, in case Archibald forgot their conversation: "Quit my job. May be back in fall. Bird whistle is for cardinals." He signed the note "Harp."

He set the whistle on the page, gazed again fondly at his friend, then left, making sure the door was tightly shut.

Yale half leaned, half sat against the derrick's cable drum. After a minute he realized his butt was getting cold from the metal. He stood up. Damn. Grease on his overalls. He'd have to be more careful. He wondered if police labs could analyze grease types. Probably. He was slipping. Had to pay attention to details.

The derrick hutch was made of weathered one-by-six pine planks. There was no door. Yale settled himself so he could sight through a knothole straight at the shack across the parking lot. Every one or two minutes, he shifted the sandstone slab from one hand to the other. His wrists got stiff.

Harper must be a really strange guy. Yale knew he was packing up to leave since he'd quit yesterday. What in the world was he doing out here? Could it have anything to do with him? One couldn't be too careful, even if it seemed paranoid. You had to analyze things from every angle.

Somebody must be living in the shack. The snow was melted off the roof: the place was heated. Once Yale thought he heard music, but wasn't sure. He caught himself staring, focused on the wall instead of through the knothole. He was thinking about Lorna. She was getting too skittish. This next insemination had become the most important one ever to him. Since he'd first seen Tobie in Mr. Chays's office, the idea'd been there like the tiniest seed. Seed. He chortled and startled himself.

He heard a loud creak and a slam. He stood up, every nerve alert. His throat was throbbing. He made himself breathe deeply, his litany for control. Four times.

Harper started across the parking lot toward his car, toward the derrick hutch, toward Yale. When Harper'd just gotten into his car, that's when he'd take him: he'd be focused on starting up the engine, and the noise would drown out Yale's footsteps.

Harper started whistling, fancy whistling, his bird whistling. He stopped and blew on his hands, warming them and his face against the bitter air. Then he started walking quickly.

Yale shifted inside the hut to get a view through the next crack, and made a crunching sound on the gravel floor. Harper looked in his direction. Yale froze. But Harper kept on, whistling again. Yale licked his cracked lips. Gripped the rock, flexed his wrist. Harper had a bouncing, cheerful walk. Poor fool. Idiot, really, thinking he'd catch Yale. Harper was a threat, but it would be over soon. Excitement thickened in Yale's throat: the terror of being found out, the adrenaline rush before bold action. The fittest would survive.

Harper strode to the side of his car. Yale sidled out from the hut's cover. Harper's hand dropped away from the door handle, he rubbed his nose. Yale stopped, his muscles tight as a tiger's about to spring. Harper turned toward the pit, walked toward it slowly, his back toward Yale.

Harper picked his way carefully to the lip of the quarry. It was amazing what man could do to the earth. The hole looked like a wedding cake reversed, except that some of the icing had worn off the doe-beige stone ledges. Wedding cake. He sure seemed to have marriage on the brain. How would his father take it if he married Sarah? Probably okay. Harper was all the old man had now. And he was so important to

Harper. He'd taught him when he was little that being a teacher was the best job in the world. Not the best-paying. But the best. Because you got to help others be excited about your favorite things.

He should have worn a warmer coat. Not to mention a hat and gloves. He slapped his arms around him and bounced up and down a little to keep warm. His jacket's noise kept him from hearing anything else, until he heard the crunch of snow right next to him. He turned. Yale Kaltmann was coming at him, something raised over his head. A brick. Harper's arm shot up and he yanked back toward the quarry. Yale stumbled but kept coming.

Kaltmann was the one. The thought flashed through Harper's mind. He'd killed Penny. He was impregnating the girls. The brick kept coming. Harper knew with a shocking clarity that Yale was the criminal. Brick. Matt, he had to tell Matt. The brick. An explosion in his head. Falling, dream-like. Harper had told his father he'd be in Boston next week. He'd never broken his word.

It was impossible to feel Harper's pulse; either Yale's hand was desensitized by the cold, or Harper had no heartbeat. He knelt and peered closely at Harper. He didn't seem to be breathing. He felt for the pulse again.

Stupid, he chided himself. What difference did it make whether he had a pulse? By the time he was at the bottom of the quarry, he wouldn't for sure. That was a slip, a small slip. He had to watch himself carefully. He was wasting time. He peered around at the distant shack. Was there someone in it? Watching? He lifted Harper's feet and set him parallel to the cliff edge, then rolled him over once. Blood was left in the snow. He rolled him again, and the body plunged over. It took a few seconds for it to land.

Yale carefully leaned out to look. The body was far away, face down, right arm crooked over its head. Yale picked up the sandstone chunk he'd used for a weapon and threw it far out into the pit. He picked up the bloodied snow around him with some dead grass clumps and tossed it over the side, too. It was good Harper hadn't had a chance to struggle. There weren't too many marks on the ground, and the ones there were would soon be covered by new snow.

Now to the shack. He had to hurry. As he strode across the parking lot, his panting breath formed huge clouds in the air. He headed fast for the door, flung it open, and went in.

A drunk old bum. His arm was flung out over the floor off the bed. Yale jostled him. The bum grunted but didn't open his eyes. Yale couldn't take any chances. Harper might have talked to him, said something. He wasn't in here very long, but he could have revealed something. Then Yale noticed the note signed by Harper. He was safe. Harper hadn't talked to the bum either.

He walked to the door, opened it, pulled it closed with a snap behind him. He turned, sprinted across the parking lot, through the woods to the van, and drove quickly to the lumberyard in Sand Ridge.

CHAPTER THIRTY-THREE

The day after her visit to the clinic, Tobie was erratic in her moods. Sometimes she was happy, almost silly. Then she would go quiet, remembering the insistent fear she'd had that she might be pregnant.

On Wednesday, munching a candy bar and carrying the lollipops from the hamburger joint in her backpack, she raced from home ec, where she'd sewn rickrack around the bottom of an apron, to phys ed for her favorite sport, even more favorite than softball, acrobatics. But shortly after Miss Petit announced that today they'd practice forward cartwheel flips, she paused and told three girls they had to go to the nurse to be rechecked.

Tobie's head was light, giddy, as she walked out of the gym class with the other two girls, Pam and Wendy. Before going to the doctor, she'd felt like her body was as heavy as an elephant's. Now she was a feather. Nothing could depress her.

"Have a lollipop," Tobie said.

She pulled two out of her small backpack, along with her Walkman radio. She switched it on; the radio was playing "When I Was a Xylophone" by a Madonna clone.

Pam stuck her lollipop in her shorts pocket. Tobie considered Pam prissy, but she tried to treat her nicely anyway. Tobie adjusted her headphones, then gave a grape sucker to Wendy, who said, "I shouldn't, but I will," and quickly unwrapped it.

Wendy was really fat. Shadrack had once told Tobie that some boys called Wendy "porker" behind her back. "That's mean," she'd said. "That's mean," Shad had mimicked in a high-pitched voice.

Wendy popped the sucker into her mouth and sidelined it so it pooched out her left cheek. They ambled—with Tobie occasionally adding a skip—along the long, main hall. Pam stopped and put her lollipop into her locker and caught up with them again.

"My dad says your dad is in real trouble," Pam said.

Tobie loosened the earphones so they dropped down like a necklace.

"What'd you say?"

"I said, my dad said your dad could lose his job."

"What for?"

"'Cause of Evie and the others."

"It's not his fault," Tobie said.

"My dad says your dad hasn't stopped it."

"How can he stop it?"

"I don't know, but he better."

"I think you should mind your own business," Tobie said, furious that she'd given Pam a sucker.

"What if you got pregnant?" Pam asked.

Tobie was silent.

"What if *you* did?" said Wendy, her sucker slurring her words.

"If you were, nobody could tell," Pam retorted, sweeping her hands out to illustrate Wendy's fat.

"Oh, why don't you shut up!" said Tobie.

She jammed the earphones in her ears and ignored whatever Pam said after that.

The door to Nurse Ross's inner office was shut. Pam said she'd knock. Wendy and Tobie plopped onto the sofa while Miss Prissy Pants, as Tobie mentally called her, primly tapped on the door. Nurse Ross emerged, looking frazzled.

"You wanted us to redo our health checks," Pam said.

"Yes, yes. I'm sorry, girls, but I lost your last records. It'll only take a few minutes. You remember my last speeches to you, so I won't repeat them. Now, who's first?"

Pam, of course, like a teacher's pet.

"Bitch," Wendy said toward the door after it closed behind Pam. She'd removed her sucker, so the word was clear.

Tobie shrugged. Fundamentally, she was too happy to be bothered. When you've just had your whole future saved, a lot of little things don't much matter anymore. WMMS was playing one of Tobie's current favorite songs. She unplugged the headphones so Wendy could hear, too.

Just as the door opened for Pam to emerge, Tobie quickly whipped the headphones back on so she couldn't hear anything Pam said. She deserved to be insulted. Nurse Ross motioned for Tobie next. Tobie closed the door behind herself and headed behind the changing curtain as Mrs. Ross directed.

She emerged wearing nothing but her earphones. She held the tiny radio in her left hand.

"You mind if I leave this on?" she asked, lifting one of the earphones. "They're playing my very favorite song right now. It's the Bobs with 'Cowboy Lips.' My daddy taught me this song. It's from San Francisco."

Lorna had her back to Tobie, rummaging for something in a drawer. She turned to see what Tobie was leaving on. The soles of her white nurse's shoes squeaked like a gerbil. Her face was flushed.

"It'll show up in the silhouette of your posture, but it's okay. I'd rather you were as comfortable as possible," she said.

Comfortable? That was a weird thing to say. Mrs. Ross probably isn't very educated, Tobie thought. And today she seemed nervous or something. Maybe leaving the headphones on would make Mrs. Ross more "comfortable."

Tobie stood in front of the bed sheet hung on the wall for a background. Lorna flipped out the lights, snapped two photographs, dropped something on the floor, and turned on the light to find it; it was only a clear plastic glove. Then she said—Tobie could hear her through the music—would

Tobie climb up on the table like before and hold the hourglass with the sand in it?

Tobie pulled one earphone away from her ear. "I didn't do that before," she said. This must be what the girls had been talking about at the slumber party.

Mrs. Ross looked surprisingly flustered. "Oh, dear," she said. "I must've forgotten to do it the first time. Please don't mention this to anyone."

"No problem." Tobie clambered up and pulled the paper sheet over her. Her headphones slipped a little when she lay down, so she fixed them. It was the chorus. Tobie sang along under her breath.

The poster on the ceiling this time looked homemade. It said: "Stand Up Tall at All Times, Except When Reading This." Tobie held the hourglass with the blue sand—it was more lavender, really—already running through it. The color reminded Tobie of contacts. That is, the lavender reminded her of Elizabeth Taylor's eyes and *that* reminded Tobie of contacts. Hadn't her father promised her she could have contacts? Why hadn't she remembered it before? She was suddenly so excited. He'd have to do it. He'd said he would, hadn't he?

Lorna walked around to her side and said something. Tobie lifted off an earphone. Said something about "going to pinch a little." Tobie nodded. Lorna disappeared again behind the sheet spread across Tobie's raised knees.

Contacts! Verity would be so jealous. She wanted purple eyes, too. Tobie should go and visit Verity. She felt so sorry for her. She'd ask her dad about it again. If she had contacts, she wouldn't have to worry about her glasses falling off during ball games. How long would it take to get them, and did they hurt? She'd seen people squint and blink a lot with contacts. Like flirting. Only not. She'd seen other people who didn't do that, though. She'd practice until nobody would know that she even had them on. Wouldn't her dad be surprised? She couldn't wait.

Mrs. Ross was saying something again. "Did you feel anything, did it pinch?"

Tobie shook her head. She hadn't felt anything, heard anything, seen anything. She hopped off the table and headed for the changing area, then stopped. Mrs. Ross looked very weird. She leaned against the table, then walked heavily over to the chair at her desk and fell into it.

"Are you okay?" Tobie asked, putting her headphones around her neck.

Mrs. Ross nodded and hoarsely said, "I'm okay."

Tobie suddenly felt very naked without the radio's music "clothing" her, and walked to the changing area to put her gym shorts and T-shirt back on. When she came out of the alcove, Lorna was standing again with her back toward Tobie, fiddling in the drawer.

Tobie cleared her throat, and the nurse turned.

"Thank you for coming, Tobie."

Tobie gave her a quizzical look.

"I just have a headache. Sometimes I get migraines. It'll go soon."

Tobie opened the door, and Wendy heaved up from the sofa in the outer room. Pam had already gone back to the gym.

In a loud stage whisper as Wendy passed into the nurse's office, Tobie said, "Contacts!"

"What?" Wendy replied, walking sideways through the doorway.

"I'm gonna get contacts so I'll have purple eyes."

"Eeeeyuuu! Purple? Like a rabbit?"

The door closed, and Tobie fairly sprinted back to the gym to the romantic music of the Ferns.

The petals of the tulip Audrey had placed on Matt's desk fell off that afternoon. One by one over a period of half an hour. Matt noticed them, but left the tulip there as he worked. Six inky blue stamens projected upward surrounding the yellow pistil, which was pinched into three sections on the top. What was left looked like a tool of some kind. The tip of a Phillips screwdriver. The petals were as bright as ever and firm. They were just detached. Lying on the desk. Shiny, like happy children's eyes.

CHAPTER THIRTY-FOUR

Harper was dead for two days before Matt found out about it, on Thursday.

Tuesday afternoon he'd experienced the closest thing to happiness he'd known in days, weeks, even months. The fact that Tobie was not pregnant had made them both euphoric, verging on giddy. That evening they'd thawed the Lake Erie perch and eaten it, cozy inside the house while the storm dumped a foot of snow softly all over their world.

Then, on Thursday afternoon, Matt remembered Audrey telling him that Harper had stopped in the office Tuesday, upset about something and saying he'd come back. Matt stuck his head out of his office and asked her if Harper'd contacted her again. Odd that he hadn't.

Matt let the phone ring at least fifteen times at Harper's apartment. He checked to see if Harper's new car was in the parking lot. Matt walked upstairs to look in the lab. Papers were scattered all over the desk. Two partially filled boxes sat on the floor. Half the girlie magazines he'd confiscated were on the desk. Harper must've thought he was coming back fairly soon. Something was wrong.

When he called the police, he learned that they'd had a report from Archibald at the quarry that a blue car had been parked there for two days. The old man didn't know

Harper'd bought a new car, so it had sat there for a full day before he grew suspicious. Later that day, the police found Harper's body, hoisted it up from the quarry frozen like a slab of meat, bloodied snow caked to his head and face.

When he saw Harper's body, Matt felt as if the top of his own head had cracked open. First he wanted to throw his arms around him, to say he was sorry, sorry, sorry. Then he felt his chest explode in fury. Outraged at the people who'd hounded Harper. Furious that the school was still open. Guilty that he'd done nothing to save his friend. Then the coroner ruled the death an accident or a suicide. Matt didn't believe it. Harper just wouldn't have killed himself. He was thinking about marriage. Depressed, maybe, but not suicidal.

During the next week, Matt felt he was being sucked deeper and deeper into a quicksand of gloom. Somehow he coped with Harper's father, who came to pick up the body and take it back to Boston. Winston Harper looked just like his son would have in thirty years—same height, build, a similar goatee, but grayer and thicker. Winston Harper didn't want the new car. He told Matt to sell it and use the money to buy science books for the school library.

CHAPTER THIRTY-FIVE

Orville swung into the Chays's driveway, opened the door of his pickup, and lumbered down from the driver's seat. He rounded the long front of the truck, ponderous as an ox. He opened the other door and reached up his mammoth hand to assist Verity. He had become very solicitous the past two months as she ballooned in imminent motherhood. It was the first of February, and the baby was due the fourteenth.

Verity slid her long legs down the side of the cab. The stretch was awkward from the full-sized pickup.

She groaned, her mind, as always, on her girth. Verity had not returned to school when it reopened. She was overwhelmingly embarrassed and, in his intensified solicitude, Orville had allowed her to stay home.

Orville put his hand under Verity's elbow while she grasped the handrail and heaved herself up the steps. Matt and Tobie both stood at the open door.

Both girls said hi shyly, Tobie first. Then Tobie stretched out her hand and took Verity's, gently drawing her inside the house.

After fussing about whether Tobie had everything she needed to fix the frozen pesto, while Tobie pressed her lips as thin as a rubber band and rolled her eyes upward at his over-concern, Matt left and drove off to Cleveland to see Niccole.

Verity looked like Humpty-Dumpty in children's clothes, egg-shaped. Her flowery print dress with ruffles around the collar, yoke, and sleeves made her look like a doll. Tobie was polite. She talked about the pesto she was putting together. She and her dad had frozen the basil and cheese last fall and this was the last container, she said. Verity had never eaten pesto, so Tobie explained what it was.

While the pasta boiled and Tobie groped for what to talk about, she hit on the idea of a tour of her menagerie in the basement. But that was not a very good idea after all. Verity had to lean heavily on the wall going downstairs because there was no handrail. At one point she lurched and bumped against the wall, knocking askew the blackboard that Tobie and Matt used for leaving each other messages. She didn't really seem interested in Tobie's tales of derring-do and derring-don't, the latter being mistakes she'd made in taking care of the animals.

When the meal was ready, Verity sat down at the table very slowly, putting her hand back to feel her way like an old woman. She was enormous and uncomfortable.

When Tobie was half finished eating but Verity's plate was already clean, a silence fell between them like a disagreement. The more they tried to ignore it, the bigger it grew. Tobie wracked her brain but couldn't think of anything more to tell Verity. Ah, ask her about herself!

"So, whataya been doing lately?"

Verity burst into tears.

"Whassa matter?"

"What'd ya think I been doing?"

Silence, while Tobie shrugged awkwardly.

"Growing," Verity wailed, angry, hurt, and confused. Tobie didn't know what to do or say.

"I know I look ugly and fat. Go ahead and tell me."

"It just takes some getting used to," Tobie said after a pause.

Verity had shoved her chair away from the table and a single heartrending sob split out from the center of her body. Maybe straight from the baby, Tobie thought.

"Oh, Tobie, I'm so scared."

Her voice was barely audible. Tobie couldn't think of anything to say.

"I wonder if I'll die. I ask my mother what it's like to have a baby, I say, 'Does it hurt?' And she says, 'Oh, yes, real bad, but then afterwards you forget about it.' I wish it was already afterwards. I want to know what the baby will look like, since God is its father and my dad can't tell me."

"Your father's real nice to you," Tobie said.

"My mother says I should be grateful that Dad thinks it's God's baby, otherwise he would be whipping me."

"Do you think it's God's baby?"

Verity blew her nose on the paper napkin. She shook her head, but she moaned, "I don't know, I don't know. Who else's could it be? Tobie, I never let a boy touch me. You probably don't believe me."

"Sure I do. I know you're honest. I have something to tell you."

Verity hardly noticed the portent in Tobie's voice but Tobie plunged ahead.

"I thought I was pregnant, too." Verity looked interested. "But I wasn't."

Verity looked amazed.

"Why did you tell me that? Is that supposed to make me feel better?"

"I thought you would see that I can imagine how you feel."

"But you can't. You aren't pregnant," she wailed.

Verity pushed herself up from the table and headed toward the couch. Tobie followed her, leaving her half-eaten meal.

"Hey, Vare," Tobie said.

She sat down beside Verity, timidly stroking her upper arm.

"It's not fair," Tobie said. "I know it's not fair and I guess I can't understand, but, well, I can try, can't I?"

Tobie got up and went into the bathroom near the kitchen and brought back a tissue for Verity, who took it and dabbed her eyes.

"I know you're my friend," Verity said. "You're my best friend."

"Can't you talk to some of the other girls, you know, like Amber Smith, to find out how she's doing?"

"She's not my friend."

"I know who you can talk to!"

Tobie jumped up and ran upstairs to her room. She came back with Niccole's business card.

"Remember Niccole Epps?"

Verity looked puzzled.

"The woman who interviewed you."

Verity nodded.

"She's really nice. She helped me when . . . when I thought I was pregnant. She's really nice. She doesn't act like adults usually do, you know, treat you like you're a kid. I'll copy the phone number for you."

Suddenly Verity said, "Oooh," and shifted on the sofa. She clasped her belly for a moment. Then she smiled.

"I can feel it kick."

"Yeah?"

"The first time it happened, I didn't know what it was, I was so surprised."

She surveyed Tobie with a long look.

"D'ya wanna feel?"

Tobie's eyes enlarged. She nodded yes. Verity reached out and took Tobie's hand, spread her fingers out, and placed them on her belly.

"Feel that?"

"No."

They waited. Thump.

"Oooh. He's kicking?"

"Maybe she. I want her to be a girl."

The baby kicked again. Verity smiled weakly through her fright.

"Will you come see me in the hospital?"

"Sure I will."

A pause.

"How're you going to take care of your baby and go to school?"

"Dad says he and my mother can take care of her, only he wants a boy."

"She'll get to watch a lot of soap operas with your mother," Tobie said, and giggled.

Verity sort of smiled.

"I been watching some lately."

Tobie felt another wrench of recognition that, through no fault of their own, they were drifting apart. Their lives were going to be so different. They already were. It must be horrible. And it had nearly happened to her, too. Oh, it wasn't the same. Poor Vare.

"I've got two weeks to go."

"I'll come and see you," Tobie said.

"I wish it was over."

Verity's voice was low and ghostly and pleading. It sank into Tobie's consciousness like a quiet and profound throbbing, a premonition of finality. The future seemed terrifyingly amorphous. Verity's fear clutched at Tobie's throat with its scrawny, dead-gray, Dracula hands.

CHAPTER THIRTY-SIX

The bright, clear air of the last weekend in February had warmed to just above freezing at midday. The snow that clung to the eaves dripped off but was arrested in mid-melt, like a promise, by the cold evening air. On his way to take the week's trash out front for pickup the next day, Yale stood on his porch, feeling as if his head were in a crystal chandelier. Icicles hung all around, adding to the crusted Victorian trimmings, lightening the house's gloom.

The trash bag was unusually heavy this week. The wood shavings and cuttings added up. He'd abandoned the oak rocking horse; carving the hard oak had been a problem, and besides, in the middle he'd decided to use his own creativity. He'd started out following a pattern for the horse, but gradually the notion of designing and carving his son's or daughter's toy consumed him. He wanted to make the grandest gesture he could to show his gratitude to Verity. He started over, in softer poplar wood, and began fashioning a rocking dog.

Soon, soon, he thought. He whistled short snatches of songs.

If they only knew, he thought. But, of course, they couldn't know. That was probably what made him so giddy. Nobody knew but him. And Lorna. Oh, well, Lorna.

Yale placed the trash bag on the mound of snow near the curb. His birthday was coming. He'd be forty-seven on the first of March. Tuesday. Maybe the baby'd come on his very own birthday. That would be another intimation of immortality.

He returned to his living room, which had been totally transformed into a woodworking shop. A table saw stood along the wall; the iceboat had been shifted to the right to make room for it. On a worktable, an orbital sander stood upright like an iron, its sandpaper worn white from use. Planes of various sizes dangled from hooks on a pegboard behind the table. A grinder for sharpening tools sat at one end of the table; a router and numerous clamps were piled on the other. Sawdust and wood chips, coiled like Shirley Temple curls, covered the floor.

Drawknives, spokeshaves, chisels, and rasps were arrayed on shelves along the wall. Yale had spent hundreds of dollars on his equipment. There'd be no scrimping for his children.

Propped against one leg of the table was his first effort, a crude rocking horse in pinkish oak. He'd learned a lot from carving that piece, and his second attempt was more impressive. He'd chosen the softer poplar, which had a light yellow heartwood, white sapwood, and an obscure pattern that would be easy to paint over. Originally he'd planned to put the rockers and body together with dowels, but, just as he'd learned the limitations of carving with oak, so he'd decided screws and glue would be just as effective.

Yale straddled a low bench he'd constructed to facilitate his work. Bent over the carving, a lock of his black hair falling forward, he looked every bit an old-time cobbler crouched over his work.

He hadn't been so happy in a long time. Since the school board had reopened the school, things had been going his way. When he paced, assessing his next carving move and stroking the dog, he smiled. His pacing reminded him of expectant fathers, fretting and worrying in a hospital waiting room.

Next to his imminent fatherhood, Yale was most pleased about the fact that Tobie had been impregnated. He was sure Tobie would make an absolutely lovely mother, with her spunk and her underlying sweet disposition. He'd stayed away from Lorna on that day, even though he'd watched Tobie come up the stairs and go down the hall to Lorna's office. Then he'd seen her exit, too, skipping down the hall with her headphones on.

He waited till two days later, when he was walking past Lorna's apartment building. She was just stepping into the street, obviously to go shopping since she carried a bag. She looked kind of tired, depressed, he thought. If she'd done well, he'd find a way to cheer her up. She had her back to him, pulling the front door closed, when he approached.

"Did it all go okay?" he asked.

She jumped, making a gasping noise. She gave him a nervous glance and cast down her eyes as she walked out in front of the bakery.

"Did it?" he repeated.

She stopped, turned her back to him, and pretended to look at the cakes in the window. "Yes," she said.

She stood up straighter, squaring her shoulders. He thought she seemed proud of having done her job well. She might have her deficiencies, but this time she'd done it right. Yale couldn't see the expression on her face in the glass since it was dusk. But when she slumped again, he suddenly felt a surge of compassion well up in him. She must be lonely. Her baby dead and all. And no friends really. He was glad she didn't have friends, but still he felt pity for her.

Without giving it a day's thought, like he always had in the past, he offered her a visit to Buford. She was really quiet again. Then, to his amazement, she said, "No."

"No?"

"No."

"Well, I just wanted to thank you for all your good work. At times I've had my doubts about you, but it turns out you've done a yeomanlike job on this."

He paused. She said nothing. He shrugged.

"If you change your mind, you can let me know." He paused. "Did Tobie act suspicious at all?"

"Leave me alone," Lorna said.

She tilted her shoulder away from him and began walking at a fast clip down the street. Her plastic bag flapped on her wrist. Yale sped along beside her.

"Well, hey, listen, I'm sorry you're upset. I just wanted to thank you."

He touched her shoulder. She drew away like he was fire. It's rejection, he thought. Of course, she's probably jealous. Then he let her walk off.

The thing about a rocking dog, just like a rocking horse, was that it was good for either a boy or a girl. Sunday night Yale worked late on the carving. He knew he was supposed to want a son, but he thought he'd prefer a girl. The baby should be healthy and big. These girls would someday be grateful to him, that he had such a good body and no addictions or diseases.

Yale turned over the nearly complete wooden dog, spread glue on the feet and the rockers and carefully matched the pieces, then inserted the screws into its feet and tightened them. He turned it back over and patted the smooth, sanded back. It stood in a pool of light in the middle of the room.

The other thing that made him happy, though a bit anxious because they might not have "taken," was that two other girls might soon discover they were pregnant. Any day now, one or both of those girls who'd been impregnated before Christmas could discover the happiest news a female could know, being expectant with a child.

He would make a special toy for each one of his children. They would all be treated fairly and equally. He wouldn't play favorites.

That would be hard with Tobie's, he had to admit. He wanted that one intensely, more than anything he'd ever desired. With Tobie pregnant, there would be no more. The project was complete. He could relax and watch his perfect children grow up. Like them, he would be innocent.

He took one last look at his rocking dog before going to bed. It looked so sweet. He couldn't bear to leave it in the dark, now that he'd carved it into life. He switched off all the lights but one, which suffused the carving in a soft, white glow. Tomorrow he'd paint the dog, black spots on white: a dalmation.

CHAPTER THIRTY-SEVEN

Matt was sitting in his office, his door closed, a stack of bills on his desk, a thermos of coffee open next to it. Things weren't going badly in his life; they just weren't going well. Tobie's period was late again. He kept telling her that there was absolutely nothing to worry about, that she couldn't expect to be regular yet. His life seemed gray, like the interminable winter. He missed Harper. He had a gnawing, isolated, lonely feeling, like a bird that had mistakenly stayed north.

Matt signed an invoice to authorize payment of the school's electric bill. He dated it February 28. Tomorrow was the twenty-ninth. Leap year day. Who needed it? Who needed one more day in this miserable year?

It was Monday. He hadn't seen Niccole over the weekend, hadn't seen her since the previous week. She'd come to Sand Ridge to see Verity Molway, and had phoned him ahead of time to arrange a meeting. Niccole said she'd just begun a new law course at the university, and that it required enormous amounts of homework.

They'd met at a pizza joint five miles out of Sand Ridge.

"I'm afraid of the time commitment a relationship now would require," she said. "I have to decide exactly what I want. Oh, I don't know what I want. That's the problem."

She waved a thin, graceful arm and looked mystified both as to what she wanted and how to convey it to him.

"You should take all the time you want, and if you don't want to see me in the end, well, I'll be very sad. But that's how it'll have to be." He smiled a forced smile.

"I'll call you," she whispered.

He'd felt she was taking control away from him. Don't call us, we'll call you, he thought. He nodded and said, "I hope you do."

Then she left quickly.

At first Matt had thought it odd that Verity would ask Niccole to come to Sand Ridge to see her, until Niccole told him that Tobie had suggested it. Poor Verity, Matt thought. When they had their talk, Verity had asked Niccole simple questions about having a baby, what it was like, what she could expect, explaining that she had no one to talk to, not her mom, not her dad. On her way there, Niccole said, she'd stopped in a shopping mall and bought a book on pregnancy and birth for Verity. When she gave it to her, Verity had clutched it as if it was her life preserver and she was afraid of sinking. She was by now two weeks late in delivering.

The phone rang, jarring Matt out of his reverie.

"Mr. Chays, bad news, I'm afraid," Audrey warned him. "Another girl is pregnant. Donald Mead is on the line. Apparently, his daughter Karen is pregnant. You want to take it now?"

"Oh, God, I guess I'd better," Matt said. "Wait, before you connect me, which one is Karen, do you remember?"

"She's new in town. Eighth grade. Remember, she was the one who got the tip of her finger cut off in biology, cutting up frogs?"

"Oh, right."

"Big girl, shy, real sweet," Audrey added.

They all are, Matt thought. He recalled his confident assurances to Tobie about her late period, and his feeling of doom returned. He could picture Karen Mead now as she'd galumphed down the hall before Christmas, a day or two before he closed the school. She'd been swinging her white, bandaged finger with her arm far out, away from her side; it had reminded him of a flashlight baton, the kind used by parking lot attendants at ball games.

"Mr. Chays, maybe your secretary has told you what I'm calling about?" Donald Mead asked.

"Yes, I'm very sorry to hear this."

"I'm sure you are," Mead said softly and sincerely.

The tone was more painful to Matt because it was subdued. He could have stood it better if Mead had been screaming and cursing.

"My wife said we should be quiet about this and do whatever we're going to do, but I said no, this is more than a personal matter, we have to consider the community."

"Mr. Mead, I appreciate very much that you've called me. I have one question."

"Sure."

"How far along is Karen?"

"The doctor thinks it's about two months and three weeks, but he's not certain, of course."

"Before Christmas. That was before I closed the school the first time. Or it could have been just after, I guess. At any rate, Mr. Mead, I know this is all very awkward, but would you mind if state officials and their lawyers come to interview your daughter? I would certainly understand if you don't want to, but it may be the only way we can get to the bottom of this."

"Maybe. I'll talk it over with Karen and my wife. You know . . ."

He paused, debating whether to go on.

"I asked Karen if she'd ever taken off her panties. Pardon me for being so blunt."

Matt murmured a sympathetic sound.

"She said no, only for the school nurse, but she was wearing a paper shirt at the time. You know, Mr. Chays, she couldn't have had sex. She's just not the type. We moved here from Detroit last year, mainly because we thought Karen would grow up in better surroundings, where she wouldn't be so shy."

Matt couldn't remember afterward how he got through the rest of the phone call.

Matt's exhaustion intensified. He was tired of the phone calls bringing doom. He was tired of having to squelch any feelings of optimism, of hope, with the realization that things weren't getting any better. He was tired of trying to stay hopeful, and then being crushed. He wanted to get Tobie out of Sand Ridge. He was angry that the school was still open, against his better judgment. He was furious that Harper had died and was completely skeptical about the official "accidental death or suicide" explanation.

The time for passivity was over. He'd close the school first, and tell the locals later. If they wanted his head on a platter, they'd have to fight him for it, all the way to the state board and into the courts. He was tired of being pushed around; he was going to push back.

Matt called Blair and made an appointment for the crusty editor to come see him. A notice would appear in the paper tomorrow announcing the school's closing. Next he informed the local radio station, asking them to broadcast the announcement beginning later that afternoon. Calling the state Department of Education, he informed them of the emergency closure. He called Dorothy Mattingly and asked her to inform the school board.

Two and a half months since Karen had become pregnant. Two and a half months. How many more victims since the school had been reopened?

The phone rang. He hadn't expected the outside world to intrude so fast. The person on the phone was a woman from UPI who had been informed of the planned closure by the local radio station. Matt told her that another girl was mysteriously pregnant and that he felt he had to close the school to protect the other children. The story would be on the wires all around the state in an hour. The media would descend, looking for the sensational angle. He knew it. He could feel it in his journalistic bones.

Matt turned on the public address system at the beginning of the morning's fourth period class. Throughout the school building, he heard hundreds of babbling voices overflow the rooms after he announced that school would be closed at the end of the fourth period. He told the children why and said that they would each be given a mimeographed notice explaining the crisis. They were to carry it home to their parents. After he shut off the PA system, he stepped from Audrey's office into the hall for a moment, just long enough to hear a delighted whoop from some boy jubilant about getting a holiday.

The mimeoed sheets, prepared by Audrey in record time, were picked up by a squadron of representatives sent from each class and distributed by the teachers. The final bell rang, and the children surged out into the hall, collecting their coats, stuffing their sheets of paper, still smelling of the duplicating fluid, into their pockets and backpacks. Matt saw one kid poke his into his snow boots.

That evening, Matt's house was surrounded by newspeople. Tobie was in the basement feeding her animals when the first two TV crews arrived simultaneously. A third TV channel appeared a half hour later. Matt gave full interviews, explaining the town's torment and his position. It would lead the news at eleven that night. The story was too hot to ignore. The various crews were in competition.

At one point, Brad Velnick, a slick investigative reporter for one of the Cleveland TV stations, pushed to the front of the crowd, cameraman in tow, shouting, "Mr. Chays, you have a daughter. How 'bout a shot of you together?"

"This is not a photo opportunity," Matt snapped. He didn't want to subject Tobie to the publicity.

That night after Tobie was in bed and asleep, Matt switched on the news. He sat in the gloomy living room with no other lights on. The blue of the tube cast an eerie glare. There it was. The school exposed. He'd had no choice, he figured. This crime, if that's what it was, had to be solved. Beachley was interviewed after Matt and was taking the position that girls should be kept home, but the school should remain open for the others. After the close-up, Arnie was shown with his children, all boys. Even the most dense observer had to have noticed.

"The small town of Sand Ridge is coming apart at its seams, many of its residents said today. Perhaps time will explain these mysterious occurrences, seven girls strangely pregnant. Meanwhile, life is increasingly bizarre in Sand Ridge. Principal Matthew Chays is in a very hot spot."

The anchorman went right on with the next story, about a bedding store that had inflated a water bed with helium and moored it to an air vent so that it floated over the store's roof. Now the water bed was loose, flying somewhere over Cleveland.

"If you see it, please phone Waterbed Dreams at 555-2091," the reporter said.

Matt clicked off the TV and sat for a long time in the dark. Even Niccole was gone. Slowly, like liquid spreading in a cloth, he absorbed the realization that his last meeting with her had been the end. She'd said good-bye as gently as she could.

He was facing this chaos alone. He went to bed abysmally depressed, slept fitfully, and dreamed he was mountain climbing by himself. He kept crawling to the edges of cliffs, retreating, going another direction, only to look over another cliff. He couldn't find the way to safety, the way back to civilization. He woke up in a cold sweat, and realized that the cliffs were like the quarry walls where he'd found Evie's body, where Harper was killed.

CHAPTER THIRTY-EIGHT

The venetian blinds in Lorna's office were lifted and the sun streamed in the window. Spring, remember spring, the brilliance seemed to say. A robin hopped around on the mulberry tree outside the window. He might seem to be a forerunner of better weather, but Lorna knew that robins actually hang around all winter. Still, she was cheered today by the prospect of spring.

She felt greatly relieved that the school was closed. Yale couldn't make her inseminate any more girls. He hadn't ordered her to do it for the past month, not since Tobie. But she'd been living in terror until Mr. Chays closed the school yesterday. She really didn't know what she would have done if Yale had commanded her to carry out the despicable deed again.

When Yale had tried to reward her by inviting her to visit Buford, Lorna had surprised herself, as well as Yale, by refusing. She'd been so disgusted by Yale and what he had made her do that for a moment her fear of him evaporated. Afterward she'd watched his face. He registered surprise, then shrugged and walked away. She'd thought about the encounter a lot since then. She'd even practiced a speech for when Yale next asked her to carry out his plans. Then, last week, she'd written a letter to Niccole Epps.

She reached into the top of her uniform, and pulled a photocopy of the letter out of her bra. She removed her bulky blue cardigan, hung it on the chair, and sat down at her desk. The letter was in longhand. On Saturday she'd photocopied it at the post office for a quarter. Because she was terrified that Yale would walk into the post office and see her, she had carried the letter between the pages of a *Family Circle* magazine and also copied a knitting pattern on page thirty-two along with it. Yale didn't come in, and Lorna had mailed the letter that day to Niccole. It might arrive today. Letters to Cleveland wouldn't take longer than the mail she sent to her family in Toledo, which always seemed to take three days.

She smoothed the crumpled paper against her blotter to read it again, holding it at arm's length in order to see it clearly. Perusing the letter infused her with courage. After each reading she thought about Yale with mixed emotions, with defiance, but also with panic when she imagined his reaction to her refusal to cooperate. Her long-ago torture when he sliced off the tip of her finger had left a deep fear in her brain, a feeling of panic, an image of blood.

Dear Miss Epps:
    I'm the nurse at Sand Ridge school who you talked
to in December. I'm writing you because I'm scared
and I want to know about lawyers. I need help. I
know who got the girls pregnant . . .

A firm, cheerful knock on the door of the reception room echoed through the office. Lorna grabbed the paper and mashed it back into her uniform, turning her body so that her back was to the door. Her heart was pounding.

"Happy Leap Year Day," Yale said.

"Umm," she murmured, rotating her body back to face him.

"Once every four years, time gets longer," he said.

The memory of Yale's basement full of clocks flashed through Lorna's mind. Then she thought what so many females think when Leap Year Day is mentioned: it's the only time when girls can legitimately ask boys to marry them. How could she ever have wanted to marry Yale? She must've been crazy. He might be handsome, but so selfish, she thought. He just wanted to reproduce his genes because he was convinced he was so superior. She hated him with a deep, burning fury.

Yale strode across her office holding an oilcan in his left hand. Lorna watched him but remained immobile. She was worried that the letter wasn't quite hidden or was lumpy.

"How're the stirrups?" he asked. "Do they squeak again?"

As he bent over the examining table, she surreptitiously checked the letter, tucking it in farther and smoothing her uniform. Why had he come in here? It couldn't be about any squeak in the stirrups. She bet he wanted to talk about Karen. He was probably gloating, and she was the only one he could talk to. You wouldn't think he would be so cheerful with the school being closed, she thought. Yale waved the stirrups back and forth.

"Guess not," he said. "Must've done a good job of oiling the first time." He straightened up and set the oilcan on the edge of the table. His denim overalls were crisp and neat, deep blue and new.

"Real nice about Karen Mead, isn't it? You did a good job and I would like to thank you. She should be a good mother. She's a big girl and should produce a baby that will grow up quite large. Maybe an athlete. I'd like one of my children to be a famous athlete. Girl or boy, it doesn't matter to me."

As he talked he walked into the reception room, drew the rocking chair from there into her office, and sat down. Lorna didn't like his sitting down. He wanted something. He started rocking. He smiled when the linoleum made a sticky sound beneath the rockers, like Velcro pulling apart, but he kept right on rocking. Lorna felt like her face was frozen; she couldn't smile in return.

"I'm making a rocking dog for my first baby. I painted it this morning before I came to work."

She kept looking up at him warily as she fidgeted on her chair.

"Don't you want to know what a rocking dog is?"

She shrugged.

298

"Like a rocking horse," he said, "only this is a dalmation dog, with black spots on it like my dog when I was a boy."

Lorna was thinking of Buford's toys, of how Yale wouldn't let her bring Bu's toys when she visited. How could this man be so cruel? He didn't seem cruel when he talked about his own children.

"Have you heard anything about Verity?" he asked.

"No," she said.

"She's overdue by two or more weeks, isn't she?"

"I guess so."

"My children are all going to be quite different from each other, I bet. Most parents don't get to have that kind of variety."

She felt nauseated. What did he want? He knew she couldn't inseminate any girls with the school closed.

"Tobie should find out pretty soon if she's pregnant. Have you heard anything?"

He really was just there to gloat. She pursed her lips in disgust, then realized he was watching her closely. A shadow crossed his face.

"Have you?"

"No."

She paused for courage or for an adrenaline rush to help her. She remembered Buford chanting "No, no, no, no," once when she told him it was bedtime. It was no wonder children liked the word "no." It bestowed power.

"No," she said again.

He sensed a change in her attitude.

"Well, could there be any reason that it didn't work? Did you do it right?" His voice was low and threatening.

"I didn't do it," she said.

Her pulse pounded in her ears. She squared her shoulders. Yale's face slowly solidified like concrete. The muscles in his jaw rippled once. He stared at her without saying a word for several seconds.

"You told me you did."

"Yes."

"That was a lie?"

She nodded. He stopped rocking. Panic flew into her chest, caught in her rib cage like a trapped bird flapping its wings. She put her hand on her bosom, forgetting the letter, remembered, took her hand away lest the paper crinkle. Yale stared at her. He couldn't seem to absorb what she'd said. He slowly rose. He shook his head incredulously and kept looking at her.

"You didn't do it," he said slowly, menacingly.

He stood several yards away from where she sat, his arms akimbo. His gaze drifted out the window, as if he was thinking what to do next. With measured step he turned and walked into the reception room. She gasped for breath. He was leaving.

His steps slowed. She could hear him turning. He walked back, his footsteps now firm, and suddenly was looming over her.

"Get up," he said.

She looked up and was shocked to see the blood vessel in the center of his forehead throbbing, the skin over it inflamed and red.

"Why?" She rose as she asked.

"You're going with me."

She pulled away toward the window.

"Where?"

"My house."

Dear God, help! He was going to take her and have her watch him unplug Buford's capsule. She thought she'd faint. She wished she would, but she didn't.

He moved toward her and she shrank away. He lunged and grabbed her arm, holding it so tightly he was bruising it. She moaned in pain.

"You better not cause any trouble or I'll break your arm."

He put his left hand on her shoulder as he twisted her arm behind her back.

"No," she said.

"Yes, you're going to do it. Say yes. I don't want any more noes. Say yes."

He pulled her arm up, and the joint cracked.

"Yes, yes, yes," she whimpered.

"Okay, let's go." He pushed her forward into the reception room.

"My sweater," she said. If only she could delay, maybe get

rid of the copy of the letter, if he'd wait for her in the reception room while she retrieved her sweater. . . . She was terrified that somehow he'd find she had it, force her to give it to him, and learn that she'd mailed the original to Niccole. But he followed her back into her office, watching her every move. His mouth was set in a perfectly horizontal line. She fumbled her sweater off the chair back and put it on. He gave her a shove back toward the reception room.

"You'd better not do anything to arouse anybody's curiosity," he said. "No noise or anything. If you do, you'll be very sorry. Wait," he ordered as they approached the door.

He pulled her behind him and put one foot out to look down the hall.

"If you see anybody while we're going down the hall, just keep walking, out the door into the parking lot."

He pushed her slightly in front of him to the left.

"Walk slowly," he hissed.

The hall was empty. The student lockers stretched down the hall like orderly soldiers on parade. She wished she were wearing loud shoes, heels or something, but she had on her crepe-soled nurse's shoes, and Yale's shoes were also rubber-soled. Occasionally Yale touched her back, reminding her of his threat.

When they were halfway down the hall, a door opened. It sounded like it was from the principal's office. Yale seized her arm and pulled her into a small alcove. They could hear footsteps. A woman with heels. It must be Audrey, Lorna thought. The water was running in the water fountain. Audrey was filling her watering pitcher.

Lorna wished she could scream. But her voice stuck, dry and noiseless, in her throat. Maybe he was going to kill her. Why hadn't she thought of the scissors in her desk? Maybe she should let him break her arm. God, she hated pain. And who knew, he might do something worse. She glanced at the hammer hanging from the loop on his overalls.

A sound started to come out of her throat. He grabbed her by the neck and pressed his fingers against her esophagus for ten seconds. When he let up, she gasped deeply for air. Maybe Audrey would hear her. The footsteps went back across the hall. The door clicked shut.

"Okay, let's go," he growled, twisting her arm and pushing her back into the hall but in the opposite direction, back where they had come from.

"What . . . ?"

"To your office," he said.

He prodded her back through the reception room.

"I forgot something," he said.

She turned to look at him.

"Get your syringe," he ordered.

"Why?"

"Just get it and shut up. You've done enough damage."

She walked across the room away from him, rubbing her arm where he had squeezed it. She pulled open the top drawer of the cabinet and withdrew the catheter and the accompanying bulb.

"Here, give it to me."

She handed it over. He detached the tube from the bulb and dropped them into a large front pocket of his overalls. She again thought of using the scissors in her desk as a weapon, but he grabbed her elbow and moved her toward the door.

The hall seemed interminably long. This time no one came out. Oh, how she wished they would! She'd seen a couple of teachers earlier this morning. As they arrived at the outside door, the bell for the end of fourth period suddenly resounded through the building.

"Damn," he said. "Keep walking. To the right. My car is that brown van over there. I want you to go to the passenger door. I will open it for you. I want you to get in and fasten the seat belt. I want you to act normal."

"Normal?" she croaked.

"Shut up. I'm not going to hurt you or anybody else if you cooperate. I don't want to hurt anyone. I want you to do just what I tell you. Is that clear?"

Silence.

"I said, is that clear?"

"Yes," she said.

She was defeated. Maybe if she went back to cooperating, he wouldn't do anything to her. She walked around to the door of the van, he opened it, and she climbed in. He pushed down the lock and slammed it shut. All this time he didn't touch her. He walked around the front of the van, watching her through the window. He hoisted himself into the driver's seat and started the car, then ground the gear, trying to put it into reverse.

"Fuckin' car," he said, and drove off.

CHAPTER THIRTY-NINE

Matt had come to work this Tuesday morning feeling a bit better. The governor had publicly backed his decision to close the school. While he was dressing for work, he'd had the TV tuned to a morning news show to which he was only half listening. He didn't at first notice.

Tobie, who was brushing her teeth across the hall, shouted, "Sand Ridge, did you hear that?"

The clip showed reporters surrounding the governor last night after a speech he'd given to supporters in Cleveland. They were badgering him about the scandal in Sand Ridge. Should the school be closed?

"It's a local decision," Governor Dixon said.

"There's dissension on it locally. What do you think?"

"I think the principal there is handling the case well. You know there are legal issues involved, and I can't comment on those. But in this case I think caution is the best position."

"Does that mean you think the school should be closed?"

"Yes."

Yahoo! Matt thought. Take that, Arnie Beachley and Hector Pickett! But then his feeling of gloom returned. His own battles weren't important as long as the girls were still getting pregnant.

Matt leaned back in his office chair, sighed, and started to put his feet up on the desk. He changed his mind. He'd forgotten he'd worn his heavy hiking boots because it was wet outside with the snow in a steady melt. Spring was on its way, he thought.

He removed his boots, put his feet up, and read the morning paper. He'd had a radio on for half an hour, tuned to a talk show. The main concern of the callers was the Sand Ridge issue, which was variously called "the virgin affair" and "the pregnancy mystery." There was an undertone of panicked identification. In fact, a lot of callers said the affair shouldn't be publicized because it would encourage copycats of this new form of terrorism.

Matt had been trying to read his papers all morning, but he'd been constantly interrupted by phone calls. Most of them were from the media, local and national, including *Time* and *Newsweek* reporters. Just as he was halfway through a local paper's editorial that came out for virginity at least until the age of seventeen, the phone rang again. Audrey was out of her office, and Matt picked it up, simultaneously turning off the radio.

"Hi, 's me."

He'd recognize Niccole's mellow, lilting voice anywhere.

"Hi, you. What's up?"

He hoped she'd seen him on TV and decided to ask him for a date.

"Saw you on TV last night. You did a good job."

"Thanks."

"I'm calling from home. Shadrack Molway just called. Verity is on her way to the hospital to deliver, and he called me because she wanted me to come see her."

"Wow."

"Wow?"

"Yeah, finally we'll get to see what the kid looks like."

"You can't usually tell what they look like at first."

"Maybe this one will have a startlingly distinguishing feature. But you're right. Probably not. So?"

"So, I'm on my way. I'll be at Sand Ridge Hospital in forty-five minutes. One more thing. Shadrack said Verity wanted Tobie there and asked me to contact her."

"I'll go get her and we'll meet you."

"You'll probably beat me."

"Yep."

"See you."

"Ditto."

Audrey was back, watering her plants.

"Verity's gone to the hospital," he called to her. "I'll phone Tobie and go."

He swung his chair slowly and looked out the window as he finished dialing home. The fourth period bell went off. He'd have to tell Yale to disconnect the bell for the duration of the school closure.

Speaking of Yale, there he was. Out the window. Walking with Lorna Ross. Maybe he'd decided to date her after all. He walked with her around his van, helped her up onto the high seat, and closed the door for her.

Tobie answered after four rings. She'd been in the basement feeding the animals and was out of breath. When he told her that Verity wanted her to come to the hospital for the birth, she said, "Oh." The quality of that "oh" was too complex to describe. Matt said he would be at the house in ten or fifteen minutes to pick her up.

He hung up and bent over to lace his boots back on. He folded up the newspapers, picked up his parka from the chair where he'd dumped it. It was sunny this morning, but it was still bitingly cold. That made him wonder. Yale and Lorna hadn't been wearing coats.

"I'll let you know about the baby," Matt promised Audrey on the way through her office.

"The first of many," she said grimly.

CHAPTER FORTY

Niccole pulled her red down coat from the closet, preparing to head for the hospital. She'd last seen Verity several days ago at the Pronto hamburger joint in Sand Ridge. The girl'd had to sit sideways so she could fit into the booth.

"First, I wanted a girl," Verity had said. "But the more uncomfortable I get, the more I want a boy, 'cause a girl would have to go through this like me."

Niccole was not exactly the praying kind, but as she pulled on her coat she sent up a small prayer that Verity wouldn't have too much pain for too long and that the baby would be born healthy. She fastened the toggles on her coat and looked at herself in the full-length mirror on the back of the bathroom door. Wouldn't do. She took off the coat and quickly made a bun of her hair, smooth as a ball of flour dough. She removed her large, brassy earrings, in the form of Chinese characters that translated as "may you live in interesting times," and replaced them with demure pearl studs.

Verity had continued: "Gloria said she definitely wanted a boy because maybe he'd be the Second Christ. My dad told Gloria to go away to have her baby, did you know that?"

Smart move, Niccole thought, and shook her head. Gloria's past dating activities cast doubt on Orville's virgin-mother theory, so it was better for Orville to get her out of town. Niccole wouldn't touch Verity's Second Christ story with a ten-foot pole, let alone a comment. Whatever she said might get back to Orville. She'd suppressed her various sacrilegious thoughts.

She pulled on her coat again, checked her watch, and sped down the stairs to the lobby. She unlocked her mailbox, rummaged in it to remove all the pieces, and, without looking at any, stuffed them into her voluminous denim purse. Waiting rooms in hospitals were usually a bore; she'd read her mail there.

The front door of her apartment building opened practically right onto the river. She backed out the door, making sure it was locked, and when she turned around, found a giant, high-riding freighter floating past the end of the small yard. A sailor on the bridge hooted at her and waved.

She loved this, looking out her apartment right into a ship. How could she ever leave this and go live in a place like Sand Ridge?

But why was she thinking of moving? She had been trying not to think of Matt. In fact, she'd been putting him out of her mind for the past month. Often, however, her memory roamed back to three scenes. The first was when Matt had emerged from the Sobo restaurant, registering amusement and amazement as he saw that she'd flattened the parking meter with the rental truck. Second was the endearing, platonic panic on his face as he ran over to her on the ice after their near miss. Last, her sexual memory took several forms, but a major one was when he'd leaned back afterward, drowsy and blissful, and run his finger sweetly around the shape of her ear as if it were the dearest possible object.

Am I a fool? she mused as she nosed her car onto the highway toward Sand Ridge. Why was she saying no to this man? Was it a false fear that she wouldn't be able to do what she wanted if she got together with him? Obviously, he couldn't move to the Flats. She'd have to move there. Why couldn't she keep her apartment on the river as a pied-à-terre and stay overnight sometimes when her classes or work required? Slow, slow, slow, she cautioned herself. She didn't want to get trapped.

Then there was the aspect of becoming an instant step-

mother if she moved in with him. Was she jumping ahead?
Maybe, but she had to be practical and self-protective. One
reason she'd stayed away from Matt was that when he talked
he was dangerous. He was so eloquent that she imagined he
could talk apples off trees if he set his mind to it.

He and Tobie should already be at the hospital when she
arrived. In her mind, she braced herself to resist him. She
turned into the parking lot and started to search for his car.
It was not in sight. She rode around and around the lot, but
there were no empty places. She looked back out onto the
street and saw cars parked for two blocks in either direction.
She turned onto a side street, finally found a spot, and
parked.

Half the town must be there for Verity's baby. Niccole was
reminded of the church parking lot the day of Orville's
virgin sermon.

She saw three enormous TV news trucks; electric cables
ran from them into the emergency entrance of the hospital.
Poor Verity. The publicity was growing.

The lobby was jammed. Niccole recognized faces from
the school board meeting and the church service. The
grapevine was obviously working well in Sand Ridge. She
wove her way through the milling people across the lobby
toward the information counter, and leaned over to talk
discreetly to the middle-aged woman with a frazzled air
behind the counter.

"I've been asked to come here by the Molway family. Can
you tell me where I should go?"

"Lady, half this crowd says that they've been invited here
by the Molways."

"Verity herself asked me," Niccole said.

"Look, I'll tell you what I'm telling everyone. There's a
waiting room upstairs where they show the new babies. Up
the escalator over there. If you can find space in the room,
you can go up."

"Do you know if she's had the baby yet?" Niccole
whispered.

"Dunno, but I doubt it," the woman said, not lowering
her voice. "I think I would've heard if she had."

"You know the family?" a tenor voice behind Niccole
asked.

"Yes," she said with hope in her voice.

Maybe this was someone who would assist her. The man was several inches taller than Niccole, probably in his thirties, and cute, with snapping blue eyes and curly blond hair. He was dressed in jeans and a sweatshirt. Didn't look very official.

"Maybe you could tell me about them."

That seemed a bit pushy and peremptory. She looked him in the eye and said, "Why? Who are you?"

"I'm with channel three. Brad Velnick. Glad to meet you."

He stuck out his hand. Niccole ignored it.

"Hey, unfriendly, huh?"

He paused, stepped back to survey her.

"I like red hair. It's mmm," he said, following the "mmm" with a kissing noise against his fingers and a dramatic gesture.

"Maybe you should go buy a red wig, then," she said.

She walked away from him toward the elevator. He stumbled a little—she couldn't tell if it was deliberate or not—and tagged after her. She sped up, threading through the crowd. Nobody could beat her at evasive crowd maneuvering, especially someone taller.

A sign had been posted on the elevator, reserving it for hospital staff and patients. Niccole entered the stream of people flooding into the stairwell. The crowd slowly ascended, with a few people struggling down, pressed to the left wall. Brad scrambled behind her, trying to pass on the left, but he kept bumping into those coming down. Niccole twisted past some slow climbers on the stairs. Brad shouted from behind her.

"Are you one of those who believes Verity is having a virgin birth?"

He was out of breath.

"Are you going to quote me?" Niccole shouted toward the ceiling.

"How can I? I don't know your name."

"You'd call me an unidentified observer."

Two people who were descending smashed into Brad; he had to turn sideways to let them by. He lost ground, and redoubled his efforts.

"The labor pains have been going on for two hours," he said, broadcasting the information for all to hear.

"Who said?" Niccole asked.

"Orville Molway. You know him?"

"Actually, I don't."

"No? I thought you were a friend of the family."

"Verity asked me to come."

He caught up to her at last, despite the agitation of those he'd pushed aside. They stepped through the door out of the stairwell simultaneously. They were face to face in the waiting room.

She said in her most scathing voice, "I think you ought to leave the poor girl alone. Don't you think it's bad enough without all this publicity?"

At that point, Brad noticed that Orville was coming in their direction.

"The man himself," he said in a stage whisper.

Orville held out his massive hand and shook Niccole's.

"I want to thank you for helping my daughter. It's been a rather difficult time for her. She told me that she really liked you a lot and that you had been sweet to her. That was her word, sweet."

Niccole figured that Verity hadn't told her father what they'd discussed, and that Orville was just "vaguing it," as a lawyer friend called the practice of a witness throwing sand in the air.

"You have a lovely daughter. I hope she's doing okay. Have you heard anything?"

"Fifteen minutes ago the doctor said everything was going normally, but he couldn't say how much longer it would be."

The reporter cleared his throat, and Orville turned in his direction.

"Mr. Molway, I'm Brad Velnick with channel three. I wonder if I could ask you a few questions?"

"Sure, son."

Brad waved his crew over from across the room. They quickly set up. Orville smoothed back his hair as the klieg lights snapped on. Niccole drew back and faded into the crowd in the waiting room. When several people stood up from benches in the center of the room, she sat down.

Brad asked Orville to explain his belief that the pregnancies in town were virgin conceptions. Orville put on his preacher's voice and explained that God sometimes moved in mysterious ways that human beings couldn't comprehend. When Brad asked if he then believed that the babies born were like Christs, Orville hedged.

"I cannot prophecy that. It may be, but the message I got from the Lord was only that the births were virgin, that we were visited by the rushing of angels' wings."

"I have to ask you because you're sort of like the father, though I know you're not. You're the male in charge. Do you want a boy or a girl?"

"I'll take whatever the Lord God gives, and be glad with a joyful noise."

Niccole thought Orville's body movements were just like those of a stereotypical father, proud swagger and false modesty. She was glad to get a seat. No telling how long they'd have to wait. If the hospital wasn't letting Orville in with Verity, there was no chance for her. Wanda Molway was sitting in a chair next to the wall. Several women stood around her talking, but Wanda looked spacey, as if this had nothing to do with her.

Suddenly some more klieg lights flashed on. A cameraman aimed his lens at the large window behind which newborn babies were displayed. A nurse entered the room behind the window carrying a bundle. People were bobbing in the back like pogo sticks, trying to catch a glimpse. The third TV crew switched on their lights. The waiting room was heating up rapidly. Niccole wished she'd brought sunglasses.

The commotion made Orville turn and peer over the heads of everybody in the room. He moved toward the window.

"Maybe that's him," he said.

The cameras rolled. The crowd surged forward to get a look. Niccole sat still. She could see through the shifting people that the nurse was waving her free arm and shaking her head. A doctor emerged from a side corridor into the waiting room.

"That's the Bilby baby," he shouted.

The lights suddenly blinked off and the room seemed plunged in darkness until Niccole's eyes adjusted. The

amily who belonged to the baby were trying to shove to the
ront. The crowd, seeing their plight, cleared a way for them,
ind then began milling again.

The doctor called for Mr. Molway. The crowd tittered and
craned their heads. Orville stepped down the corridor a few
steps and disappeared into a small room. When he returned,
ie announced so that all could hear:

"Friends, the doctor says Verity is doing fine, and he will
probably be announcing the birth soon."

That still could be a long time, Niccole thought. Remembering her mail, she unzipped her purse, removed the mail,
plopped the bag between her feet, and began to sort it out.

CHAPTER FORTY-ONE

After Matt called, Tobie dashed upstairs and swung open the closet door. What should she wear? Would she get to see Verity? What would it be like in the hospital? Would there be tons of people there? What about her jumpsuit?

Verity would probably be in a room away from everybody and the baby would be brand-new and she wouldn't get to see Verity or the baby. Nobody would care what she wore.

Her stomach felt queasy. It was hard to imagine Verity having a baby.

Tobie heard the front door open. She was still wearing what she'd had on all day. She turned, started over to the stairs, and, trying to sound cheerful, called out: "Daddy, is it okay for me to wear jeans?"

At the landing she stopped, looked down. Those weren't her father's legs. She bent down. Standing at the bottom wasn't her daddy. It was Mr. Kaltmann. Nurse Ross was with him. He was holding her arm.

Matt gazed down, mildly irritated, at the flat tire. How had it happened? Oh, well, it had. He didn't want to take the time to fix the flat now. He and Tobie could ride their bikes to the hospital. That would take only twenty minutes. The weather was crystal clear and nippy. Matt began the walk home.

He thought he should phone Audrey when he reached home and ask her to call the service garage and tell them to go fix the tire.

It would be a beautiful day, if it weren't for this dreadful sword of Damocles that hung over him. If only Matt could grab the sword and threaten whoever was causing all of Sand Ridge's problems. He was not a violent person, but he'd been having fantasies of bludgeoning the shrouded figure he imagined had caused this horror.

As he rounded the corner and walked across the front of their yard, he spotted the snowdrops Tobie had planted last fall without his knowing. For several mornings last week, he'd noticed that Tobie would dash out onto the porch before breakfast. She said she was "testing the air." Then this morning she'd called him out to show him the white, bell-shaped flowers nestled in the snow.

"You like them?"

"It's spring," he'd said, hugging her.

"Well, not quite," she'd said, and dashed back inside to stop shivering.

Matt leaped two steps at a time up to the front porch, pulled his key from his pocket, and unlocked the door. As he did, he noticed in his peripheral vision something sitting on the porch. It was Tobie's Walkman. She wasn't usually that careless with her possessions, especially her favorite ones. He picked it up and went inside.

"Tobie," he called.

No answer.

"Tobe, are you ready to go to the hospital?"

Silence.

He hung his parka on the coat hook and noticed that his straw hat was off the closet shelf and on the living room floor. Odd. He walked upstairs. Maybe she had the door to her room closed and couldn't hear him, or maybe she was in the bathroom.

The bathroom was empty. The door to her room was open. A record was out of its jacket on the bed. That wasn't usual. Matt squeezed up the narrow, curved steps to the attic and called her name.

She must be in the basement with the animals. He headed downstairs. In the kitchen, a loaf of bread was open, a slice on the breadboard half slathered with peanut butter. The knife, a glob of peanut butter still on it, was stuck on the table. It looked like she'd left in a hurry. Maybe something was wrong with an animal and she'd rushed down to it.

"Tobie," he called downstairs.

He opened the basement door. Wig let out a squawk, resembling no human word. Matt descended to the halfway landing, then noticed some writing on the blackboard where they left messages for each other. It was scrawled and ran down at the end.

"Yale," it read.

Yale? The only Yale he knew was Kaltmann. He'd just seen him with Lorna. Maybe that wasn't innocent. Yale was suspicious. Could Yale be the person impregnating the girls?

The sword of Damocles was suspended on a thin thread over Matt's head.

Tobie was missing. She'd left in a hurry. The record, the peanut butter, the straw hat, the Walkman. Yale must've taken her. How had she managed to get down here to write his name? Smart kid.

His heart was pumping fast. Time was of the essence. What would Yale do with her? Would he try to impregnate her? He certainly hadn't done the others this way. Maybe he was a copycat criminal. Maybe someone else had done the other girls.

Matt charged up the stairs, tripping near the top and scraping his shin. Given his bad leg, he wasn't the fastest man around. But he was now driven by a force greater than any passion he'd known. *Save Tobie.* That command pounded in his brain.

He sped through the living room, yanked his parka off the hook, and swung it on as he opened the door. He pulled it to, leaving it unlocked. Down the steps, again two at a time.

Yale lived several blocks away. It'd be faster to bike. Matt ran to the garage, unlocked it, and rolled out his bike. He'd gone two blocks when he realized he'd forgotten to phone Audrey. He slowed a little, debating whether to go back, not for the tires but to tell her where he was. He couldn't go back. He imagined what Yale could be doing to Tobie. He pedaled faster.

The town was empty. The residential street was silent. Possibly everybody was at the hospital.

He roared across the bridge over Heron Creek and started up the hill. Yale's high fence came in sight. That must've cost a lot—that amount of treated lumber. Matt was glad of the fence. It hid his approach. He slowed, stopped, and looked around. He left his bicycle on the sidewalk ten yards from the gate. Yale's mailbox was stuffed with mail.

Something bright green caught his eye, on the ground next to the front gate. He leaned down to pick it up. One of Tobie's plastic bracelets. She'd left a clue. Reading all those Nancy Drew mysteries had been useful for something.

Matt sized up the gate, walked back a few yards, sprinted toward it, and vaulted over. Not great on the leg. He crossed the yard, mounted the steps slowly and stealthily. On the porch he listened, heard nothing. He quickly bent over, unlaced his boots, and stepped out of them.

He slowly walked to the door and gradually opened it. It was whisper quiet. Yale kept his hinges well oiled.

CHAPTER FORTY-TWO

In her mail Niccole found a *National Geographic,* an ad
from a shoe company for women with small feet, several
letters. All of them wanted money. Everybody always
wanted money. How did she manage without lifting a finger
to get on so many mailing lists?

Wait. Here was an envelope that was handwritten. The
sender was L. Ross, no address given. Who could that be?
Niccole reached into her purse and removed a fingernail file.
She slit the envelope with it and pulled out the letter, which
was also handwritten. Her eyes fell to the signature first.
Mrs. Lorna Ross. Oh, the school nurse. Niccole's fruitless
interview with Lorna in the Café Rififi flashed back.

Dear Miss Epps:
   I'm the nurse at Sand Ridge school who you talked
to in December. I'm writing you because I'm scared
and I want to know about lawyers. I need help. I
know who got the girls pregnant. Yale Kaltmann.

Niccole gasped and crushed the paper to her chest in
horror.

"Oh, my God!" she said softly several times. She looked
back at the letter.

He made me inject his sperm in the girls. I thought
he would kill me. Will you please help me find a
lawyer? I don't have much money. I'm sorry I didn't
tell you more when you were asking me questions
before. But I was afraid. I still am.

My number is 555-8341.

Yours truly,
Mrs. Lorna Ross

She had to tell Matt. Why wasn't he here? What could
have happened to him? She felt a flutter of panic.

"Who's Yale Kaltmann?"

Niccole spun around. Brad Velnick was standing behind
her. He straightened up.

"You were reading my letter!"

"I was."

"How dare you!"

"Easy. I'm after a story."

She jumped up and glared at him.

"So you're not going to tell me who Yale Kaltmann is, the
man who's caused all this? I guess I'll have to ask Orville
Molway. He seems rather forthcoming."

"I suggest you don't," she said.

"Why not?"

She didn't have a good answer, just a foreboding of chaos.
She'd better locate a phone and call Matt. She turned to
explore, and found a phone on the west wall of the waiting
room. It was being used. She tapped on her watch and
looked quizzically at the woman who was speaking. The
woman nodded and gestured that she would be finished
quickly.

Niccole looked back at Brad. He crossed the room and
was talking to Orville. The woman hung up. Niccole
snatched the receiver and dialed Matt's home number. No
answer. She watched Brad waving his arm toward her.
Orville was going to come over any minute. She phoned
Matt's office. Audrey answered. She said Matt had left the
office more than half an hour ago, and she thought he would
be at the hospital.

When Niccole hung up the receiver, she dropped the letter
on the floor and bent to retrieve it. As she straightened up,

319

she saw Orville's bulk looming over her. His face was flushed, the birthmark deep purple.

"This man here, uh . . ."

"Brad Velnick," Brad said.

". . . Brad Velnick is a journalist, and he says that you have a letter telling you that some man was impregnating girls. Yale Kaltmann, he said. Is that true? Do you have a letter?"

She didn't see how she could refuse to show Orville the letter, especially since she couldn't reach Matt.

"Ordinarily I wouldn't do this," she said. "I'm not a lawyer, but it seems to me that lawyer/client privilege would usually apply here. But I think these are unusual events and people's lives may be threatened."

She smoothed out the letter and handed it to Orville. It was better not to announce it to the crowd. He took his reading glasses from his shirt pocket and began reading. He looked shocked. He must've gotten to Yale's name. He looked down as if baffled about what to do. His jaw hardened.

"Mr. Molway," the voice of the doctor rang through the waiting room.

Orville turned.

"Your baby, I mean, Verity's baby is coming into the viewing room in a second. He's a boy. Seven pounds, eight ounces. The mother is tired but in good shape. You'll be able to see her in a few minutes."

A cheer went up from the crowd.

"Up front, up front," someone shouted, wanting Orville to move to the window to see.

He did not look happy, but most people seemed not to notice. A man grasped Orville's elbow and maneuvered him to the window as a nurse carried the baby out. The TV lights blazed on and the whir of the cameras was like locusts in the middle of a summer day. Everybody craned to see.

"What color is he?" an elderly, slightly deaf woman asked loudly.

"Shh," was the answer.

"What do you mean, shh? I can't see. What color is he?"

"White, Granma," a child's voice said.

"Praise the Lord," she answered.

A brief chorus of "praise the Lords" rippled around the room.

"Mr. Molway, how do you feel at this moment?" asked a man with Channel 8 emblazoned on his lavender T-shirt.

"Uh . . ." Orville was at a loss for words. He shuffled his feet.

"Don't be shy," a man shouted.

"I'm, uh, happy the baby and Verity are healthy, uh," he said.

He suddenly turned and looked toward Wanda, who was still fading into the woodwork at the back of the room.

"Where's Shadrack?" he asked.

Wanda looked around as if she'd been mugged.

"Do you know where he is?"

She shrugged. "Last I knew, he was running up and down the stairs with Huey."

Shadrack's head came into view through the door to the stairwell. Orville headed toward him.

Oh, God, now what? Niccole wondered. She followed Orville, who still held her letter in his hand.

"Shad, I want you to come with me."

"Where're we going?"

"Just come, don't ask questions."

He spun the boy by his shoulders and urged him back down the stairs. Niccole followed them. Behind her was Brad. She could hear him.

"Bring that camera, fast! Forget the tripod. Don't lose sight of him."

She glanced back and saw a second TV crew alarmed and deciding to follow.

Orville pushed Shadrack in front of him through the lobby and out into the parking lot. Niccole was losing ground, so she sprinted after them.

"Mr. Molway," she shouted.

He kept trundling along at a fast clip. She ran after him all the way to his pickup. As he opened the door, she rushed to his side.

"You've still got my letter. Can I have it back?"

"Oh." He looked surprised, as if someone had thrown an obstacle in his way. "Oh, sure." He handed it to her.

"Where are you going?" she asked.

"Where do you think? I have a few questions for a certain electrician who lives in a mansion on the hill."

Niccole didn't know where Yale lived. She'd have to trail Orville if she wanted to be at the scene. She stuffed the letter into her purse and turned, jogging out of the parking lot to her car.

CHAPTER FORTY-THREE

The house was quiet as a mausoleum. And about as big, Matt thought, gazing up toward the ceilings. Must be fifteen feet, if not more. Baseboards and ceiling trims were of oak, darkened with age, and the walls were painted a dark color. A light was on in the living room over a woodworking bench. In the center of the floor was a carved and painted dalmation puppy mounted on rockers. The tools were impressive. To the right against the wall were the shiny hull and outriggers of an iceboat. A chill ran up Matt's back. Was it the same iceboat?

Matt was afraid to move. Old floors usually creaked. Maybe nobody was here. But Tobie's bracelet . . . A bird squawked from another room. A murmur of voices drifted from the same direction as the bird. Matt tensed. A pain shot through his bad knee. He slid his stockinged feet along the floor. If he could only will himself to be lightweight. Like Alice in Wonderland shrinking and growing according to what she ate.

The murmur was suddenly louder. A man's voice. The door groaned. Matt hoped the talk was loud enough to cover the sound. The voices were coming from the direction of the kitchen. Matt moved carefully. Or if he could change his walk into a slither like a snake, he thought in the Wonderland vein. He edged his head around the doorjamb to look into the kitchen.

The bird exploded in a trill. He spotted it in a cage next to the sunny window. A cockatiel. He hoped the bird wasn't capable of giving a warning to its master. He could now tell that the voices weren't coming from the kitchen, but from behind a door that was closed.

Good and bad. Good, in that he could move through the kitchen fairly quickly without being heard. Bad, in that he had to open the door, and he hadn't a clue whether someone would be watching on the other side. If the front door was any sign, the hinges on this one would be quiet, too.

He leaned over and looked into the keyhole. The view was blocked by a key. He put his ear next to the door. The voices seemed to be traveling up. Must be the basement. That meant chances were good that he could maneuver through the door without being seen. It was like stalking an enemy in war: holding his breath and trying to move like a cloud. Listening, as if he were an owl and could even hear rodents' heartbeats.

He couldn't move agilely with his coat on. He slipped it off and left it on the kitchen floor.

"Hello, hello," a voice warbled. Matt jumped at the bird's shrill outburst.

Jeez, scared the wits out of him. His heart pounded. He turned the glass doorknob, slowly, slowly, as far as it would go. He began to ease the door open. The voices kept on. He could now tell it was Yale and a woman. Must be Lorna. He swung the door open in slow motion.

He was right. It was the basement. He looked down. The walls were bright white, the carpeted stairs were white. The floor at the bottom was barn red. The basement was well lit. He lifted his foot to take a step, then noticed something on the top step. Shoes. Lined up neatly. A man's, a woman's— and Tobie's. Her red rubber boots. Last time he'd seen them, they'd been on the front porch. Should've brought mine in and lined them up, he thought sardonically.

His heart was thumping in his throat. He carefully stepped over the first step, placing his foot sideways on the stair. How dangerous could Yale be? He remembered the iceboat, then the wheel on his car that had fallen off. The fetus. Shit, Matt'd forgotten the fetus. Disgusting. Harper— he must've killed Harper.

"You are going to do it, understand?" Yale shouted.

Lorna cried out in pain.

Matt quickly and quietly went down three steps, ignoring the pain in his left leg. He slowly sank down two more to the landing. Behind him was a door. Useful to know. He looked at it more closely. No, it was boarded shut.

Someone moved across the concrete floor, a long stride. Must be Yale. A door opened and shut. It had the whump sound of a vacuum closing like a refrigerator or freezer.

Matt realized he could observe the scene if he squatted down and peered through where the wall was cut away. He sank gradually into a hunkering position and leaned his head down.

"What're you trying to make her do?" Tobie asked.

At the sound of her voice, Matt caught his breath.

"Maybe I can do it," she added.

Matt could tell by her constricted tone that she was frightened, but trying to be brave.

"You can help," Yale said. "But you can't do what she has to do."

Yale's voice was cloyingly sweet. Patronizing. Tobie hated it when adults patronized her, and she often told them off. Matt hoped she wouldn't say anything now. No, she wouldn't: he could tell just by looking that she was too scared to think of Yale's tone.

She was standing on Matt's right, half facing in his direction. Lorna was next to her, and Yale on the other side of Lorna, walking toward them holding something in his hand. Tobie's hair was disheveled. She had on jeans and a chartreuse sweatshirt that said "Umpire" in black letters. She wore only one orange plastic bracelet. Her coat lay crunched up on a chair at the end of a white table that stood across the room.

What a weird room it was, Matt thought. All those clocks and all that white. There were dozens of three-foot-long white cylinders stacked on shelves all around the room. One row of them ran across the wall behind where the three of them stood. Just above that long shelf was a window filled with glass bricks. To Matt's right in a small alcove sat a humming compressor, attached to a six-foot-long steel capsule. A green light glowed steadily near the gauge at the far end.

Along the wall to Matt's left were a refrigerator or freezer, a sink with a pegboard over it full of tools, then more shelves with cylinders on them. The long table in the center of the room was about six feet long, with a cabinet beneath it.

Lorna had pulled up the sleeve of her cardigan and was rubbing her right arm, which was red. Suddenly one of the clocks began to bong. Halfway through its chiming, a second began, and a third. It was eleven forty-five.

"Gee, how come you have so many clocks?" Tobie asked.

"Pretty nice, eh? To make time longer. You should understand that. If I have more clocks, I have more time, don't I?"

Yale was just like the Mad Hatter, Matt thought.

Yale lifted what he held in his hand toward Lorna.

"I'll put this in hot water. It'll be ready in no time."

He walked over to the sink, set the object down on the edge. Matt shrank back for fear Yale would turn his direction. When Yale turned his back, Matt looked and could detect that it was a jar. Yale rolled up his shirtsleeves, exposing his tattoo. He turned on the faucet and ran the water until it was scalding, filled a pan, and placed the jar in the water. It bobbed and floated a bit. He walked back across the room.

"Now, I want you to tell Tobie what you are going to do," Yale said to Lorna.

"Why don't you?" she said wearily, rubbing her arm some more.

Yale glared at her and she drew back, all the time watching his eyes. "Because it's not appropriate," he said.

Yale had lost control of the situation the moment he'd kidnapped Lorna, because he hadn't planned it beforehand. But he was certain he could regain power through his strong will. He grabbed Lorna's arm. He didn't have to twist.

"No, no," she moaned.

"Tell her."

"He wants me to put his sperm inside you so you'll get pregnant," she blurted out, and averted her face from Tobie.

"Oh," Tobie said, as if somebody had kicked her in the stomach.

She backed toward the wall and something clattered off the shelf behind her. She didn't look at it.

"It's you?" she said.

Her voice was a whisper of horror. Matt could hardly bear it, wanted to run to her. But he had to wait. He didn't know why, but he knew this wasn't the moment.

"You killed Evie," Tobie said, her hand over her mouth.

"I didn't kill her," Yale said gently. "She killed herself. Great pity. I don't want to hurt anyone. I want only to bless. Motherhood is the greatest blessing a woman can know. You want to be a mother, don't you?"

Tobie stared at him.

"Mrs. Ross pretended to do this to you once, but she's now confessed that she lied and didn't do it. Remember when she examined you at school? Now, that didn't hurt at all, did it?"

Matt felt nauseated.

Yale crossed in front of Lorna and reached out to pat Tobie reassuringly on the head.

"Don't touch me," Tobie hissed; she jerked sideways and shot up her hand.

"Honey, I don't want to hurt you," Yale whined, aggrieved. "All you have to do is get on this table," he added. "You can take that white apron over there and use it as a sheet and just act the way you did at school."

Tobie stared at him.

"Oh, you're worried I'll see, aren't you? Well, I won't. I'll turn my back. I would leave the room, but I can't trust her. Now, why don't you just climb up on that table?"

He moved toward Tobie again. She dashed over to the opposite side of the table to get away. Yale followed her around the table. Tobie flung his arms away when he put his hands on her.

"I said, don't touch me," she said grimly.

"Okay, okay. Just hop up on that table."

Tobie put her back to the table and hoisted herself up to sit on it. As she did, she caught sight of her father, and her face lit up. Matt quickly put his finger across his lips for her to keep quiet. Fortunately, Yale at that moment had turned to go check the temperature of the jar. Matt could tell from Tobie's posture that she was transformed. She thought all was okay now that he was there, that he would save her. God, he hoped he could. As Yale walked to the sink, Matt disappeared up a step.

"It's ready," Yale said.

He lifted the jar out of the water and dried it off with a dish towel hanging beneath the sink. Holding it proudly, he turned to Lorna. With his left hand, he pulled the catheter and bulb triumphantly from his overalls pocket.

"Now, I want you to do it," he said.

Tobie had turned sideways on the table to follow the action.

"No, no, no," Lorna whimpered, refusing to take the items he was holding out to her.

Yale lifted the jar and rapped it down on the table behind Tobie. The stuff slopped inside the glass. Both Tobie and Lorna flinched. He set the catheter next to the jar.

"Are you going to do what I tell you, or am I going to have to do something to your beloved Buford?"

Lorna looked at Yale sullenly.

"Buford is dead," she said.

"But he can come back."

"You're lying," she said.

Yale raised his hand as if to hit Lorna just as Tobie chimed in, "Who is Buford?"

Her tone was too cheerful, but Yale didn't notice.

"Buford is her baby. He's dead—I mean, he's just sleeping, right?" he said, and shoved his toe against Lorna, who had her arms over her lowered head.

"He's frozen over there in that steel capsule," Yale said. "Actually, it's a great scientific experiment with liquid nitrogen, but it could all go up in vapor if she doesn't cooperate."

Lorna wailed a wordless cry—a mother in despair, a woman enraged.

Yale walked over to the capsule. Lorna raised her head and watched, horrified. He reached up and pulled out the connecting cord. The green light suddenly flashed red, and kept flashing.

"Now are you going to do what I say?"

She raised her head defiantly.

"No," she said.

"It's no again, is it?"

Yale reached down to the wooden cabinet beneath the table, opened the top drawer, and pulled out something gleaming silver. He set the scalpel on the edge of the table.

Lorna snapped her hands behind her back. Tears were streaming down her face. She let them bathe her chin. She was familiar with that knife, Matt thought.

Yale seemed desperate and, curiously, almost distraught, as if he really didn't want to be doing this, but couldn't help himself.

"Why do I have to do her?" Lorna said between sobs and sniffs. "I can give you a baby."

"Can't you get it through your head that I don't want your baby?" Yale said in exasperation. "It would be a waste of my potency, an inferior child. I want the best."

Lorna was distracted, semicrazed, and didn't seem to hear him.

"That's what I used the jar for last time," she said. "Buford, my Bu."

"What did you say?"

Yale slapped her.

"What did you say?"

She put her head down and held her jaw.

"I'm going to have your baby," she said, not looking at him.

Yale snatched up the scalpel and raised it.

"Stop!"

Matt's voice rang across the basement. He jumped up and stumbled down the stairs, his knees aching from their squatting clinch.

"Don't do it," he shouted.

Yale dropped the knife and reached down to the cabinet.

He crashed open the drawer and yanked out a tiny, silvery gun. He pointed it directly at Matt and crouched in an aiming position.

"Daddy!" Tobie shouted.

She started to dash in his direction. Yale grabbed her wrist with his left hand and jerked her back so hard she screamed.

CHAPTER FORTY-FOUR

Matt couldn't swallow. He remembered how Yale had been described as moving like lightning when he put out the fire in the school kitchen.

"Yale, I think you don't want to hurt anybody," Matt said, fighting to keep his voice low, controlled. "Isn't that what you said before?"

Yale stepped back one step. He adjusted the gun to get a better grip on it. The center of his forehead was inflamed and pulsing where the artery was. Matt had never seen anything like it. A red, throbbing ribbon.

Matt made the usual calculation: could he take him? If Yale didn't have a gun, it'd be a toss-up. He was lighter than Matt but looked very fit. Probably both of his knees worked right.

"Were you the one in the iceboat?"

Yale stared at him hostilely.

"Were you trying to kill me then?"

"No."

"How can I believe you? Sure looks like you wanted to."

"I wanted to put you out of action," Yale said, "so someone else would take over as principal and keep the school open. I did not intend permanent damage to you or your friend."

Matt was surprised at Yale's carefully worded answer. The conversation seemed to calm him down. The red ribbon was fainter.

Lorna had moved toward the alcove that contained the cryogenic capsule. Getting behind the capsule would be a good shield, Matt thought. She didn't take her eyes off Yale. Her knees were shaking. Matt could see her trying to steady her legs with her left hand.

"What about the car wheel? Did you unscrew the lugs?"

"I only wanted to scare you."

"You succeeded."

Yale began to look impatient.

"The puppy fetus?" Matt asked. "You sent that to Niccole?"

"I didn't kill the mother," Yale protested. "She was dead, hit by a car. I found her."

He gestured with the gun as he answered. Matt decided not to press the issue of Harper's death. If Yale knew Matt suspected him of murder, he'd become even more dangerous. Tobie shifted and groaned lightly, putting her hand to the arm that Yale was clenching.

"Right now you're hurting my daughter," Matt said. "Why don't you let go of her?"

"She'll run to you." Yale adjusted his grip on Tobie. "And besides, I need her," he added.

"It's too late," Matt said, in as calm and definite a voice as he could muster.

"What do you mean?" Yale asked. "Isn't it just the right time of the month?"

He glanced up, confused, at his calendar on the pegboard.

"No. You'll have to go with what you've done so far, the girls you've already made pregnant. Let go of Tobie. Tobie, don't move. Yale can trust us, can't he?"

"How do I know?" Yale's voice faltered.

"You have my word. You know, Yale, you've been a good worker. I've never had any complaints. You're a reasonable man, like a scientist."

Matt could see the effect of his flattery. Yale relaxed another notch. Mr. Chays still considered him a reasonable man.

"I am a scientist," Yale said.

"So we can talk about your work," Matt replied gently.

Yale loosened his grip on Tobie's arm, then dropped it.

"See," Yale said, sweeping his free arm around the basement. "I had a great experiment, worth the Nobel Prize, but she fucked it up." He jerked his head in Lorna's direction. "Excuse me," he added, turning to Tobie.

She shrugged awkwardly.

"But your experiment worked," Matt said. "It's just that this series of experiments has come to an end."

Yale lowered the gun, a questioning look on his face. Matt tried not to watch the gun.

"A real scientist like you doesn't waste his efforts. With Verity, you have succeeded, right?"

Yale nodded once. This was a tight situation, but if he remained in control, he figured, he could come out of it in good shape.

"If a great scientist's experiments succeed, then it's time to move to another problem, to be more creative. The scientist doesn't just keep doing the same thing. He's logical. That's the way he succeeds in the first place; that's how he'll continue to succeed. He has to be courageous and take on new challenges at the frontier of his work."

That's what he'd already decided, Yale thought. Then, when Lorna'd said Tobie hadn't been "done," he'd ended up here. He'd go back to his plan to give up on the project, including Tobie, though that made him sad.

Matt was getting a headache.

Tobie shifted her feet. Yale whirled and raised his gun toward her. She shrank back, crossing her arms over her chest. Her eyes enlarged in fear. Matt desperately wanted to rush over and hold her.

"She's not going anywhere," Matt said.

Yale lowered the gun and turned back.

"If you do anything to hurt us, you are going to be in a great deal of trouble. We're in your house. You can't get away with it. It's not logical."

Yale knew it was true. He shrugged ashamedly and ran his left hand through the black forelock that had fallen into his eyes. So far Mr. Chays didn't suspect him of killing either Penny or Tom Harper.

"I'm not going to hurt you," Yale said.

"Then why don't you put down that gun on the table and let us go?"

Yale raised the gun tantalizingly, pointing it at Matt.

"You don't believe me?" he charged.

"I beli—" Matt was interrupted by the blast, and something whizzed past him and lodged itself in the carpet on the second-from-bottom stair.

"See," Yale said, and smiled triumphantly, the gun warm in his hand.

Shit, Matt thought, this is supposed to make me trust him? What a crazy.

"But I already believed you," Matt said. "I think you have the will to live now, because you have a child."

"Oh, Verity!" Tobie exclaimed, then instantly put her hand over her mouth.

"What about Verity?" Yale whirled toward Tobie.

"She probably has already had your baby," Matt said, drawing Yale's attention back. "You're a father by now."

Yale's gun arm went slack, almost as if he'd forgotten what he was holding.

"Don't you want to see your child?" Matt asked.

"Now that everybody knows, they won't let me," Yale said resentfully.

"I understand your fear: I'm afraid for Tobie right now," Matt said. "But they can't keep you, the father, away from your child; he or she is yours. If you let Tobie go, I'll help you. I promise."

Yale looked skeptical.

"I promise."

Matt knew Orville would never let such a visit occur.

"I have a toy I carved," Yale said. His voice was tentative and tender.

"I saw it upstairs," Matt said. "It's wonderful. A perfect toy. You'll be a wonderful daddy."

Suddenly a bong filled the basement and resonated from stone to stone, rolling around like thunder. They all turned to the grandfather clock in the corner of the alcove. Another clock chimed in with a high castrato's tone. A third, and a fourth. Then it was difficult to say if there was a fifth or not. It was like being inside a cuckoo clock, Matt thought.

Yale smiled and reached over to place the gun on the table

next to the scalpel. There was time for him with his child after all. He didn't really need Tobie. With an eye on Yale, Tobie craned to examine a clock that really was a cuckoo clock, with farm animals moving in and out. In the process, she managed to move a few feet farther from Yale.

The last noontime chime vibrated out of existence.

"Hold it right there!" a voice shouted from the stairs.

Matt didn't turn. He saw Yale reach for his gun, but freeze before he got to it. Matt recognized Orville's booming voice. He must've come inside and downstairs with his noise cloaked by the clock chimes' din.

His eye was fixed behind his rifle sight, and the gun was riveted on Yale. Orville was wearing a gray wool suit with a pink paisley tie. He sat on a stair, his back to the wall, one leg outstretched, the rifle braced against the bent knee.

Matt saw the red ribbon reappear on Yale's forehead. Matt turned. Above Orville, he could see Shadrack peeking down from the landing.

Matt heard voices up the stairs.

"What's he doing?"

"Who's down there?"

"Can you get a shot?"

"Hell, man, who do you think I am, Houdini? Besides, that's a big fucking rifle!"

"Is the kid in the way?"

Orville seemed distracted, almost ready to turn his attention toward the voices.

Immediately, Yale grabbed for his gun, but miscalculated the distance and pushed it off the table. Matt saw Orville's finger tighten on the trigger, and launched himself across the few yards that separated them. He leaped into the air and slapped the rifle barrel with his palm. Orville's knee kept it from moving sideways, but the force of Matt's blow knocked it upward.

The shot went off. The enormous blast pounded Orville's arm and shoulder backward.

Matt turned to follow the shot. It'd struck one of the white-painted cylinders of liquid nitrogen stacked against the wall at the level of Yale's head.

The bullet sheared off the valve on the cylinder's narrow top. A jet of liquid nitrogen shot from the cylinder. Great billows of steam boiled out from it. The gas and liquid struck Yale's neck and head. His mouth gaped open in horror. He swayed, crumpled. He fell to the floor, his head making a resounding crack on the red cement.

Lorna moaned, "Oh no, oh no, oh no. Oh, God."

She stood slightly behind the head of the capsule, clutching her arms around herself. Suddenly she stretched up, and with great force sprang the latch on the door and window of the capsule. She reached in and pulled out the tinfoil-wrapped Buford.

She screamed. He was cold. Too cold to hold. Buford crashed to the cement floor, face down. Lorna sank to her knees, nestled her hands beneath her skirt to protect them, and turned over the frozen baby. Still on her knees, she rocked to and fro, alternately moaning and murmuring, "Buford, my baby."

Matt glanced quickly at Tobie, saw that she had shoved herself safely into the small nook next to the sink. He limped across the room to Yale. He'd twisted his knee jumping to stop Orville.

The nitrogen had dissipated. Matt knelt down to feel Yale's pulse. Nothing. He turned him from his side onto his back. Yale's neck was blue, his face contorted and stiff. Where his frozen scalp had hit the floor, hair had come off and lay damply on the concrete. Matt set the heel of his hand on Yale's breastbone and pushed, trying to restart his heart. Live, damn it. Live and be charged with murder, you bastard, he thought grimly.

"Anybody up there know CPR better than me?" he shouted back over his shoulder toward the stairs.

He could hear the question being passed up. After four or five seconds, he heard a reply.

"Yeah, here he comes."

Almost immediately, a man was next to Matt on the floor, pumping Yale's chest, then listening for a heartbeat. Nothing. Finally, he said, "It's no use. The guy's gone."

Matt tilted back on his heels, clasped his forehead in his palms for a few seconds, then arose, turning toward the stairs.

Niccole was downstairs holding Tobie, who was sobbing and gasping. Niccole nestled her against her shoulder and stroked her hair down her back, murmuring, "It's okay, it's all over. You were very brave."

Matt walked over and encircled both of them in his arms. Tobie clung to him. Then he looked over at the stairs and noticed Orville. Matt pulled away gently, leaving Tobie and Niccole together, and walked over to him. Matt's arms felt loose in their shoulder sockets and he was weak from the release of tension.

Orville sat at the foot of the stairs, the rifle propped between his knees. Shadrack stood beside him, wide-eyed, looking down at his father's tearful face in awe and embarrassment. He'd never seen him cry before. Up the stairs, Matt noticed reporters and TV crews with cameras and sound equipment.

Orville's tears coursed down; he was sobbing loudly and praying. Every once in a while he choked.

"I killed him. God forgive me. Will God ever forgive me?"

Matt took the rifle and set it on the floor. He stood up and put his hand on Orville's arm.

"Orville, the gun went off when I hit it. And you didn't shoot Yale. You shot a gas bottle. It was an accident," Matt tried to assure him, half believing his own words. "And anyway, Yale was going for his gun."

Orville sobbed. "Thou shalt not kill. I wanted to kill him. I had hatred in my heart. I pulled the trigger. I would have shot him if you hadn't hit the gun. The Lord can see into the heart. He knows."

"Is Verity okay?" Matt asked.

Orville sobbed again.

"A baby boy," Shadrack said. His voice cracked slightly, and went back down deep.

"Make way for the police," a voice in the kitchen said. "Make way."

Lorna had hesitantly placed Buford on the table. Her face was streaked with dried tears. She stood still, both hands on her stomach, as if her unborn baby were already big. She seemed unaware of her action. Her eyes, which looked as exhausted as the rest of her body, were fastened on the stairway, expecting the police. She lifted her left hand limply and brushed it over her forehead in a gesture more of resignation than foreboding. The flashing alarm light on the capsule, which had been throbbing like a heartbeat next to her, finally stopped.

Chief Leland trundled down the lushly carpeted stairs, his bloodhound jowls wobbling like Jell-O. He looked with trepidation at Orville.

"Of all people," he said.

He turned to inspect the body from a distance. He pulled a walkie-talkie from his belt and summoned an ambulance.

"We're going to have to have depositions from everybody, so I want you to give your names and phone numbers to my lieutenant who's coming down the stairs there."

Watching Leland operate, Matt was certain that his questions about Harper's death would never be resolved.

Leland turned back to Orville, pulled an absurdly tiny notebook from his pocket, and drawled, "I believe you have the right to keep quiet and have a lawyer, but, Orville, maybe you'd like to tell me what happened."

CHAPTER FORTY-FIVE

"Verity looked really tired, didn't she?" Tobie said.

"Small wonder," Niccole replied.

She was driving them home from the hospital. Tobie sat between her father and Niccole on the front seat of Niccole's Pontiac.

"She had dark circles under her eyes," Tobie continued.

"The least of her beauty problems, I'd say," Niccole said.

"I don't think I want to have a baby," Tobie said.

Matt and Niccole looked at each other over Tobie's head. He wasn't sure what the glance said. Maybe it was just contact. Niccole slowed the car for a traffic light.

"The grass is turning tweedy," Matt said, surveying a field off to the right.

"Tweedy?" Tobie mocked him.

"Yeah, tweedy. See, it's not just beige anymore. It's got green in it, so it looks like an English country gentleman's walking jacket."

"Like Sherlock Holmes?" Niccole asked, her eyes twinkling.

"Yup," Matt said, grinning. "Everything's more beautiful when you've been close to death," he added soberly.

"Verity liked her necklace, don't you think?" Tobie asked, glancing up at her dad and squinching close to him.

"That was a good idea," he said, patting her shoulder.

Tobie had made them go to the local jewelry store and buy a mother-of-pearl necklace. "To replace the pop-pearl one I gave to her in church," she explained. "She's a good friend."

Niccole pulled into a gas station, rolled down her window, and asked the attendant to fill it up.

"The baby sure was wrinkly," Tobie mused, wrinkling up her nose.

"Just like your nose," Matt said, touching it.

"Was I that ugly?" she asked.

"Oh, no, I thought you were the most beautiful baby that had ever been born into the world."

"Silly," Tobie said, cuffing his bicep.

"Really. 'Course, I imagine every father believes his child is the most beau—"

He stopped, and they all knew why.

"Daddy, was he really a mean, evil man?"

"Yeah, in a way, honey, but he was psychotic, crazy."

"Do you think Mrs. Ross will go to jail?"

"Maybe, but the court or judge might decide that she's crazy in some way, too, and send her for care."

"Will she have his baby?" Tobie asked, stressing "his."

"I imagine she will," Matt said.

"Can she keep it?"

"I guess that depends on what happens to her."

"How could she do that to Verity and Evie?"

"Honey, she was afraid she'd be killed."

Niccole nosed the car out of the gas station and turned down the Chays's street.

"By the way," Matt said, "how did you manage to write 'Yale' on the blackboard?"

Tobie grinned slyly, pleased at the tone of admiration in her father's voice.

"Easy. I told him I had to go to the bathroom before I'd go with him. He said okay. Then I slid through with the door to the basement barely open so he couldn't see it wasn't the bathroom, and I went in and wrote it."

"Impressive," Matt said. "You've got a cool mind in a hot spot."

"Thanks," Tobie said, beaming.

There was a moment of silence crowded with emotions and memories.

"Miss Epps . . ." Tobie said.

"Call me Niccole, for heaven's sake," she said, smiling at Tobie.

"Niccole, when do you think we could start our karate lessons?"

"Right away," Niccole said. Her arm was over the back of the seat. Matt reached out. Their hands held hungrily behind Tobie's back.

"I think we need it," Tobie said.

"Where are you going to take karate?" Matt asked, surprised.

"We'll check it out," Niccole said.

"By the way," Tobie said, "it's perfectly okay if you two hold hands."

Both of them looked astonished, and a bit sheepish at being caught.

"Don't underestimate the little kid," Tobie said.

Niccole and Matt roared with laughter.

"The kid's not so little anymore," Matt said between chuckles.

Niccole pulled into the Chays's driveway.

"You gonna come in for supper?" Tobie asked.

"Well, thanks for the invitation. Believe I will."

Matt's and Niccole's eyes locked.

"So?" Matt said.

"So, let's," Niccole replied, opening her door.